As they tu ⟨...⟩ er hand. He tried ⟨...⟩ only think about kissing her. Holding her in his arms and touching her soft skin. Knowing he could never get much beyond that, a lump formed in his throat. She might not allow more than that anyway.

Shaking his head, he focused on the vows.

"I, Erik, take you, Tessa, to be my lawfully wedded wife."

She gazed at him with such delight on her face, he was humbled. This beautiful woman was giving up her life to help him keep custody of some children who weren't hers and dedicating herself to be married to a scarred and crippled ex-soldier. Not much of a bargain but he'd damn well make her as happy as he could.

"I, Tessa, take you, Erik, to be my lawfully wedded husband."

A few minutes later they were slipping rings on one another's fingers and being declared husband and wife.

"You may now kiss the bride."

Planting his feet as securely as he could, he lifted both hands to cup her face. This was the part he'd been waiting for. To show her, and everyone else here, he wanted her for his wife. No room for doubt.

This is a work of fiction. Names, characters, places, and incidents are either the product of the author's imagination or are used fictitiously, and any resemblance to actual persons living or dead, business establishments, events, or locales, is entirely coincidental.

Elusive Dreams

COPYRIGHT © 2019 by Kari Lemor

Cover Art by *Kim Mendoza*

The Wild Rose Press, Inc.
PO Box 708
Adams Basin, NY 14410-0708
Visit us at www.thewildrosepress.com

Publishing History
First Champagne Rose Edition, 2019
Print ISBN 978-1-5092-2718-1
Digital ISBN 978-1-5092-2719-8

Storms of New England, Book 1
Published in the United States of America

*Kari
Lemor*

Elusive Dreams

by

Kari Lemor

Storms of New England, Book

Dedication

To my husband and children,
who have been my biggest cheerleaders
as I continue on my writing journey.
I love you all!

Acknowledgments

So many people had a hand in getting me to this place, it's hard to thank them all. To all the military men and women who dedicate their lives to keeping us safe in our land of the free, I salute you! To my father-in-law, Mac, who helped me with all the military aspects and even made a few suggestions that added to the story.

To Samantha for making sure all the psychology and counseling angles were covered. To Susan for your expert Physical Therapy review and advice. To Judi, my editor, for helping me clean and polish this story and making it shine. To Pamela, for holding my hand and staying by my side through this whole submission and contract process.

To my beautiful, wonderful, talented, amazing TEAM who is always there helping me wordsmith and rearrange, making me look good! Emily and Kris, my betas, you are precious beyond words and I don't know what I'd do without your support. MA Grant, my valued Critique Partner, you are my rock who helps me stay focused and on task. What a gift you are to me.

AND to the beautiful region of New England, and all its small towns, thanks for being my inspiration!

Chapter One

Save my babies, please.

The words echoed through Captain Erik Storm's head like an eighty-mm mortar attack. Reaching for the crutches, he slid out of the minivan. The images of the bombed-out cellar, where he'd spent four days of misery, flashed through his mind like sniper fire.

Fuckin' hell. What had he been thinking? No way he was in any shape to take care of two young children. It didn't matter if they were arriving in four days or four months. He couldn't even walk on his own. And who the hell knew if he ever would? The doctors hadn't even been sure.

But he'd promised. Sure, only to reassure Matteen and Kinah's dying mom that they'd have a good life in the States versus whatever hell awaited them in a Kandahar orphanage. And with their grandfather having been British, their chances of surviving until adulthood were slim. He'd gotten to know them during the ordeal. Their silly games, their precious smiles, even their inability to stay quiet when he needed them to. When the mortar fire had exploded above them, he'd kept them occupied. Sacrificed his water and MREs to keep them somewhat hydrated and nourished. Held and rocked them when they were tired but too scared to sleep. Then comforted them when their mother had finally succumbed to her injuries.

He slammed the car door, which gave him only a momentary satisfaction, then shifted the crutches under his arms and hobbled to the back of the vehicle. Somehow he needed to get the food into the house. There was no grocery cart here to wheel it along.

The salty scent of coastal Maine assaulted his nostrils as he opened the back of the van. He'd loved coming here as a kid. His grandparents had decided not to sell the place after they'd moved back to New Hampshire, and for that he was grateful. It was perfect for what he needed to do. The next step in his life.

But now he needed to get everything inside. The groceries he could bring in a few bags at a time, but what about the other supplies? Like the baby crib and high chair? Maybe he should have taken his brothers up on their offer to help. But no, he had to be a stubborn marine and show he could do everything himself. Maybe he could leave the heavy stuff in there for a few days, eat some crow, and call Alex and Luke. They'd bust his balls, but what did that matter, it wasn't like he'd be using them anymore. His bashed in leg and hip had resulted in other damage. Stuff you couldn't see.

He gritted his teeth and pushed those thoughts back in the furthest part of his mind, then reached in for the grocery bags. His left crutch slipped as he grabbed a second bag, and he swore again as he bumped into the side of the van. Even after a month, the friggin' wounds were still tender. Maybe he could use just one crutch. The shattered knee and fractured pelvis were both on the left side. Switching the right crutch to his left arm, he slid his right hand through the handles of several plastic bags. See, manageable.

Until he took a few steps. At the pressure, pain

sliced through his left leg, and he stumbled, dropping the bag the eggs were in.

"Shit, damn, fuck."

As he bent to pick up the bag, the brace holding his knee in place was too bulky and threw him off balance, tossing him on the ground. The driveway met his ass, sending his hip into spasms. Heat surged through him along with the pain, and he flung the crutch at the car. It smacked into the bumper and fell with a thud, a good five feet out of his reach.

"Nice going, dickhead. Now you need to crawl across the ground to get it."

Maybe he could sit here and wait for his knee and hip to heal enough so he could actually move. Right, 'cause that was sensible. At this moment he didn't feel like doing sensible. He felt like punching something. Hard.

He took a few deep breaths and called on the control the corps was so famous for. Before he could start the familiar army crawl, a soft voice floated over.

"Do you need some help?"

****

"Shit, damn, fuck."

The words drifted over to Tessa Porter as she opened the door to let her cat, Calico, into the house. Her gaze moved to the Storm's house next door where a light blue minivan sat in the driveway. It didn't belong to Hans or Ingrid, but they had three sons and ten grandkids. It could be any one of theirs.

More grumbled swears made their way over, and she took a few tentative steps down from her porch. Did someone need help? It wasn't obvious from her position, so she walked closer, waiting to check what the situation was. The Storms were all nice, but she wasn't the type to barge in where she wasn't needed.

A crutch bounced off the back fender, startling her. A crutch? Did the person swearing need it? Probably, if the cursing was anything to go by. She moved around the end of the vehicle and there, on the ground, sat Erik Storm, his face a mixture of pain and frustration.

Erik. Why did it have to be Erik? Of all the Storm cousins, he was the one she'd had the biggest crush on. And most likely he knew it. She'd avoided him like the plague and had barely been able to string two words together when he was near.

"Do you need some help?"

Stupid question. The huge brace on his knee, poking out from his cargo shorts, attested to some sort of injury, and the crutch only confirmed that. Actually there was another crutch sticking out from under the other side of the van. Had he been injured in the war? His grandparents had told her he was oversees. Obviously not anymore.

He gazed up at her, his expression thunderous. She took a step back. Maybe she should turn around and go home. Run home. Fast. He didn't look like he was in a good mood.

"Tessa." Her name came out softer than she would have imagined with the scowl still on his face. "I'm fine. Thanks."

Giving a quick nod, she backed away, but he swore under his breath and called her again.

"Tessa, sorry. No, I'm not okay. But I'm being stubborn. If I can swallow my pride for a minute, maybe you can give me a hand."

"Sure." Had she been loud enough to hear? She

moved forward again but slowly.

A smile, a real one this time, formed on his lips. He held up his hand. "Could you get the crutches? Please."

The last word was like an afterthought. But Hans and Ingrid had hammered manners into all their grandkids. There was no way he could be rude.

Picking up the crutch closest to her, she handed it to him, then retrieved the other one. He struggled for a minute, folding his good leg under him, and attempted to push himself up with a crutch in each hand.

"Do you want help?" Why had she opened her mouth and asked? He'd probably just scowl at her again. Touching him wasn't in her plans either. Not good for her nerves.

He clenched his teeth and faked a smile. "If you don't mind."

She moved up behind him, put her hands under his arms, and lifted. The muscles hidden by his T-shirt strained as he pushed on the crutches, but soon he was standing. For a moment he balanced, then took a deep breath in. As soon as he seemed stable, she let go. Those few seconds had been far too long for her.

"Thanks. I'm not usually so clumsy, but well…" He glanced at the metal and fabric wrapped around his leg. *Look away from the muscular calves, or you'll be stammering like the idiot you usually are.*

"No problem. Do you want help getting the groceries inside?"

Throwing her a wry grin, he nodded. "Sure, I've got no pride left anymore. What the hell."

"Is the door unlocked?"

He shook his head. "I just got here. Stopped at the store first. Didn't figure I'd have any problems. Dumb ass." The last words were muttered under his breath, and she pinched her lips together to keep from smiling. This self-deprecating Erik was kind of adorable.

When he grinned again, heat rose to her cheeks. God, why couldn't she be normal around him? Around any guy? It had been over ten years. She wanted to be normal.

"Why don't you unlock the door, and I'll bring in the bags." There weren't too many, and she could loop the handles around her hands and carry more of them.

He sighed, maneuvering his way up the few porch steps and into the house. Once she grabbed some bags, she followed him. Already he was setting a few bags on the counter. She walked through the large family room with the gorgeous ocean views and entered the airy kitchen.

She'd always loved this house. The windows on the ocean side were large and unobstructed, and it felt like you were practically standing in the waves. Usually the breeze blew through, and you could smell the salt air. Not today. The house had been closed up for a few weeks at least. That was the last time Hans and Ingrid had been here.

"Your grandparents were up a short while ago but didn't say anything about you coming here." She dropped the bags on the kitchen table.

"They didn't know. I only got back home last week."

"There're a few bags left. I'll get them while you put the food away." Erik wouldn't want to look like he couldn't handle a task, so she'd given him something to do. His crooked smile told her he appreciated it.

When she came back in, he was studying the

contents of the egg carton. He held it up and smirked. "Want an omelet? A few of these are cracked, but I think I can still use them."

"Thank you but I'm—"

"It's the least I can do. Give me a little of my masculinity back by accepting my offer. I make a mean omelet."

"I know you do. I've had them at The Boat House." Years ago when she bussed tables and he cooked. And she'd dropped silverware every time he'd looked at her. God, how embarrassing.

"That's right," he chuckled. "You used to take any of the extra parts that didn't fit on the plate when I had an order."

Should she stay and let him make her an omelet? That meant she'd have to talk to him. It wasn't something she did all that well and especially not with Erik Storm. But his eyes were begging her, and she never could resist anything he asked of her. Luckily, he'd never asked too much.

"I don't want to put you out and eat all your eggs." One last chance to let him get out of it.

Erik limped to the counter and pulled out a bowl. "I need to use the broken ones now anyway. And there are…" He looked in the egg carton, then back up. "Five of them. I like to eat, but I think five eggs is a bit much even for me. You'd be doing me a favor. And letting me pay you back for getting me up a few minutes ago."

"Okay, but let me help." At his tired look she added, "I always wanted to learn your secret for perfect omelets."

His lips twisted, and one eyebrow rose. "The secret's in the way you cook it, not the ingredients. Can you grab the frying pan in that cabinet?"

He pointed to the one she was standing near, and she bent over to retrieve it. Taking it from her, he placed it on the stove. After cracking open the already fractured eggs, he started whisking them with a fork.

"Is ham and cheese okay for today? Onions and peppers will take too long to chop up."

She nodded. For today? Did that mean he'd make her some another day? Did she want to sit with him and have conversation more than once? Although maybe when he realized she sucked at small talk, he wouldn't ask again. That's what most people did. Her extreme introversion made most people uncomfortable.

"I'll get a few plates." She bustled around the kitchen so she wouldn't have to chat, and he wouldn't need to find something to say. Although he'd always been outgoing. Conversations flowed freely around him. She sighed. Wouldn't it be nice if she could be that way? After so many years of trying, she wasn't sure it would ever happen.

When dishes, napkins, and silverware were on the table, she sat down and watched as Erik chopped the ham and finished creating his masterpiece. She took the opportunity to really study him. While he rested on his right leg, his left leg stayed slightly bent with the brace. What happened?

His blond military cut, she suspected, was a little longer than was traditional. When had he been injured? Wide shoulders filled out the T-shirt in ways she shouldn't be thinking about and then narrowed down to slim hips. She'd seen him before he was deployed, and he'd been much bulkier, more buff. Had he lost weight with his injury? Or being in a war zone? He still looked amazing to her, though. Always had.

Her gaze moved to the scar on his face running from his hairline and crossing through his right eyebrow. When he turned to grab the spatula, she saw another, deeper one, starting on his jaw line and ending at his left ear. It should have taken away from his good looks, but it simply made him look more human. He'd always been far too perfect.

"Can you grab these plates so I don't end up with egg all over my face, literally?"

Bouncing up, she took the plates he held out and returned to the table so he could shuffle over on his crutches without an audience. Being seen as weak would be something he'd hate since he'd always been so athletic and in shape. And would be again when this injury healed.

"Let me know if cracked eggs work as well as whole ones. I'm kind of curious."

She bit into her omelet but couldn't help notice Erik glanced down at his leg when he'd mentioned the cracked eggs. Did he wonder if he was still as good as someone whole?

She closed her eyes at the taste of the eggs, ham, cheese, and spices, all precisely blended together and cooked to perfection. Heaven. Just as she remembered.

"It's amazing, like you always made them."

"Thanks." The gratitude in his voice surprised her. He'd never been the timid type or in any way lacking self-esteem. Suddenly he was in need of praise?

She took her time eating the meal so she didn't have to come up with conversation. He didn't seem to mind the lull and paid attention to his own food. How long would he be here? A few days? A week or more?

How could she avoid him if he was staying here? Their houses were fairly close, and their driveways were side by side. And she worked out of the house, so she was home every day. If at all possible, she steered clear of going out anywhere.

The weather this July had been beautiful and not too humid. Spending days outside and working with her computer from her back deck was typical. The thought of staying in all day so she didn't have to see him wasn't a pleasant one. And to get to the path leading to the ocean trail, she had to go past his house.

"So how've you been?" he finally asked, having eaten most of his omelet.

She swallowed what was in her mouth. *Don't let me have anything stuck to my teeth.* "Fine." Oh, great answer. Now ask him something back. But not how he's been since, duh, brace on his leg.

"How long are you staying here?" Lifting her fork, she finished her last bite. It was his turn to speak. She could risk it.

"Actually I'm moving in. I'm buying the place from my grandparents and planning on living here year round."

The fork dropped from her hand and clattered on the table.

Chapter Two

The clink of the utensil hitting the polished wood startled Erik. Tessa's wide eyes stared at him as if he'd announced he was planning to swim from here to England. What had he said?

"Tessa? You okay?"

She immediately dropped her gaze and covered the fork with her hand. "Fine. Sorry, I…I'm kind of clumsy."

Keeping her eyes lowered, she took a deep breath. Had he scared her? Since she'd always been skittish, most people pussyfooted around her to keep from alarming her. No one knew exactly what she'd gone through in her early years, but it had been something. When she'd come to live with the Millers, at around fourteen, she'd been wound tighter than a drum and usually preferred to stay as far away from people as possible.

Looking at her now, he could see she'd matured and blossomed into a beautiful woman. It wasn't surprising, though, since she'd always been a pretty girl, just extremely timid and reserved. His sister, Sara, and some of his cousins had managed to get her to actually hang out with them when they'd visited in the summers. He thought she'd finally accepted the Storms as people she could trust. Yet here she was still fumbling in his presence.

"Are you done with the food?" When he reached his hand out, she shrank back, her doe-like eyes filled with anxiety. No-Touch Tessa. That's what some of the kids had called her when she'd been younger. He wasn't sure if she'd ever heard, but she wasn't stupid. Since some of them weren't all that discreet, she must have known. And it looked like she still didn't like to be touched. What the hell had she gone through to be so scared of everybody? It kicked up the protective older brother in him and made him want to go bust a few heads.

"I'll clean up the plates and wash them. You cooked."

He allowed her to do this, but only because he figured he'd drop the damn dishes on his way, and then he'd need to clean up that mess too. With his injuries he'd end up on the floor again. It would be nice if she could relax in his presence.

"There should be some dishwashing soap under the sink as well as a sponge."

When she bent over, he sucked in a deep breath. Her denim cutoffs hugged her ass, and suddenly that older-brother feeling he'd had earlier vanished. But this was Tessa, and he doubted she'd let him get beyond a casual friendship anyway. *You have two children coming to live here soon, and your focus needs to be on them.* It wasn't like he was in any shape to be romancing a woman, now or in the future. That part of his life had effectively ended in a bombed-out cellar in Kandahar.

"What are you doing now for work? You were in community college last time we chatted." Actually, she'd been with Sara and their parents, but he'd been nearby and heard the conversation. She pushed her wavy, light-brown hair over her shoulder and licked her lips, then turned away to squirt dish liquid onto the sponge.

"I do medical billing from home. It pays well, and the commute is awesome."

When she actually chuckled, his stomach did something weird. Maybe it was digesting his meal. But hearing her laugh was such a rare occurrence.

She rinsed one of the plates and set it in the drying rack, peeking over as she did. "Why are you moving here? Is there a marine base nearby?"

Sighing, he gritted his teeth. Damn fucking war. But he'd known the price he might have to pay when he joined the corps, and he was more than willing to make those sacrifices. If it kept his family and the people of this country safe, then he'd do it all again and pay a higher price if needed. A bum leg was nothing compared to what many of his brothers had given. *Stop feeling sorry for yourself. You still have your legs regardless of whether they work or not. And you're alive. Be thankful.*

"No, I'm on disability if you couldn't tell by the lovely accessory I have decorating my knee. I'll be doing physical therapy but most likely honorably discharged when it's done." No idea when that would be. If ever. Did they finally reach a point where they told you they couldn't fix it?

Her shoulders rose and fell as she rinsed off the utensils. "So you decided to move here. Wouldn't it be easier back home with your parents and family nearby?"

He'd been asked that a million times already.

"I don't need someone else taking care of me," he growled, then closed his eyes when he saw her flinch. Clenching his fists, he reached for that marine control.

"This house is all one floor so it's easier to maneuver." He lowered his voice this time. "And I have two kids coming to live with me soon, so I need more room than my parents have. Especially since they're moving into some fifty-five plus community, and Alex is buying the house."

She turned all the way around this time. As she wiped her hands on a towel, her tongue poked out to rest on her upper lip. A habit she'd had since he'd known her.

"Two kids?"

The expression on her face showed interest, but she'd never been one to stick her nose in other people's business. It was surprising she'd even asked.

He pointed to the seat she had just occupied. After looking nervously around the kitchen, she finally succumbed to her curiosity and sat.

"We were helping a village rebuild a school when insurgents started shelling the place. We each grabbed as many children as we could to evacuate. I was going from house to house to make sure we hadn't missed anyone. There was a woman hiding with her two children, attempting to get into her cellar. I'd almost convinced her to come when the house was hit by mortar rounds."

She sat still, listening intently. "Is that how you got injured?"

"Yeah, the shelling didn't stop for almost a day. And the enemy continued to comb the area, so we couldn't even radio out to get help. We had to keep the kids as quiet as possible to avoid detection."

That tongue poked out and hugged her top lip again. Too distracting. Swinging his gaze around the room, he continued. "The woman was injured worse than me and didn't end up surviving. She made me promise to bring the children back to the States and give them a good life."

"She spoke English?"

"Yeah, her father had been a British soldier, but she'd been raised there. Her husband was a doctor and had been taken by the Taliban to serve them. They—he died." No reason for her to know all the gory details of what those brutes did.

"So where are the children now?"

"They stayed in the German hospital I was in to be treated for their injuries and malnourishment. I was there for a month before coming back. Now they're in the infirmary at Hanscom Air Force Base waiting for final clearance to be released to me."

"How old are they?"

Digging in his pocket, he pulled out his phone, flipped through his pictures, and held it up. "This is Matteen. He's three." He swiped his hand over the phone. "And this is Kinah. She's a year old."

Her face lit up, and he couldn't stop staring at her. When she smiled, she was gorgeous. She looked up, and he blinked, then glanced at the pictures on the phone. No sense her getting the wrong idea with him staring at her. There was nothing he could give to any woman. He had to focus on the kids.

"They're adorable."

Yeah, they were. No denying it. They'd wormed their way into his heart easily. It wasn't until he hadn't seen them for a week he'd realized how much he missed them.

"They are. They'll be here Friday, so I need to get this place ready for them."

Looking around, he sighed. So much to do.

"That's only four days from now." She paused as if considering something. "Do you need any help?"

His first thought was no, he was fine by himself. But honestly, there were things he couldn't manage with this damn brace on his leg and his balance still off. He'd only gotten out of the wheelchair a few days ago.

"Are you really offering? I know you must be busy with work, and I'd hate to keep you away from anything you already have planned."

She lowered her head, but he'd seen her eyes roll.

"I'm not really a big party girl, and I usually do my work first thing in the morning. I've actually already done this weeks' worth of assignments."

He raised an eyebrow. "It's only Monday."

She shrugged. "I know, but I get my work on Fridays, and sometimes I do it over the weekend. Get it out of the way, you know."

He drummed his fingers on the table. *Suck it up and accept her help.* "Well, if you do have some time, I wouldn't say no to a hand. My grandparents keep the place in good shape, but I still need to baby proof everything and set up the kids' rooms."

"I can help. Tell me what to do."

Reaching into the pocket of his shorts again, he pulled out a folded sheet of paper. "My mom helped me make a list of what needs to be done. It was the only way to keep her from tagging along and doing it for me."

"What's wrong with asking for help, Erik? Especially when you've got an injury. I'm sure your whole family would be willing to give you a hand. I'm surprised Sara isn't here with you. She was always following you around like a little duckling."

He chuckled. Yeah, Sara had been a major pain in the ass especially when he was trying to score points with some local girl. When you were nineteen, you certainly didn't want your thirteen-year-old sister getting in your way.

"Luckily ten years ago you came along, and she turned her attention to making friends with you. And she's down the Cape this summer working. I think she likes her independence." As he leaned back in his chair, he stretched his leg out. "So, this list. I need to set up the crib in the smaller bedroom, put the baby locks on the cabinets with any cleaning stuff in them, and make sure the door to the cellar is secure."

"Sounds easy, just time consuming. Where's the crib?"

"It's in the van. I hate to admit to being such a wimp, but I could barely get the groceries in. I think the crib's going to be a bigger challenge."

"Let's go out and take a look."

She got up and walked away from him. Rising, he grabbed his crutches to follow. As her hips swayed from side to side and her long hair cascaded down her back, he was very happy to take a look. Unfortunately, that's all he could ever do.

****

"Okay, I'll do a little mea culpa on this one, Tess. You were right."

Tessa glanced up from tightening the screw on the

17

last part of the crib. Erik sat on the floor doing the same thing on the other end.

"Yeah, I was right." Her smile slipped. "About?"

He narrowed his eyes, but his crooked smile softened the hard expression. "I wanted to put this together in the living room because I'd have more room to lay out the pieces. You said it wouldn't fit through the door once it was together. You were right. Thanks for keeping me from doing something stupid."

No way she'd tell him she'd done exactly that with a large bookshelf a few months ago. A girl had to have some secrets. Although maybe she had more than most.

"Anytime. What else do we have to do?"

Erik looked around the room at the trash from the crib box and sighed. Popping up, she started grabbing it and putting it all in the large garbage bag they'd brought in earlier. When he attempted to stand, she pushed at his shoulders and glared.

"Just sit there and think what we need to do next. I'll get the trash."

Flopping back on the worn carpet, he stared at the ceiling, his face deep in thought. He turned his head and studied the walls and the floor.

"These rooms need a good painting and new carpet. Damn, I wish I had known. I could have found someone to do it before the kids arrive. It's too late now. I don't want them inhaling the fumes after they're here."

She looked at the room. It wasn't horrible, but it could use a fresh coat. "Painting a room's pretty easy."

He shot her a look that turned her insides to mush. Stupid, considering she could barely speak to the man without gibbering away like a chipmunk. Although this afternoon she hadn't stammered too badly. She'd simply kept herself busy and concentrated on the work that needed to be done.

"Easy for you maybe, but I've got a bum leg. I can't really see myself taping windows and standing on a stool to get the tops of the walls. I might be over six feet, but these are eight-foot ceilings."

Don't do it. Seriously, don't do it. Her mouth wasn't listening to her brain, and it opened of its own accord.

"I could paint them. The rooms are square, and there's only the one big window in each that'd need to be taped. I could have it taped tonight. It's warm enough you could do two coats tomorrow. And then touch up anything that needs it Wednesday. Keep the windows open, and the fumes should dissipate by Friday easily."

Sitting up, he pursed his lips as he crossed his arms over his chest. She stared at the muscles and bit her lip. He'd never use those muscles to hurt anyone, right? A few times when she'd first moved here, he'd defended her. But he'd been at war for the past…how long had he been overseas? Hans and Ingrid had talked about his leaving last summer. Had he been in war-torn conditions for a year? Who knew what he was capable of with those muscles that stretched the sleeves of his shirt and rippled under the soft material?

"I don't want to take up all your time. It was nice of you to help me with the crib and locks."

He didn't want her here any longer. Typical. They'd chatted a bit but mostly about how to put the crib together or which cabinets needed to be baby proofed. Soon enough he'd want real conversation. Not

19

something she could provide.

Tossing the last of the trash in the garbage bag, she pulled it together to tie it closed. "I'll bring this to the bins outside so you don't have to go up and down the stairs again."

She wanted to thank him but knew it would be stupid, and he'd think she was a freak. Well, everyone thought that, but she'd kind of hoped the Storms had been a bit kinder. They probably just thought she was strange. But this afternoon she'd actually enjoyed herself. The silence hadn't been uncomfortable, and they'd talked when they needed to. It wasn't often she had company. Yes, by her own choice, but there were times even she liked to have another human to talk to. Her cat didn't count.

As she moved toward the door, Erik looked around the room, lost in thought. She didn't want to disturb him, and he probably wouldn't even notice she was gone. Or care.

"Tess?" His voice was distant, and she turned to see him still studying the walls. "Would you really be okay with helping me paint the walls? I could pay you."

Was he serious? She didn't care about money, but he hadn't been turned off by her slim conversation this afternoon? "I'd be happy to do it. And you don't have to pay me."

He scooted over and grabbed onto the crib to pull himself to standing. "Well, I'd owe you big time. What do you want?"

What would he say if she said she wanted *him*? Like she'd ever verbalize that. Relationships weren't her thing. Not romantic ones. She didn't have the right stuff for them to be successful. But a girl could dream.

And Erik Storm was certainly the stuff dreams were made of.

"How about…could I…?" An idea formed in her mind, but she wasn't sure he would go for it.

"Anything. What do you want?"

Biting her top lip, she then took a deep breath for courage. "Could I paint a mural on each of the kids' walls?"

"You want to paint a mural?" His face scrunched up. "How is that *you* getting something? It's *you* doing more for *me*."

"No, I've always wanted to do a really big painting. I've done a few little things around my house, but I guess I still don't always feel like it's my house. It's the Millers' house, and they just let me use it."

He limped closer, and she held her breath. Would he try and touch her again? Could she hold still long enough to allow it?

"You've lived there for ten years. How does it not feel like your home?" He didn't touch her. Was she relieved or disappointed?

She shrugged. "It still has all their things in it. I mean, I got rid of their clothes and stuff, but it's the same décor and furniture they had when I moved in."

"Why haven't you changed any of it? Made it the way you want it to be? Mrs. Miller passed away over two years ago."

Why hadn't she? Did she still think someone would come along and tell her it was time to move on again?

"New furniture and stuff costs money," she stated, though it was a bad excuse. The Millers had left her enough to live on for quite a few years, even without working. Her job paid well, and she certainly didn't spend it on anything extravagant. She was still driving their old 1980 Chrysler LeBaron.

"Yeah, it does," he agreed. "The mural? Won't that take a lot of time to paint? And you want to do one for each room."

"I don't have to paint the entire wall. I could do a few little pictures here and there to add character. Do the kids have any special toys they like or movies they've watched?"

A grin broke out on his face and turned any sour expression into pure masculine magnetism. She forgot to breathe. How could she be near him all the time if he caused her internal organs to go on overload and stop working? Could she convince him not to move in?

"Matty was mesmerized by the boats in the ocean when we first got here. He'd never seen anything like them or seen water like that. The nurses at the hospital bought him a toy pirate ship with little figures he plays with all the time."

"And Kinah, is there anything she likes? I know she's only a year, but I didn't know if she had some stuffed animal or something she was fond of?"

Pulling out his phone, he flipped to his pictures again and showed her. She moved closer, hoping her heart wouldn't completely close down.

"This is Kiki's favorite toy. It's a fairy doll, and it's soft and cuddly. She's slept with it every night since we left Afghanistan. I wrapped part of her mom's head piece around it, so it could be she likes the smell."

Tears filled her eyes, and she blinked them back. Memories of the rose scent her mom had always worn swirled through her mind. Even after all these years, she still remembered. Kinah, Kiki as he'd called her, was only a year old. Would she keep that memory, or would it fade with time?

Rotating slowly around the room, she pictured what she could do here. Fairies. Yes. And maybe little trees where they lived. And a castle in the background. Every little girl needed to have a castle where she could go to escape when the big ogres came looking for food to eat. Hopefully Kiki would never have to go find that castle like she had on more occasions than she could count. She'd paint her one anyway so it was always there.

"I can paint a few little fairies flying around. It shouldn't take too long."

"That'd be cute. Don't kill yourself, though. I'm sure I can buy some pictures or something to hang on the wall later."

"I could do a pirate ship riding on the waves in Matty's room."

"Perfect. I know he'd love it."

She'd love it too. She couldn't wait to get started. "Do you want the rooms any specific color?"

He looked around again. "I guess we'll need to get paint, huh?" He glanced at his watch, then looked back at her. "I couldn't talk you into going to the hardware store with me, could I? Tape and paintbrushes are easy enough to get, but picking colors aren't really my thing. Think you could give me a hand there?"

The look he gave her was one she'd seen him use on so many girls when he wanted something. She wasn't one of his girls, though. Never would be.

"Sure. I can go with you." Toss her damn pride down the drain, but she did offer to help.

"It's a little after four right now. How about we visit the hardware store, bring the stuff back here, then I'll whip up a fabulous dinner. We can tape the room after that."

"You're going to feed me twice in one day? I may never be able to eat my own boring cooking again."

Erik grabbed his crutches and started for the door. When he got near, he stroked her arm. "Thanks. You're doing me a big favor here. And for that I should make you meals every day for the rest of your life." As he hobbled out of the room, her skin tingled where he'd touched it.

Following him, she let out the breath she'd been holding. Damn, had he heard how shaky it was? His statement had been meant innocently enough, but the thought of him making her meals and eating together for the rest of their lives was an elusive dream she couldn't even begin to hope for.

Chapter Three

"Enchanted or Lovable?"

Erik turned his head and stared at Tessa sharply. "What?"

She held up two of the color samples she'd been looking through. "This one's called Enchanted, and this one is called Lovable. What do you think?"

"They look pink." What was he doing here looking at pink paint samples?

Tessa pursed her lips. "They are pink. But this one's a bit softer than this one. Or maybe you'd prefer Rosebud or Demure Pink."

She was serious about this paint color thing. He figured they'd come to the hardware store, tell the clerk they wanted a few gallons of pink and blue paint. Who the heck came up with all these colors? And the stupid names to go with them?

Without looking, he stuck out his finger and pointed at a color. "That one?"

Her full lips frowned.

"What? It's not a good one?"

"It's called Party Time. And if you put this bright pink on the walls, you'd need sunglasses to walk in the room. Something softer will look better. Or we can go with one of these peach colors."

When she picked up a few more sample cards, his head began to swim. He limped a few yards away, allowing her the time to analyze the colors. There were thousands of them. How was anyone supposed to be able to choose?

A family walked through the aisle with some teenage boys who were teasing each other. They weren't watching where they were going and bumped into Tessa. As she whipped around, she dropped the cards and pulled her hands up tight to her chest. Her eyes widened, and her mouth pinched closed. What the hell?

The damn crutches made it impossible to move quickly toward her. She stared at the teens as they jostled past, and one said a casual, "Sorry, lady."

"Pick those up for her," the mom ordered, and both boys scooped the samples from the floor and held them out for Tessa. She looked at them as if they were poisonous snakes.

Reaching out, he grabbed the cards. "Thanks."

The boys took off, muttering under their breath. What they said wasn't totally clear, but the word *weirdo* floated back at him. If he thought he wouldn't have landed on his ass on the floor, he would have smacked them.

When he turned around, Tessa was facing the display. Her head hung down, her shoulders sagged, and her hands gripped the edge of the display case tightly. Damn. Why hadn't he been more aware of their surroundings? She'd been excited about the paint colors, and now she was closing up like a freakin' clam. Something she'd done often in the past, not today, though.

Sifting through the paint cards, he grabbed one and thrust it at her. "Are any of these colors okay? I really need your opinion, Tess."

She looked up, and her tongue hugged her top lip again. The pain in her eyes killed him, and he wanted to wipe it away. Wanted to make sure no one ever hurt her again. Damn, what was his problem? He had enough to worry about with the kids coming soon.

"Or how about this?" He held out another random card. "Peach Fuzz, Spun Sugar, or Soft Apricot? Any of these look good?"

Taking a deep breath, she slowly reached for the two cards he held out. "I liked the colors on these two, especially the Soft Apricot. Do you like that one?"

He leaned in, pretending to look closer at the colors. She stiffened. Backing off, he smiled at her. "How about you pick the color you think will go best with the little fairy world you plan on creating."

It was only a few seconds before she took one of the cards and tucked it in her pocket. "This one. I think we'll need two gallons to cover the walls with a few coats. We need to pick something in a soft blue for Matty now. Did you see anything you liked?"

Shit, she'd given him the job of finding a blue color, hadn't she? It had been too nice watching her get excited about paint. Making a face, he closed his eyes. When he opened them again, a tiny smile played about her lips.

"Okay, so we know I'm a dismal failure in the paint-picking-out department. Kind of why I brought you along, I think. You know what you want to paint on the wall, so you'll know what's best for the rest of the walls."

"Okay, give me a few minutes. Is that all right? I'll try and be fast. But I'll need a few quarts of some other colors for the trees and the boat."

He dropped the other sample cards on the shelf. "You do what you need to. I'll stand right here on guard duty."

Turning his back on Tessa, he stood between her and any other customer who might wander by. He tilted his head a few times to see what she was doing and noticed her body was more relaxed, and she was smiling again. It took another twenty minutes to pick out more colors, but she finally held up a handful to him.

"We need to get them mixed now."

After he adjusted his crutches, they walked to where the paint was mixed. When the associate asked how he could help them, he indicated Tessa and her samples.

"Whatever the lady needs."

As time passed, his hip began to throb. He'd been standing for a while now, and even though it'd been over a month since the injury, it still bothered him. The doctor had said the pelvic fracture could take a while to heal. And his medication was in his bag in the van. Glancing at Tessa, he wondered if she'd be okay if he trekked back out to get it.

"Are you okay, Erik?" Her warm blue eyes held concern. Did he look that bad?

He gritted his teeth and tried to smile. But damn, the pain was getting unbearable. Checking his watch, he realized he should have taken his pills a few hours ago.

"Good, just hate using these crutches. The arms get a little sore." That wasn't exactly a lie.

"Here you go, ma'am. Is there anything else I can get you?"

Tessa pulled their carriage over and lifted the gallons and quarts of newly mixed paint into it. "Brushes and rollers, but we can get them. Thanks."

She rolled the cart away from the counter, then looked his way when he shuffled behind. "Do you want to go get in the car, and I can grab the other stuff we need?"

"I'm fine," he growled. He had to be, didn't he? There were two children who would be depending on him to take care of them very soon. "I need to pay for this stuff. I'm not letting you do all the work and fork out the dough for it, also."

Quickly, she threw rollers, drop cloths, tape, and paint brushes into the carriage, then pushed it toward the check out. After paying the cashier, he pocketed the change, then followed Tessa as she maneuvered through the aisles and into the parking lot. Opening the back of the van, he helped toss the items into it.

When he swung into the driver's seat, he couldn't keep a groan from escaping at the twinge in his leg and hip. He twisted in his seat and struggled to get his duffel bag.

"Do you need me to get you something?"

He pointed at his bag. "Bottles. Side pocket."

She turned and pulled the orange phials from his bag and handed them to him. After twisting the cap off one, he popped a pill in his mouth, washing it down with the water bottle sitting in between the front seats.

"Sorry."

She stared at his leg, then glanced up at his face. There wasn't any pity, only curiosity. Good, he hated pity.

"Is it broken?"

Broken? You could say that, but shattered was more like it. But he didn't want pity, so he'd give her the simple diagnosis. "Kneecap needed reassembling, and I've got a pelvic fracture." No need to mention the amount of damage to his muscles and tendons.

"Pelvic fracture? And they're letting you walk around?"

"It happened over a month ago. I was on bed rest for a few weeks and only got out of the wheelchair a few days ago. I'll need the crutches for another couple weeks, and then I might be able to graduate to a cane. After that, they couldn't promise anything."

The blue in her eyes looked almost stormy. "But it'll get all the way better, right?"

God, he hoped so. Shrugging, he started the car. "Thanks for coming with me and choosing the colors. I'm completely out of my element with anything decoration oriented."

She stared at her hands. "I was happy to do it. I'm looking forward to painting those murals."

It had been obvious how enthusiastic she'd been choosing the colors. The next few days she'd spend in his house helping him get the rooms ready for the kids. After the cellar in Kandahar, his life had looked pretty bleak. Now he had something to look forward to.

****

Erik clenched his teeth as he slid out of the van and grabbed his crutches. He hated to admit it, but he'd pushed himself too much today. The drive down to Hanscom to visit the kids had been long, but he wanted to let them know he'd be bringing them home tomorrow. They'd been excited to see him and hadn't wanted to let go. God, he'd missed them. Then he'd spent what felt like hours finishing up the paperwork for taking custody. For right now it was simply foster care, but he'd already filed papers to adopt them. There was a ton of red tape involved, and it could be a while before it came through.

After the two hours back to Maine, he'd gone to the new physical therapist he'd be seeing. More paperwork and questionnaires then a two-hour session had drained him and left him as limp as a wet rag. How the hell was he supposed to take care of two active children after PT sessions like that? And who would watch them when he was there? Damn, why hadn't he worked some of this out before he came up?

Sure, his mom had offered to help, but she had her own job. Yeah, it was summer, so the school she worked at wasn't as busy, but still she only had a limited amount of vacation time. No way in hell he'd make her take it all for him. And he was two hours away.

Grabbing the two grocery bags from the car, he maneuvered his way into the house. Even though he was getting better at the crutches, the damn knee brace was still cumbersome and nearly made him lose his balance often. His physical therapist, Sue, had told him he might be able to start wearing one without the metal bar soon. His leg needed a bit more strength in it first.

The fresh smell of the ocean drifted through the open windows of the family room as he made his way into the kitchen. Was Tessa still here? When he'd left this morning, she had been sketching on a pad of paper, and it was now almost six. After finishing the little pictures, she'd most likely gone back home. It was time to eat. Some food and a few Vicodin were top of his list. Maybe he'd even forego the food and just take the pills and crash.

Dropping the groceries on the counter, he limped into Matty's room. The color they'd picked out looked nice. The soft blue was calming and warm. His eyes opened wide when he saw the ship Tessa had painted. It took up almost the entire wall. Puffy clouds floated above it while frothy waves churned underneath. A few comical pirates worked on deck, and the sails almost looked like they were flapping in the wind. Over in the corner was a small island with a palm tree, and under it sat a pirate's chest with gold coins spilling over onto the sand. She'd totally outdone herself. He'd expected a small boat on the wall, not this masterpiece. Matty would love it.

He stared at it a bit longer, figuring she couldn't have gotten anything done in Kiki's room yet. That was fine. The child was only a year old and probably wouldn't notice.

Hobbling to Kiki's doorway, he peeked in.

"Holy shit!"

Tessa turned, and her face scrunched up, her tongue at her top lip again. "You don't like it?"

The transformation from pinky-peach colored room to fairy kingdom was astounding. A dozen trees lined two walls split up the middle by a sandy path leading to a turreted castle in the distance. Tiny flower vines crept around the tree trunks while fairies danced in the air, flittered in the trees, and strolled on the path. Each tree had a small rounded door in the bottom and lights that seemed to twinkle among the branches. How did they do that?

Looking at Tessa, he suddenly realized she was

nervous about his reaction. He put as much energy into his smile as he could. "This is amazing. How the hell did you get it all done in one day? Did you have fairies come to help you?"

The anxiety on her face decreased, and her tongue poked back inside her mouth. Good, because it always gave him ideas about what he wanted to do with it. No sense believing that was anywhere in his future.

"The trees were easy. Just some long lines. I used wide brushes to fill them in, then covered in a few spots to make the bark look real."

Tilting his head, he stared at the shiny fairy lights. "How did you get those to look all sparkly?"

She pointed to a tray on the floor. "I had some glitter paint from a project I did a while ago. It also glows in the dark. I thought it might be nice to know the fairies were here to keep Kiki safe while she slept."

Something in her expression told him those words held more meaning than the simple sentence. Would he ever know what she'd gone through before she came to live next door?

"I'm sure she'll love it. It's remarkable. Have you always been this talented?"

She shrugged. "Paper and pencils were usually accessible in whatever home I was in. Paints not so much. But Mr. and Mrs. Miller were very generous and bought me lots of them. Over the past ten years, I've improved a little in my painting skills."

The scene now decorating almost half of the room made him shake his head. It didn't look like the same place they'd painted a few days ago. The new crib stood regally on the far wall, overlooking the magical kingdom. He craned his neck, noticing matching sheets now covering the mattress.

"Where did the sheets and comforter come from?"

Her face turned pink. "When I started thinking about what to paint, I looked up some ideas online. I found that comforter and the sheets, and they were a perfect match for what I wanted to do. So I bought them. Are you mad?"

Anxiety filled her eyes again, and her shoulders hunched. What did she think he'd do to her? And why hadn't she gotten over it in the ten years she'd been with the Millers? They had treated her very well.

"It was really sweet, Tess. Thank you. But how did you get them here so soon? Overnight delivery costs a fortune."

She kept her head down. "I do a lot of online shopping, so I have free two-day shipping on my account. They came today."

He thought back to Matty's room and realized there had been a different bedspread on that bed too. Damn, he should have thought of that. Sheets hadn't been anywhere in his mind, though they were most likely on the list his mother had made for him. The one he hadn't looked at since Tessa agreed to help him paint.

"That was really nice of you. Let me know how much I owe you."

She looked about to object, so he glared at her, gently, but it was still his don't-mess-with-me expression he gave his troops. Nodding, she bent down to pick up another container of paint. "I've got the invoice at home. I'll bring it over later."

The activity of the day suddenly weighed on him, sapping his energy. To keep from actually falling on his face, he leaned on the door frame. It was bad enough he moved like a sloth in mud. He didn't need her witnessing his complete inability to function.

"I'm going to grab a small bite, then get off my feet. It's been a long day." Understatement but she'd seen him the last few days and knew he wasn't in great shape. Not once had she treated him like an invalid. He appreciated it.

"Have you eaten yet?"

She took her eyes off her creation long enough to glance at him. "I had some of the leftovers from the pasta dish you made last night. I hope that was okay?"

"The least I can do is feed you. Are you done? It looks great."

"I have a few more fairies to paint, but I'm almost there. Did you want me to leave so you can rest? I don't have to stay. I can finish while you get the kids tomorrow."

Get the kids tomorrow. It was exciting to finally see them again for longer than a few hours, but when he listened to his aching bones, fear crept along his spine and threatened to strangle him. How the hell could he do this? Right now, he felt like shit. Sure, if he had to, he could find the strength to continue, but he'd end up paying for it later. With the kids here, though, later would find them here with him still their only means of care.

Kiki was still so wiggly, and she hadn't started walking yet. Which meant he'd have to carry her. What the fuck had he been thinking? He was still dependent on his crutches to even walk. Maybe he'd have to break down and ask one of his brothers to take the day off and help him bring the kids back here. They'd do it with no argument. But he wanted to prove he didn't need help. Damn pride.

His gaze skimmed over the newly decorated walls and then landed on Tessa. She already knew he needed help. Could he…? Would she…?

"Tessa?" Good decision? Bad decision? At least she wouldn't babble on incessantly while they drove. Would she agree? She'd freaked in the hardware store, and that was right down the street.

Turning, she smiled at him. "Did you want me to make you something to eat? You look tired. I can't guarantee it will be anywhere near as good as what you make, but it should be edible."

"Thanks, no. I actually had a really big favor to ask, and I want you to feel free to say no if you aren't comfortable with it."

That tongue poked out again and played on her lip. Poker would not be her game.

"I realized Kiki will need to be carried to and from the van when I get the kids tomorrow." He glanced down at his legs. "You've seen my ability to walk at the moment and how dependent I am on these stupid things." The crutches rattled as he scowled.

"Would you consider coming with me to get them at Hanscom? If you have other plans, or don't want to for any reason, it's okay."

She looked around the room and then at his damaged knee but didn't say anything for a while. He sighed. It was a long shot. But no way he'd want to make her uneasy.

"It's okay—" he started, but she interrupted him.

"If I didn't go, how would you get her to the car?"

He shrugged. "I'm sure someone there can help

me." But would that convince anyone he was able to take care of the kids?

"Would they still let you take the children? Foster parents are *supposed* to be…capable."

Her tone made him think she'd had some that weren't. Damn. It was his turn to look at his feet. He didn't have an answer for her.

Waving his hand, he turned. "Don't worry about it. I shouldn't have asked. You've already done so much."

After hobbling to the kitchen, he put the groceries away, then pulled a piece of fried chicken from a container and sank into the chair. That's when he realized his meds were in the cabinet, and he wasn't sure he had the energy to actually get up again.

"I'll go with you." The tiny voice drifted his way as Tessa stood in the doorway staring at him.

"I shouldn't have asked. You've already done so much."

Her step closer was tentative. "I'm happy to do it. You know I don't like big crowds, though. But we're just getting them and driving most of the time, right?"

"Yeah, I did all the paperwork today." He scrubbed his hand through his short hair and down his neck, trying to ease the tension.

"Do you need your medication?"

Could she read minds, or did he look as bad as he felt? "How could you tell?"

Shrugging, she moved to the cabinet. "I saw it in here earlier when I got a bowl for my food. And you were gone all day. Most medicine is every four or six hours."

He grimaced. "Yeah, I didn't realize I'd be gone so long. I'll get it in a minute."

She opened the cabinet, took out the bottle, and set it on the table in front of him. "What do you want to wash it down with?"

A cold beer? Maybe not too smart with the heavy drugs but boy would it taste good. "I'll get some water."

When he started to rise, she put her hand out. An inch from his shoulder, she seemed to realize what she was doing and stopped.

"I'll get it. You wanted to rest." After filling a glass, she put it on the table. "Do you need anything else?"

"It's not your job to wait on me." Although right now he was eternally grateful he didn't need to get up.

"I don't mind. If you're all set, I'll go finish up the fairies, then get out of your hair."

Before he could thank her again, she scooted out of the room. It seemed he'd been thanking her a lot in the last few days. His grandparents had mentioned she might be helpful, but he hadn't planned on asking. After a few days on his own, he now knew he might have to screw his pride and put himself out there. At least she wouldn't gloat like his brothers or smother him like his mom.

When the chicken leg was picked clean, he rinsed his hands in the sink and hobbled his way past Kiki's room to poke his head in the door.

"I'm going to get off my feet for a while. If you need anything, I'm right here."

Tessa sat cross-legged on the floor, concentrating on a tiny winged creature. She stroked a gossamer wing and looked up.

"I'll finish the last few fairies, then go home. What

time do you want me tomorrow?"

"Kiki usually takes a nap around noon, so they suggested we get there a little while before, and she'd probably nap in the car on the way home."

Would this place ever really be home to the kids? He'd come here since he was a baby and felt comfortable, but how would they feel? Although it had been a month since they'd left Kandahar, and by all accounts they'd adjusted well.

"Is nine thirty okay?"

"I'll be ready."

He pulled his phone from his pocket. "Would you mind putting your number in here in case anything changes?"

"No problem." She rattled off her number, and he punched the buttons. "That's the house. I don't have a cell phone since I don't really need one."

That was strange, but he didn't question. She'd come to his rescue too many times in the past few days. And she was doing it again tomorrow.

"Night."

Turning back to her paintings, she murmured, "Night."

After stumbling into his room, he collapsed on the bed, letting his crutches fall to the floor. He didn't even have the energy to remove his shoes properly. Somehow he managed to get his bad leg off the floor and on the mattress but knew that was as far as he'd go right now.

Typically he wouldn't be able to sleep well knowing someone was roaming his house, but for some reason having Tessa in the next room didn't bother him. Had she painted some fairies in this room too who watched over him and helped him feel safe enough to sleep? His mind started to whirl with thoughts of tomorrow and how he'd take care of the kids. But Tessa's sweet face appeared in his mind, and suddenly the worry settled, and he drifted into a deep sleep.

****

Tessa cleaned up the last of the paint and stored the brushes in her case. The room had to be perfect for when Erik's new children arrived. Children. It was something she'd never allowed herself to think of. She loved watching them play and gallivant around in all their innocence but knew there was no way she'd ever have any. Not any of her own. There were times she'd considered adopting like Erik was doing but wasn't sure she'd be any kind of decent mother. Her role models had been sorely lacking in maternal skills.

Glancing around the room one last time, she made sure everything looked perfect and she hadn't left anything on the floor. Kiki was only a baby and might put stuff in her mouth if she found it. The room looked great. Pride filled her but also longing. What would it have been like to live in a room like this? To have a parent who cared about you and wanted only what was best? One who pushed aside his own pain to make sure you had what you needed?

She'd never know. But these children would. He hadn't ever struck her as the paternal type, but when he'd shown her the pictures of them, his eyes had lit up, and he couldn't hide the grin that crossed his face. He cared for them already, and they weren't even his. And she knew how proud he was. But he'd pushed that aside to ask for her help, in not only preparing the room but in bringing them safely back here. Yeah, he'd be a great dad.

Leaving her supplies in the hallway, she tiptoed to the door of Erik's room. When she was younger, she and the girl Storm cousins had hung out in the window seat overlooking the ocean, playing all sorts of games. Only when the weather was poor, though. Otherwise they'd drag her along the shore, looking for shells and other sea trinkets. It had been tough at first, but she'd come to trust this family.

He rested peacefully on the bed, his face calm. Unlike during the day when pain shadowed his handsome features. Not that he'd admit it, but she could see his discomfort. How would he manage once he got the kids? Would he ask her for more help?

Did she want him to ask her for more help? That was a good question. One she wasn't sure she knew the answer to. Most people made her uneasy, but the last few days with him hadn't been as nerve wracking as she'd thought it would be. The lack of conversation hadn't bothered him, and he'd seemed satisfied with the small amount she'd managed. And for some reason, after her initial anxiety, she'd felt a little more comfortable with him.

Maybe she was finally getting over this fear she had. *Don't count on it.* Deep inside anxiety still clung to her nerves and lived in her blood. It was a part of her.

Erik grunted, turning on his side, and she backed away so she was mostly out of sight.

As she stared at the huge king-sized bed, she wondered what it would be like to sleep in it beside him every night. Right, like that would ever happen. First of all, he'd never want someone like her there, and she'd break into frozen little pieces if she ever tried.

It was a nice dream.

Backing out of the room, she left the house. Dreams were great, and she allowed herself the indulgence often. But they were all she'd ever get of the family she wanted.

Chapter Four

"You're all set, Captain Storm. Do you need directions?"

Erik took his military ID back from the soldier at the gate and shook his head. "I was here yesterday. Thank you, Airman."

Tessa unclenched her fists and waited as he drove through the grounds of Hanscom Air Force Base. The ride down had been quiet, though she was used to quiet. The few times they'd spoken had shown her he was pretty nervous about getting the children and being responsible for them on his own. It was too late to rethink at this point.

"You're in the marines. How come the kids are at an Air Force base?"

He glanced at her, then put his eyes back on his driving. "It's the closest military base with an airfield and a hospital."

They pulled into a parking spot near a long, low building, and Erik sat staring at the steering wheel. He took a deep breath in and then let it out again slowly. After a few more times she began to get nervous. When was she not nervous? It was her theme song.

"Are you having second thoughts about taking the children?"

That seemed to wake him from his stupor. "No, no, I...really care for these kids, and I promised. It's

43

just…" He turned to look at her. "Thank you for coming with me today."

And that was it. His thought was never finished. The confident Erik was back in place, and he got out of the car, grabbing his crutches. She met him on the sidewalk and followed him into the building where an older woman greeted them.

"Captain Storm, Mateen and Kinah have been eagerly awaiting your arrival. I couldn't really get them to eat anything for lunch. I'm sorry. I know you have a long ride ahead of you."

"That's okay, Mrs. Cooper. We'll stop and get something before we hit the highway."

It took a second, but he seemed to realize she was there and gave introductions. She hoped it was just because he wanted to see the children.

"I thought it might be nice to play with the children a few minutes here before you take them. Even though they love seeing you, they haven't really been away from the base for two weeks."

He shifted his crutches, then continued on. "I understand. I figure there'll be a bit of an adjustment period…for both of us."

Mrs. Cooper laughed. "I'm sure there will be."

They entered a room at the end of the hall, and she stood back while he hobbled forward. Two children sat on the floor playing with wooden blocks. The boy kept piling them up while the young girl knocked them over and laughed. They were still able to laugh after what had happened. That was good.

As Erik leaned down to sit on a chair, the boy, Mateen, got up and raced toward him.

"*Pedar*, you come?"

When Erik scooped the boy into his arms, enveloping him in a warm hug, her heart twinged. Why, she didn't know. It's not like she was comfortable around touch, and a hug was the worse contact she could think of. It totally invaded your space and made you vulnerable.

The girl crawled to Erik, so he slid Matty to one knee and slung his arm around Kinah, pulling her to sit on the other. Reaching, she clung to his neck.

"Did you miss me, Kiki? I was just here yesterday."

The change in him was astounding. His typical scowl melted into something softer and unbelievably warm. He held the children as if he'd never see them again. It made no sense. They were going to his home to live with him every day.

He looked up at her, and the hand that held Matty made a motion. "I have someone I want you to meet. Her name is Tessa, and she's going to be with us on our ride home."

She stepped closer, not exactly sure what he wanted her to do.

"Hi Matty. Hi Kiki. I'm glad I finally got to meet you." She'd been about to say he'd told her all about them but didn't know what they called him. Or how they thought of him. Essentially he would be their new father. But she'd had foster fathers who she never called anything but their formal names. Most she'd been happy to stay away from and not call them anything.

"What are you two building here?" Erik slid the kids to the floor and managed to get himself down near the blocks too.

Matty piled a few blocks on top of each other. "I do this and Ki—"

The baby pushed at the blocks, and they tumbled to the floor. Both children laughed, and Erik joined in.

"Can I build one?" Erik started stacking blocks and playfully telling Kiki to wait. Crawling over his leg, she pushed them over anyway. A determined young girl. The family scene made her insides twist. The Storms had often made her feel that way. They would tease and torture each other, but they did it with so much love you couldn't help but envy them.

Standing, Matty walked over to her and reached up. Panic set in. What did he want? She put her hand in his, hoping that would be enough. After grabbing it, he pulled her to sit with them on the floor, then slid a few blocks in front of her. "You do it."

"Okay." She piled the blocks, and they stayed put as Kiki was knocking over the ones Erik had stacked. It should make her happy no one ruined her blocks but for some reason it didn't.

Kiki laughed, then noticed her sitting there. Or maybe she noticed the blocks because she crawled over Erik and in seconds had Tessa's blocks tumbling to the floor.

"I guess we'll have to make sure you have some blocks to play with at home."

When he glanced up at her, she realized she had said home. Would he think she meant she now thought of it as home? Her own house wasn't even considered home most of the time.

"Good idea." He winked at her. "Can you remind me to get some? I have a feeling I may be preoccupied with other things this week and forget."

"Sure."

She and Erik took turns stacking blocks and Kiki made sure to knock them all over. At one point she crawled into Tessa's lap and rubbed her face against her shirt front.

"Hey, you okay, sweetie?"

"She's probably tired." Mrs. Cooper had stood in the doorway the whole time. "She woke up very early this morning."

"Maybe we should get going then and give her the chance to fall asleep in the car." He looked at Mrs. Cooper.

"Their bags are ready and right there. I packed some diapers and wipes since I wasn't sure if you'd remember to bring any."

His expression was sheepish. "Thanks. Yeah, Tessa, another reminder for diapers."

She chuckled. Erik was so damn cute when he was chastising himself. Standing, she handed him his crutches, and scooped Kiki off the floor. Matty looked curiously at Erik, then at the crutches, and held out his hand to her. Guess she was elected to hold his hand.

Taking the backpack Mrs. Cooper handed him, Erik put it on, then slung the diaper bag over his wide shoulders. Should she offer to carry one? But he slipped his crutches under his arms and made his way to the door.

"Thanks for all you've done with them," he said to the woman who was giving the children hugs.

"It was my pleasure, Captain Storm. They're lovely children. You've got my number if you have any questions. Congratulations and good luck with everything."

When they got to the car, the children were wide eyed and excited. It took more than a few minutes to get them settled in the new car seats, but they finally managed.

Shifting in his seat, Erik groaned.

"Do you need your pills?"

He shook her off, the pain lines evident now he wasn't playing with the children. "The Vicodin makes me drowsy. It's fine if I'm only going a short distance, but two hours of highway driving and I'll be falling asleep at the wheel. I'll take some when we get back."

"I can drive if you want." It wasn't something she did often since she never had any place to go, but she had a license and certainly knew how.

After starting the van, he patted her knee. He snatched his hand back fast and sent her an apologetic look. "Thanks, but I'll be fine. We can stop at one of the fast food places off the highway. There should be a few on the next exit."

As promised the next exit had an abundance of restaurants as well as the mall. She didn't say anything but hoped he wouldn't pick the mall food court. She'd probably break out in hives and start twitching.

"I'm not much of a mall rat. Can we do this place? I want to get in and out fast."

Her shoulders sagged with relief. "Perfect."

It took another few minutes to get the kids out of the seats and at a table. Erik dragged over a high chair for Kiki and snagged a booster seat for Matty. Pulling out his wallet, he tossed it at her.

"Do you mind getting the food, and I'll stay with the kids. The inept one is finally conceding he can't carry a loaded tray with these crutches."

Once he'd rattled off what he wanted, she got in line but kept her eyes on him and the kids as the food was being prepared. He tickled Kiki, and she started to squeal. A smile popped on her face. What a great way he had with them. He should have a whole passel of children. Maybe that's what the minivan was for. Did he have a mother all lined up too? Female company wasn't anything he'd ever lacked before. The thought was depressing.

When the food was ready, she brought it back and settled on the bench seat across from Erik, next to Kiki. Matty slid off his chair and bounded around to climb on the seat next to her.

"I sit here."

She peeked at Erik to see if he was upset. Apparently not since he was grinning.

As she spooned the yogurt into Kiki's waiting mouth, Erik broke apart the hamburger for Matty and squeezed ketchup on his fries.

"Make sure you eat, too, Tessa."

"I will, but I can eat in the car while you're driving. You and the kids can't. Kiki looks like she's about to fall over."

The look Erik gave Kiki was so precious she stopped breathing. How come he already cared so much for these kids and none of her foster parents had ever looked at her that way? Cared for her that way? *Because you aren't lovable.* Some of the other foster kids had taunted her with that. No one had ever kept her longer than a few years except the Millers. And by that time Mr. Miller was sick, and Mrs. Miller had needed someone to help her care for him.

Kiki blew a raspberry, dribbling yogurt all down

her front.

"Oh, sweetie, you're a mess now. Finish this off, and we can clean you up."

Erik dug in the diaper bag and pulled out a packet of baby wipes. "Here, these might help. I'm going to get a cup of coffee for the road."

When Kiki had finished and been wiped up, she removed her from the high chair. The child snuggled right up to her, so Tessa kept her in her lap. Matty had eaten as much as he could and leaned against her side. Putting her arm around him, she stroked his back. It was what she should do, right? Help these children to feel safe and wanted. Something she'd never felt.

Yeah, that's exactly what they needed. Erik should be the one who did this, but maybe they needed it from as many adults as possible. She was up for the challenge, wasn't she? Sure. They were small innocent children. They certainly couldn't hurt her. But they could *be* hurt. And she'd never let anyone do that.

When Kiki rested her head on Tessa's shoulder, warmth crept along her spine and filled her with…what? What was this feeling she was having? It was unbelievable. And maybe somewhat familiar. But from way too long ago to really remember.

Pulling both children closer, she closed her eyes, trying to recall. Images of someone holding her floated back, but she couldn't grasp them. Never could. What did it matter, though? They probably weren't real. She'd never had anyone hold her like that.

But these kids would. Maybe only today, but she hoped they'd remember and have more times of being held. With Erik as their dad, she was sure of it.

"You look like you're ready for a nap too. All set

to head out?"

He slung the diaper bag over his head again, then scooped Matty off the seat. She continued to cradle Kiki. The child was nodding off already. Was she that trusting?

When they got to the van, she didn't want to let Kiki go. The fresh baby scent and soft skin was heaven, and something inside her just felt like home. Only no home she'd ever had. But like the ones you saw on TV with the perfect family who all loved each other, and all was at peace.

"Do you need help getting her in?" Erik had finished putting Matty in his seat.

"I'm all set. I don't want to wake her. She fell asleep." Good excuse and it was true. Just not all of the truth. She gave the child another squeeze and inhaled before strapping her in and making sure her head was at a comfortable angle.

As he turned into traffic, she pulled her meal from her bag and began to eat but also turned around often to check on the children. Matty also fell asleep, and she adjusted his head to a more comfortable angle. Luckily the van had bucket seats in the front, and she could walk in between them to reach the back. Erik could never have done this in his old car.

"What happened to your Camaro?" She wasn't sure if she should even bring that up. He'd adored that car and treated it better than any other possession.

He threw a swift glance at her but stayed focused on the road.

"It's in the garage at my parents' house. Alex says I can keep it there even when they move out. Of course he says he'll charge me an exorbitant fee."

Would Alex really do that? The smirk on his face told her no. Family helped each other out. The Storm family did anyway. Matty and Kiki were lucky to now be a part of that family. She'd simply have to watch and enjoy from afar…as she always did.

But when they got back to Maine, he would need help carrying Kiki inside. That would give her one more opportunity to snuggle with the child. And she'd enjoy every second because it was as close to being a mother as she'd ever get.

****

Erik looked at the running bath water, then at a naked Matty and diaper clad Kiki sitting on the bathroom floor. The logistics and tactics of how he would give both of these kids a bath weren't adding up.

At first he'd figured they'd sit in it and he could scrub them leaning over, but now he realized, with his knee's inability to bend, that wouldn't really work. Matty might be okay washing himself, but Kiki, no way. She was as squirmy as an eel, and he'd bet when she was wet, she'd be as slippery as one too. No way he'd take the chance of her getting hurt. Maybe they didn't really need a bath tonight.

As he glanced at Matty putting the bath towel over his head and playing peek-a-boo with his sister, he knew spaghetti and sauce may not have been the best thing to give them for dinner. But Kiki only had a few teeth so far, and he'd cut it up really small. There was no baby food in the house. Stupid. Why hadn't he thought this out more?

"We take a bath?" Matty moved to the edge of the tub, watching the water level rise. How high did you fill the tub? Damn, maybe he should call his mom and ask.

That wouldn't solve his problem of actually bathing the children.

Tessa? She was right next door, but she'd already done so much for him he hated to ask for more. When she'd helped him bring the kids in this afternoon, though, she'd almost seemed disappointed he'd told her he was all set with them. Maybe she wouldn't mind coming over for a few minutes. It couldn't hurt to ask.

Pulling his cell phone out of his pocket, he pressed her contact number. It rang a few times, and he held his breath. Maybe she wasn't home. It was Friday night after all.

"Hello."

"Tessa, hi, it's Erik."

"Erik? Is everything okay?"

"Um, yeah, I, uh…have another small favor to ask. I'm sorry. Seems I've been doing that a lot lately."

"It's no problem. I'm happy to help. What do you need?"

"I'm about to give the kids a bath and realized I can't really bend in the way I need to. I suppose I can wipe them down with a facecloth, but I gave them spaghetti for supper, and they're a mess. If you're on your way out, though, don't worry. I'll manage."

Her laugh warmed his blood. It wasn't something she did often.

"I'll be over in a minute. Don't stick them in until I get there."

As promised, it was barely a minute before he heard the door open and footsteps down the hallway. Seconds later, she appeared in the doorway.

"Oh, my." As she spotted the dirty hands and faces of the children crawling on the bathroom floor, she laughed. "I guess you really enjoyed that spaghetti. Let's see about getting you cleaned up."

After glancing in the tub, she quickly shut the tap off. "That's more than enough water. We could actually let a little out. I used to help give baths to a few of the younger kids at one of my last foster homes, and the mom there said only to fill it a few inches."

He leaned over and drained a small amount out as Tessa removed Kiki's diaper.

"Here, sweetie, we're going to clean you all up. Are you ready, Matty?"

The boy bounced up and down, the towel still in his hand. Taking it, he placed it on the counter. Tessa knelt on the floor and swished Kiki's feet in the water first, then lowered her slowly.

"Do you like this, sweetie? It feels nice and warm, huh? Matty, come join your sister."

He scooped the boy up and slid him in beside Kiki, then pushed the shower curtain back so he could see the kids as Tessa bathed them.

"Can I have that face cloth?"

Picking it up, he handed it over, then leaned back against the counter. *I can't even freakin' do this simple task.* Yet another reminder why maybe he wasn't the best person to care for these kids. But every time he thought of handing them over to another family, his stomach turned and his hands shook.

While she gently washed the children, she played with them too. Man, she was so good with kids, keeping them occupied so they didn't splash. Not much. After a while she picked Kiki up and kissed her nose.

"Open the towel, and I'll hand her to you."

Grabbing the towel, he sat on the closed toilet seat.

He didn't dare carry the baby yet. Tessa flew the dripping child through the air, with Kiki giggling and flailing her arms and legs. When she settled her in his lap, he closed the towel around her.

As usual, Kiki wiggled, but he scrubbed the towel over her soft skin, getting the excess water off. Tessa clicked the drain open and grabbed another towel to wrap around Matty. Lifting him out, she set him on the bath mat and began to rub the towel over his skin.

What a domestic scene. A few months ago he'd never have pictured anything like this any time in the near future for him. Was he crazy? Something about Tessa chatting to Matty had him remembering his mom giving them baths. All three boys would be stuck in the tub at the same time. As he got older, he'd hated having his little brothers there too and had insisted he get his own. That's when he'd been introduced to showers and had thought he was cool stuff.

Matty and Kiki couldn't reach that age for a very long time. He wouldn't let them. The way they were now was how he wanted to enjoy them. His stomach turned sour. That was something their real parents wouldn't be able to do. Their biological father had barely known Kiki before he'd been pulled away from his family. Erik grew determined to give them the best life possible with lots of love and support. It was how he'd been raised.

"Are they getting into their pajamas now?"

His musings cut short, he planted raspberries on Kiki's belly. Squealing, she kicked her chubby little legs. Hearing her laugh would never get old. Joining in the fun, Matty jumped up and down in his towel.

"Yeah, I left them in the bedrooms, though. Maybe

someday I'll get this parenting thing right."

She threw him a strange look. "I think you're doing better than a lot of parents."

Again there were hidden meanings in her words. Would he ever find out exactly what she meant by some of what she said? And did he really want to know? Yeah, he did. For some reason her background intrigued him. Maybe it would give a clue to her personality.

"Why don't I take Kiki?" she suggested. "And you can do Matty since he can get there on his own."

When she scooped up Kiki, she immediately snuggled the child to her chest. She really seemed to enjoy holding the baby. Maybe it wasn't such an imposition after all.

"Come on, pal. Let's get those jammies on and get ready for bed. It's been a long day."

He hobbled after Matty, wondering when he could finally get rid of these damn crutches. The child was dancing around the room naked and waving at the painting on the wall.

"Do you like your pirate ship?"

Jumping up and down, Matty chanted, "Yup, yup, yup."

"Make sure you say thank you to Tessa because she put it there."

Matty scrambled to the door and called out, "Thank you, Tessa."

Her chuckle floated back. "You're welcome, sweetie."

The soft voice continued to drift in as she chattered away, explaining to Kiki what she was doing. What a great mom she'd be someday. The thought made him pause as he pulled Matty's pajamas from the bag. Did she have a boyfriend or someone special in her life? Over the past week she hadn't mentioned anyone, but then he'd never asked. And she hadn't gone anywhere when she wasn't helping him either.

Not that he'd admit he kind of kept tabs on her. It was simple curiosity, and after being in a war zone, he made sure to be aware of his surroundings at all times. She was part of his surroundings. And the protective military aspect of him wanted to make sure she was safe. Which was silly because she'd lived on her own since Mrs. Miller died two years ago.

"You need help with these, pal?" He tossed the pajamas to Matty who shook his head and started pulling his pants on. The top did need to be turned around the right way, but soon Matty was ready. Patting the bed, he hoisted Matty on top and under the covers, then stood up, grabbing his crutches.

The boy's eyes widened, and he looked scared. His bottom lip trembled, stopping Erik in his tracks.

"What's the matter?"

"You going away?"

"No, pal," he assured him. "I'll just be in the other room. I'll keep the door open so I can hear you if you need me."

Tears filled Matty's eyes, and he clamped his lips together. What in the world was wrong? Hobbling back, he sat on the bed. Matty climbed in his lap and snuggled into his chest.

"What's wrong, Matty? It's time for bed."

Matty clung to him and whimpered. After a few minutes his tiny voice floated up. "You stay."

"You want me to stay until you fall asleep?"

"You stay," he repeated and pointed to the second twin bed he hadn't had time to get rid of yet. Hadn't had the *ability* to get rid of yet.

He frowned. "I have my own bed in the other room. I showed you, remember?"

The boy held on to him tighter. What the hell was he supposed to do now? Would Tessa know?

Standing, he picked up Matty, struggling to stay upright. The child didn't weigh much, but he could barely support his own weight, never mind hold someone else up. But he gritted his teeth and took the steps to Kiki's room, the pain ripping through his hip and leg. While balancing Matty on one hip, he held the wall and doorway with his other.

"She almost asleep?"

Tessa sat in the Canadian rocker, holding Kiki nestled against her. The baby's eyes flew open at his voice.

"Not yet." Her expression said Kiki had almost been asleep.

"Matty wanted to say goodnight to his sister." Maybe that's all it really was. Why hadn't he thought of that a few minutes ago? These two had been sharing a room for a long time.

Rising, Tessa walked closer with Kiki in her arms. Matty squirmed, and Erik almost fell over. He grabbed the railing of the crib as Matty leaned to kiss his sister.

"Careful, sweetie. You're going to knock over your…" Her eyes asked a question.

"*Pedar* is the formal version of father. Maybe once they've been here awhile, they'll start calling me Dad."

She put Kiki next to Matty so he could hug and kiss her. Then the boy leaned in for a kiss from Tessa.

For a second she froze, then shifted Kiki to one hip and gave Matty a hug and kiss. She was so close he could smell her. Something rose scented and baby shampoo. It was intoxicating.

"Night, Kiki." He kissed the baby, then grinned sheepishly at Tessa. "Matty's a little nervous about sleeping alone, I think. Do you mind getting Kiki settled? It might take a bit for Matty to fall asleep."

"No problem." She walked back to the rocking chair. As he left the room, he heard her whisper, "Means I can hold you for a little longer."

The words allowed him to release some of the guilt he felt at asking her to do so much. He lowered Matty to the floor. "Can you walk for now, pal? I need to get my medicine before I sit with you."

Matty held on to his pant legs as he held the wall up on his way to the kitchen. Quickly he took his meds, then went back down the hall to Matty's room. A quick peek showed him Tessa holding Kiki snuggly against her, eyes closed and a content smile on her face, rubbing the baby's back.

Matty got back in bed, and Erik pulled the sheets over him. The angle he was sitting at was torture for his hip, so he scooted Matty over and settled next to him in the narrow bed.

"Do you mind if I stay next to you for a while?"

"You stay." Matty snuggled up against his side, and Erik threw his arm over the child's shoulder. At times he'd been with his dad like this when he was younger. It was a good memory, and he wanted Matty and Kiki to have great memories too. So far in their young lives, they hadn't had too many.

Tessa's sweet voice drifted over to him as she sang

to the baby in her lap. He hoped Kiki would settle quickly so she didn't have to stay too late. Although if he was truthful, he realized he wouldn't mind having her nearby. Next to his boisterous family, she was calm and peaceful. Never asking for his constant attention or nattering on in his ear about silly things. As the events of the day weighed on him, and Matty's drowsy body relaxed against him, he knew having her nearby was a very nice thing indeed.

Chapter Five

"Damn it. They're here already." Erik looked away from the window and closed the tab on Kiki's diaper. The child's wiggling body made it difficult to get her one-piece romper thing fastened.

"Tess, my folks are here."

Tessa appeared in the doorway of Kiki's room, Matty at her side. His outfit was free of the breakfast mess he'd made. Live and learn. Getting them dressed before breakfast did not make things easier. Good thing she'd stopped by this morning with the milk he'd forgotten to buy last night. The kids had been tired, and there was no way he'd be able get around the store with them.

What would he have done without her? Having her around the last few days had been damn helpful, and he was man enough to admit it.

"I'll take off, then. Matty's all cleaned up. You've got Kiki?"

Lifting the baby onto his hip, he grabbed one crutch. This was doable, right? Not like he had much choice. Apparently, Tess didn't want to stick around. When he took a few steps, she watched him anxiously. Heat rose in his face, but he managed to get halfway across the room before the pain in his hip made his knee give out.

"I've got her." Tessa grabbed Kiki. "I'll bring her

into the family room."

Matty walked over with his other crutch, and he faked a smile. "Thanks, pal." Even a three-year-old saw how pitiful he was.

"Erik? We're here." His mother's voice rang through the large family room, and he smiled. Molly Storm might be strong minded and a bit pushy at times, but everything she did, she did out of love for her family.

Hobbling into the room, he found not only his mom and dad but his grandparents as well. Tessa stood by the windows with Kiki in her arms. She held herself stiffly with a forced smile. Damn. The last few days she'd been more comfortable, but now she seemed to close up again.

"Tessa, I told Erik you'd probably be available to help him," his grandmother said. "I'm so glad he took my advice." Ingrid Storm was another gentle lady who was fiercely devoted to her family.

Tessa's smile grew warmer as she looked his way. "I was happy to." Leaning down, she rubbed her nose in Kiki's hair as her cheeks turned red.

"She didn't have much choice with me on my as...uh, butt in the driveway, cursing up a storm my first day here. Luckily, she took pity on me and helped me get everything inside."

"And Erik's been feeding me home-cooked gourmet meals ever since."

His mom's eyes twinkled, and he knew she had matchmaking on her mind. Yeah, like Tessa would ever want someone as bent and broken as him. What woman would?

"So are you going to introduce us to these

grandchildren of ours?" Pete Storm put his arm around his wife's shoulders and moved her forward in the room. "That's the whole reason we came."

When the adults had come in, the boy had wrapped himself around Erik's leg and hidden, so Erik took Matty's hand and pulled him out.

"Matty, these are my parents and grandparents. *My pedar* and *madar*." He pointed to Pete and Molly. "And these people"—he indicated Hans and Ingrid—"my *pedarbozorg* and *mâdarbozorg*."

Matty gave a tiny nod, then stuck his face in Erik's pant leg again. "This is Mateen, and the lovely little princess Tessa has is Kinah."

He threw his parents and grandparents an apologetic look, but his mom shook her head, her short blonde bob bouncing softly. "Oh, sweetie, they're precious. And it'll take some time for them to be comfortable with us. They've gone through so much in their short lives. We won't try and rush them."

"But we will try and feed them," his grandmother pointed out as she lifted a casserole dish. "I thought we could do a nice brunch. This will need to go back in the oven to warm, though. I made it last night."

"The kids ate a short while ago but only cereal. I'm sure they'll be hungry again soon."

His dad laughed. "They take after you already, Erik." As he placed some bags on the floor, he continued, "I'll go get the rest of the stuff we brought." He and Gramps walked out the door.

"What stuff?"

"Oh, just some things your aunts and cousins thought you might need for the children." His mother waved her hand in the air. "Let's get this food in the kitchen. Tessa, do you want to help?"

Her gaze flitted around the room, and he wanted to make her more comfortable, but he didn't know how.

"I should let you have your family time. I'll head home if someone wants to take Kiki."

"Nonsense, honey." Gram patted her arm. "You've been hanging around here long enough we think of you as family too."

Her shoulders lowered, and her face softened as she followed his mom and Gram into the kitchen. Since the Millers has been best friends with his grandparents, Tessa had been around them more than anyone else in the family.

"Come on, Matty, let's see what all this stuff is they're talking about." Wobbling to the door, he went out onto the porch. The bags coming in were filled to the brim, and he sighed. Forget doing this on his own. His family wouldn't allow it. Felt kind of nice, though.

The sound of a car got his attention, and he clenched his teeth as his prized Camaro zoomed into the driveway. Lukas exited the driver's seat and came onto the porch, Alex right behind him.

"Pouring salt in the wound, Luke?"

"Who me?" Luke's angelic expression didn't fool him. "Thought you might like to visit with the old girl."

Alex stuck out his hand to shake. "We know you have Mom's minivan but figured you might want this here too. We can hitch a ride back with them if you do."

Pumping his brother's hand, he sighed. "I'm sure that wasn't Luke's intention but nice try, Alex. And this freakin' leg isn't in any shape to work a clutch." The need to tell his brothers the doctor wasn't sure it would ever totally heal was strong. But more pity wasn't what he needed. The women in the family had that covered.

Alex squatted down and peered behind Erik's leg. Reaching down, Erik ruffled the child's thick locks. "This is Matty. His sister is in the kitchen with the ladies."

"Where they belong," teased Luke, looking around, probably to make sure no one else heard. He'd catch hell for even joking about something like that in their family.

Cautiously, Alex put his hand out. "I'm your Uncle Alex. I'm the nice brother."

"Brother?" Matty glanced up at him with a question in his eyes. His English was improving, but he was hardly fluent.

"*Barâdar*," he supplied as he pointed to his brothers. "Alex. Luke. Your...*amu*." He always had to think about which word to use since Farsi had a different word for maternal and paternal uncle.

A shy smile crept onto Matty's face, and he slowly put his hand into Alex's. After shaking it gently, Alex stood and ruffled the boy's hair too.

"So have Mom and Gram started the food yet?" Luke asked. "I'm starving."

Alex narrowed his eyes at their youngest brother. "You had three donuts on the way up here. How could you still be hungry?"

"Have you forgotten who you're talking about, Alex? Luke's always hungry. Someday it'll catch up with him, though."

"I just make sure I do lots of vigorous activity to work it all off." Luke winked.

Alex shook his head as he moved toward the door. "One of these days you'll regret all your wild ways and

wanton woman. It'll come back to bite you in the ass."
Luke's only reply was a snort.

Erik guided Matty back inside and thought of the
vigorous activity Luke was talking about. Deep regret
sliced through him. Not that he'd ever been the
Casanova his brother was, but he'd had his share of
female encounters. Now he had to focus on the children
and forget that part of him ever existed.

A few hours later, when brunch had been cleaned
up and everyone oohed and aahed over Tessa's amazing
wall creations, the gifts were unpacked and sorted into
the correct rooms. Now they all sat in the family room,
enjoying the sound of the waves against the shore and
the salty breeze blowing in the windows.

"So what do you still need for these cuties, Erik?"
his mother asked, a notepad in her hand. His mother
and her lists. She was famous for them.

"I think you brought more than enough. I can get
things as I need them."

His mom rolled her eyes. "Men. Tessa, maybe
you'd be a better person to ask. Is there anything you
can think of my grandchildren will need over the next
few weeks or so?"

As she glanced at him, her tongue touched her top
lip. Could she stop doing that? It made him want things
he couldn't have.

"They could use bathing suits. We went down on
the beach yesterday, and they had to play in their
shorts."

His mom scribbled on her notepad, then looked up
with her *I've-got-an-idea* face on. "Tessa, sweetie,
would you mind coming with Gram and me to the
Walmart in Brunswick? It's only fifteen minutes, and

maybe you'd be able to think of more things these children need as we go through."

The anxiety on her face was obvious, so he interceded. "Mom, I'm sure I can get anything they need later. You don't need to drag Tessa out now."

"Erik, you know I'm concerned about your being so out of the way here. The closest stores are in Brunswick, and anything more you need is in Portland, and that's forty-five minutes away. We might as well get stuff now since we're here."

"Don't argue, Erik," his dad said. "You know you can't win against your mother."

Yeah, he knew, but he still glanced at Tessa holding tightly to Kiki, her eyes only on the baby.

His mother looked at Tessa. "You don't mind, do you? We can take Kinah with us and leave all the men here to...well, do whatever it is men do when women aren't around."

"You mean relax," Luke muttered under his breath. Alex smacked him on the head, and their mother scowled. It was so familiar, and he wondered again at his decision to live almost two hours away from his family. Looking at Matty and Kiki, he knew he had a new family now.

Tessa and Kiki were dragged away, and his dad and Gramps started talking about the various repairs the house needed.

"Might as well get them done now while we don't have the ladies under foot," Gramps stated with a twitch of his lips. "Pete and I will take Matty and work on trimming those bushes out front. You boys see if you can fix the loose boards on the back deck."

"I thought we were supposed to relax when the

women left," Luke complained, then ducked to avoid Alex's swinging hand. He'd gotten better at it.

It took less than an hour to get the boards nailed down tighter and to replace the two that needed it. He settled into an Adirondack chair near Alex as Luke brought out two beers and a can of soda.

"Sorry, bro, Mom left explicit orders not to let you drink." Luke took the chair on his other side and cracked open his brew. He chugged it loudly then moaned in satisfaction.

"Nothing like an ice-cold beer after a day of hard work."

Alex laughed. "Or an hour of hard work, in your case, Luke."

"Whatever, it was still work."

"You have too many of those, and you can forget about driving my Camaro back home. I'll keep it here just to spite you."

"Only a few, I promise. That car is a huge chick magnet, you know."

"I know." He sighed. "Not that you need anything to attract more girls. How many do you need at once?"

"Only one at a time, dear brother, but must have another in reserve. In case the first falls through."

Clearing his throat, Alex said, "Speaking of girls, Tessa has matured quite nicely, huh? I've only seen her a few times in the last couple of years, but she's a far cry from when she first moved here."

He glared but remained silent. Staring at the waves, he remembered how she'd helped him with the kids on the beach yesterday. What insanity had made him think he could actually bring them down there on his own, he didn't know. Maybe it was Matty's puppy dog eyes as he asked what the water felt like. The poor kid had never been in an ocean before. Erik had grown up minutes from the sea and wanted to allow the kids the chance to enjoy it also.

But walking wasn't something he could do at the best of times right now, and trying to do it in the sand, with a baby in one arm and a three-year-old running in circles around him, was more than impossible. Tessa must have been watching because she showed up after only the third time he'd landed on his ass. But sweetheart that she was, pretended she'd just been going for a walk along the shore path.

"What's that stupid grin for?" Luke asked, and Erik wiped his face of any emotion, pissed he'd allowed Tessa and her graciousness to give away his thoughts.

"Nothing, Puke," he reverted to the teasing nickname he'd given his youngest brother as a kid. "Trying to enjoy a few minutes without having to run after a couple of kids."

"It was your choice to take care of them, Prick." Luke paid him back with the juvenile label. "You could have left them there."

"No, I couldn't." His jaw tightened when he thought of his kids in an orphanage in that hell hole. His kids. In such a short time, he already was so attached to them. What the hell would he feel like if he'd had a blood child of his own? It didn't matter because it wouldn't happen.

"It's just rough right now because my leg is still sore and doesn't bend correctly. Once it's better, it won't take so much out of me."

"Does the medication help at all?" Alex leaned closer, his face filled with concern.

Shit, he hadn't meant to give away how much the leg bothered him. At least he had hedged and said it would get better. No need to have anyone feeling sorry for him. He loved his brothers, but they could get overprotective of him too.

"It takes the edge off," he said to Alex, then turned to Luke. "I want the kids here. No child should have to live in the piece of crap place they did. Here they'll have someone to be a good father to them." He hoped. They'd all had the best example in Pete Storm, so as long as he followed by example, he couldn't do too poorly.

Luke made a face. "Better you than me, bro. I like my life with very little responsibility to anyone except me."

He closed his eyes and turned his face to the sun. Once, he'd been like that too. Not anymore. Luke was in the Air National Guard, but he hadn't been deployed yet. It would be a pretty quick lesson if he had to live in a shit hole in the Middle East. Erik hoped he never had to, though. It was a crappy way to learn a lesson.

"You'll be a great dad," Alex said softly. He appreciated his brother's confidence and wished he had the same. "Anyone around that might be a great mom?"

He narrowed his eyes at his brother.

"Yeah," Luke joined in, "I have to admit Alex was right. Tessa has grown up nice. And filled out nice too."

"Keep your eyes in your head, dipshit. She isn't the type of girl you ogle and talk about. And she's been really helpful this past week. God knows what I would have done without her helping me with the kids."

Luke waggled his eye brows. "Imagine what else she could help you with. It gets awfully cold up here in the winter."

This time Erik swatted him in the head. "Fuck off, okay. She's just been helping me as a friend. Get your mind out of the gutter."

Lukas sat back and muttered, "Sorry. I didn't mean anything by it."

He knew Luke was only kidding around like they'd done all their lives. But for some reason he felt protective of her. With all she'd gone through, though he didn't have a clue as to what most of it was, and all the help she'd given him this week, she deserved some protection.

When he sat back, his brothers did the same, but he didn't miss the scathing look Alex threw Luke. The one that said *back-off before I thrash you myself.* Alex might be the milder brother, but he was no lightweight. He could do it.

"I'm glad you have someone here, a friend, to help you when you need it."

Luke looked properly chastised and agreed. "Yeah, me too."

His brothers would be here in a minute if he ever really needed them, and he appreciated it. But when he thought of Tessa, he was glad she was around, and he could call her friend.

****

"Do you want to put Kinah in the carriage?"

Tessa swallowed while her stomach muscles tensed. She looked at Molly Storm and attempted a believable smile. "Thank you, but no. I think she's still a little skittish around new things. I don't mind holding her."

That last part was true. Over the past few days,

she'd found it quite easy to hold Kiki. And when the child wrapped her arms around Tessa's neck, none of the feelings of panic at being touched ever appeared. But then she knew Kiki would never hurt her. The child was the weaker one and in need of protection.

"Of course, dear," Ingrid replied. "But if she gets too heavy, we'd be happy to help."

"Thank you," she repeated. *Always be polite. Never argue. Keep the attention on everyone else.*

"Why don't we head over to the children's section?" Molly suggested, steering the carriage in that direction. "We'll probably find most of the stuff we need there."

How much more stuff was needed? The Storm aunts and cousins had sent tons. Although much of it was toys and other safety essentials. They hadn't sent clothes because they hadn't known the kids' sizes.

Molly and Ingrid moved up and down the rows of supplies, asking what the children already had. As she walked along behind them, she answered in as few words as possible. Big stores with lots of people were not her thing. Sunday at Walmart was always crowded, and with the summer vacationers here, it was worse than ever. The noise and activity made her skin crawl.

A large man pushed past them to reach for a car seat, and she jumped back as if she were burned. Holding Kiki tighter, she turned so she was between him and the child. The man threw her a look, one she knew well, grabbed the large box, and lumbered away. *Deep breath in, let it out slowly. Stay calm. No one's going to hurt you. It's just a store, and people are in a hurry.* It drove her crazy she had to talk herself through something as simple as being in a store. Online shopping was essential to her well being.

"Tessa," Ingrid called out. Her face, lined with her years of wisdom, was filled with compassion. She'd lived next door for many years and had been good friends with the Millers. Tessa's quirks were nothing new to her. "Do you think a stroller would be good to have?" *Shift attention to something mundane.*

Ingrid knew the tricks too, though she would never mention the minor freak out she'd just had. Too sweet and nice. Heat rose through her cheeks, knowing she'd overreacted again. Like with the boys in the paint section of the hardware store. Erik hadn't mentioned anything then either.

Shaking her head, she put her attention back to Molly and Ingrid who were looking at a variety of strollers. That might make it much easier for Erik to bring the kids around places. But then maybe he wouldn't need her as much anymore.

"I think so. Do they have one that fits two children? Matty can walk, but if he's tired, he wants to be picked up. Erik can't really do that right now."

"I know." The expression on Molly's face as she sighed showed the pain she felt at her son's injury.

What would it be like to have someone who cared for you so much they hurt when you did? Not that she'd ever know, but she often dreamed of it. Dreamed of having a family like the Storms who loved each other so much and would do anything for each other. In her little fantasy world, she'd created parents who loved her but were torn away from her by extreme circumstances. It helped a little to erase the taunts of the other children as she moved to yet another foster home. *No one loves you. No one will ever love you because you're a freak.*

You aren't lovable.

But in her dream world, her parents loved her, and one day they'd come back and tell her every day how much they loved her. How much they missed her. And then…then she'd wake up. Alone in a house left to her because she was the only one around.

"They've got a few that would fit two children. Front and back or side by side?"

Moving closer, she examined the strollers. Which would be easiest for Erik to handle? And be most convenient for him?

"I think this one." She pointed to a moderate-sized stroller that had a few spots for storing supplies. "The side by side is kind of wide, and with Matty weighing more it might not be balanced well. I wouldn't want Erik…I mean, the stroller to tip and fall."

Damn. Erik would be pissed if he knew she'd mentioned him falling. But he had quite often since he'd been here. Having his mother and grandmother know would embarrass him.

"Hmm, yes, good point. And it has places to put cups and bags and extra diapers if needed. Nice choice. Thank you."

Molly pushed the stroller along as she and Ingrid tossed items into the carriage that Ingrid pushed. Tessa gave Kiki the sippy cup she'd brought along, and the child drank rapidly. After finishing it off, she settled onto Tessa's shoulder, popping her thumb in her mouth.

"It's almost nap time," she explained as Molly smiled at them.

"She seems quite comfortable there. I'm so glad you've been around for Erik. He likes to play the tough, independent marine, but I know his injury is worse than he lets on. Sometimes you just need to ask for help."

"And he has. I'm happy to do it." As Kiki snuggled into her, she knew she was. This child and her presence had made all the anxieties and fears she usually felt in a large, crowded place almost disappear. She didn't know what magic the little girl had, but it was something. Maybe the fairies from around the castle had sprinkled her with fairy dust, and it was rubbing off on Tessa.

"Let's get a few bathing suits and some more outfits, and that might be it. Unless you can think of anything else, Tessa."

Giggles floated over to the group as they dug through the racks. A pack of teenage girls flipped through the displays in the junior department, holding up clothes and laughing.

"Ohmagawd, are you kidding me? I wouldn't be caught dead in that shirt. Unless I wanted to look like Abby Wood." The girl snorted, and her friends did too.

The words drifted by, and she was taken back to when she was young. Her clothes had been either hand-me-downs or cheap bargain stuff her foster parents picked up at a thrift shop. She'd never fit in with the popular kids. Not that she cared. They were usually mean and snotty. But they were also well-dressed and pretty and liked by all the boys and the teachers. Tessa had never been around long enough to make many friends. And every new foster home seemed to mean moving to a new school if not a new town.

"This is gorgeous and would look so amazing with those boots I got from American Eagle. It would be totally shabby chic. Right?"

The other girls, all pretty with nice figures, agreed with the girl who was most likely the ringleader of the group. She turned away and thumbed through a rack of matched outfits for young boys.

"Look at how cute this is." Ingrid held up a one-piece outfit, Matty's size. It was bright yellow and had turtles all over it.

Laughter rang out from the girls across the aisle. She flinched. *They aren't laughing at you. They don't even see you. Pay no attention to them. They can't hurt you.*

It didn't stop her from glancing over her shoulder to make sure they weren't looking at her, then she turned back to Ingrid.

"It's on clearance for only two dollars."

Understandably. While it would be adorable on a baby Kiki's age, if Matty wore that to preschool, the other kids might laugh and make fun of him. The poor boy already had enough points against him in a new country with English being his second language. Weird clothes would make it worse.

"It would probably be too warm to wear it now. It has long sleeves and might not fit by the time the cooler weather comes." And she'd have to hide it if Ingrid insisted on buying it. No way she'd let Matty wear that and be teased. She looked across the aisle again as the girls picked up items and carelessly tossed them down.

"Hadn't thought of that." Ingrid replaced the outfit. "It's been a while since I bought clothes for little ones. I do like a bargain, though."

So had many of her foster parents. That's why she'd worn a plaid wool dress with long sleeves for one of her school pictures…at the beginning of September. It had been a horrible combination of lime green and yellow, and the collar had been this huge monstrosity that nearly choked her. The worst part had been they'd had gym class before pictures were taken, and she'd been so hot and sweaty her hair had matted into knots, and her face was beat red. And that was the picture they'd put in the end of the year memory book for her class. The one she'd burned when she'd moved to the next home. Those weren't the kind of memories she needed.

Closing her eyes, she hugged Kiki and rubbed her back. The child was asleep, but somehow her magic still worked. The soothing calm entered her and assisted in getting those memories into the back of her mind. Holding this baby close helped her make new memories. Better ones.

They spent the next hour picking out clothes for the children, Tess giving her opinion much more than she'd ever done. But she didn't want to see these kids teased and taunted for something they couldn't control.

As they left the children's department, the giggling teenagers appeared beside them.

"Ohmagawd, look at her."

Tessa's heart dropped as they pointed at her. Heat rushed across her face and down her neck. She glanced at what she wore. Casual tan shorts fit well over her slim thighs, and her top was one of the cutest she owned. It was a white, no-sleeve with eyelet lace on the bottom which skimmed the top of the shorts. It was hardly daring, but occasionally it gave a peek of her stomach. Her figure was decent, and she'd almost hoped Erik would approve. Silly, yes, but she hadn't wanted to look like a frump when she saw him this morning. Sticking around all day hadn't been in her plans. Or going out in public.

The girls surrounded her, and the leader peered down at Tessa's shoulder. They were looking at Kiki.

"She's so adorable. What's her name?"

She turned to show them the sleeping child better but shushed them. "Her name is Kiki. I'd like to keep her sleeping if possible."

The girls all nodded vigorously and murmured more words of how cute the baby was. She smiled and walked away, following Molly and Ingrid. As the girls headed into the next aisle, she heard them say, "That baby was so cute, but man, did you see the mom? I'd kill to have legs like that."

A tiny burst of excitement bubbled in her chest as she adjusted Kiki and rubbed her back. Those girls were probably the mean ones at school, and what they thought shouldn't affect her at all. But the timid teenager in her thrilled they hadn't put her down and made fun of her. She'd take it for now.

Chapter Six

"Be good now, Matty, this lady is important." Erik hugged the child and sat him on the couch in the family room. Checking Kiki was settled in her bouncy chair with a toy on the tray, he took a deep breath. This interview had to go well. The fate of these two children was in her hands.

The doorbell rang, and he groaned. "Are you kidding me?" She'd gone to the front door. He grabbed the one crutch he was currently using and hobbled into the living room. After his PT session this week, he was close to losing the crutch, but he wasn't there yet. Thank God for Tessa. While he'd been at therapy, she'd watched the kids and allowed him time for a cool shower after.

When he pulled the front door open, his stomach dropped to his toes. Holy shit! The Wicked Witch of the West, in human form. What was her name, Miss Gulch? His gaze shifted behind her to see if she'd come on her bicycle and had a basket for Toto.

"Mr. Storm?"

"Hi, yes, I'm Erik Storm. You must be from Child Services. They said you'd be here some time this afternoon." Earlier would have been better so the kids wouldn't miss their nap, but Murphy had other plans apparently.

The woman's narrow eyes got smaller, and her

already pinched lips tightened. She peered at the large utilitarian watch on her wrist and frowned. "They said between two and four o'clock, and it is now precisely three forty-five. Well within the parameters set. Is there somewhere more important you need to be, Mr. Storm?"

"No, no, come on in." Stepping back, he allowed the woman to enter. "And technically, it's *Captain* Storm." Would his service to their country soften her up a bit?

"Yes, that's right. Your file says you're in the military."

"The marines," he corrected.

"Yes, well." Her gaze roamed the living room and peeked down the hall to the bedrooms. "I'm Gertrude Abernathy. I've been assigned to your case. Where are the children, Captain Storm?"

"Um, in the family room. This way." He tried not to wobble as he walked, but since he hadn't taken his meds today, the pain was more than usual. The Vicodin made him feel out of it, and that couldn't happen today.

Miss Gulch, uh Abernathy followed him and muttered, "You left them alone?" A small notebook came out, and she jotted something in it.

"Just to answer the door. I thought you'd come in the other way."

"Accidents can happen in the shortest amount of time, I assure you."

"I know." He swallowed the bile in his throat at the apparent black mark he'd already earned. "I'm sorry. They're right here."

And they were. Matty on the couch exactly where he'd been and Kiki happily spinning the little monkey around the tree on her play seat. The woman hadn't even smiled. How could you not smile when you saw them? They were adorable.

"Matty, Kiki, this is Ms. Abernathy. Please have a seat, ma'am." He indicated the chair by the window, hoping the beautiful ocean view would help this lady peace out. Once she sat, he followed suit on the couch next to Matty and within reach of Kiki.

"It is *Miss* Abernathy. I don't go for all this new-fangled way of mixing married and unmarried women into the same mold."

He sat up straighter, like he'd been scolded. "Yes, of course, Miss Abernathy."

"Now let's start with a few basics. I have here Matteen and Kinah Samad have been placed temporarily in your care until it has been determined you are a good fit for adoption or another more suitable home is found."

He clenched his jaw. Suitable? That was a good question. But he loved these kids already. Wasn't that enough?

"I've been with them almost the whole time since the bombing. I'd think that would speak for something."

Matty snuggled against his arm, anxiety on his face. The child might not understand every word they said, but he guessed the boy had an idea what was going on. Putting his arm around Matty's shoulders, he squeezed, smiling down at him.

"Did you want to play with your blocks?" See if he could get Matty's mind on something more fun.

Matty shook his head and burrowed deeper against him. Erik looked back up at Gertrude Abernathy. Did her eyes ever open into something other than a slit? Or maybe the bun she wore pulled her face so tight she couldn't. The thought made him want to laugh, but the circumstances kept him quiet.

"Let's discuss your military career, Captain."

"What would you like to know?" Should he rattle off all the commendations and awards he'd gotten? Or mention the heroic act of saving the children, although unfortunately not their mother?

"I'd like to know if you plan on staying in the military. It can't be good for children to travel from place to place while their father is off fighting in a war."

She made it sound like that was a bad thing, for men to defend their country. But his answer hopefully would please her.

"I'm actually on the disabled list for now. When I'm done with my physical therapy, I'll be honorably discharged."

"And do you have a job lined up to support these children?"

"Yes." Uncle Sam wasn't going to be footing his bill if that's what she was getting at. "I'll be working as a chef at The Boat House. It's a few streets over on the harbor. I worked there during high school and college, and the owner assured me I have a job as soon as I'm able to work."

"You are currently unable to work? Due to your disability?" She threw a furtive glance at his crutch, which leaned against the side of the couch.

"I'm getting there."

Her face pinched tighter. "Hmm, well, let's find out a bit more information, shall we?"

For the next half hour, she asked him everything she possibly could. Did he drink, smoke, take drugs or other medications, play sports, own a gun, what shows did he watch on TV? And so much more. He was waiting for her to ask his shoe size and if he preferred boxers or briefs. Could he get a rise out of her if he divulged he preferred boxer briefs? Or he slept in nothing at all? But she'd probably mark it in her notebook and frown.

She finally closed her notebook and looked around. Kiki started to whine. The little girl didn't like being immobile for so long, but he could hardly let her crawl around while Miss Gulch was here. The old witch would surely have something to say about her safety. He was concerned too.

"Perhaps you could give me a tour of your house, Captain Storm. I need to assure myself this is a safe environment for the children."

"Of course." He levered himself on the edge of the seat and pushed. Matty jumped up and grabbed his crutch.

"You have him well trained." Damn, if only he could read her thoughts. Her face constantly looked like she'd eaten a handful of lemons.

"He's a good boy." Erik leaned down to kiss Matty's head. "He just wants to help me. I shouldn't need this much longer, though. My physical therapist said my knee and hip are getting stronger."

Waving his hand in the air, he said, "This is the family room. It goes out to the wrap around deck, which leads to the driveway also."

"And are these doors always locked so the children can't get out?"

He bent over to pick up Kiki, then adjusted her on his hip as best he could. Matty handed him the crutch, and Erik shifted it under his other arm. "I lock them at night but not during the day because the children are never out of my sight."

"Except when you answer the front door."

Shit. "No one ever comes to the front door."

She tilted her head and pursed her lips. "Apparently they do."

He sighed and turned away before she saw the fury on his face. It wouldn't do for her to know he had murder on his mind at the moment. "As you can see, this whole room is open. The dining room is here and then the kitchen through the large archway."

As his leg hit the floor, he grunted, gritting his teeth, and managed to get into the kitchen without dropping Kiki. Matty followed close to his side. Miss Abernathy thoroughly checked out the formal dining table and hutch, then cruised sedately into the kitchen. Would she take out the white glove and run it over the furniture? Not that she'd find anything, though. He and Tessa had polished this place to shining in the past week.

"Normally we eat in here. It's more convenient and casual for the kids. They're kind of messy when they eat. Especially this one—" He nuzzled his nose into Kiki's neck, making her giggle. "—who's just learning how to use a fork and spoon."

"And what type of food do you feed them?"

This was his specialty. "I'm a chef. I can make all sorts of healthy food taste amazing even to the picky eater." He named some of the dishes he'd made since the children were here. Abernathy walked around, opening cupboards and checking the baby latches on the cleaning supply cabinets. When she opened the fridge, he smiled. There were only healthy foods in there.

"You have alcohol in here?"

Fuck. How could he forget his brothers left that here? "Um, my family came to visit last weekend, and my brothers brought that up."

"And they left the rest for you?"

"Probably just forgot it. I haven't had alcohol since before my injury."

She didn't ask any more questions, simply closed the fridge door. "I see."

Out came the notebook. His heart raced thinking about the things she could be writing.

"Here's the main bathroom, and as you can see, it has two doors. It exits here in the kitchen and near the bedrooms in the front of the house."

"Why don't you show me where the children sleep?"

"Sure." He'd been leaning against the kitchen counter but now straightened up and hoped he could get down the hall without dropping Kiki. The baby rested her head on his shoulder, making her dead weight.

He held out his hand to indicate Miss Gulch should precede him. One eyebrow rose, but she walked down the hall ahead of him. To ease Kiki's weight, he leaned against the wall as they walked.

"The door on the left is Matty's, and the second one is Kiki's." He didn't bother going in, simply waited at the doorway as she looked around, inspecting everything. She checked the outlets for covers and peeked in the closets. After she'd appraised his

85

bedroom, she checked her watch, then actually attempted a smile. It didn't make her any less scary. "Do you mind if I use your powder room?"

"Of course not. I'll wait for you in the family room."

"Thank you. I just have a few more things I'd like to discuss."

More? Holy hell. How much more could she find out? He hoped to God she didn't want to go into the cellar. Those steps were steep, and he'd never get down them with Kiki in his arms.

The sound of water started but also cabinets being opened. Damn. This woman was snooping into every last crevice there was. Good thing he'd stuck his meds in his dresser drawer.

"Come on, Matty. We'll go play in the other room."

He managed to get Kiki into her seat, though she wasn't happy about her almost nap being postponed. Moving to the door, he looked out. Tessa stood on her back deck staring in his direction. She'd said she'd be available if he needed her. Should he send out smoke signals? He'd never needed her more.

As he drew the letters SOS in the window, a noise behind him made him turn. Abernathy was watching Matty stack his blocks on Kiki's tray. It kept the baby occupied and not whiny. God bless him.

He limped to the couch and sagged against it. Why bother pretending any longer? This lady didn't like him, and he didn't know why.

"Well, Captain Storm, I have to say you have a few points stacked against you. A single man, on his own, will have a much harder time taking care of two children. And have you thought of what you'll do with the children when you go back to work?"

"Well, yeah, I thought—"

A light rap sounded on the door, then it opened. Tessa's beaming face gave him hope.

"I'm sorry I'm late. My errand took a bit longer than I planned."

****

"And you are?"

Tessa stared at the buttoned-up old woman sitting ramrod straight in a chair by the window. She looked like something out of an old movie. Hair scraped back into a low bun, half-moon glasses perched on her nose, and a high-necked, crisp blouse tucked neatly into a long, straight gray skirt.

"Um, Tessa Porter. I live next door. I help Erik with the children."

Glancing at him, she hoped it was the right thing to say. His relieved expression told her it was. She crossed the room and shook the lady's hand. It was like ice. On a sunny day in July?

"Miss Gertrude Abernathy," Erik supplied for her. "She's from Child Services. I've shown her the house, and we've chatted about the kids."

Kiki looked about to keel over, so she pulled her from her seat and snuggled the child to her shoulder where she stuck her thumb in her mouth and closed her eyes. Poor thing was exhausted. Erik didn't look much better. The strain around his eyes told her he'd neglected his medication again. And if they'd had a tour of the house, he'd been walking on his leg, most likely carrying Kiki. Had he dropped her? Is that why the SOS signal?

"So you help with the children, Miss Porter? It is Miss, isn't it?"

"Yes. And I, uh, help Erik whenever he needs it."

"And what do you do for work, Miss Porter?"

"I do medical billing. From home," she added, realizing why the woman was asking the question.

"And what is your schedule for this medical billing?"

She swayed side to side, keeping Kiki blissfully asleep. "I don't have a set schedule. I can do it whenever I have free time. Often at night after the children are asleep." That sounded good, right? Like she didn't do it while they needed her.

"Sounds convenient." Miss Abernathy wrote something in her notebook. Erik looked resigned. "How often are you here with Captain Storm and the children?"

"Since they've come, she's been here a lot," he said. "She keeps an eye on them when I've got my PT and if I have to run errands."

"Is that so? But what about the middle of the night? I've noticed, Captain, you aren't exactly steady on your feet. You can barely carry that child"—she pointed to the baby on Tessa's shoulder—"and I'd hate to see her injured due to your...disability." She made the last word sound like a curse.

"I've managed okay so far." His tone was sharp. Hopefully he wouldn't say something he'd regret.

"I help him bathe the children and get them ready every night for bed. We tuck them in, and I make sure they're all set before I leave. They're very good sleepers."

Miss Abernathy's hard eyes drilled into her, and

she tried to hide her flinch. She didn't like this woman. Why would someone like her, old and obviously not a family person, be in this job?

"It's a problem if you can't be here in the middle of the night."

"Well, I…"

The woman's shrewd eyes cut deeper. "Unless you are here. Except that's not a very good role model for children, now is it? Having a *friend* sleep over." When she turned her gaze full power on Erik, he sat up straighter and rubbed his hands down his pants.

"I don't stay over."

"Well, then, I don't know how you, Captain Storm, can possibly take care of these children with your injury. Perhaps in another few months, I could come back and reevaluate, but for now I have to report this isn't the proper and safe placement these children need."

Erik's eyes grew dark and his jaw hardened. "I'm the one who promised their mother I'd take care of them."

"I don't care what you promised a dead woman, Captain. My job, and my only concern, is these children. I must ensure they are in a good environment."

She gritted her teeth. No one had ever cared whether she was in a good and safe environment.

"They know me. They want to be with me. I could have left them in a Kandahar orphanage." His fists were clenched. Would he say something to make it worse?

"But you didn't, and they are here now and in my jurisdiction, so I'm the one to make these decisions. They are hardly of an age to choose what's best for them."

Miss Abernathy closed her notebook and started to rise from her chair. No, she couldn't take these children away from Erik. He needed them. Maybe more than they needed him. She'd seen how much he cared for them, but also how he changed around them. The gruff, arrogant soldier melted into the background, and a man whose main concern was their welfare came forward. *Do something! But what?*

"Erik knew I'd be here to help him when he got back." She paused. Her idea was both brilliant and stupid. Would he thank her or hate her? And would it even work?

"And once we got married, I'd be here permanently."

"Married? You two are getting married?" Abernathy's glare moved over both of them. "You've just moved here, haven't you?" She looked at Erik. "How long have you known each other?"

"Ten years," they said in sync.

"I moved here when I was fourteen. Erik's grandparents lived here, and he visited often. Plus, he worked here during the summers."

The smile he flashed her almost made her knees buckle. Okay, so he wasn't mad at her impromptu ad lib?

"We've been close ever since."

That fib made her want to laugh. If they'd ever been close, she'd broken out in hives. Only recently had she been able to control that.

Miss Abernathy's gaze ping-ponged back and forth between them. "And when is this wedding?"

Shit. What was her answer for this? Something

vague maybe? "Well, Erik was deployed, so we hadn't set a date. We figured sometime after he got back."

"I was supposed to be there another eight months when I got injured."

Miss Abernathy slipped her notebook into her purse and hefted that into her arms as she stood. "Well, I suppose that changes things, however I don't condone people living together in sin with children in the house. It's a bad influence. I can't recommend they stay here unless someone else is here to keep them safe all the time. You are hardly capable presently, Captain Storm."

He flashed his hand in her direction. "But if we're engaged, wouldn't it be—?"

"Engaged is *not* married. Propriety. Now if you happen to move the wedding up, I might see fit to ignore a week or two of impropriety. But not much more. I really should be going."

Miss Abernathy walked through the house to the front door. Erik hauled himself up with Matty by his side. She followed, holding Kiki.

As Miss Abernathy opened the front door, she turned and stared at Erik. "I'd suggest you get back to me with any other details you want to give me. I pass in my report at precisely three p.m. tomorrow."

With that she left, closing the door with a definite finality.

A long sigh escaped his mouth as he turned and leaned against the door.

"Let me put Kiki down, and we can talk."

By the time she got the child settled and went back to the family room, Matty lay next to Erik on the couch, his eyes closed. Erik sat sprawled, his head back and eyes also shut. She sat in the comfy chair next to the couch and waited for him to notice her.

Silence hung in the air for a few moments, then he spoke softly. "Thank you for trying to help. I appreciate it. I'm not sure anything would have worked."

"Erik, these kids need you. I'm sorry I jumped in with that marriage thing, but it was all I could think of so you could keep them."

"It was a great idea, Tessa. I can't ask you to do that, though."

Her heart broke into little pieces at his words. *It was a great idea. Just not with you.* Isn't that what he meant? Maybe it would have worked with some other pretty girl who wasn't a freak of nature. Who could be in a crowd and actually talk to people without twitching and having a fit.

"Maybe if I call and ask for a different social worker."

"Maybe." Nothing else would come out.

When Miss Abernathy was here and she'd mentioned the marriage thing, Erik had perked up. It hadn't been her imagination. Obviously, it was only because of the children. When he actually thought about it, he must have realized what life with the frigid freak would be like. And even the children couldn't make him do that.

For a few short minutes, she'd actually thought she could have Erik Storm as her husband. The elusive dream she'd tucked away since she was a teen. Not that she wanted him forced against his will. But it would have gone a long way toward fulfilling her dreams of a husband and family.

Matty slept soundly, and Erik looked like he might be too. She swallowed the sorrow that rose up inside her. It wasn't like this was any different than anything else in her life. Why should she be disappointed now? Because she'd stupidly believed for one brief moment she might have a normal life. Kind of.

Standing quietly, she walked toward the door. Would he even know she'd left? If he needed her, he'd call. Maybe he wouldn't. It might be too big a price to pay.

When she twisted the knob, he rustled on the couch.

"I need to think about this, Tess. Let's sleep on it and talk tomorrow."

Translation: *I'll figure out a way to keep the kids without marrying you.*

Chapter Seven

Erik barely slept and by noon was ready to polish off the rest of the beer in the fridge while popping the entire bottle of Vicodin. All right, maybe not that bad but the thought of losing the children tore his heart out. How could he let them be taken and given to someone else? Someone who hadn't held them while bombs went off overhead or given up his water supply to keep them hydrated and alive. Damn, Miss Gulch. Didn't she see that? No one could love them the way he did. Except maybe Tessa.

For the past few weeks, he'd watched her with Matty and Kiki. Twelve days really. It had taken her some time to get involved, but she'd done it. In that time, he'd seen her closer to these kids than she'd been to anyone else she'd ever hung out with. His sister and cousins included. There was no doubt she cared for Matty and Kiki.

And finally, she seemed comfortable with him, too. Occasionally joking a bit and laughing at times. And every time he walked in the room, she didn't jump. Her company was enjoyable too. A lot. It wasn't scintillating conversation, but she was intelligent, sweet, and she made him feel comfortable. No worries about putting on airs or acting all rugged and macho in her presence. He could be Erik Storm, the guy, not marine.

Being married to her wouldn't be a chore. But would she want damaged goods? It's not like he could make love to her like a husband was supposed to, but he could still please her if she wanted that. Or maybe she wouldn't. His scars and disability were enough to make any person reject his touch.

It was her suggestion, though. Had she meant it? Would she go through with it? Only one way to find out. The kids were napping, so there was only a small window where they could talk privately. After pressing her numbers, she finally answered.

"It's Erik. Can you come over to talk about…well, what happened yesterday?"

A few minutes later she walked in. Her gaze stayed low, like the Tessa of a few years ago. Where had the new one gone? The one who had been such an integral part of helping him parent the kids? The one who had thrown out the idea of getting married?

When he pointed to the space next to him on the couch, she sat near the edge, her hands in her lap.

"Were you serious when you talked about getting married to help me keep the kids?"

Her gaze lifted quickly, her eyes wide. Why? It's what they'd talked about. What she'd suggested.

"But you don't want to marry me."

He let out a deep breath. "If it means keeping the children, I'd do almost anything."

Pain filled her eyes. What had he said to hurt her feelings? She couldn't possibly *want* to marry him.

"Well, maybe not anything," he added, then grinned. "Not murder. Although I might not object if a little arsenic found its way into Miss Gulch's tea."

"Miss Gulch?" Her face lit up in understanding.

"Yes, Miss Gulch. *Before* she wrote her report, of course."

He chuckled at her dry sense of humor.

"I have to know you'd be okay with marrying me. It wouldn't be a traditional marriage, obviously. I wouldn't expect anything from you...you know...in that way. It would be a marriage of convenience, in name only. Is that acceptable?"

She nodded, then looked down again.

"I don't understand why you'd want to get married this way. Are you sure you want to shackle yourself with a broken-down husband and some ready-made kids?"

She threw him a skeptical look. "I know you've heard what people call me. No-Touch Tessa. No guy would ever want to marry a freak like me."

When he started to object, she leaned forward. "I've grown to love Matty and Kiki. I won't ever have kids of my own, so this is a way I can have both, kids and a husband. Plus you keep the kids with you. But I'm not sure why *you'd* want that kind of marriage? I'm sure someday you'll want more."

How to answer? She deserved the truth, especially after all she was willing to give up for him, after everything she'd already done. He took a deep breath to bolster his courage. This wasn't anything he'd shared with anyone. Not even his family.

"After the bombing, I figured I wouldn't get married either, definitely not have any kids of my own. My face is scarred, and I can barely walk. What woman would want that?" Shrugging, he gave her a wry smile.

"Plus my injuries were severe. The pelvic fracture resulted in other...things being affected. Nerve damage, muscles, tendons, and other…organs…stopped functioning properly." Shit, this was so embarrassing, but she needed to know what she was getting herself into.

"You being skittish with touch is fine. I can't offer any woman what she needs in a real marriage." Did she understand what he was saying?

Her face had a myriad of emotions running across it. Finally, she pursed her lips, trying not to grin. "No-Touch Tessa, remember? I'm okay with that."

He managed to smile. "I guess we're the perfect pair, then." If she could joke about it, so could he. And she was serious about this marriage thing.

Her tongue poked out as she glanced at the floor. "You really want to marry a freak?"

"You really want to marry a scarred, impotent soldier who can't walk?" There, he'd said it, and the world hadn't ended. And she hadn't walked out or looked at him with pity in her eyes. That's what he dreaded most. The pity.

She moved closer, closer than she'd voluntarily come before. "I think your scars make you look more human. You always were too perfect."

A laugh escaped. She'd thought he was perfect. Well, not anymore. Lifting his hand, he stopped and merely waved it in her direction. He itched to touch her, though. Wanted to caress her skin and see if it was as soft as it looked.

"You, Tessa Porter, are no freak. I see a beautiful woman who is sweet and kind. She gives her time and energy without asking for anything back, and she's a wonderful mom to these kids. I would be honored to have you as my wife."

He wanted to do this right, but his damn leg wouldn't cooperate. Sliding halfway off the cushion, he made a face. "Pretend I'm on one knee, okay."

She giggled. Should he be insulted or pleased with that kind of reaction? "Tessa Porter, will you marry me? Be my wife and help me raise these children as our own."

Tears glistened in her eyes, and his stomach clenched. "Oh, shit, I made you cry."

She brushed the tears away. "No, I never thought anyone would ask, especially not the heartthrob Erik Storm. I had a huge crush on you when I was a kid. You probably never noticed since most of the girls around here did too."

"Is that why you always dropped things when we were near?"

"One of the reasons."

"You still haven't answered my question. You're making me nervous. I'm wondering if you're stalling, trying to think of an excuse that won't hurt my feelings."

She wiped another stray tear, then took a deep breath. "Yes, I'll marry you, Erik. I would be honored to be your wife."

Looking at her beautiful face and the happiness he saw shining from it, he could almost believe this marriage would be real.

"Thank you. I'll do everything I can to make you happy. I don't ever want you regretting this."

"I won't. Like you said, it's the perfect arrangement for us."

They'd have to tell his family. What the hell could he say to them, though? Lying wasn't an option with his family, but if he told them the exact situation, it would embarrass her. And give up his worst secrets.

"How about we keep the details of the arrangement to ourselves? Obviously Miss Gulch can't know."

Tessa snorted, making him chuckle. "But maybe we can give my family limited information. I don't think they need to know all the intimate details."

"Or lack of intimate details."

Damn, there was that humor again. Another benefit of this marriage. "Or lack of. We tell them we're getting married sooner to benefit the kids. That's not a lie. They don't need to know Miss Gulch made a veiled threat to take them away."

"That's what you call a veiled threat, huh?"

"I was trying to be polite. But we should get married soon. Is next weekend too quick for you?"

She froze, then shrugged. "I guess I'm not doing anything, so it's fine."

"Can we seal the deal?" He held his hand out, and she looked at it cautiously. It was only a moment before her tiny hand filled his larger one. Soft as he'd imagined.

"I know you aren't big on touching, but is that something we could work on?"

Her eyes opened wide.

"I only meant maybe we could do a few couple things in public, like holding hands. I promise I won't hurt you." Her doe-like gaze mesmerized him.

She glanced at their entwined hands and covered them with her other one. "I trust you, Erik. It would be nice if people didn't always see me as a freak."

Pulling on her hands, he lowered his face in front of hers. "I don't want to hear you call yourself that anymore, okay? From now on, you'll be my beautiful wife and the mother to our amazing children. Are you good with that?"

"It's hard to shrug off what I've always been. But if you don't see me that way, maybe I can start believing it too."

She still hadn't pulled her hands away, and she'd stopped staring at them like they were poisonous snakes. Could he push a little more? Raising his free hand, he gently slid his fingers down her cheek. Her breath went in and held, and her eyes went wide, but she didn't move away. Good sign.

"I really want to kiss you." Where had that thought come from? In truth, it had been in the back of his mind all week. Knowing her background, he'd ignored it.

"I know the whole touch thing scares you, but…think you could do this once for me, and then if you really hate it, I won't bring it up again."

When she licked her lips, he stifled a groan. Did she have any clue what that little tongue did to him? Well, parts of him, though not the parts he wanted reacting.

"It *would* seem strange if we don't at least kiss at our wedding." Her words were soft, but there was strength in them.

"It would. You haven't pulled your hands away yet. Does that mean it isn't totally repulsive?"

"Not totally." Her mouth twitched.

He leaned down until his lips almost touched hers. "Last chance."

Her smile was answer enough.

****

Tessa closed her eyes as Erik's lips touched hers.

She'd forgotten how to breathe. But instead of the panic and revulsion she expected, like she'd had with Jeremy, his lips were soft and sweet. Like he was with the children. His hand caressed her cheek, holding her firmly in place. For some reason it didn't terrify her like she'd thought it would. He wouldn't hurt her.

When he eased back, disappointment railed through her. Disappointment? Really? A familiar emotion but not one she'd equate with someone backing away. Relief, usually.

Opening her eyes, he stared, a tiny smile playing about his lips.

"Was that okay? I didn't hurt you?"

Shaking her head was all she could do. Would her voice even work? He still held her face, and her stomach fluttered wildly, but she kind of liked the feelings he incited in her. Could she admit that to him? After so many years of avoiding people?

She cleared her throat. "It was fine. And I didn't freak out."

He ran his fingers over her cheek, then pushed her hair behind her ear, his mouth still so close to hers. "No, you didn't. I'm proud of you."

His gaze lowered to where she chewed her lip. It was a bad habit when she was nervous. Would he kiss her again? How weird she kind of wanted him to. If only to make sure she could do it without flinching.

"Do you think we could practice a few times before the wedding? I don't want to look awkward."

A grin lit his face. "No time like the present." As his mouth lowered to hers again, she gave in to the kiss. This time she kissed him back, following his lead. Her hands curled into her lap so she wouldn't touch him.

What? Aside from her one disastrous encounter, she'd avoided physical contact with anyone.

But his touch called to something in her and made her answer. His lips tasted of chocolate and…something minty. Had he given the kids ice cream for dessert and thrown in a Girl Scout cookie? He'd done that a few times last week. When he pulled back this time, she wanted to scream, but he kept his forehead against hers and his hands in her hair.

"I could get to like this."

"Me, too," she whispered against his lips.

"I know I said that I couldn't…that we wouldn't…but do you think this type of thing would be okay every once in a while?"

"Mm hmm. Of course." Except she wouldn't be able to think, her mind was so muddled.

"I mean…only if you're comfortable. Like you said, it would look awkward if we didn't kiss at the wedding. Or every now and then. It's what married couples do."

Yeah, real married couples. That got the fog out of her head.

"Yeah."

"And I hate to say this." He looked down, and she waited for the bad news. "Those lips of yours have been teasing me all week. You don't know how badly I wanted to kiss them. To kiss you."

Her gaze flew up. Was he lying? He'd wanted to kiss her?

"Really?"

Nodding, he rested his head against hers again. "If we get married, I'll get to do that whenever I want. I mean…when you want too. Are you sure you're okay with that? Don't let me do anything you aren't comfortable with, Tess. I don't ever want you to feel uneasy around me."

"I don't, Erik. I've seen how gentle you are with the kids, and it's helped me trust you. You've always been there for me when I needed you."

He laughed. "When have you needed me? You've kept to yourself so much it seems like you didn't need anyone."

Memories slipped out of the box she'd locked them in. Or tried to lock them in. Somehow they always seemed to find a way to escape at the worst time.

"My first month here, down by the marina."

He narrowed his eyes, then rolled them skyward. "You mean those jerks who were teasing you. They're idiots. They needed to be put in their place."

Calling on her courage, she moved her hand to his knee. "You were my hero. I don't think you realized it."

"I was hardly a hero for that. I'm glad I was in the right place at the right time."

"And when I first started working at The Boat House, I know you spoke to some of the staff so they wouldn't make fun of me."

He shrugged like it wasn't a big deal. But it had been huge to her. To be able to go to work and earn some money of her own, money she could spend on decent clothes and shoes, had been vital to her survival. He'd always been aware of how great he was. But the past few weeks, she's seen a humbler Erik. One who wasn't so sure of himself and his abilities. It made her feelings for him even deeper, filled with more respect.

"You're a nice person, Erik Storm. I'm happy to be marrying you."

"You're a nice person too, Tessa Porter. I honestly didn't think I'd get married after what happened, but now I see our future, I think it's going to be good."

He kissed her again, and her whole world spun dizzily. When he let her up for air, he cupped her face and smiled. "Yeah, I think this is going to be very good."

And for the first time in her life, she actually believed it.

Chapter Eight

"Okay, deep breath. Here we go."

Erik parked in his parents' driveway and patted Tessa's hand. When he'd called, he hadn't mentioned why they were coming down. What they planned on saying about their marriage had been discussed a fair amount.

"You're absolutely sure you want to marry me?" she questioned for about the tenth time in three days. "Last chance to get out of it. If I know your mom, she'll have all the plans done within an hour of our telling her. Unless she objects."

The lack of confidence was nothing new for her, but he hated seeing it. Not when it involved him. Leaning over, he slipped his fingers into her hair, pulling her closer.

"I'm not letting you get out of it that easily. And my mother has always liked you. What could she possibly object to?" He kissed her thoroughly so she wouldn't answer. Knowing her, she'd have a list.

Once they got the kids out, Tessa carried Kiki while he took Matty's hand and strolled up the walk toward the huge Victorian.

"This is the house I grew up in, Matty. It's where your grandparents live right now."

Matty nodded, his eyes almost bugging out of his head. He'd probably never seen a house so big.

When they stopped on the porch, Tessa moved to his side, her face anxious. "Erik, what if—?"

Shifting his crutch, he captured her mouth. This method of stopping her from questioning things was one he liked. When she sighed against his lips, desire surged through him. Damn, not like he could do anything about it.

"Erik, it's so nice—" The door swung open, and his mother stood there, eyes wide and twinkling when she saw them kissing.

Tessa pulled back and stuck her nose into Kiki's neck, making the child giggle. He simply grinned. This hadn't been in his plans, but it worked to their advantage.

"Hey, Mom. Glad you guys were home."

"Of course, Erik. Tessa, it's lovely to see you again. I wasn't sure if you were coming. I'm so happy you did."

His mother stepped back, and they followed her down the hallway. Tessa handed Kiki over and had a pleased look on her face. He'd told her his mother liked her. Maybe she'd believe him now.

"I just made sandwiches and salads for lunch. Everyone's on the back deck."

They walked through the kitchen. "I'll need to get your brothers to bring out the salads."

"I can get something," Tessa offered.

"Thank you, sweetie." His mom directed her to the fridge, and he handed Matty a bag of napkins to bring out. Alex and Luke sat on the deck with his father, looking up when they walked out.

"Erik, good to see you again. Here, have a seat."

He gritted his teeth at his dad's words. Did his

father see him as a cripple who couldn't stand on his own? The man was still fit and healthy even at fifty-six. Erik had always wanted to be exactly like him. You couldn't always get everything you wanted.

"I'm fine, Dad. I want to make sure Mom's got everything."

"Your brothers have two legs. They can help her." He nodded at Alex and Luke who jumped up and strode into the house.

"So do I, Dad."

Pete Storm turned to him, and he saw pain cross his father's handsome features. "I'm sorry, Erik, I didn't mean—"

Attempting a grin, he touched his dad's shoulder. "No, I'm sorry. Touchy subject, I guess."

"Well, don't get used to it." Luke stepped onto the deck with a tray of sandwiches. "Because once that leg is healed, you're paying us back for all this labor."

Once the leg was healed. Or should it be *if* the leg healed? No doctor had given him any guarantees yet.

Food and drinks were passed around. Kiki sat on Tessa's lap, and Matty sat next to his new grandpa. Matty had talked a lot about Erik's dad and grandfather allowing him to cut some of the shrubs in the front of the house.

"So we never did decide what these children should call your father and me. I was thinking I'd like to be Nana and your father insists on Papa. Does that sound agreeable, Erik?"

He laughed and looked down at Matty. "What do you think, kiddo? Nana and Papa okay?"

Matty nodded. "Nana and Papa."

"Pa-pa," Kiki repeated, and they all laughed.

He pretended to scowl. "Hey, how'd you get that before I even got a Daddy?"

"Daddy?" Matty looked confused.

"It means the same as *pedar* or *baba*."

"I say Daddy?"

A huge lump formed in his throat as he looked at Matty's serious face. "I would love that."

Tessa's eyes glistened. Could he get the kids to call her Mom one day? Would she want that?

After a few more bites, he cleared his throat. "I, uh, wanted to make an announcement."

All eyes turned to him, and for the first time ever he was nervous about talking. But this was his family, they'd support him in anything he asked.

"With my injury and all, it's been a bit difficult taking care of the kids by myself. Tessa has been fabulous, and I couldn't ask for anyone better to help me."

She gazed at him like he'd hung the moon. Seriously? How could she look at him like that? He was crippled, scarred, and not a complete man. But she'd said marrying him would make her happy. Could he have that same happiness too?

"Tessa and I have spent a lot of time together the last three weeks, and it's been nice having someone with me to take on some of the burden." He ruffled Matty's hair. "Not that I consider them a burden."

She nodded, giving him confidence to finish. "We've been talking a lot and realized it would be more convenient if she was around permanently."

"Permanently?" Alex asked. "What do you mean? She lives next door."

"If the kids need something in the middle of the

night, she isn't there to help. I can't always hold Kiki if she's wiggling too much."

"Are you planning on moving in, Tessa?" The strange expression on his mom's face was one he couldn't interpret.

Reaching for her hand, he squeezed it. "More than that, Mom. We decided to get married."

The silence that followed was hard to read. He'd definitely shocked them. But what did they think?

His mom was the first to speak. "Do you *need* to get married?"

He laughed. "No, Mom, I've only been up there three weeks. It's not like that. But we *want* to get married."

Tessa's cheeks were crimson, her eyes glued to the table. He squeezed her hand again. "We've known each other for ten years, but the last three weeks have been amazing. We care for each other a lot, and we care about these children. We want them to have a great life, and we think getting married will be the best thing for all involved."

His father grinned, and his mother's eyes twinkled again, like they'd done when she saw them kissing earlier. His brothers sat with their mouths hanging open.

"Congratulations, Erik." His father stood and shook his hand. "That's a great deal of responsibility. But with all you've been through, your military training and service, I think you're up for the job."

His mom brushed what looked like a tear from her cheek and came around to hug Tessa. "We couldn't ask for anyone better for Erik. You've always felt like part of the family. Now it will just be official."

She kissed Tessa's cheek, which now also held tears. Damn, these women and their crying. They better not expect him to start bawling too. But her tears were happy ones, and she deserved to be happy. Hopefully she'd always be that way with him.

"No comment, Luke? Like 'better you than me'?"

Luke smirked but merely said, "Congrats, bro. And condolences, Tessa. Are you sure about this?"

Alex smacked him on the head and sighed. "I think it's great. Congratulations to both of you. Have you set a date?"

He threw a glance at his mom. "We wanted to get married next Sunday."

"Next Sunday?" his mom yelled. "You mean a week from tomorrow? Why ever so soon?"

Tessa sat up straighter. "There's a woman from Child Services who doesn't think Erik is an ideal candidate for taking care of the children right now. We didn't think it was a good idea for them to be placed in another home until she thought he was. They've already had so much upheaval."

Yeah, the looks on his family's faces said they'd figured out what really happened, but no one said anything. His mother merely ran inside and got a notepad and pen.

"You're right, these children need stability and they've got that with you two. Now, let's get to the business of this wedding. We can have it here."

She looked up to see if anyone dared contradict her. The smug smile Tessa threw his way said, *I told you so*. Yeah, she'd called it. His mother was in her element.

As lunch progressed, Molly Storm took over and

made list after list. They'd have to come back during the week to get a marriage license. Tessa needed a dress, and she knew the perfect boutique downtown that had darling vintage dresses that would look stunning with her coloring. Would he be wearing his dress uniform? Invitations would take too long, but she could call all the cousins and invite them personally. Who would stand up for them?

"Tess, do you have a best friend who you want as your attendant?"

"I thought maybe Sara could be my maid of honor. If she's able to come. I know she's working down the Cape. If not, then Sofie or Leah, maybe, if they were okay with it. I don't really have a whole lot of close friends."

His mother patted Tessa's hand. "I'm sure Sara would be more than happy to stand up for you. I'll have to call her tomorrow. I know she works Saturday nights."

"And what about your best man, Erik?"

"Hey, Alex?" Erik cocked his head at their mother's question.

Alex grinned and nodded. "Sure."

"What about me?" Luke squabbled. "And what if I had plans next Sunday?"

Their mother quelled that thought with a single stare. She was incredible. And beautiful and she'd made Tessa feel so welcome in the short time they'd been here. No lingering questions or doubts, only acceptance. The way his family had always been. His parents were amazing, and they loved each other unconditionally. That's what he'd always wanted in a marriage. Had always wanted to be like his dad, providing for his family and giving them everything they needed.

Not that he couldn't do it with Tessa and the kids. Financially, they'd have no problem. His military disability check was decent, and he knew Sid Greene at The Boat House would pay him a good salary. But he couldn't run around with Matty and play tackle football or soccer like his dad had taught him. Would he ever be able to run again? Not if the damage to his leg was as bad as the doctors had hinted.

And Tess, could he give her what a woman needed in a husband? Probably not. Definitely not. Even if she said she didn't want touch. Her responses to kisses had more passion than many of the girls he'd dated. And they'd practiced the kissing many times in the past few days. She wasn't experienced, sure, but that almost made it better, more intoxicating. He was introducing her to a side of herself she hadn't known was there. Would she eventually want more than he could give her? Damn.

And how had he not noticed exactly how amazing she was? He'd always thought her pretty and sweet, but he'd never gone beyond that. The fact she was only fourteen to his nineteen when they first met probably had something to do with it. But he'd also been more involved in the physical side of relationships. He hated to even admit he'd chosen girls for certain physical and social attributes they possessed. Shit, he'd been shallow.

She smiled at him, then turned back to the wedding plans his mother was elbow deep in. She looked happy. Really happy. And if he had even a tiny bit to do with that, he was glad.

****

"Okay, now we can't touch anything in the store. Do you understand, Matty?"

Matty nodded as Tessa lifted him from the stroller. "Kiki touch?"

Chuckling, she pulled Kiki from her seat and settled the child on her hip. "No, Kiki can't touch anything either. But she'll be in my arms. I expect you to stay near my side. No wandering, okay?" He'd been good on the half mile walk here, so she figured he'd behave inside.

The boy nodded again, his eyes anxious. She pulled open the wooden screen door, allowing Matty to go in. Willie's Country Store was always a favorite of hers, with its antique look and old-fashioned decor. But Gladys Williams was the best thing inside. She always had been.

The bell tinkled as they entered, and Matty reached up for her hand. She took it as they walked over to the counter where Gladys stood.

"Tessa," the woman called out. "It's so great to see you. I got in another shipment of that rose-scented lotion you like."

Gladys settled onto a stool behind the counter and tilted her head as she stared at the kids. "And who do we have here?"

"This is Matteen and Kinah. They're staying with Erik Storm."

Gladys narrowed her eyes, but a genuine smile crinkled the already lined face. "I'd heard some scuttlebutt about that but wasn't sure if it was just people spreading rumors. You know how some of them get when it's too boring around here."

Yeah, she knew. Many a bored townie had made

her the topic of conversation. Luckily she'd always had Gladys to defend her. The woman had been Mrs. Miller's best friend forever. And when she'd come to live with The Millers, she'd become a great friend to Tess also. Gladys always made it a point to order anything she needed. She knew of her fears of public places so provided all her groceries here. Anything she couldn't get, Tess ordered online.

"So why do you have these two darlings today?"

Handing Kiki over to Gladys, she helped Matty slip onto a stool at the serving counter. "Erik's got physical therapy today in Portland. I've been helping him take care of the kids since he got here. I even painted a mural on their bedroom walls."

When Gladys clapped her hands, Kiki mimicked her. "Oh, maybe someday he'll let me see. You have such talent. I keep telling you to make some stuff for the tourists, and I'd sell it here."

"Maybe someday, Gladys. Right now, I'm busy with these kids and my work."

"I bet Erik's happy to have your help. I heard he got pretty banged up in the war. Now I don't like to listen to gossip, but some say it's bad."

She loved how Gladys didn't come right out and ask about his injuries. The hinting was there, but she'd never say anything again if Tess didn't give her any information.

"It's mostly his leg and hip. He's still on crutches, which is why he needs a hand every now and then. Kiki's a bit wiggly, as you can tell."

"Yes, she is." Gladys leaned down and stuck her nose in Kiki's hair. There was something about smelling a baby's head that made things right. "Why don't you take her, and maybe I can get these two a small dish of ice cream. Is that okay?"

"Thanks. I'm sure they'd love it. Vanilla for now. Kiki likes to wear her ice cream, and this outfit is new. Molly and Ingrid were here last week and spoiled them."

The ice cream was scooped into small cardboard cups and set in front of the children. She spoon-fed the ice cream to Kiki while Matty dug into his own.

"Um, Gladys, there's something else I wanted to tell you."

"Sure, honey, what is it? You know if you ever need anything, I'm here for you."

"I don't know what I'd do without you."

She scooped another spoonful into Kiki's mouth. "Erik had a problem with the child services lady who came out last week. She didn't think he was fit enough to take care of the children."

"Erik Storm, not fit." Gladys frowned. "That sounds a bit strange. That boy was about the fittest young man I ever saw. Pretty much all the girls around here thought so too."

"Well, it's a bit difficult carrying this one around. But I think we found a way around it."

"Good. What did they object to? Erik being single?"

"Well, it wasn't so much him being single as being injured. But even when I came over and said I've been helping, she wasn't impressed. So...Erik and I are getting married. To help the kids. Not for any other reason. And we...well...it's for the kids. He needs them."

"Married? Woo hoo! Honey, you don't know how

115

long I've waited to hear you say that."

She frowned. "Gladys, you know why I've never had any boyfriends."

"Well, there was that one, Jeremy." Gladys scowled. "Stupid boy."

Jeremy was the last thing she wanted to talk about. Or why he'd dumped her so fast. But she didn't want Gladys to think she and Erik would have a happily ever after either. She wasn't stupid enough to believe it, even if she wanted it more than anything in the world.

"We're getting married Sunday in Squamscott Falls. At his parents' place. You wouldn't be able to come, would you? I know it's short notice, but I can't imagine anyone I'd love there more."

"How about that handsome new husband you'll have? You'll want him there."

She rolled her eyes and grabbed a napkin to wipe the ice cream dripping from Kiki's face, then handed one to Matty.

"Erik's whole family will be there. But I feel like you're my only family."

Gladys reached across the counter and patted her hand. "Of course, I'll be there. I can get my granddaughter, Brianna, to bring me. She can drop me off, head to the beach, and pick me up later. You've met Brianna."

"Thank you, Gladys. Here are the details." She handed her a scrap of paper she'd put the information on.

"And you know Brianna is available for babysitting if you and Erik ever need a night out."

"I'll remember that. Oh, and here's my new phone number. Erik insisted I have a cell phone, especially if

I'll have the kids a lot."

She scribbled her number on the back of the wedding info as Gladys cleared the ice cream and spoons.

"Erik's a good boy. He'll make sure everything is good for you and these kids. I'm sure."

Heat rushed into her face. "He's already talked about getting me a new car. I tried to argue, but he's right—mine isn't adequate to drive kids around in. Not that I really want to be going many places. I like my walks from my house to here and back."

"But you'll be living with Erik now. What will you do with your house?"

She shrugged. "Nothing for now. I haven't made any plans." Selling it was too hasty. Who knew how long this marriage would last? It's not like it was a real one anyway. He'd said they were a perfect pair, but she still had a hard time believing anyone would think pairing with her would be perfect.

"You let Erik take care of you. He's a Storm. I'd trust them all with my life. The whole bunch of them were brought up right. From Ingrid and Hans right down to the youngest, which one is that now?"

"Amy's the youngest." She had the Storms all memorized. They were the family she'd always wanted. The family she'd always dreamed of. And now she was actually going to be part of them. But would she be good enough?

"Amy, right. But Erik, he's one of the oldest, and he's always been a solid person. I don't think you have to worry, honey. He'll treat you right. And if he doesn't, he'll have to answer to me."

Chapter Nine

"You sure you'll be all right here?" Erik checked Tessa's face as he grabbed his overnight bag from the minivan.

"I'll be fine. I have the kids with me, and Sara and your mom have been great."

He wasn't sure he believed her, but he didn't have much other choice. The wedding was tomorrow, and his mom had insisted he stay at Alex and Luke's house tonight. No seeing the bride before the wedding.

Hanging with his brothers tonight? They'd probably ask all sorts of personal questions he didn't want to answer. Stuff that wasn't any of their damn business. But TJ, Sara's boss, had driven her back from the Cape for the wedding and was staying with them also. He might diffuse any awkward questions. The man looked about as thrilled as Erik felt since he'd only met them all once about a month ago.

"I'll see you tomorrow." He gave Matty and Kiki hugs and kisses. "Be good for Tessa. As of tomorrow, she'll be your new mom."

"Ma-ma," Kiki squealed, and Tessa's eyes filled up with tears. Reaching out, he wiped one away, then leaned down and kissed her.

"If you need me, text or call. My mother won't let us see each other, but she didn't say anything about phone communication."

"Can I call?" Matty asked. The phone had fascinated him as Erik taught Tessa how to use it.

"Maybe before you go to bed, okay. But you aren't to play with the phone. Understand?"

"Yes, Daddy."

His heart squeezed at the name. Matty had called him that all week, and it still hadn't gotten old. After another hug and kiss, lingering on the one with Tessa, he walked away to where his brothers waited.

"You finally done?" Luke grouched. Alex's hand went up, and Luke ducked.

"Just wait until you're a father, then we can talk."

Horror crossed Luke's face. "That won't be for a very long time, bro. Take my word for it."

"Could I ride with you, TJ? I need to keep away from Laurel and Hardy for as long as possible."

The man agreed, and they got into his truck and ambled down the road. He adjusted the cane he'd finally graduated to and stretched out his leg. All week he'd been practicing. No way he'd stand to say his vows with a pair of crutches at his side. The only thing he wanted there was Tessa. And the kids.

"Thanks for driving Sara back home. I appreciate it."

TJ shrugged. "No problem. Your mom needed help today, and I didn't want Sara taking a bus from the Cape. They take forever."

TJ looked at the road. "Plus Molly invited me. Hope that's okay?"

"The only person I need there is Tessa. Anyone else is surplus but welcome."

He directed TJ to the house Alex rented with Luke. Pretty soon, though, his parents would be moving into their retirement community, and Alex would be buying the Victorian. It was good it would remain in the family. It was a great house. Too bad he couldn't have bought it, but the narrow, steep stairs made it impossible for him to maneuver.

Today he'd felt like a damn invalid as his family got the tent and chairs set up for the ceremony. He'd almost fallen over stakes and ropes a few times and Kiki at least a dozen. He'd told Tessa he'd watch her so his mom could do the last-minute adjustments to her dress. Though she refused to tell him what she was wearing. Her secret smile told him she liked it.

Alex and Luke came through the door a few minutes later with two pizza boxes. "My timing was perfect," Alex bragged. "It had just come out of the oven. Piping hot."

"And I've got the beverage to wash it down with," Luke called out, carrying a case of Sam Adams.

He slumped into one of the comfy chairs lining his brothers' living room. The place was a total bachelor pad except for the fact it was immaculate. Alex hadn't earned his nickname Felix for nothing. Luke tried his hardest to live up to the Oscar Madison part.

Luke pulled a few brews from the case and pointed one in his direction. He took it, then tossed it on the couch next to where Alex walked in with napkins and a knife. "This doesn't go too well with some of the meds I'm on. You'll have to drink my share tonight."

Luke made a face, then held up the bottle to TJ. The man shook his head and claimed another chair.

"I'll keep Erik company tonight and stay sober."

Alex passed out plates of pizza and Luke popped in a DVD.

"There's soda in the fridge if you guys want some," Alex offered, fiddling with the remote.

TJ stood and tilted his head at him. "You want a soda? I'm getting one."

"Thanks." He liked this TJ. He offered to do stuff but was so cool about it that it never seemed like he thought Erik couldn't do it himself. Which right now was debatable. He'd been on his feet all day, chasing after the kids. They'd been hyped up on excitement at being with their new family and the cookies he knew Sara had been giving them when he wasn't looking.

"Hey, how much baking did Sara do before she came down? She looked like she had enough for a friggin' army."

TJ handed him the soda, then sat again. "She baked all day yesterday. I think I gained at least ten pounds."

"Sampled a few, did you?" Alex asked and TJ grinned, rubbing his stomach.

"What are we watching tonight?"

Luke held up the DVD case. "Lots of action and hot sex. Mom forbade us from having a real stag party with strippers, but I figured we could still get our jollies another way."

Typically, he'd have loved partying with his brothers and friends and doing the whole bachelor-party, naked-girl thing. But for some reason it held no appeal to him anymore. To be honest, TJ didn't look all that thrilled either. Alex chowed on his fourth piece of pizza and his second beer and casually leaned back against the couch. This was about as wild as Alex ever got. Somehow all of that had bypassed him and gone straight to Luke.

His phone vibrated, and he pulled it out to check

the screen. It was a text from Tessa. The kids were ready for bed and wanted to say good night. Was it a good time?

If he was truly going to be as wonderful as his dad, it would always have to be a good time. Pressing the speed dial for Tessa, he waited. Matty picked it up.

"We ready a bed. Night, Daddy."

"Night, pal. Did you brush your teeth?"

"Yup, real good 'cause I had cookies."

He laughed. His mother never could resist spoiling a small child. "I'll see you in the morning. Make sure you're good for your mom and grandparents. Let me say good night to Kiki."

"Okay, see you in a mornin'."

"Kiki's right here, Erik." Her soft voice came through the phone. Damn, why hadn't he insisted he be there to help her with the kids? *Right, like you aren't thinking of her perfect lips kissing yours.*

"Hey, Kiki. Have a good night. I'll see you soon."

"Say good night to Daddy, sweetie," she encouraged the child.

She repeated it again, then he heard Kiki chirp, "Da."

It was close enough. "Tessa, you there?"

"Yes, I'll be fine, Erik, you don't need to worry." How did she know what he was going to say? "Oh, and tell Alex and Luke your mother is expecting them on Thursday night for dinner."

"Will do. And if you need me at all tonight, call. It's not a problem."

"I know. Thanks. Good night."

"Night, Tess."

After pressing the button to end the call, he looked

at his brothers. "Mom is expecting you both Thursday for dinner."

Luke tore his gaze from the couple gyrating on the screen. "What's she making?"

"I didn't ask. I'm not eating it, so I don't care."

"And you don't care about your brothers?"

TJ chuckled. "Is your mom not a good cook? The stuff she had out today seemed fine."

Alex sat up straighter. "No, she's a great cook. But every now and then, she makes one of these really weird dishes she thinks is amazing. And it isn't."

Luke made a face. "Like that sauerkraut dish."

He cringed at the same time as Alex. "That one's especially nasty."

Luke shivered, then the naked acrobatics on the TV caught his attention. Alex sat back and watched, but TJ's gaze moved around the room, taking in the details.

Looking down at the phone still in his hand, he wished it would ring and she'd need his help with something.

"You just have to get through tonight, then you can spend *every* night with her."

He looked up at TJ's words. Obviously the man didn't know the circumstances behind their marriage, but his words rang true. Even though it wouldn't be a real one in many ways, he was still looking forward to spending every day and night with Tessa.

****

"Your dress is beautiful, Sara."

Tessa sat still as Erik's sister pinned her hair into gorgeous ringlets on top of her head. It was a good thing Sara was here because she probably would've stuck it in a ponytail or left it loose. Fancy wasn't really her thing. No mother or sisters around to fuss with what she looked like. Sara and her cousins were as close as she'd ever get.

"Thanks, Tessa, but today is your day. No one's going to notice me. You're the bride. They'll all be looking at you."

She fiddled with the lace on her dress. "I really wish they wouldn't. Maybe you could keep them distracted while the ceremony is going on."

Sara adjusted one of the small flowers she was adding to her hair, then stood back for a second glance. Did they look ridiculous? Would *she* look ridiculous standing in front of a preacher and saying vows to a man who didn't love her? Would everyone know and whisper behind their backs? But she was marrying Erik Storm. Did she even care?

Sara held a mirror for her to see the back of her hair. It was nice, but her stomach was twisted into knots at the thought of what she was about to do. Lowering the mirror, Sara took a chair and sat in front of her.

"Are you okay?" Sara took her hands. "Is there some reason you aren't as excited as I thought a bride should be? Did Erik do something to get you upset?"

"No," she replied. As she shook her head, she could feel the unfamiliar curls bounce. "Erik's been great. I guess I'm a little nervous. You know I've never been one for the spotlight."

Sara squeezed her hands, sending warmth along her spine. Is this what love of a good family felt like? "I know my mom can be a bit like a steamroller when she has things to do. Did you want something different for a wedding?"

Standing, she gazed at herself in the mirror. She

didn't look half bad. Actually, she looked really nice. Maybe he wouldn't regret marrying her. At least not today. "Your mom's been great. She helped me pick this dress and even asked what I wanted for flowers and decorations. It doesn't really matter. I never figured I'd get married, so I didn't have anything special in mind. What she's planned is beautiful. I love it."

The vintage dress Molly had not only helped her find, but insisted on paying for, was beautiful. The V-neck lace wrapped nicely around her figure, and the short sleeves showed the tan she'd gotten from her hikes along the water. It fell to the floor and had a satin sash that flowed behind her. It was such a light shade of pink it almost looked white. But only virgins were supposed to wear white. Wouldn't Erik, and everyone else who called her No-Touch Tessa, be surprised at that?

"Do you love Erik?" Her head whipped up at Sara's softly spoken question.

She closed her eyes for a moment, then opened them and took a deep breath. "This marriage isn't really about love. It's about helping Erik so he can keep the children. He needs them, you know."

Tears filled her eyes, and she tried to blink them away. Sara's eyes also looked suspiciously damp. "He needs me too. Even if he won't admit he needs anything."

Sara chuckled. "Yeah, that's my brother, the big strong guy who won't ever ask for help. He can do it all."

She gave Sara a real smile. "And he can do it all. But not right now and not without some help. I'll be there for him and make sure the kids are safe and taken care of. Make sure they have a family. And I'll do anything else he needs me for. I do care for him, Sara. Erik's always been nice to me, even when others haven't been. He's a good man."

A tear slipped down Sara's cheek. This family truly cared for each other. She was getting the better end of this deal, and she knew it. Hopefully she'd be able to live up to her side of the bargain.

Sara wiped her cheek, then looked around the room. "Do we have everything? I think it's time to head downstairs."

She had a sudden longing and pulled Sara in for a hug and held tight. It wasn't something she typically did, but Sara was going to be her family now. It was time to start trusting people and letting them in. Allowing them to be in the space she'd marked as her own for such a long time.

As she let go, Sara kissed her cheek. "I'm glad I'm finally getting a sister. I've been outnumbered too long in this house. Welcome to the family."

Molly had said those same exact words. The family. Something she'd never had. Not a permanent one anyway. Could she really have one now even if the reason for this marriage wasn't the usual one? Or should she run as far and as fast as she could before they discovered she was a fraud? That she was too weird and damaged to be a part of any family.

No, she'd do this. It had been her suggestion, and he needed it. Needed her. And she'd do everything she could to be a good wife to him. Maybe they couldn't do the intimate stuff married couples did, but they could keep each other company and raise their children.

She squared her shoulders and nodded as if trying

to convince herself of this. They walked downstairs, and the next few minutes felt as if time had frozen. Hans Storm had offered to give her away. He'd been good friends with Armand Miller and felt it was his duty. She wondered what it would be like if she'd had her real father here to give her away. Not that she knew who he was.

Reaching up, she touched the locket hidden under her dress. It held a picture of her mom and the man she assumed was her dad. She only vaguely remembered her mother, snips of images here and there. But she had no memory of the man in the picture. Who was he, and why hadn't he wanted her? Why had her mother dumped her in a hospital waiting room? Had she been that much of a problem even back then they couldn't handle her? Or was she truly unlovable as some of the foster children had taunted her with?

Hans steered her toward the makeshift aisle in the Storm's backyard. The wedding was small, and only the aunts, uncles, and cousins, whom she'd known for a long time, were there. Mrs. Mazelli next door. And Gladys. She sat near the front and smiled so wide Tessa thought her face might crack open.

When she looked to the end of the aisle, there stood Erik, and her heart actually stopped. But when it started again, it beat triple time. God, how could any man be so devastatingly handsome? His marine uniform was blue from broad shoulders to above his spit-shined shoes. The red stripe down the lighter blue pants focused attention on his long legs. His white cover sat on top of the fresh haircut he'd gotten two days ago, and the amount of decorations he had on his chest filled her lungs with air and pride. This was no mere mortal. This man was a hero, and for some strange reason he'd agreed to her stupid suggestion of getting married. There were a dozen women in town who he could have asked who would have agreed to marry him to keep the kids. Then told Miss Gulch she was a liar, and he had a different wife in mind. One who was much prettier and not such a fr…introvert.

He looked up. His eyes glowed, and a huge grin crossed his face. It was similar to the one he'd worn the times they'd practiced kissing this week. Forget about her heart. Every damn organ stopped functioning. How would she get the last few steps to reach him?

"Don't keep him waiting, dear," Hans whispered in her ear. "It's obvious he's a mite impatient."

She took a step and then another. Soon she was close enough, and he shifted his cane and reached out with his left hand. Putting her hand in his, she held on tight. For Erik, she'd hold on as tight and as long as she needed to.

Chapter Ten

The music floated from the speakers of the stereo as Erik watched his sister walk down the aisle. She looked pretty in a lacy dress with some pink slip thing underneath. But he didn't care what his sister was wearing. Was Tessa okay? And was she actually going through with this?

This morning he'd woken in an icy sweat, and at first thought he was getting cold feet. Then he realized he was afraid Tessa would get them and back out of the wedding. Or more likely run away. Although she didn't have a car. They'd driven down here together with the kids. But she was a survivor, and he wouldn't put it past her to find a bus leaving town and get on it.

Sara stepped aside as the bridal song came on, and he strained his neck to see. Tessa walked on his grandfather's arm toward him. God, so beautiful. How had he missed it all these years? And why had he never done anything about it? He was doing something about it now, though.

Tessa's gaze flittered from person to person and finally landed on him. His grin couldn't be held back. Kissing her in a few minutes, when they were declared husband and wife, was all he could think about. Damn, he wanted to do so much more.

Clutching Gramps' arm like a lifeline, she looked around the crowd. Would she make it the last few steps? His grandfather whispered something in her ear that brought a tiny smile to her lips, and she moved forward. He shifted his cane and held out his left hand. The energy coursing through his arm when they touched was a reminder of what she did to him.

As they turned to face the priest, he squeezed her hand. He tried to listen to the words but could only think about kissing her. Holding her in his arms and touching her soft skin. A lump formed in his throat, knowing he could never get much beyond that. She might not allow more than that anyway.

Shaking his head, he focused on the vows.

"I, Erik, take you, Tessa, to be my lawfully wedded wife."

She gazed at him with such delight on her face he was humbled. This beautiful woman was giving up her life to help him keep custody of some children who weren't hers and dedicating herself to be married to a scarred and crippled ex-soldier. Not much of a bargain but he'd damn well make her as happy as he could.

"I, Tessa, take you, Erik, to be my lawfully wedded husband."

A few minutes later they were slipping rings on one another's fingers and being declared husband and wife.

"You may now kiss the bride."

Planting his feet as securely as he could, he lifted both hands to cup her face. This was the part he'd been waiting for. To show her, and everyone else here, he wanted her for his wife. No room for doubt.

"Gladly," he answered, lowering his lips to hers. A soft sigh floated out, and she closed her eyes as he skimmed his lips over hers. A few hoots and hollers let him know he'd fulfilled his duty. People were convinced. But he saw pain beneath the joy in her eyes.

"You are absolutely perfect." He wanted to alleviate her fears. "I couldn't have hoped for anyone better in my life."

Tears filled her eyes, but a genuine smile lit her face. "Me too."

They stood staring at each other until the spell was broken by the announcement. "I present to you, for the first time, Captain and Mrs. Erik Storm."

He swooped in for one more kiss, then allowed himself to be dragged down the aisle where his family all converged to congratulate them. Once hugs and slaps on the back were administered, people scuttled off into the house for food while others moved tables and chairs. He and Tessa were told to simply relax and enjoy being waited on today. Tomorrow they were on their own.

"Where are the kids?" she asked frantically. "Your mom had Kiki during the wedding, but she's carrying food out now."

He scanned the small crowd. "Right there with Gladys and my grandmother. And Matty's attached himself to Ryan." He pointed to his cousin Greg's son, Ryan, who was about eight. The two boys were farther back in the yard, kicking a soccer ball around.

Once the food was out, and he and Tessa had some at the central table, the guests got theirs. She picked at hers, glancing nervously around the yard.

Patting her hand, he said, "You know almost everyone here. You have nothing to be afraid of."

She sighed. "I know, but you're aware you married a weirdo, remember."

"But you're my weirdo now."

She nudged him in the side and giggled. He felt lighter than he'd felt since mortar rounds had left him damaged in a blown-out cellar with two kids and a dying woman. What an effect she had on him.

Suddenly, Sara rose and walked over to where Alex had moved her old keyboard. She nodded at TJ, then smiled at her audience.

"Can I have everyone's attention? TJ and I prepared a little gift for the bride and groom. This is a new song he wrote this summer, and we've been practicing it all week. Congratulations Erik and Tessa."

TJ sat behind the keyboard and started to play while Sara picked up her guitar and joined in.

"*Gray skies filled my world as I passed through yesterday,*" TJ's deep vocals joined Sara's higher ones. "*Never knowing which path I should take along the way.*"

He listened to the lyrics, watching how Sara and TJ gazed at each other while they sang. Something was going on between these two. "*But you stepped into my life, and the sun began to shine. I see the path I need for happiness to be mine.*"

Was that possible? Could they be happy with a marriage of convenience? Making Tess happy would be a top priority, but there was so much he couldn't give her. Not just physically, emotionally too. His parents had spent thirty years together, deeply in love. He'd wanted that, too. More than anything.

"*You said, 'Put the past behind you and live for today.' You taught me how to love and see beauty along the way. Now we're walking hand in hand down a road I've never known. With promise of tomorrow, you have*" *given me a home."*

They sang the chorus again, then ended the song. Sara walked over and hugged him. "That was beautiful, Sagey," he whispered. "The best gift ever. Don't take what you have for granted." Her beautiful voice and the love he suspected was growing between her and TJ. Tessa had tears in her eyes when Sara moved to embraced her. As TJ shook his hand, he heard Sara's lowered voice. "Be happy with him."

Tessa nodded, then kissed Sara's cheek. His family applauded, then his mom stood and ordered everyone to eat.

He and Tess were kept occupied with feeding the kids and chatting, with the occasional clink of glasses.

"Do you know what that means?" he asked after his cousin Sofie had done it the first time.

"I've never been to a wedding before." She shook her head.

He smirked. "It means we have to kiss. They'll keep banging on the glass until we do."

Her eyes wide, she looked out at all the faces lit with anticipation. Leaning over, he stroked her cheek.

"A quick kiss is fine. We don't have to put on a show." He took his time, though, with the kiss, and when he was done, she was breathing hard. He loved her reaction. And that she trusted him enough to get that close.

****

"Where do you want your bag?"

Tessa looked up as she closed the door to the room. Erik stood with both bags in his right hand as he clutched his cane in his left. His white cover was tucked under his arm, and he looked every inch the marine.

133

"The bed is fine for now." Such an impressive room. But The Inn at the Falls was well known for its prestige as well as its exorbitant price. They'd simply wanted to drive home to Maine, but his family had already paid for a night here and had insisted. Every couple needed a wedding night without their kids. Even ones pretending to be in love.

He tossed both bags onto the large double bed that was the central focus of the room. A Queen Anne's chair sat in one corner next to a writing table with a rolling chair tucked under it. A dresser with a TV sat in the other corner. The last wall had a door to what she assumed was a bathroom.

As she turned, she tried to avoid looking directly at Erik. They'd been alone before at his house in Maine, but they'd always been fixing something or taking care of the children. Now it was only the two of them…and they were married. It was their wedding night, and people would expect them to…oh, shit. But he'd said that wasn't part of the deal. Even hinted he couldn't— God, that must have been difficult for a man as virile and strong as Erik to admit what his injury had done to him. Truthfully, it was the only reason she wasn't running out of the room screaming.

When he slid into the upholstered chair with a big sigh, he leaned his head back and closed his eyes. The pain lines on his face were apparent. Over the last three weeks, she'd come to know what they meant.

"Can I get your medication for you?"

Cracking open one eye, he smiled. "I didn't marry you so you could take care of me."

No, it was to take care of the kids, but they weren't here right now. So why not throw him into the mix? If she could get him to relax, it would be worth it.

"It's been a long day on your feet. Are they in your bag?"

This time his eyes stayed closed. "The side pocket. Thanks."

She grabbed the two bottles and got a glass of water from the bathroom. When she moved toward him, she noticed he'd kicked off his shoes.

"Here. Would you be more comfortable out of the uniform?" Damn, that was stupid. It wasn't like she wanted him stripping in front of her. Those muscles in his snug T-shirts sure were fine, though.

Sitting up, he took the pills, then handed her back the glass and looked at his watch. "It's after ten. Honestly, I could just crash."

She was tired too, but nerves kept her body on full alert. "I'm glad we put the kids down before we left your parents. Hopefully they'll sleep all night without a problem."

When he started undoing his white belt, she turned away to return the glass to the bathroom. Should she stay in here until he was done? But what if he stripped down to nothing? Then what would she do? And where the hell would they both sleep? In that big bed? Her stomach flipped a few times, and she had to take deep breaths to calm her racing heart. Maybe she could go sleep in the van. No one would think that odd, right? Sure, they'd probably have her committed. Then where would Erik and the kids be?

Peeking through the doorway, she saw him hanging up his uniform jacket. He leaned against the wall for a second, and she knew he'd be too tired to try anything. Not that he could, she had to keep reminding herself.

"I think I'll take a hot shower before bed to work out some of the kinks. My mom said there's a hand-held shower head I can put straight on my leg."

She looked back in the bathroom. "There is." She held her tongue before offering him help there. In the shower he was on his own.

He limped toward the bathroom and stopped in front of her. "Do you need anything in there before I go in?"

"No, I'll just get ready for bed. Take your time."

After he hobbled in, the shower started. She moved their bags to the suitcase rack and rummaged through until she found her pajamas. Molly had insisted she get a nightgown and matching robe and had even paid for it. All brides needed something pretty to sleep in on their wedding night. She hadn't the heart to dissuade her. But she made sure the nightgown was as conservative as possible and had a robe to go over it.

Pulling out the ice-blue, silky material, she held it up. *Put it on quick before he finishes*. She hustled into it and slid her hands into the robe. Only then did she pick up her wedding dress to hang next to his uniform.

As she tidied everything else, the bathroom door opened. Steam wafted out, then Erik's damp head and torso followed. His uniform pants were draped over his arm, and his undershirt was wadded in a ball in his hand. A towel lay over his shoulders.

"Can you get my cane, Tess, please?"

Grabbing it, she stepped toward him. When his eyes grew intense, she realized her robe was still open.

"Here, do you want me to hang these up too?" She reached out for his pants. All he wore was a pair of white boxer briefs. Damn, damn, damn. *Move away and don't stare.*

She put his pants in the closet and tied her robe snugly around her body as he sat on the bed, running the towel over his head and arms. His injured leg rested on the bed, and she saw for the first time exactly how serious his wounds had been. The skin was puckered and pink from below his knee all the way up and disappeared under the edge of his shorts. It didn't look like a simple surgical incision either. There had been some major damage there.

"Oh," he groaned and covered his leg with the towel. "Sorry, didn't mean to put that out on display. It's not very pretty."

She forgot all about being nervous and sat on the end of the bed near his foot. "I wish I could make it stop hurting. Did they say how long until it's better?"

His jaw clenched as he lowered his eyes to the floor. "Maybe never. There was lots of damage. Stuff they couldn't fix."

He'd said something like that before. She thought he was just being dramatic. When she patted the towel on his leg, he flinched. "I don't need your pity. I'll be fine."

"You think I pity you?" She pointed to his leg and the scars on his face. "That's only physical, Erik. You have so much going for you. You have an amazing family who loves you so much. I'd give both my arms and legs to be a part of something like that."

His scowl softened, and he reached for her hand. For some reason she couldn't pull away, even though she wanted to.

"You don't have to give anything. You're a part of

them now, Tessa. They're your family as well as mine. And they accept you as such."

She knew what he was saying, but it still didn't stop her from thinking of her own blood family, what she knew of it. Which wasn't much. She fingered the locket around her neck. Lifting his hand, he traced his fingers over hers.

"What's this?"

After undoing the clasp, she took the chain off. "I don't always wear this, but it was my something old for the wedding."

His expression showed his curiosity, so she pressed the small latch, and the piece of jewelry opened.

"This is the only thing I still have from when I was little. I had it on when they found me."

"Found you? What do you mean, found you? You grew up in foster care, right?"

He shifted on the bed until he was sitting next to her. She sidled closer so he could see inside the locket. Two pictures lay side by side, old and somewhat faded.

"I was put in foster care when I was about four. I was abandoned at a hospital in Portland, and they never found my mother. This is her, though, in this picture. I remember that much."

Her fingers traced the face of the woman in the picture who stood next to a handsome man in a uniform.

"Is this your father?"

She shrugged. "I don't know. I always assumed he was. The date on the back of the picture is about ten months before the date on the back of the baby picture."

Popping open the frame, she lifted the picture of a smiling infant from the locket and turned it over. "See,

March tenth. And the year shows it's most likely me."

He touched the words written in feminine handwriting. "It only says Tessa. If they knew your last name was Porter, why couldn't they find your family?"

The emptiness she always felt thinking about her past enveloped her again, threatening to smother her. With Erik beside her a little bit faded away.

"I wouldn't talk to anyone when they first found me. They gave me crayons and paper, and I wrote Tessa on it, but I didn't say anything for a long time." Whenever those memories surfaced, ice cold fear filled her.

Lifting his hand, he ran it up and down her back. For some reason she didn't flinch and move away, though. She let him touch her. A far away image of the woman in the picture rubbing her back and singing to her floated through her mind. His touch brought back the soothing emotion, and she allowed it to calm her.

"The first family I went to was named Porter, so they gave me that last name. I only stayed with them a few years, but the agency didn't want to keep changing my name, so they kept it as Porter."

After putting the picture back in the locket, she closed the sides but didn't want to leave his touch. A far cry from her usual behavior. But she stood and placed the piece of jewelry on the dresser.

He cleared his throat and started to stand. His leg was bothering him, but he kept his stoic expression in place. "I'll, uh, sack out on the chair, and you can have the bed."

The chair? Seriously? He'd be in agony by morning. If anyone took the chair, it should be her. But as she opened her mouth to say that, something completely different popped out.

"There's plenty of room on the bed for both of us. No one should have to spend their wedding night in a chair. Regardless of what kind of a marriage it is."

He glanced around the room, then stared at her. "Are you sure, Tess? I don't want you to be at all uncomfortable."

"But it's okay for you to be uncomfortable sitting up in that chair all night?" She gave him a look and crossed her arms over her chest.

"If you're sure, then fine. We can share the bed. Would it be too much to ask you to grab my sleep pants in my bag?"

"What? I'm taking care of you now?" she sassed, and he laughed. After throwing his pants at him, she grabbed her toothbrush and disappeared into the bathroom. When she came out, he was under the covers on the left side of the bed. Probably so she wouldn't accidentally bump his injured leg. Hopefully the bed was big enough she wouldn't bump into any part of him.

But his hand felt so nice rubbing your back. It did, and she didn't know what to make of that. For most of her life, she'd resisted touch, so why was she now accepting it? That was a good thing, right? Especially with her husband. The person who had every right to touch her.

After sliding into bed, she took the robe off, tossing it near her feet. She glanced at him reclining against the plump pillows with one arm behind his head.

"Thanks for doing what you did today. You saved me and the kids. I'll do everything I can to make you happy. I hope you'll never come to regret this."

"You said I now have a family, right? That's something I've always wanted. I not only have you and the kids, but I have your huge extended family as well."

He reached up to touch her face. He'd done this often, and she found it was another thing she was getting to like. He didn't say anything, just stared at her like she was the most beautiful woman he'd ever seen. Not that he could possibly think that, but she could pretend. Screwing up all her courage, she did the thing she'd wanted to do since they'd said, "I do." She leaned down and kissed him.

It was meant to be a light touch of her lips to his with a hasty retreat, but somehow it didn't end up that way. Was it because Erik tightened his hand in her hair? Or because her lips enjoyed the taste of his too much and refused to leave? Whatever it was, the kiss was long and deep. But it was also sweet.

She finally eased back and shut off the light. Settling back against the pillows, she pulled the sheet up under her arms. "Good night, Erik."

Reaching over, he took her hand. They'd practiced this enough she didn't jump out of her skin at the contact. He didn't pull her closer, he simply held her hand.

"Good night, Mrs. Storm."

Mrs. Storm. Yes, as of today, she was now Mrs. Erik Storm. It had been a dream of hers for so long she couldn't quite believe it. But it had been a childhood dream. One she never expected to come true. As she held on to his hand and slipped into slumber, she could almost believe it had.

Chapter Eleven

"He has big muscles like you, Daddy."

Erik glanced at the cartoon character on the TV screen. They were allowing the kids a movie before bed and had settled on the animated Hercules.

"I'm not sure mine are as big at that, Matty. Are yours?"

Matty flexed his arms. "Now you, Daddy."

Chuckling, he held up his arms in a traditional muscle pose.

"What is this, the gun show?" Tessa quipped as she walked in with a freshly pajamaed Kiki in her arms.

"Comparing ourselves to Hercules. What do you think?"

Tessa slid Kiki next to her brother and pretended to squeeze Matty's bicep. "Ooh, so strong. Good thing Kiki and I have you tough men here to protect us."

Matty giggled, leaning against his side to watch the movie. This was different from last night with he and Tessa at the Inn. It hadn't been as bad as he'd expected, though. The scars on his leg were obvious, but she hadn't looked revolted or disgusted. Had even sat next to him on the bed while his leg had been up there.

A bit more of her background information had also come to light. What could possibly have made her parents desert her? And was that what happened? The man in the picture wore an army uniform. Could they get any information from it? Find out who he was and if indeed he was her father?

Kiki slid off the couch and cruised around the furniture, showing off her steady legs. Tess sat on the floor and moved Kiki in front of her.

"Let's show Daddy what you did in the other room."

The baby girl took a few steps toward him all on her own. Seriously walking.

"Woo hoo, look at you go."

When he scooped her up, he planted a kiss on her cheek, then placed her back on the floor where she proceeded to wobble back to Tessa. Only two months since he'd known these kids, and they were growing up so fast. With the way Kiki was moving now, pretty soon she'd be walking better than him. That was a depressing thought. Why did everything have to come back to his injury? He had a beautiful wife now and two amazing kids. And he was thankful, he was. But the spoiled boy in him that had once been as strong as Hercules couldn't help but compare the two. He came up seriously lacking.

After walking back and forth, Kiki snuggled into Tessa's lap on the couch near Matty. A nice family scene, watching TV like his parents and siblings had done often. After seven years in the military, maybe he was ready for something calm and uncomplicated. Simpler. Could be that dream of having a marriage like his parents had wasn't so far off. In some ways. Not all.

After a while both kids fell asleep, and Tessa stood, keeping Kiki snuggled against her.

"I'll put her down and come get Matty."

He clenched his jaw. What kind of a freakin' hero

was he that he couldn't even carry one of his kids to bed? On the screen Hercules got batted around by some one-eyed creature. Bad day for him too.

As Hercules finally outwitted the enemy, who fell to his death, the buildings around the hero began to shake and crumble. Sweat broke out on his face and back as he started to tremble. Flashes of mortar shells exploded around him, and the house rumbled. Matty moaned, and he pulled him closer. *Don't let the children get hurt. Protect them.* The noise echoed through his head, and he couldn't make it stop. Dust and debris rained down, and he crouched into a ball, keeping Matty safe. Damn, when would this freakin' shelling stop? How many of his men hadn't gotten clear?

Sharp pains sliced through his leg and hip, reminding him they'd been buried under all the rubble. Rocking back and forth, he held Matty, whispering words of assurance to him. They had to stay strong. Had to hold on until help came. And it would as soon as the fuckin' enemy stopped attacking. If they stopped. Maybe they'd all be dead before that happened.

His breath came in gasps as he stroked Matty's hair and stared at the precious face, eyes closed in slumber. Or was it death? Had he failed already? Been incapable of keeping this child alive? How many days had it been? Two? Four? The water had run out yesterday. They couldn't last much longer. Not in this heat.

"Erik? Erik?" The worried voice penetrated into his subconscious. Had his men finally found them? Could they dig them out in time?

Something touched his arm, and he bolted up, the room spinning furiously around him. What was happening? Where was he?

"Erik, you're scaring me. You'll wake Matty if you keep moving around like that."

Someone tried to remove the child from his arms. No, they couldn't. He had to protect Matty.

"No, keep him safe."

"I'm just going to put him to bed. I'll be right back."

Back where? In the bombed-out cellar? "No, too dangerous. Need to get out."

And Kiki? Where was she? Shit, had he lost her already? What kind of marine was he to lose his charges?

"Erik." Something stroked his face, and he reeled back, trying to focus. He blinked his eyes a few times and saw Matty being carried away. When he reached out for him, his hip gave way, and he crumpled into a ball. But he was on something soft. There was nothing soft in the hell hole they'd almost died in. Where was he?

He took a deep breath in, then expelled it slowly. Another one and another. Blue plaid made its way into his sight, and he pushed himself up. His grandparents' sofa in Maine. He was in Maine. With Matty and Kiki and…

"Erik, are you all right?"

Tessa. His wife. Who stood ten feet away, looking at him like he'd been dancing the hula.

"Tess."

He closed his eyes, then opened them again. Still there, her expression filled with concern. Not fear though. Good. It would kill him if she was ever afraid of him.

Stepping closer, she said, "What happened?"

Yeah, what the fuck *had* happened? One second he was watching the movie, and then…he was back in Kandahar. Since leaving there he'd had nightmares but never during the day when he'd been awake. Shit. This wasn't something he could be doing with the kids around.

He stuck his fingers into his hair and rubbed his thumbs over his eyes. "I'm sorry, Tess. I don't know what the hell happened. I was suddenly someplace else."

Cautiously she sat next to him. "Is there anything I can do to help?"

Put him out of his misery? No, what the fuck was he thinking? He had a family to take care of. *Get your shit together and be there for them.*

He shook his head, gritting his teeth. "No, I'm fine. I'll be fine. Thank you for putting Matty to bed. I didn't hurt him, did I?" That thought made his heart beat triple time.

She reached out and patted his thigh. "He was asleep. The last few days have been busy. I'm sure he never noticed."

"Noticed his father had a complete freak out?"

She leaned in, grinning. "I have freak outs all the time. Welcome to the club."

Laughter bubbled up inside him, and he wrapped his arms around Tessa and hugged her. At first she stiffened, then slowly relaxed and hugged him back. Her laughter joined his.

"We probably shouldn't be too loud, or we'll wake the kids."

Sobering up, he sat back, missing the warmth of

her arms. "Are you okay?"

She shrugged. "I'm fine. No need to worry about me."

"I'm your husband. It's my job to worry about you now."

"And I'm your wife, so it's my job to do the same."

The room grew quiet as the credits of the show scrolled over the screen. She grabbed the remote and shut the TV off.

"Maybe we can avoid that movie for a while, huh?"

Yeah. What else would trigger an episode like that? He'd have to be extra vigilant. "I know it's still early, but whatever the hell that was, it left me feeling like a wet rag."

"Moving all my things over here today made me pretty tired too." Her eyes lowered to her feet, and she blushed. Like she'd done when they woke up together this morning. He'd been staring at how peaceful she looked in sleep when she opened her eyes. Her cheeks coloring, she'd barely said two words, then scooted out of bed and into the bathroom to change. Was she thinking of that now?

They hadn't discussed their sleeping arrangements here. Last night at the Inn, she'd been gracious, but what about now? Especially after his little episode?

"I can bunk here on the couch. You take the bedroom."

That tempting tongue poked out and caressed her upper lip. "I don't think you'll be comfortable here, Erik. You're longer than the couch."

"I know but..." He wasn't sure what he should argue about.

"It's easier for me to stay on the couch."

"No. You totally rearranged your life for me and the kids. There's no way you're sleeping on a couch every night."

When she glanced around the room, her face turned red again. "You have a king-sized bed. That's bigger than what we shared last night. We can avoid touching if you want."

Is that what *she* wanted? Lifting his hand, he stroked his fingers down her cheek. She held herself stiff but didn't flinch or move away. He wanted to touch her, but he knew her limitations, even though they'd dwindled in the past week.

"If you're sure."

She handed him his cane. Hefting himself up, they got the house shut down for the night and them ready for bed. Stripping down to his T-shirt and shorts, he slipped into bed, his left leg closest to the side, while Tessa brushed her teeth. His mind still raced from the flashback, so he focused on the pattern on the ceiling. When she came out and rounded to her side, disappointment slammed into him. T-shirt and loose pajama shorts, not the sexy number she'd worn last night. The one he couldn't stop thinking about and had kept him awake for hours.

She slid in and moved the covers over her. The windows were open, and the ocean breeze held a slight chill. He wondered what she was thinking. Last night she'd made the move to kiss him. Should he do it tonight?

"Good night, Erik."

Lifting on his elbows, he leaned over and pressed his lips to hers. She reached up and held his face as they kissed. Minty toothpaste. And she smelled like strawberries. He wanted to feast on her all night. Gathering his courage, he pushed her hair behind her ear, then skimmed his fingers down her neck. A soft moan escaped her lips, and he got braver, allowing his hand to glide to her shoulder and along her arm to where she touched his face.

He turned her palm and kissed the center. "Thank you for not running from the room screaming tonight."

"You never ran from me."

"And I won't."

He kissed her one last time, then settled on his back. She shut the light off, and he tensed. What if the stupid images came back? What would she think then?

Her hand snaked out and took hold of his, like he'd done last night.

"I'll be right here if you need me, Erik."

The thought brought him comfort. He might actually be able to sleep tonight. Because he knew she would be there.

****

"Kiki's out cold. I'm going to put her in her car seat down below."

Erik turned to Tessa who rose from her seat at the back of the power boat with the sleeping child in her arms. He leaned on the captain's chair but extended his hand to grasp her elbow.

"You want help?" She wouldn't accept, but he figured he'd offer anyway. If he'd learned anything about her since their marriage two weeks ago, it was she was damn independent. But she was the first one to offer help for the kids or him.

She pursed her lips comically. "I think I can

manage."

Oh, he wanted to kiss those lips, but Kiki was awkward in her arms with the large flotation vest around her. She stepped down into the small cabin and got the baby settled. Baby. Kiki toddled all over the place lately, and he hated to admit maybe the baby phase was ending.

"Grab some soda or juice boxes while you're down there, please," Greg, his cousin, yelled down from his perch at the helm. "The boys might be thirsty."

After Tessa got Kiki settled, she bent over to retrieve the drinks. God, that view. A loose cover-up was all she wore over her bathing suit, and it road up as she leaned over, giving him a nice glimpse of her perfect legs.

"Looks like you won the jackpot with that one, huh?"

Greg also checked out her form, and he gritted his teeth. "Keep your eyes on the waves, hose jockey. Nothing to see down there."

Chuckling, Greg stared straight ahead. "Plenty to see, cousin, just not much I can do about it. But you can. That's why I said you won the prize. Nathaniel and I got married before you did, but let's face it, you have a higher chance of success with this one."

When Tessa appeared with a few cans and some cardboard boxes, she smiled at Greg. Greg grinned back and took one. "Thanks."

He wanted to wipe the grin off the man's face, even though Greg was his favorite cousin. They'd grown up across the street from each other, and along with their other cousin, Nathaniel, had all been in the same grade together. But Nathaniel's upper-class wife had cheated on him with his law partner and gotten pregnant. Greg's wife had died in a car accident when Ryan was only a few months old.

"Do you still miss her?" he asked as he popped the top of his soda can.

Greg looked confused, so he elaborated, "Wendy. I know it's been eight years, but I didn't know if it was still painful."

Throwing him a strange look, Greg turned away for a second. When he faced Erik again his expression was as composed as ever. "We were married for less than a year. And you know the circumstances of that. I'm just sorry Ryan never got to know his mother. But everything happens for a reason."

Greg had only been dating Wendy a few months when she got pregnant, and they'd quickly gotten married. This was as close as his cousin had ever gotten to admitting the marriage hadn't been perfect.

Looking over, Tessa laughed at something the boys said, and he wondered about his own marriage. No way she'd cheat on him. Not with her fear of new people. And she certainly wouldn't get pregnant by him. Even if he could manage the act, he remembered the doc telling him something about not producing sperm due to the injuries he'd sustained. He had to be happy with the two great kids they already had. They weren't blood related, but he would love them like they were. He had a feeling Tessa would too.

"I'm glad you were able to come today." Greg took a sip of his soda, then replaced the can in the holder. "Ryan's been talking about Matty since the wedding, hoping we could get together again. This is the first cousin he's got."

"Thanks for asking us. We didn't get a chance to chat all that much at the wedding. How close are you to that promotion to captain?"

Greg shrugged. "Probably a few years before someone retires. But what about you, Captain Storm? What's your military status?"

He explained about his disability leave and mentioned The Boat House. It would be at least a few more weeks before he started there. Now he needn't worry since Tessa would be with the kids while he was working. Marrying her really had been a godsend.

When he glanced back, she'd slipped the cover-up off her shoulders and sat with her face to the sun. Several tendrils of hair had loosened from her ponytail and whipped around her cheeks. Gorgeous, absolutely gorgeous.

Greg killed the motor. "Thought we'd float here a while. Ryan wanted to cast his rod into the water and try and catch a shark."

"A shark, huh? Big goals."

As Greg instructed the boys where to stand and how to hold the pole, Erik walked back to where Tessa sat. The boat bounced softly, and he clenched his teeth, trying to keep his balance. The cane was in the seat next to Greg's.

"Big waves coming in," Greg called out as the boat tipped, and a wave swelled and crashed over the side, soaking them.

Tessa's arms were suddenly around him, and he twisted, landing on the bench seat with her in his lap. "Are you okay, Erik?" Her eyes widened with anxiety. For him?

"I'm fine," he snapped. "You don't have to coddle

me like the kids." Or treat him like the damn cripple he was.

When she stiffened in his lap, he regretted speaking to her that way. But dammit, she was his wife, and he should be protecting her. He looked up, expecting a hurt expression, instead her eyes lit up mischievously.

Leaning in close, she whispered in his ear. "Fine, next time I'll let you fall on your ass and get washed over the side of the boat."

A laugh erupted from his throat, and he couldn't stop it. This wife of his was growing a set, and he liked it. She struggled to get off his lap, but he held her in place.

"You're not on my life insurance policy yet, so you might want to behave." He put his hands around her tiny waist and enjoyed the feel of the skin on her back. Would she allow it or have one of her freak-outs, as she called it?

She stilled and grabbed his shoulders as another large wave hit the boat. Greg had the boys under control. He was going to enjoy this. Pulling her in closer, their faces lined up.

"Life insurance, huh?" she teased, her eyes still glowing. "How much? I've always wanted to go to Hawaii."

"Hmm, I'm beginning to think you and Miss Gulch manufactured this whole thing so you could get a free vacation in paradise. Do you admit it?"

As he pressed his lips to hers, she sighed. Her body physically relaxed, and she kissed him back. God, her reaction to him today, from just a few weeks ago, was so different. She liked this. Liked kissing him. And he couldn't say he didn't enjoy it himself. Her lips were like candy, sweet and addicting.

"Big wave," Greg called out, and Erik pushed her down to cover her as the ocean splashed over them. The chilly water slid down his back and cooled his desire. But seeing her spread out under him on the bench warmed it right back up again. He kissed her once more, then sat up and helped her sit too.

Her lips were closed tight, and he could tell she was trying not to laugh. He was drenched. When he started to lower his head for another taste of her lips, Kiki's cry rang from below.

Tessa's eyes held disappointment, but she popped up and went to get the child.

The rest of the afternoon flew by, and soon Greg was tied up to the dock at the marina, and Tess was gathering their things.

"Thanks for taking us out. Matty had a blast with Ryan." He shook hands with his cousin, and Greg clapped him on the back.

"We should do it again soon. Get the kids together again anyway. I'd love to see Tessa again. She's really come out of her shell with you and the kids. Totally different from the shy wallflower she used to be. You two look good together. Like you fit."

He glanced over as she picked up Kiki to snuggle on her shoulder. Looking his way, she smiled shyly.

"We're getting comfortable with each other. She's definitely more than I expected."

"Hope it works out for you." Greg slapped him on the back again, and Erik picked up their bags and hobbled with his family to the minivan.

"I think they'll sleep well tonight with all the water and the waves." Tessa pointed to his still-damp shirt.

"You caught quite a bit of that too."

"Yeah, I kept you from getting soaked."

She gazed at him with stars in her eyes. "I know you did. You're my hero."

Hero, hardly. But the way she looked at him, he felt like one.

Chapter Twelve

"How many stories did you end up reading?"

Erik stepped through the sliding door from the family room down to the deck and the Adirondack chairs. She watched for signs of pain around his eyes as he walked. He still leaned heavily on the cane, but his balance seemed much improved from a month and a half ago.

"Only four tonight." He chuckled, settling onto the aging wood. "He was out midway through the last one, though. I thought you said the sun and water would make them both go out easy tonight."

"What do I know? I've only been a mother for two weeks. That's limited experience, and I shouldn't be held accountable for any maternal advice I give."

"Actually it's two weeks tomorrow. Should we do something for our anniversary?"

She watched the waves roll in as the sun sank behind them. It had seriously been two weeks since she'd been married. And to Erik Storm. Never in a million years would she have imagined that happening.

"A cruise to the Caribbean," she teased, peeking at his handsome face. The scar on his forehead was still visible, but the red skin had softened to a light pink. One day she wanted to be brave enough to kiss it. But today was not that day.

"Hmm, a bit much for two weeks. How about we

save that for the one month? Maybe a walk along the beach and playing in the waves. It's supposed to be hot tomorrow. You can wear that cute bathing suit you had on today. The one Greg couldn't stop staring at when you took your cover-up off."

"He wasn't staring at me." Heat rose to her cheeks. "And if he was, it's only because I actually spoke words today. Growing up, I didn't often talk to him."

"You didn't talk to most of us. Gave me an inferiority complex."

She snorted. Not very ladylike but his words were ridiculous. "Right, like you ever worried about what I thought of you. You were too busy with your beach babes and macho fan club."

"There was no *official* fan club." He winked at her, and heat crawled from her face down into her chest and lower. Did he have any idea what effect he had on her? With his long muscular legs, clad in camouflage shorts, stretched out in front of him. His strong arms clasped behind his head and his eyes closed, face tipped to catch the ocean breeze. She could only stare and wonder what she'd done so right in her life to deserve this man here by her side.

"Hey."

Erik grinned, staring at her. Damn, he'd seen her gawking. She chewed on her bottom lip and faced straight ahead to watch seagulls diving for their last meal of the day.

Reaching out, he entwined their fingers, settling their hands on the arm of her chair. A smile then he closed his eyes, resting his head back. "I couldn't think of anything more perfect than this."

She couldn't either but Erik? Wouldn't he prefer

some vivacious blonde with an hourglass figure and skimpy clothes simpering over him? Her loose top and drawstring pants weren't exactly fashion model friendly.

But he was here with her, holding her hand. She'd never complain about that. Leaning back in her own chair, she closed her eyes. The kids may have gotten all worked up from being out on the ocean today, but she was exhausted. Constantly watching to make sure they weren't too close to the side of the boat or that Erik had a firm grasp of something nearby whenever the ocean rolled too much had sapped her strength. It still felt as if she were bobbing around like a cork. But Erik's hand in hers was a reminder she was anchored here with him.

She must have dozed because when she opened her eyes the sky was black and filled with stars, and the breeze had picked up. Erik still sat close, their hands resting on the arm of her chair.

A small light soared across the sky, and she remembered the town was shooting fireworks off tonight at the marina. Color exploded in a huge circle, lighting the dark, and she tensed for the big boom that would come.

At the sound, Erik's eyes flew open and darted around the deck. Two more were launched, and the whistling noise echoed through the air. Looking at her frantically, he reached for her shoulders.

"Erik, it's just fire—"

He slammed into her as the second boom rocked the sky. They landed on the deck, and she couldn't breathe. His entire body trembled as he lay on top of her with his head tucked down. What the heck was happening?

More fireworks crackled overhead, and she suddenly knew. Like the movie a few weeks ago, he was having some sort of flashback.

"Erik, it's me, Tessa. It's only fireworks. It's okay."

"Stay down. Safer here," he mumbled, then twitched as another few crackled in the sky above them.

Wrapping her arms around him, she whispered soft encouragement. Could he even hear her? His head jerked back and forth, his breathing heavy. The weight of him almost crushed her, and her heart began to race. This full body contact was new and reminded her of her time with Jeremy. This was different, though. He was just making sure she was safe.

"Erik, I'm okay. We should go in the house. They won't be so loud in there. Can you get up?"

Half a dozen lights zoomed across the sky. Shit, the sound in a few seconds would be terrifying to a battle-torn soldier.

Lights exploded around them, and he flinched. His hands shook as they clenched her shoulders tighter. She managed to twist to her side and hold his face.

"In the house. Now, marine, now!" she yelled, and he perked up enough to look around. His eyes glazed over, obviously not seeing her. "Let's go."

As they moved into the family room, she heard Matty screaming. Damn, of course he wouldn't like the sound either. She left Erik sitting on the couch, then rushed to Matty's room. The poor child sat up in bed, crying, covering his ears.

"Come here, honey. I've got you." She picked him up, holding him close. Fireworks weren't something he'd know about, so no sense explaining right now.

When she peeked in Kiki's room, all was still except the glowing light and soothing noise from the device beside her bed. It must have masked the worst of the din.

"Daddy doesn't like the noise either. We need to make him feel better too. Can you help me with that?"

With tears streaming down his face, Matty clung to her neck. They found Erik sitting on the floor in front of the couch, his good knee up to his chest, his hands in his hair. She sat next to him and moved Matty close.

"I need you to take care of Matty. He's afraid, Erik. Can you do that?"

When Erik glanced up, his eyes held recognition. They still darted around the room at each flash, but he knew where he was. Pulling Matty into his lap, he rubbed the boy's back.

After racing around the room putting on lights, she found a classic station on the radio. Soothing classical music filled the room. She moved back to Erik's side and enveloped both her boys in a big hug. Erik attempted a smile. Until another boom shook the house. His arms tightened around Matty, and his face buried itself in the boy's hair.

"I'm sorry, Tess. So stupid. But I can't…"

She kissed his cheek, then stroked Matty's back. "Fears aren't stupid, and we can't always control them. Believe me, I know." She snuggled in closer. "We wait it out and support each other as we do."

They spent the next twenty minutes huddled close. Matty started singing a song, and she listened to the soft voice.

"We did this when we were buried in the cellar. It helped to soothe Kiki too."

"Whatever works, Erik."

She picked up the simple lyrics and sang along. Erik started to relax, and Matty's head bobbed as he tried to stay awake but soon lost the battle.

Staying close, she listened as the end of the show drew near. They usually shot off a few dozen fireworks in succession, which would be tough for him to handle if his earlier reaction was any indication.

As if on cue, the sky outside exploded in a cacophony of sound. She tightened her grip on Erik and hummed louder to distract him. He started rocking back and forth and humming too. Was he trying to keep Matty asleep or keep himself from a further flip-out?

The noise finally ended, and Erik panted like he'd run a marathon. Yup, knew that feeling. A busy store usually did it to her. Her heart raced, and she couldn't breathe.

"It's all over now."

Erik inhaled deeply a few times, then let it out slowly. Finally, he turned to her, and his eyes held such pain she couldn't help but reach for him and kiss him. As she moved her lips over his face and traced his scars with her fingertips, he simply sat there. Kneeling, she moved her lips first to the scar on his jaw and then touched the one through his eyebrow. The sigh that hissed from his mouth dripped with relief. Apparently today was that day.

"Let me get your cane, and we'll put Matty to bed."

She quickly returned with it and lifted the child into her arms. Erik struggled to rise, but she allowed him to do it himself. After what happened he needed a small victory.

After getting doors and lights, she placed Matty back in his bed. The child didn't move. They both pressed a kiss to his forehead.

"I'm going to hit the sack, if you don't mind."

They moved the few steps to their room, and she went about getting ready for bed. Water splashed in the bathroom for a few minutes, then he came out and slid into bed. She joined him a few minutes later.

Before she could shut the light off, he cleared his throat.

"Tess, listen I—"

"Don't say anything." She reached for his hand. "I know how it feels to be unable to control something."

He glanced down at their clasped fingers. "Why are you so good to me?"

The brave part of her, that had kissed his scars a few minutes ago, kicked in stronger. "I'd do almost anything for you. Haven't you figured that out yet?"

"I'm starting to. But what can I do for you? It feels kind of one sided here."

Seriously, he thought that? This marriage gave her more than she'd ever dreamed of. "You've done a lot, Erik. You've helped me get in touch with some of my fears and start working on overcoming them."

As his thumb stroked her hand, he actually grinned. "Yeah, you've done an awful lot of touching for someone who doesn't like touch. Especially tonight."

"I guess the fear you and Matty had took precedence over my own."

He lay down, and she shut the light off. His hand immediately reached for hers. This time, though, he pulled. And kept tugging until she rested against his side.

"Is this okay?" His voice held uncertainty. "I don't ever want you to be uncomfortable with me."

She leaned her head against his arm and inhaled. God, he smelled good. There might be some discomfort here, but it sure wasn't the kind she usually had.

"I'm getting used to it. I guess you're growing on me."

"Like mold," he joked but pressed his lips to hers, making her forget the teasing. Forget everything except the taste of his mouth.

"I had to face some of my fears today. Seems like you've been getting closer to combating yours. Maybe the day wasn't a total loss."

When she snuggled against him and didn't have an overwhelming urge to run, she had to agree.

****

"Keep your head down. Stay safe."

Bright flashes slipped through the ravaged floorboards, lighting up the cellar in bits and pieces. Mortar exploded overhead, echoing around the confined space. Erik huddled around the children, protecting them from the debris raining down upon their heads with every shell.

"Take care of them for me. Don't let anything happen to them."

Footsteps above drowned out the pleas of the woman. They couldn't be found, not yet. Not by the enemy. They'd kill him for sure. But the children wouldn't survive either. He had to hide them, keep them safe. And their mother. He needed to get help for her.

"Maman!"

He couldn't let the children speak, or they'd be discovered. The voices above were not the ones who would help them. He glanced at the woman who was now silent. Her brown waves fell across her shoulders as her eyes stared into the distance, lifeless and cold.

"Tessa? No, you shouldn't be here."

He crawled through the rubble to get to her, save her. Where were the children? He looked around but couldn't find them.

"Matty? Kiki? Tessa?"

"Erik? Are you okay?"

The soft voice penetrated his consciousness, and the warmth against his side brought calm to his heavy breathing and rapid heart rate.

Tessa's brown waves tickled his chest as she leaned over, her expression concerned. The pre-dawn light was just enough to make out the frown on her full lips. Her hand rested near his navel and moved soothingly over his skin.

He was in Maine, in his bed. With Tessa right beside him. Closing his eyes, he released a sigh.

"Erik?"

"I'm okay." The clock showed it was still too early to be up. "Go back to sleep." He slipped his hand around her back to hold her in place against his chest.

Her head settled on his shoulder, and her sleepy voice mumbled, "You were talking in your sleep."

"Only a dream. Nothing to worry about. Sorry I woke you." More like a nightmare; one where she died, and he hadn't been able to save her.

She simply hummed and snuggled closer. God, she felt good. Never before had she been this close, practically lying on top of him. Most likely unaware of her position. He was certainly aware and enjoying the sensation of her hand resting on his stomach, her breath tickling his shoulder.

As he glanced at her, he was thankful for the tiny bit of light coming in the windows. Her serene face was so beautiful, and his heart hammered wildly, knowing she was his wife. Thank God she'd suggested this arrangement. He didn't deserve someone as good as her, but he was so grateful he had her. But would she stay? The whole no-touch thing had started fading since they'd decided to get married. Would she regret he couldn't give her everything a woman needed?

The large night shirt she'd worn to bed fell off her shoulder, exposing more skin. Damn, more than her shoulder showed. The curve of her breast peeked at him from the gapped material.

As he ran his hand over her back, another sound, like the purr of a kitten, slipped from her throat, and she adjusted her position. Holy shit, now it was his turn to moan. Her top slipped again, exposing one plump breast to his view. It was round and firm like a fresh, ripe peach with the tip of her nipple a shade of darker pink. His mouth watered, imagining his lips there, tasting her.

Desire slammed into him hard and fast, and he swore his cock twitched. Nah, had to be his imagination. That part of him had died months ago. There hadn't been any proof otherwise. He'd looked through enough girly magazines to try and jump-start things. It hadn't worked.

Sliding his other hand down his side and between his legs, he froze. Holy Christ. It hadn't been his imagination. He wasn't standing at full attention, but by God, he was at least half mast. Could he get the rigging to go full sails?

Taking himself in hand, he also caressed Tessa's bare skin. Was this smart, though? He'd finally gotten her to let him touch her, if only briefly. If she woke up to him fully aroused, would it scare her back to where she'd been a month ago?

Too soon, he realized, that wouldn't be a problem. Damn, and he'd actually gotten excited for a few short minutes. That didn't mean he couldn't fantasize about feasting on her gorgeous breasts and tasting everything else on her. Dream of easing her back on the bed as he licked his way up one side of her body and down the other. The sounds escaping from her throat would spur him on as his tongue delved into her private places.

Moving his hand away, he wondered if that would be a good thing, though. If she started wanting touch, would she also want to have her happy ending? He could pleasure her, he had no doubt. And he'd enjoy every delicious second of it. Most likely, she'd enjoy it, too. When they kissed, he could feel the passion she'd hidden for so long. If he unleashed it from its hiding place, would she be able to settle for the little bit he could give her? Or would she want more? Want the one thing he couldn't give her?

He pressed his nose into her floral-scented hair, inhaling her memory. He didn't want to think about anything beyond that right now. She was in his arms, and he'd cherish every second.

****

Erik slammed the door of the minivan and leaned on his cane. Damn freakin' leg and hip throbbed like a bastard. Sue had pushed him at PT seriously hard today. *After* she'd lectured him about taking the anti-inflammatory medicine to keep the swelling down so he didn't make it any worse. It had been well over two months since he'd been injured. How long did he need to be dependent on these drugs? Although right now he could use a few hits of the Vicodin. If at all possible, he'd been studiously avoiding taking them. Too many guys he knew got hooked. The last thing he needed was some fucking addiction on top of all his other problems.

Limping up the stairs to the porch, he gritted his teeth at the pain. To add to his frustrations, he'd talked to his mom today. They'd moved to their new place in the fifty-five plus community. He felt like such a slug that he hadn't gone down to help them. It was one more thing making him feel useless. But what the hell could he do with his crippled leg? Not much.

Then she'd told him Sara had been offered a singing contract along with the opportunity to go on tour with a big-name band as their opening act. His sister had left a week ago for rehearsals in California. No one had thought to tell him. Damn, he wasn't in the Middle East anymore. He was here in New England.

His mom had apologized but hadn't wanted to interrupt his honeymoon period. What fucking honeymoon period? Holding hands and a few hot kisses were as far as he and Tess had gotten. Unless of course he counted his dreams. Day and night, he thought of what he'd like to do to his wife. And when he'd gotten a peek at her breast last week, it had made him realize exactly what he was missing.

Then he'd been stupid and actually growled, "There's no honeymoon, Mom. Tessa married me to help with the kids."

"I know you need to take it slow with her, sweetie, but she's so much better than before. It shouldn't—"

"It's not Tessa. It's me. My stupid injury left me imp—" He'd almost said the word…and to his mother. "Damn, forget I said anything, Mom."

He told her he loved her and tried to say goodbye. But not before he heard the tears in her voice. Shit. Nice way to break that little piece of news to the family. How could he even look her in the eye next time he saw her? Or his dad. His parents didn't keep secrets from each other, so she was sure to tell him. It was something he loved about them. He'd always wanted to be just like Pete Storm, to make his father proud of him. That goal kept moving further and further away.

He pushed the door open, wondering why he'd told Sid he'd start next Friday. It was only the lunch crowd, but weekends were crazy busy during the summer. It was the day after PT, and he always felt like shit. Why hadn't he used his brain and asked to start a week later, after the Labor Day crowd had dissipated?

When he stepped into the family room, chaos surrounded him. Shouldn't the kids be down for their naps by now? Instead, Matty beat a stick against a drum in some off-beat rhythm while Kiki squealed and shook two of her rattles. Toys littered the floor.

"Hi, Erik." Tessa looked up and smiled as she tried to snap Kiki's romper after an obvious diaper change. "Can you keep an eye on them while I get rid of this and wash my hands?"

He grimaced but nodded. She gathered up the old diaper and scurried into the kitchen. What had they eaten for lunch? The room smelled toxic. *Air. Get some air in here.*

Hobbling over to the slider, he pulled it open, then turned and tripped over Tessa's cat.

"Jesus Christ! Get that damn thing out of here. It's going to kill me one of these days."

Tessa rushed back in, grabbed the cat, and pushed it out the door. "I'm sorry. You said it was okay to bring her here."

"It's fine," he grumbled. When she started to respond, he scowled and shouted, "I said it's fine. I just had—" His foot stumbled on a block, and he dropped into the nearest chair so he didn't end up on the floor. One of Kiki's toys went off, playing the obnoxious song it sang over and over.

"Fuckin' hell! Can I have one stupid moment of peace?" When he pushed the toy away, it crashed into the wall and shattered into several pieces. Kiki began to cry, and Tessa scooped her up. They all stared at him silently. He'd fucked up again. *You are no Pete Storm.*

"Just get them out of here. I can't deal with this right now." His tone was harsh, but he didn't have the energy to make it softer. Within seconds, they were gone, and he felt like the biggest loser in the world. *Way to love your family, dipshit.*

After a few moments of self-pity, he hauled himself up and limped into the kitchen where he proceeded to shove aside matches and Band-Aids while he got some Vicodin and something to wash it down with. The desire to take the whole damn bottle was strong, but he wouldn't do it. That was the coward's way out. He might not be exactly like his father, but he could be there for his family. If they were still talking to him after the way he treated them.

He slumped into a chair at the table and rested his head in his hands. *Get your act together, marine. You've got a mission to accomplish.*

In the service, he'd be lucky if his recent behavior didn't get him court-martialed. Where the hell had all this crap stuff come from? Freaking out over a stupid children's cartoon, completely losing it during the fireworks, dreaming about Tessa dying, and now this. Fucking basket case.

The house was eerily quiet. Usually when the kids went down for naps, there was chatter and stories read, but all was still. Where the heck was Tessa? The kids usually went down without a fuss. Pushing himself out of the chair, he grabbed his cane.

His overused muscles and tendons screamed in agony as they objected to his walk down the hall. When he peeked in both of the kids' rooms, no one was there. Weird. Tessa was going to put them down for their nap. Had she let them sleep in their room? He walked the few more steps, but the master bedroom was empty too. Where the hell had they gone? They hadn't walked past him in the kitchen, so they hadn't gone outside. Unless they used the front door.

He hobbled back down the hall to the living room, but when he saw the deadbolt still on, he knew they couldn't have gone out that way. What the fuck? Had he been so out of it he hadn't seen them go back through the family room? His heart picked up speed as he rushed through the house, bumping into furniture in his haste and clumsiness.

They had to be here somewhere. Moving down the hall again, he slumped against the wall, trying to figure out what the hell he should do. A bump followed by a tiny voice turned his head. As he entered Matty's room, he heard it again. The song they'd sung in the cellar to keep the kids calm. It was coming from the closet.

What the hell was Matty doing in the closet, and where were Tessa and Kiki?

"Matty?" He pushed the bifold door to the side, his breath freezing in his lungs. Tessa sat on the floor, both kids in her lap. She trembled violently, but her eyes spit fire.

"Don't you touch them," she growled, her voice low and determined. "I won't let you hurt them."

Hurt them? She thought…

He staggered back as if punched. He couldn't breathe. His heart pounded fiercely in his chest. How could she think he'd…?

Matty's bed bumped against his back, and he couldn't keep his liquefied legs holding him up any longer. Sliding to the floor, he stared at her agonized face. The children huddled close but watched him carefully. Were they scared of him, too? Had he ruined the best thing he'd had in his life?

He pulled his good knee up to his body and dropped his head onto it, his hands pulling at his hair. Sobs shook his whole frame, and there was nothing he could do to stop them.

Chapter Thirteen

Erik's face paled as he bumped into Matty's bed. Tessa kept her eyes on him and held the children close to her. Stumbling back, he landed on the floor, his expression one of horror. She wanted to feel bad for him, to comfort him, but the tremors shaking her body reminded her of the past and the fear she'd never been able to get under control.

There was no attempt from him to move toward them. His face crumpled, then fell onto his raised leg. His fingers slipped into his hair, gripping it tight, shoulders shaking as his breath came out in heavy pants. Was he…?

"Daddy cry," Matty whispered in her ear. "Mommy cry, too."

Matty kissed her cheek, and she realized she had tears streaming down her face. She glanced at Erik who curled into himself near Matty's bed. The boy hugged her neck, then loosened his grip.

"I kiss Daddy, too."

"No, sweetie, stay here."

Matty kissed her again, then pulled away. "I kiss Daddy."

She couldn't stop him without leaving the confines of the closet. It was safe in here, wasn't it? She needed to protect Kiki also. But if he made one move to hurt Matty, she'd stop him.

This is Erik. He'd never hurt you or the kids.

Her heart knew this to be true, but her mind, and all the memories of foster parents and siblings, were stronger than her reasoning. She'd trusted Mr. Carter at first, but too many bruises convinced her hiding in the closet or under the bed made more sense. Mrs. Simmons had seemed nice at first, but after a few drinks, her shrill voice screamed some harsh words. Words no child should ever have to be subjected to.

But he's proved himself to you. He's from a good family and has never done anything to hurt you.

What about the tantrum he just threw in the family room? The sound of the toy smashing against the wall echoed through her head, bringing back memories of one toy Santa had brought her. The one Mr. Carter had thrown against the side of the house because she hadn't shut it off quick enough.

Matty walked slowly toward Erik and knelt in front of him, titling his head to try and see Erik's face. The boy's hand touched his father's head. "Daddy, I kiss you better."

When Erik looked up, his eyes were liquid pools of agony. His trembling lips clamped together as he took Matty's hand.

"I'm so sorry." His voice was like sandpaper. Lowering his leg, he pulled Matty into a hug, his face in the child's neck, still whispering, "I'm sorry."

She watched carefully, but he simply held Matty, rubbing his back and hair, talking softly. The child hugged him back and kissed his cheek.

Kiki stirred in her arms and wiggled to get free. No, she couldn't go.

Erik won't hurt her. Let her go.

She knew this but didn't want to release her hold on the baby. If she did, she'd be vulnerable. Alone and unable to hide behind the child. All the calm Kiki brought to her would be gone, and the fear would rush back like floodwaters.

"Dada." Kiki twisted, and she let her go. Pulling herself up on the doorframe, the child toddled to Erik. He looked up, his face still haunted. His hand reached around the child and pulled her to his other shoulder. Kiki settled there with her thumb in her mouth, no hesitation even after the earlier outburst.

She scooted closer to the doorframe, needing some sort of protection from the maelstrom swirling inside her. Part of her wanted to comfort Erik. The strong, vital man rocked the children, still muttering, "I'm sorry. I'm so sorry."

The other part of her had settled into survival mode. *Remain in the background. Stay quiet. Don't do anything to draw attention to yourself. Remove yourself from any situation that could become volatile.* How could she forget the years she'd spent learning how to get by? These lessons were so deeply ingrained in her she didn't think she could ever get them out.

You don't need them with Erik.

Her heart kept repeating this, but her head, filled with harsh memories, wouldn't let her get past it. She wished she could be as forgiving as the children, but their innocence was still somewhat intact, even with the reality of what their life had been like before this. She should be able to do this too, but she wasn't strong enough.

Matty lifted himself from Erik's arms long enough to grab his security blanket and pillow from his bed and drag it back to settle his head in his father's lap. When Erik ran his hand over Matty's head and back, the child's eyes drifted closed, like his sister's. Erik glanced over at her, and she pressed closer to the doorframe.

"I'm sorry, Tess. I'd never hurt you. I promise. I'm so sorry." His Adam's apple bobbed up and down as he swallowed.

She clamped her lips together to keep them from trembling, then swiped her hand over her face to erase the evidence of her fear. *They'll use it against you. Use your fears to control you.*

Erik wouldn't do that. He cares for you. He's been good to you. He had, but was it because of the children? And did it matter? This was Erik Storm. The man she'd dreamed of for ten years. But she'd never dreamed of him throwing toys against the wall and yelling like he had. Could she find out what caused it? Was she brave enough?

"You scared us, Erik. It isn't like you."

"I know." His face twisted in agony. "I don't know what the heck is happening to me. My control is shot to hell, and it seems I can't do anything about it. I swear, I'd never hurt you or the kids, Tessa, but I'm starting to doubt myself and my sanity."

She'd heard of soldiers returning from war to face similar things. Maybe it was time he admitted he needed help.

"Lots of military get that post-traumatic thing after fighting in a war. Did any of your doctors talk to you about it?"

He closed his eyes and sighed. When he opened them, she saw resignation. "There's a VA in

Brunswick. I've only been once to set up my PT. Guess it's time to see what else they can do for me."

She nodded, and he went back to rubbing Matty's back and kissing Kiki's head. He couldn't be comfortable with both children like that, but she wasn't sure she had enough courage to approach him. And maybe, like her, they helped him regulate his out of whack emotions. Children had such a calming effect. If only they could bottle it.

They sat in the room for a while, both trying to get their emotions under control. She wanted to be close to the children too but wasn't sure she was ready to leave her safe harbor. Watching from a distance, she saw the notable difference in his body tension. His expression was still regretful, but he'd stopped shaking, and his eyes had dried up. She swiped at her face again, knowing she needed to do the same.

"You're still hiding in the closet, Tess," he said softly, his gaze roaming over her. "Think there might be a little post-traumatic stress going on with you too?"

A grin tugged at her mouth while she shrugged. "Maybe. I never thought of it that way." Her trauma hadn't been one incident, like fighting in a war. It seemed her whole life had been fighting to survive.

"I'll call the VA in the morning to see what they suggest. Maybe we could find a counselor who'd give us a two-for-one deal."

His humor had returned. Maybe they'd be okay. In all these years, with all her quirks, no one had ever suggested she seek counseling to help her cope. But in a few short weeks, he'd helped her get past a few of her fears. Would the counseling get them both to where they could have a normal life? She'd been so far from normal forever, she wasn't sure she'd know what it meant.

****

"Are you ready?"

Erik opened the door of the Community Based Outpatient Clinic and let Tessa go in first. He wanted to put his hand on her back, but since the episode a few days ago, she'd been back to her skittish behavior. Still polite but distant. If she got any closer to the side of the bed at night, he thought she might roll off onto the floor. His actions had made her revert to where she was six weeks ago, and he hated it.

She simply nodded as she walked in front of him. Glancing at the piece of paper in his hand, he looked up and checked the sign.

"Dr. Sullivan's office is down this hall to the right. Room 117."

Tessa chewed her bottom lip, twisting her hands together. Could she give him a sign she didn't hate him? He'd apologized so many times he'd lost count. It was fine, she always said, and she understood, but things had changed between them. They hadn't held hands or kissed at all since his screw up. He missed it. Thank God the kids hadn't seemed as affected by his atrocious behavior.

The door was open, but he still tapped on it. The man inside stood and waved for them to come in. He was a bit shorter than Erik with gray brushing the temples of his dark hair.

"Come in. You must be the Storms. I'm Dr. Sullivan, but you can call me Harry, if you like."

Tessa's gaze scanned the room, from the desk in the corner to the sitting area that housed a small couch and a few upholstered chairs. Still anxious.

Dr. Sullivan came forward and shook his hand. "Captain Storm?" He had a firm grip but nothing too overwhelming.

"Erik is fine. This is my wife, Tessa." It still felt weird to introduce her that way, but he kind of liked it.

The man held out his hand, and she froze. Dr. Sullivan quickly moved his hand to point to the seating area. "Why don't you have a seat?"

As he sat on one end of the couch, he wondered if she would choose to sit next to him or take a seat of her own. When she chose the couch, he let out a breath of relief, though she made sure there was space between them.

Dr. Sullivan closed the door and took one of the chairs. "Why don't you tell me a little about yourselves and what brought you here?"

He glanced at Tessa, knowing she wouldn't initiate the conversation. On their way here, she'd made a comment that her issues were so old they probably couldn't be fixed. He knew better. She'd come so far in the short time they'd been married. Now they needed to get him in better shape so he didn't scare her, or the kids, again.

"I had a tour in Afghanistan that ended with me coming home in a wheelchair a few months ago."

Sullivan glanced at his cane. "Looks like you've made good progress in that area."

"Some, yeah." Not as much as he wanted.

"Tell me how you got injured."

Launching into his tale of the shelling and trying to evacuate the village, he tried not to make it sound too horrible, even though memories of it still sent chills through him. As he spoke, Tessa shifted in her seat, moving closer. Was she trying to offer comfort in her own reclusive way?

"It must have been terrifying, Erik. Being responsible for two young lives while you were in excruciating pain yourself. Not knowing if rescue would arrive in time."

Terrifying didn't even begin to describe how he'd felt. But marines didn't talk about fear. They gutted it out and stayed strong. But would he get better if he did that? Wasn't part of counseling to talk it out and get past it? If he wanted Tessa to talk too, he needed to lead by example.

"It scared the shit out of me." He grimaced at his curse. "Sorry, I've been toning that down for the kids, but sometimes they still slip out."

"I've worked with military personnel and heard it all. There's no judgment in this room. I want you to speak freely, unless you, Mrs. Storm, are upset by it."

Her tiny voice piped up. "No, it's fine."

Taking a deep breath, he continued. "The not knowing was the hardest. My men had my location, but I wasn't sure how many of them had actually made it out alive. The enemy kept coming back for the next few days, so I had to keep the kids quiet. If they found us, we all would have died."

His leg cramped up, and he realized how tense he was. He glanced at Tessa as he rubbed it and immediately felt calmer. Her expression showed she truly cared what he'd gone through.

"The worst part was thinking I'd never see my family again. Did they know how much I loved them? How much I appreciated all the emails and care packages they'd sent while I was away?"

"Do you have a big family, Captain?"

"Yeah, and we mostly live near each other. I'm the oldest and have two brothers and a sister. Plus my parents, grandparents, aunts and uncles, and a bunch of cousins. We're all pretty close."

He turned toward Tessa. "You know, it's funny, I actually thought of you. As I sat there waiting for us to be blown to pieces again, or die of thirst or heat, I went back through all my good memories. The ones from Maine, with my grandparents, you were part of those."

Her face softened, her eyes suspiciously damp. Was he getting to her? Would they be able to get back to where they'd been before the closet episode?

"What about your family, Mrs. Storm? Or may I call you Tessa?"

She glanced at Erik quickly, then looked away. "Tessa is fine. I don't have any family."

"You mean they've passed away?"

Her shoulders hunched a bit as she shook her head. "No, I don't know who they are. I lived in foster care most of my life."

"But now you're part of Erik's family. How long have you two been married?"

"A little over three weeks."

The doc looked surprised. "Oh, so you're newlyweds. Congratulations."

"We got married so Erik could keep the kids."

After the kisses they'd shared, he sometimes forgot. "Uh, everything in here is confidential, right?" Had they screwed themselves by telling him this?

Sullivan nodded.

"I promised I'd take care of the kids I saved. But

the old battle axe who works for Child Protective Services didn't think I was physically capable of doing it right now. Tess had been helping me with them and was willing to get married to keep the kids with me. We don't really want that info getting out to the public."

"Understood. So had you two been dating already?"

This was the part he hated. The thought of opening up his private thoughts and failings to a stranger. Worse still, they had to share her difficulties, too.

As she stared at her hands clenched in her lap, he took a chance and patted them. A grateful smile appeared on her face.

"Tessa has some issues to deal with from her past, and she doesn't like to be around people much. It takes her a while to trust others." And he'd blown that trust to hell with his stupid actions last week.

"She didn't think she'd ever get married, and me, well, I have a few physical issues as well."

"The leg obviously." Sullivan pointed to the cane resting by his side.

"And more." He grimaced, knowing what he had to say next. "My face is banged up pretty bad. Plus the injury left me unable to…have kids or…do anything in that…area. I figured no woman would want an…impotent, scarred soldier. The deal between us worked out perfect."

The doc simply nodded, and Erik briefly closed his eyes. Taking a deep breath, he looked around the room. "I should have a huge sign made and stick it to my back. Or maybe take out an ad in the paper. *Can't have sex*."

"There are plenty of ways to have sex without

181

actually having intercourse, you know."

Tessa turned scarlet. They'd barely gotten to the kissing part, he'd drive himself crazy thinking of doing other intimate acts with her.

"Erik, you mentioned on the phone you thought you had PTSD. What made you come to that conclusion?"

"I've had a few episodes lately that are totally out of character for me. I blanked out once while watching a cartoon with Matty. I totally lost it during some fireworks last week."

"That's very common," Sullivan interrupted.

"I've had a few nightmares lately about the bombing and people dying."

"A few?" she questioned, her expression one of concern. A look he missed. "It wasn't just that one morning?"

He slid his hand close to her but didn't attempt to touch her. "More than that one. But when I feel you next to me, they seem to fade away quicker."

Her hand inched closer but still didn't connect with his. It was progress, though.

He tore his gaze away from her. "Then Thursday, after my PT, I came home in a foul mood. A bunch of stuff had happened, not to mention the pain from my therapy, and I took it out on Tessa and the kids."

"Where are the children right now?"

"We got a babysitter." Thank God for Gladys's granddaughter, Brianna.

"What did you do that was so upsetting?"

"I threw a fit and yelled, then broke Kiki's toy. I didn't mean to. I was annoyed because it plays this obnoxious song over and over. I told Tessa to get the kids away from me because I couldn't deal with them. I knew I was being a fucking bastard, but I couldn't stop, couldn't control what was happening."

She sat staring at her hands. Was she reliving the terrible moment when he lost it?

He retold how he'd gone looking for them. "I found them hiding in the closet, completely petrified of me."

His voice cracked on the last words, and he cleared his throat. God, how pathetic was he?

"Is this something you usually do, Tessa? Hide in a closet?"

It was almost a relief the focus was off him, but she looked like she was about to come apart. Regardless of her objections, he grabbed her hand and squeezed. The pressure was returned, and she nodded at the counselor.

"It is? Perhaps we need to get into your background, too. We can discuss it here, or if you prefer, we could do a private session. I'm sure Erik wouldn't mind taking a break for a short while."

"No." Her voice came out strong. Her hand clenched his tighter and actually pulled. "Erik can stay."

Chapter Fourteen

"That's fine. Why don't you fill me in on your childhood? Tell me what it was like and anything you do remember of your parents or the foster homes you were in."

She touched her chest where her locket rested. She looked around but couldn't meet Sullivan's eyes. Erik scooted nearer and took both hands, then whispered, "It's okay. I'm right here."

"Tessa, maybe it would be easier to talk to Erik. Focus on him and tell him about your childhood."

Looking at him, she swallowed. He rubbed his thumbs over her hands and smiled. Her anxiety dimmed somewhat, but he was also the cause of some of her nervousness. Talking about her childhood wasn't pleasant, but she'd promised him. After all, he'd just spilled his guts about his time in the cellar and his injury. That had to have been terrible for someone as masculine as him.

"I was about four when I went into foster care. They found me in a hospital waiting room, but nobody was with me. I kind of remember sitting there, but I get an awful feeling when I think of it, so I try to avoid that memory."

"You're doing great, Tess. Keep going." Erik continued to caress her hands.

"They brought me to the Porter's house, and I

stayed there for a few years. I don't remember much, but I know I didn't talk to anyone at first. I remember watching lots of TV."

Pulling her legs up on the couch, she tucked them under her hip. "I got sent to another home where the Carters lived. I started first grade and must have begun to talk because I remember reading to the class. But Mr. Carter wasn't very nice. He didn't want kids, but his wife did, and she couldn't have any. I think she only talked him into it because they got money for taking us in. If you got in his way or did something he didn't like, he dragged you or pushed you around. It was easier to simply stay out of his way."

"Like hiding in a closet?" Sullivan asked.

She nodded. "Or under beds. I was still small enough to do that easily."

Now that her ridiculous past was being laid open for them to dissect, Erik must be regretting their marriage.

"Did he ever hit you?" Sullivan asked. Her body tensed, and she lowered her eyes.

"Sometimes, if you got in his face or didn't get out of his way fast enough. I got really good at avoiding him, though."

She hated she'd been so weak and had never stood up for herself. But she'd seen what the man had done to the kids who mouthed off or misbehaved. At six or seven, it had scared the pants off her.

"I never stayed more than two or three years in any place. The other kids told me it was because I wasn't lovable. They said that's why my parents dumped me at the hospital and why no one ever adopted me." God, this was so embarrassing. *Move on. Next family.*

"Mrs. Simmons was really nice…most of the time. I was there next. She let us do whatever we wanted. She had a bunch of us there, and the older kids would cook and make sure we got to school on time. But she used most of the money she got for us on herself. Lots of time on wine. If she had too much, then she would yell. That was never any fun. She used to say really mean things."

Lowering her head, she mumbled, "And the kids at school made fun of the stupid hand-me-downs I wore." That was sometimes worse than the hitting and yelling.

"I'll buy you a whole new wardrobe if you want." He gazed at her with sympathy in his eyes. Or was it pity?

She pulled her legs closer. "I went to the Pitcairns after that."

Erik's eyes grew intense. "Did they hurt you?"

"No, they were okay, but they had a few kids of their own, so there wasn't much money for extra stuff. I shared a room with two other girls."

She stared at her hands. Should she tell them everything? Would it help? Finally, she looked up and took a deep breath. "One of the girls in my room was Katie. She was sixteen and real pretty. The oldest son, Richy, used to come in some nights to be with her."

Sullivan's voice broke into the little world she had going on with Erik right now. "What do you mean by 'be with her,' and did she want that, too?"

She shrugged, her gaze never leaving Erik's. He was looking straight into her soul. What did he see? The damaged freak she'd always been? Or something else?

"I didn't really know what was happening at first. I

was only eleven. Katie would groan and whimper, but Richy did, too. Later, I realized what they were doing, but as for whether Katie wanted it, I don't know. She never yelled or complained, but she never looked at Richy like she had a thing for him either. I should have asked her and maybe said something to his parents, but…"

Her voice ended with a sob, and Erik slid his arm over her shoulder to pull her close. He looked at her to finish.

"I didn't want him doing that to me." What a coward she'd been.

"I can certainly see why you're skittish," Sullivan said, and she glanced at him. She'd rather face Erik. "Can I assume you're still a virgin?"

Heat rose to her cheeks, and she stared at her hands. What would they think of her answer?

"No." Keep it simple. Maybe they wouldn't ask questions.

Erik moved so close she could feel his breath. As he touched the side of her face, fear filled his eyes. "Did someone rape you?"

"No." Though it certainly hadn't been pleasant.

When he continued to stare, she knew she had to give more details. It was so embarrassing. But no more so than a guy like Erik admitting he couldn't perform.

"Right after high school, there was this guy who asked me out. His name was Jeremy, and he was pretty cute. He was new to town so didn't know I was a total freak."

"Hey." Erik shook her hands. "We decided we'd never use that word again."

"You decided. But it's what I was. What I am. And

187

I was tired of being a freak. All the girls at school always talked about their boyfriends or guys they picked up at parties. I thought going out with him would give me a chance to be normal."

"What happened?"

"We went out on two dates. The first was pretty awkward, but he actually asked me out again. Said he wanted to get to know me better. I didn't realize that was guy talk for having sex."

"Did you want to?"

"Not really, but I hated the way people thought of me—the way they looked at me. I wanted to be like the other girls, and I thought if I had sex with a guy, all the weirdness would go away."

Erik stayed silent, watching her. She curled closer to him. If she was going to tell the whole tale, she needed some sort of comfort.

"He worked at a garage and knew where the key was. We used the couch in the office."

Could she even finish this story? The contents of her stomach planned to revolt even thinking of what had happened.

"It doesn't sound like a satisfying encounter," Sullivan said softly.

She inhaled the unique scent that was Erik. It was woodsy and smelled like strength.

"No. I didn't know what to do, so I just lay there and let Jeremy do it all. I was so scared and tried not to flinch as he touched me. I don't think he enjoyed it either. He said…" She looked away. This part was too painful to share.

Erik stroked her hair gently. "He said what?"

She inhaled that strength again. "He said it was

like…fucking a snowman. Told me I was frigid."

Erik's hands cupped her face as he stared into her eyes. "You are definitely not frigid." His lips lowered and brushed against hers. This was what she'd missed the past few days. Yes, she'd been the one to back away from him, but he had the power to hurt her, and not just physically.

His kiss was soft, gentle, and filled with a need she could understand. She felt it, too. He pulled her closer, and she responded like she had the last few weeks. His lips on hers made her feel things she'd never felt before. Passion, yes, though she never thought she'd be able to have that. But his arms also gave her a warm comfort she hadn't ever had. Unless her vague memories were accurate. She had no idea if they were.

Rough fingers caressed her face as his other hand ran up and down her back, urging her to give in to the feelings he evoked. Wanting more of this, she pressed herself to him. But he eased back and kissed her nose.

"Not frigid."

When he looked at the counselor, her face heated. How could she have forgotten they had an audience? Her husband could make her forget all sorts of things. Like the fact she hated anyone touching her.

"What do you think, doc? Can you fix us?"

"You look like you've got some good therapy going there already, Erik. For Tessa anyway, to get her past some of her physical anxiety. Tessa, you seemed fairly comfortable having your husband touch you. Your response to his kiss tells me you are definitely not frigid."

The situation should be embarrassing, but she thrilled at the thought they didn't think she was the snowman Jeremy had accused her of being. She'd hated the word but knew her response to Jeremy was abnormal.

"As for fixing you, I don't do that. My job is to help you come to terms with your problems and find ways to cope. It looks like Tessa found ways to cope with what happened to her."

She stared at him. "Hiding in a closet. Not being around people. Those aren't normal ways to cope."

"It could have been worse. You could have taken drugs or become promiscuous or resorted to violence and criminal activities. You chose to hide away from life to avoid hurt. I think marrying Erik is a huge step forward for you."

"So what do you suggest, doc?" Erik asked.

"For Tessa, I think what you've been doing is working. Plan little outings to places that have more and more people. Take it slow, but increase her exposure, not only to people but touch. Does that sound reasonable, Tessa? Do you trust Erik to keep you safe?"

"He won't hurt me."

"You didn't think that a few days ago when you hid in the closet."

"You scared me. I knew deep inside you wouldn't hurt us, but the reaction was automatic."

"Maybe if I can keep myself in better control, you won't have those memories."

He turned to Sullivan. The counselor leaned back in his chair. "I can suggest a few things that might help keep you in the here and now, Erik. What helped you get back the last few times?"

"Tess was there, talking to me, making me focus. It helped having her in bed next to me, holding my hand.

Especially with the nightmares."

"I wish I'd known you had more."

"They weren't bad enough to wake you up. I can't always get back to sleep, though. That last time, when you snuggled up on my shoulder, totally helped me relax."

"I'd suggest you continue to work on your own PT. Physical touch therapy. It seems to benefit both of you." Sullivan rose to his feet, and she realized they'd been here an hour. The man gave Erik a pamphlet with some suggestions to help him stay calm and avoid or remove himself from flashbacks, then shook his hand.

"I think we need to get a bit deeper into Tessa's background, as well as your war experience and your reactions recently. I'd like to see you every week for at least a month, and then perhaps we can cut back to twice a month. Of course, if you ever have an emergency, please contact me, and I'll find time to get you in here."

They made another appointment and thanked the counselor. Once in the car, he pulled her close and kissed her. She responded without even thinking. Tentatively at first but then with more passion than she'd felt with him before. She liked it. It made her feel ridiculous for shying away from it for so long.

"Hope that's okay." He eased back, his breath still mingling with hers.

"Doctor's orders." Damn, her voice sounded like she'd been running.

He kissed her again, then settled into the car and started the engine. "This is one medicine I won't need you nagging at me to take."

****

"I peeked in at the kids, and they're both sound asleep. Did you need help with those dishes?"

Erik rinsed the last pan and set it in the drainer, then turned to Tessa. She'd already gotten ready for bed, and he attempted to keep his eyes off her. She wore sleep shorts and a tank top. It was loose except where her generous breasts filled it out nicely.

"The dishes are all in the dishwasher, and the pots and pans are done. I thought maybe we could have a relaxing night of watching TV."

"Okay. Did you have anything in mind?"

Sure, but none of the stuff on his mind involved the television. If he claimed doctor's orders, would she play along?

After drying his hands on a dishrag, he took his cane and walked toward her. For a second her body stilled, then relaxed. When would the day arrive she simply accepted his presence without some tiny bit of fear?

"We can take a look at what's on and decide." Placing his hand on her back, he guided her to the living room where he stopped in front of the recliner. Would she go for sharing it? It was big enough for two. Barely.

"What happens if you start to have another flashback?"

"I guess you'll need to distract me."

She bit her lip. "How do I do that?"

He grinned. "You could take off your shirt." Touching the straps of her top, he trailed his fingers down lightly. "That'll probably work." Would definitely work.

She glared at him.

"Or maybe a kiss. A really passionate kiss."

"I don't do really passionate. You know that."

As he pulled her in, he lowered his lips to her gorgeous mouth and ran his hand down her back, then up again, sliding behind her neck. Her floral scent tantalized his nose, and he burrowed it deeper into her thick mane.

"How about we move this to the recliner? It's big enough if we squish. You game?"

Her cheeks turned pink, but she nodded. Yes. Score one for the gimp. It took him a few moments to get settled into the recliner with his damaged leg, but she waited patiently, then slid in next to him. When he reached for the remote, she adjusted to a position that was comfortable for her.

The TV flicked on, and he channel surfed for a few minutes, allowing her to get used to his being so close. After choosing an old sitcom, he leaned back, his arm sliding under her shoulder, pulling her closer.

"Is this comfortable? It'll give us a little more room if you rest on me."

She turned sideways and placed her head on his chest. Her gaze glued to the show, but her body relaxed against him. Good. It had nearly killed him seeing her and the kids so afraid of him, and he never wanted to upset her again.

They watched for a while, then he broke the stillness.

"Thank you for trusting me. I know what I did last week was horrible, but I promise I'll try my best not to do anything like it again."

"Erik, you've apologized a million times. Maybe I'm the one who should be sorry. For overreacting. For making you feel so bad. I promise I'll try not to do anything like that again too."

He leaned in close so their foreheads touched. "Seal the deal?"

Her tongue poked out, teasing him. He'd take that as a yes.

The show played across the room as he and Tessa kissed. No shyness this time, no reticence or reluctance. She participated actively, and he was thrilled. His tongue skimmed across her bottom lip, and her mouth opened. Slowly he explored as she became braver too.

"I thought you didn't do passionate?" he teased, her heavy breath tickling his face.

"I never have before."

"Are you okay with this? Being so close to me?"

She only nodded.

"The doc did say we should practice touching. It's good for both of us."

He lowered his mouth to hers for more kissing. She was amazing. He couldn't get enough of tasting her. Needed to touch her. More than he was. His hand slid from her back under her top, and the silky skin nearly sent him over. Shit. Could an impotent cripple still get off, and from simply caressing the softest skin he'd ever felt?

"Damn, you feel so good, Tessa. Tell me if I need to stop. But I really hope you won't. This feels unbelievable."

Leaning back, he lifted her so she lay across him while both hands now stroked her skin. She practically purred. Good sign, right? Their lips continued their mating dance, and Tessa even slipped her fingers into his hair, pulling at it slightly. He needed more, though, no matter how much his brain argued he should take his time.

Sliding one hand down her back, he slipped it under the loose waistband of her shorts. A tiny whimper escaped from her mouth as her hands clenched in his hair. Was that good or bad? She wiggled her hips and moved so his hand slipped deeper. Fucking hell. Or maybe he should say heaven, because that's what it felt like.

He nibbled across her cheek and down her neck as his other hand joined the first. Jesus, she had a sweet ass. The sensation of it at his fingertips spiked desire through him that went straight to his cock. Damn, if only he could keep it that way for a while. Would it stay longer this time? He'd never had her sweet ass in his hands before. Would it make a difference, or was he destined to get hard, then deflate before he arrived at the finish?

What the hell was he thinking? No way she was ready for anything even remotely close to that, even if he could manage to keep the sails up that long. Didn't mean he couldn't enjoy every second of having her in his arms.

"You're so beautiful. Thank you for trusting me enough to hold you like this."

Her cheeks flushed with color, but she held her head up and looked straight into his eyes. "I think I might like this touch therapy."

Gathering her close, he caressed and squeezed the rounded skin of her backside. As her lips closed in on his again, he whispered, "I know I will."

Chapter Fifteen

The door in the family room opened, and Tessa looked up from placing Kiki's bowl on her high chair tray. Erik had his first day of work at The Boat House. All day she'd wondered how he was doing.

"Hi, Daddy." Matty waved, his face covered in gravy from the meatloaf and potatoes he'd eaten. "You back from work?"

Erik's white knuckles gripped his cane as he gave a curt nod. The pain was evident in the tightness of his face. He'd deny it, but he wasn't in good shape. No way she'd ask how his first day had been. The job may have been fine, but he wasn't.

She moved to the stove and scooped potatoes onto another plate. "I made meatloaf and mashed potatoes. Probably not as good as what you cooked at the restaurant, but it's ready if you want some."

A nerve in his jaw ticked as he glanced around the kitchen. "I ate something at work. I'm going to take a shower and put my leg up." As he turned to leave, he muttered, "Thanks," and limped away.

After filling her plate, she sat between the children. Matty rattled on, half in Farsi, half in English, about starting preschool soon. He was excited about being able to play with other children his age. They'd both been building it up into a big, fun place so he wouldn't get nervous. Once they got there, he might sing another tune when he realized she and Erik wouldn't be staying.

Kiki played with her meal and managed to get some of it in her mouth. The child preferred to eat from someone else's plate instead of her own. When they were finished and she'd cleaned up the mess and the kids, she scooted them down the hall to their rooms.

"Let's get jammies on, and then we can play for a bit."

"Daddy read to us?" Matty turned toward the master bedroom.

"He's probably tired from working, but we'll see." He'd gone in at ten this morning to prep for the lunch crowd and stayed until the night chef had arrived. It was still six hours, and knowing him, he'd been on his feet for most of them. Or more specifically, on his bad leg. How he'd manage to get around the kitchen and actually cook while using the cane, she wasn't sure. But he couldn't quite keep his balance if he didn't have it. Often he'd try when he thought she wasn't watching.

She got Matty dressed first and then Kiki as Matty picked out a few toys. She helped him bring them into her bedroom and settle on the floor a few feet away from the bed. Erik lay unmoving on top of the covers, but he was awake. The pain around his closed eyes gave that away.

"Play quietly while I sit with Daddy, okay?"

Erik's eyes opened briefly at her words, and a tiny sigh escaped from his mouth. Sitting on the edge of the bed, she wondered what she should do.

"Do you need me to get your medication?"

"No," he snapped. "These kids don't need a drug addict for a father."

The urge to flee was strong, but she fought it. Her

husband was in pain and was taking it out on the nearest body. Taking a deep breath, she screwed up her courage.

"You're right. They also don't need someone who's going to ignore them."

That got his eyes open. So he could glare at her. "My freakin' leg is killing me," he growled under his breath. "I can't very well get down on the floor with them to play blocks."

"No one asked you to. But you barely acknowledged them when you came in."

He simply stared at the ceiling, his mouth in a straight line.

"Was work that bad? Should you have given yourself more time?"

Finally, he looked at her, and his mouth curved into a wry smile. "I enjoyed cooking again. That part was great. The being on my leg so long wasn't. Sid was fantastic and had a few rolling stools in the kitchen, but I didn't use them."

She hid her grin. "Stubborn marine."

"More like stupid marine. I'll use them next time."

"Promise?"

He rolled his eyes. "Promise."

"Can I help make the leg feel better?" She reached out and began to run her hand over his knee gently. She'd seen him do it before when he'd been on it too long. When he flinched, she pulled her hand away.

"Did that hurt? I'm sorry."

"No, it felt good, but you don't need to do that. I'll be fine."

"Fine, but grouchy." She began to knead the skin and muscles near his knee and then moved up to the tight muscles of his thigh. They were in such knots she didn't know how he could lay there without screaming in agony.

A small moan came from his mouth, and she paused again until she realized the pain lines around his eyes were easing. She was helping him. Moving back to the knee, she massaged up and down his leg.

"Tessa, you really don't have to do this. I feel like a flippin' invalid. And the kids are sitting there watching you do this."

"What's wrong with a wife giving her husband some comfort? Shouldn't they see their parents touching each other? We wanted them to have as normal a life as possible. And they're playing with their blocks. They aren't staring at us."

He sighed and relaxed back against the pillows. "It does feel great. I hate looking weak."

"You were out all day working and now need some chill time. Nothing wrong with that. And this fulfills our daily dose of touch therapy."

That got him to actually smile. She smiled too, thinking of what they'd been doing the last few days since their visit with Dr. Sullivan. Every night after the kids were in bed, they'd snuggle in the recliner and make out like teenagers. Not that she'd ever done that as a teenager, but he had. And most of her high school class.

If she'd known it was that nice, she might have attempted to do it earlier. Right. Who was she kidding? She'd freak if anyone even bumped into her, though she was getting better. What was it about Erik that allowed her to lower her defenses? To the point she not only let him kiss her, but run his hands over her back and butt too. And she liked it. A lot.

"I hope it doesn't fulfill *all* our daily touch therapy requirements. I kind of liked some of the other exercises we've done." His hand crept toward her hip and rubbed against her shorts. He threw her some deadly puppy dog eyes. God, he was so damn cute. No wonder she melted into a puddle whenever he touched her.

"We'll see how you're feeling once the kids go to sleep." After spending some time rubbing his leg, she moved her hand up to his hip. Because of the strange angle he needed to walk in, the hip would get sore as well. His eyes closed, and he let out a huge breath.

She glanced over at the children playing happily on the floor. Matty stacked the blocks, and Kiki knocked them down, and both giggled. Another groan came from Erik's mouth, and he started to turn over.

"Are you okay?"

Flopping on his stomach, he mumbled into the pillow. "Fine. Back muscles need work too."

She grinned. It was a good excuse, but the bulge in his pants as he flipped over had been noticeable. Often this week as they'd made out, she felt it also. She didn't know all the intricacies of men and their privates, but it seemed like what he had, worked. Was there another reason he'd said he couldn't perform? Was it her?

The sigh from the bed let her know her massage was doing the job. He certainly didn't seem opposed to her touching him. Reaching up, he grabbed his shirt by the back of the collar and pulled it over his head.

"Do you mind? The back and shoulders are a little tense from work."

She admired the sculpted muscles underneath the

tanned skin. Did she mind? For days, if not weeks, she'd been dying to touch his skin.

After making sure the kids were okay, she massaged up Erik's back to his neck, then down his arms. She practically saw the stress melting away. Hers increased, though. Not bad stress but she was definitely tenser thinking about him and how much she wanted to press her lips to his bare skin. What was coming over her? Running to another country was more her M.O., not wondering how she could get his chinos off. They did look good on him, though, stretched tightly across his bottom.

She divided her attention between the children on the floor and Erik who might very well be asleep. When she paused in her ministrations, he let out a sound of disappointment. So, not asleep. But looking at Kiki, who kept sticking her thumb in her mouth and leaning against Matty, she might soon be.

She leaned closer to Erik's ear. "I've got to put the kids in bed. Kiki's going to pass out soon. You stay here, and I'll be back as soon as I'm done."

He rolled over, grimacing as his knee tried to bend to sit himself up.

"You don't—"

He reached for her hand and pulled so he was standing. "If I'm going to be their dad, I need to act like a dad. Like my dad, who was always helping out with everything. I won't leave it all to you."

She wanted to argue he'd worked all day, but he was right. Dads shouldn't be able to get away with not caring for their kids. Mothers worked just as hard at home with the children.

"Time for bed, kiddos," Erik called out. "Whose

room do we have story time in tonight?"

"We did me last day, so this day is Kiki," Matty said. They'd been doing stories together every night as a family and alternated between rooms.

When Erik stood, Matty rushed over with his cane. Her husband's face was resigned, though he tried to smile at the boy. The fact he was dependent on the cane made her sad. Not because he had to use it, but because he hated that he did. It didn't make him any less masculine in her eyes.

He took the rocking chair with Kiki in his lap, while she and Matty sat in the window seat next to them. Erik's strong voice sent chills down her spine as he read about a bird who'd fallen out of his nest and didn't know where his mother was. Like her. *Are You My Mother* was one book she'd avoided as a child. Touching the locket under her shirt, she knew how that little bird felt. But she'd never had a big Snort to put her back in her nest.

She pulled Matty closer, wanting to make sure this boy and his sister never felt abandoned or unloved. These children were a miracle brought to her after so long thinking she'd never have children or a family of any kind. In only three weeks that thought had started to fade, and she hoped someday it would completely dissipate.

He finished the story and kissed the head of the now sleeping child in his lap. She gently lifted the baby from his lap and pressed her own lips to the child's sweet cheek, then settled her in her crib. Erik walked Matty into his room, and she followed to say her good nights as well.

When they moved into the hallway, they paused,

each looking to the other. Taking a deep breath, she did something she'd never in her life imagined.

She touched his arms and whispered, "Did you need me to finish that massage?"

His eyes blazed, and her stomach did a few backflips.

Slipping his hand into her hair, he kissed her quickly but deeply. "That sounds like a great idea. Maybe I could return the favor. It's a lot of work taking care of these kids all day. You must need relaxing too."

What he had in mind might not be relaxing, but she sure wouldn't complain if he wanted to rub her back. Or anyplace else. As they walked back into their bedroom, she wondered what else on Erik she could find to massage.

****

"Look at all these toys to play with, Matty." The child clung to Erik's leg. Tessa bounced Kiki higher in her arms as she knelt in front of the boy. "When you come to preschool, you'll get to play with them."

Matty didn't look convinced, and she didn't blame him. Anxiety gnawed away at her too. The orientation for The Lighthouse School was crowded. Parents and kids wandered around in the large open area that housed bigger toys and some physical equipment for rainy days. The half dozen classrooms surrounded this room. Maybe it would be better in Matty's classroom.

"Which room is his?" she asked as Erik stroked the boy's hair.

He pointed. "The younger kids are on this side I was told. He has Miss Meredith for a teacher. I don't know what she looks like. I only met the director when I signed him up."

The teachers all stood outside their doorways, chatting with parents. Most of them seemed very young and had huge smiles on their faces. She checked the signs on the wall outside each room. *Miss Meredith—three-year-old preschool.* That was his.

"Matty, let's go meet your teacher, Miss Meredith. She looks really nice."

Matty clung to Erik's leg, glancing around to see where she pointed. Adjusting his cane, he guided the boy in the right direction. The woman with the short dark hair smiled as they approached.

"Hi, I'm Miss Meredith." She got down to Matty's level and asked, "What's your name? I hope you'll be in my class. I need a nice, handsome boy in my class this year."

"This is Matteen. We call him Matty," Erik answered since the child seemed to have lost his voice. "I'm Erik Storm, and this is my wife, Tessa."

Meredith stood and shook his hand, then reached out for her. The old feeling of dread didn't run through her as it used to. She shook the woman's hand, wondering why she wasn't having a panic attack. The crowds alone should have sent her into protection mode, but now there was barely a trickle of apprehension.

"This is Kinah," she introduced as Kiki bounced in her arms, wanting to get down and explore. Not quite as shy as her brother, this one.

"Kiki." Matty took a step away from Erik and repeated, "She's Kiki."

Erik grinned. "Yes, her nickname is Kiki. Thanks, Matty, for letting Miss Meredith know." The teacher seemed charmed by both father and son. Who wouldn't when he smiled?

"Would you like to see the classroom, Matty?"

The child stared at his teacher, then peeked into the room. His eyes lit up at the tables, chairs, and shelves, all his size. "I go in there?"

Meredith nodded.

"Kiki come too?"

Tessa walked past the teacher and took Matty's hand. "We'll all come in and look."

"Matty's first language is Farsi," Erik explained as she took the children inside the smaller room. "The children are from Afghanistan, but my wife and I are adopting them as soon as the red tape is taken care of."

She sat on one of the tiny chairs, thankful she was small herself. Letting Kiki slide to the floor, she pointed her in the direction of a shelf that had larger toys, ones that would be okay for the little girl to use. Matty stuck his finger at some shaped blocks and shot a questioning look at her.

"You can play with them."

Even though Erik chatted with the teacher by the doorway, his eyes stayed on her and the kids. He was explaining the children's circumstances. It felt good to hear him speak about the two of them as a couple, working together to make a good home for the children. Soon he moved near them and glared at the minuscule chairs surrounding the tiny tables.

"It might be best for me to stand. If I even managed to get myself in one of those, I don't think I'd ever get out."

"It might be fun to watch, though."

Erik threw her a look that sent desire spiraling down past her stomach and lower. It had happened a lot lately, and she was still trying to figure out what it meant. Okay, maybe she knew what it meant, but she'd never experienced anything like it before.

After the children had explored the room for a while, Miss Meredith called them all to sit on the big, colorful rug decorated with colors and shapes. Some kids ran to grab a spot while others hung back and needed encouragement. Matty was one of those. Erik walked him over and kissed the top of his head.

"You can choose a purple square or a red circle. Which would you like?"

"Mama like purple. I sit here? You sit there." He pointed to the spot next to him.

"You know it's hard for me to get down, right, pal? How about I stand over there with Mommy and Kiki?"

Matty glanced nervously to where she stood near the door with the other parents. Then he looked back to where Miss Meredith sat with a basket of puppets she was handing to the children. The puppets won.

When Erik limped back toward her, Tessa's chest filled with pride, knowing he was her husband. The admiring glances of the other moms hadn't gone unnoticed by her. And she wasn't blind. He was the best-looking dad here. Even with his scars and cane. Or maybe because of them.

Miss Meredith led the children in some songs, and the director encouraged the parents to slip out of the classroom to the outer room. She couldn't help but peek inside to make sure Matty was okay. He was thoroughly engrossed in using the puppets during the song.

"He'll be fine," Erik whispered in her ear. His closeness sent shivers through her. Good shivers.

"I might not be."

"Sure you will." He touched her arm. "I'm going to find a men's room. You'll survive without me for a few minutes?"

She eyed the crowd and saw a familiar redhead. Paula Redmond. They'd gone to high school together. She hadn't been one of the super mean girls, but she'd certainly never stuck up for Tessa as she was bullied and called names behind her back. No one had.

"Tess? You okay?"

Hiding behind him seemed a good idea, or better yet running from the room and going to their nice, safe house. The music from Matty's room reminded her the small boy was in there being brave without his parents. Shouldn't she be brave too? For Pete's sake, she was an adult. She couldn't go around the rest of her life hiding. Dr. Sullivan had urged her to get out more only yesterday at their second counseling appointment. If Matty could do this, then so could she.

"I'm fine, Erik. I'm going to let Kiki play on the little slide."

He walked off, and she set the toddler at the top of the small plastic slide, then let go. It was a short ride, but the child loved it and toddled back to the two steps to get to the top. She climbed them herself, then slid down again.

"Tessa?"

Paula stood behind her. Maybe she was still a coward, but she'd hoped the girl wouldn't recognize her. Or if she did, she would simply ignore her like she had in high school. No such luck.

"Paula. Hi." What else could she say? *It's nice to see you again?* No, because it wasn't. She had lots of faults, but she wasn't a liar.

"I didn't realize you still lived around here," the redhead commented. "I haven't seen you since high school."

Thank God for that. "I live by the beach. There's no reason to go anywhere else." That was true enough.

"Do you have a child here?" Her tone indicated she was surprised Tessa had a child. Yeah, No-Touch Tessa wasn't the first person you'd think of for that job.

Kiki toddled over and lifted her arms to be picked up. Tessa did and held her close. Not for protection, she simply loved holding this child. *Sure, keep telling yourself that.*

"This is Kiki. My son, Matty, is in with Miss Meredith."

Paula studied Kiki, and her thoughts were obvious. The child's olive skin was in stark contrast to her lighter coloring.

"My husband's a marine and rescued them from Kandahar. We're in the process of adopting them."

Paula's gaze slipped to the ring on Tessa's finger, more surprise written there. "Did you marry someone local?" Her tone indicated it must be someone fairly desperate.

Before she could answer, Erik returning caught her eye. She didn't need him rescuing her, though. She had this. It would still be nice for him to be by her side as she spoke to Paula.

Paula's gaze followed hers as Erik stopped to talk to the director. "Oh, that's Erik Storm, isn't it? I haven't seen him in years. The hours I spent at The Boat House trying to get his attention." Flipping her red strands over her shoulder, the woman pushed out her chest as he walked their way.

"Erik Storm, hi. How are you? Are you living around here now?"

Erik, always polite, paused. "Uh, Pamela, right? I bought my grandparents' house. We're living there now."

"That's so great," the redhead gushed, her conversation with Tessa totally forgotten. Typical. "And it's Paula. We should get together sometime. Do you have a child here? We could do a play date."

She knew exactly what kind of play this woman had in mind, and it had nothing to do with the kids. He realized too and shifted in place. His leg hurt, she knew the signs by now.

"Paula," she said, gaining the woman's attention back, though she wasn't happy about it if her expression was anything to go by. "You asked about my husband."

Kiki squirmed and yelled, "Dada."

As she transferred the child to Erik's outstretched arm, Paula's face fell.

"You two are married? I didn't know you knew each other."

"Tess lived next door to my grandparents. We've been friends since she moved here ten years ago."

Not exactly close friends, but let the woman believe that. He didn't expand on their marriage, and she was relieved. Paula didn't need to know their business. She probably already suspected Erik was slumming by marrying her.

Paula chatted a bit, asking Erik where he was working and about being a marine. Tessa was completely ignored, but she was used to that. Whereas Erik was used to girls flirting and preening in front of him. It was something she'd seen them do a million times. Stepping closer to the door, she could see into Matty's classroom better. The little boy danced around, holding hands with a few other students. The class only had ten children in it, and Miss Meredith had them all engaged in her activities.

Erik let Kiki down again to run around the large cardboard blocks and try and stack them. Better keep her eye on the little girl too. Not that she didn't trust him, but a tiny part of her wondered if he'd be distracted by the outgoing redhead and if he preferred her company.

"Is your husband with you?" she heard Erik ask.

Paula fluffed her hair and pouted. Something she'd never learned to do.

"I'm not married. Dakota's father wasn't really the marrying kind, though he certainly helped create a beautiful child. My little girl, Dakota, is my life. I don't know what I'd do without her."

Yeah, go for the doting-mother thing. That always worked. Not. What guy wanted someone else's kid? Well, Erik obviously if he was adopting two kids from another country. Paula didn't seem to care he was married. Her flirting and casual touching of him was outrageous. Or maybe by her standards since she never touched anyone.

Not anymore. Okay, lately the touching thing hadn't been such an issue. But only with the kids and Erik. And maybe his family who had popped in a few times since they'd been married. They were a huggy group, for sure. Not that she minded. They accepted her as one of their own. Molly and Pete had even insisted she call them Mom and Dad. Keeping the tears from falling had been hard when they'd suggested it.

"How's he doing?" Erik's soft voice startled her, his breath whispering in her ear. Placing his arm around her shoulders, he squeezed.

"He's having fun, like he should."

Kiki still played with the cardboard blocks. Erik's gaze stayed on the toddler, only flicking to the classroom for a second. "I hope he'll be okay when we aren't here."

That was her hope too. She knew what it was like to be anxious in a new place. And she'd had so many new places to get used to. It seemed she'd barely get comfortable in one, then she'd be sent somewhere else.

"I'm sure he'll be okay. He's adjusted well to living with us. And this place seems like tons of fun." Unlike some of her foster homes.

Kiki toddled over, and Erik lifted her with his free hand. He was getting good at that. As she settled on his hip, she stuck her thumb in her mouth.

"She woke up early this morning," Tessa said. "Maybe she'll take an early nap today."

"Maybe this will tucker Matty out too. Then you and I can do some of our therapy while they sleep." His mouth lingered in her hair, and he inhaled. "God, you smell so good."

Tingles rolled down her arms and through her stomach. Closing her eyes, she leaned into him. When he kissed her temple, a feeling of contentment washed over her. Perfect.

The singing from the classroom stopped, and she opened her eyes, remembering where she was. He really messed with her mind at times. In a good way.

Across the big room, Paula stared at them, her

expression unreadable. It seemed a cross between disbelief and envy. Her gaze kept moving to Erik's arm around her and his lips near her cheek. She wasn't sure what made her do it, but she lifted her face and kissed him.

He grabbed the opportunity and kissed her back. It wasn't anything super passionate, but it was enough that Paula turned away to focus on some of the other parents in the room. A tiny smile made its way to her face, and he turned to see what she was staring at.

"Marking your territory?"

Damn, he'd figured her out. "Maybe. Not that I need an excuse to kiss my husband, do I?"

"Never."

That single word made her heart race and fill with excitement. His gaze held promise, and she didn't want to look away. The children rushing from the classrooms broke the spell, though.

"I'll see you all bright and early tomorrow morning. Have a great day," Miss Meredith sang out. Many of the children stopped to give her a hug. Matty stood shyly to the side, his expression unsure.

"You can hug her if you want," she said. "But you don't have to. It's up to you, Matty."

The children cleared away, and Miss Meredith waved. "I hope you had a great time today, Matty. I think I'll give you the elephant puppet tomorrow. You really seemed interested in that one."

Matty nodded exuberantly, then timidly reached for the teacher. She bent to hug him, and he clung to her neck. Tears filled Tessa's eyes at the gesture. Matty needed people to love him, and here was another opportunity for that.

"I'm so happy you're coming to my class."

"I happy too."

Tessa took the boy's hand and led him away as Erik carried Kiki and said, "Thanks."

When they got in the minivan, Matty couldn't stop talking about what they'd done in class.

"I go to bed now. Then I wake up and go to school."

She slid into the front seat, and Erik squeezed her hand.

"You can take a nap, pal, but it'll be a while before tomorrow comes."

As Matty chatted away to Kiki in the back seat, he started the car. "I'm looking forward to that nap myself."

Heat crept up her face at his meaning. She couldn't disagree, though.

Chapter Sixteen

Erik stepped out of the steamy bathroom and froze. Tessa stood in front of the mirror, her chest pushed out, hands reaching behind her back. All day at the beach, she'd worn a cover-up. Only now was he getting to see what she had under it. The bikini top was conservative with its attached skirt, but with her arms the way they were, she was spilling out the front.

Tucking the towel around his waist, he tried for nonchalant since she would hate to be ogled, even by her husband.

"I'll probably be late getting home. Saturday's a busy night. Make sure to tell the kids I love them."

She grimaced, and her hands twisted on the knot at her back. "I will. Can you possibly undo this? I want a shower before the kids wake up from their naps."

"Sure." As he stood behind her, he checked out the material. It was tied pretty tight.

"Thank you. I'm glad we got one last beach day. It's warm, especially for the second week in September."

He fiddled with the knot, tugging but having no luck. "They say it's supposed to cool down next week. I won't mind when I'm slaving away at a stove at work." Yup, discussing the weather was a great way to pretend he didn't want to rip the suit off her.

The knot was stubborn, and the intoxicating scent

of beach lingering on her skin wasn't helping. That and she was shorter by a good seven inches.

"Can we move so I can sit on the bed? This angle isn't helping my hip any."

She took a few steps back as he perched on the mattress. He moved her ponytail aside. Even with the tie this close, it didn't look any easier to get undone.

"I'm sorry, Tess. I need to use my teeth to get the fabric moving. My fingers are too big to grab it."

A shiver ran through her, and he loved he wasn't the only one affected by the proximity and lack of clothing. He pulled at her waist so she rested against the bed between his legs.

Leaning closer, he grabbed the fabric with his teeth. Damn, she smelled good, like sunshine and beach. His nose brushed against her skin, and she arched her back with another shiver.

"Are you cold?"

"Um…a little. My suit's still wet."

For now, he'd let her have her excuse. The piece that had been stuck loosened, and he pulled the rest out. The ties hung at her sides. Keeping his hands where they were, he pressed his lips to her back.

"You feel so good."

A humming sound was her only reply. He was okay with that. And with moving his hands over more of her skin. Sliding them around to her ribs, he skimmed over her flat stomach as his lips nibbled on her back.

"Is this okay?"

She leaned farther against him with a quiet, "Mmm hmm."

Pulling her to sit, he licked his way up until he

reached her shoulder and neck. Salty and sweet, all at the same time. Her belly was his next target, then the underside of her breasts.

Her breath grew raspy, and that alone had his cock hardening. Freakin' hell. Why did it taunt him if it couldn't carry through? As he cupped her full breasts and kneaded, he glanced in the mirror to see her reaction. Her head fell back, and her eyes closed as an expression of ecstasy crossed her features. His erection got even harder.

Her nipples pebbled in his palms, and he wanted desperately to squeeze them. Was she ready for that? She hadn't pulled away, and her reaction right now gave him hope she'd allow it. Caressing her again and again, he touched the tight tips with his thumbs and forefingers.

A tiny whimper escaped, and her hands grasped his thighs tightly. Shit, he was turned on. This damn injury was a pain in the ass. He needed to slow things down.

"Dr. Sullivan says there's a veteran's support group that meets on Sunday mornings. I was thinking of checking it out tomorrow if that's all right with you."

His hands still roamed. Apparently, they hadn't gotten the slow-down message.

"Support group?" Her voice was breathy and turned him on even more. Leaning forward, he tugged on the top string of her suit with his teeth until it came undone.

"It's at eight in Portland."

He rubbed her nipples with his fingers again, and her hands tightened on his thighs.

"You'll have to leave early, and you're working late tonight. Won't you be tired?"

216

When he nipped at the spot between her neck and shoulder, goosebumps appeared on her arms. "I've gotten used to not having much sleep."

Tessa stilled and turned to face him. "Are you still not sleeping much?"

Her top slipped to the floor, and she grabbed for the fabric. But he still got his first glimpse of her perfection. He reached up to cup her. "Shit, I'll never sleep knowing these are next to me now."

Placing her hands on his shoulders, she rested her head on his. "You need your sleep."

"I think I need this more right now."

His lips closed around her tight peak and sucked. Her hands clenched in his hair as her breath exhaled shakily. Sliding his hands over her back, he caressed the silky skin. God, the taste of her.

"You'll be late for work if we keep doing this." She didn't let go of his head, though. It was clasped to her breast, her heart pounding louder.

"Who cares?"

"You will if you get fired." Still holding on.

Damn, he ached. He wouldn't be able to do anything about it, though. Because he had to go to work. Because she wasn't ready to go that far yet. But worst, because the part he needed for *that* was still playing games with him. He eased her back and let his hands trail down until they sat at her hips.

"Why do you have to be so reasonable?"

She looked down and blushed from head to toe, then grabbed her robe from the side of the bed. "Someone's got to keep you in line."

As she rushed into the bathroom, she called out, "Have a good night at work."

"Keep me in line?" He snorted, then glanced down at his fricking erection standing still and proud. "I need to keep you in line. Stop teasing me and making me think you work."

Limping to the dresser, he grabbed some clothes. *Get your mind off Tessa's breasts.* It wouldn't do to walk around work like this all night.

Work. Yep, that'd do it. He'd think of the three-hundred-pound fry cook, Bernie.

****

"I'm looking for Erik Storm. I was told he'd cut his hand and was being brought here."

Tessa let out the breath she'd been holding as she rushed to the desk in the emergency room. Matty clung to her pant leg, and Kiki twisted in her arms.

"Let me check for you," the nurse responded, then started typing into her computer.

Tessa reached down and tousled Matty's hair. The call from Erik's boss, Sid, that he'd hurt his hand and needed stitches, had made her nervous. For Erik as well as her. She hated hospitals. But the busboy who'd given him a ride had to go back to work, and Erik needed a ride home.

"Are you a relative?" the nurse asked as she bounced Kiki in her arms to keep the child from trying to get down.

"I'm his wife. His work called and said he'd be here."

The woman tapped a few more keys, then looked up. "He's in the exam room with the doctor now. He'll be out soon. You can have a seat in the waiting area. There are some toys in the corner for the children to play with."

Shouldn't she be in with her husband? But really, the kids didn't need to see their dad having his hand sewn together. As she walked toward the Lego table, she wondered how bad his hand was. Bad enough to be unable to work? She'd love to have him home more, but she also knew he'd feel even more useless, the word he used to describe how he felt. He'd said it often during their therapy sessions the last month.

She set Kiki on the floor near a toddler toy with large beads hanging on thick pieces of twisted metal. Matty got to work building with the colored pieces of plastic. As her gaze flicked between the children and the door to the treatment rooms, she twisted her hands together.

"Stay right there, honey, while I talk to the lady at the desk."

The words floated through her mind, tightening her stomach. She rubbed her arms to keep the chills down.

"I want to come, Mama."

"You're always a good girl, Tessa. I need you to be one now too. I'll be right there, so just sit quietly, please."

Mama walked to the desk, glanced back at her with a smile, then sat down, her hand touching her head as if in pain. They were here because Mama didn't feel good. She said these people would help her get better. She wanted Mama to feel better. Then they could play.

She didn't like sitting here by herself, though. She wanted to be near Mama. Maybe she could walk over there. It was really close. But Mama had said to be a good girl and sit quietly. She loved Mama and always did what she was told.

Lots of noise near the door made her look that way.

People rushed in, yelling and being loud. They raced through the big room with strange beds on wheels and people sleeping in them. Why were they moving beds around? Shouldn't they be in a bedroom?

More people came in, and she got nervous. She wanted to be with Mama. She turned her head back, but too many people were in the way. She couldn't see Mama at the desk with the lady anymore. Why were all these people here? And why did some of them look like they had blood on them? Had they fallen and gotten scraped like she had last week? Did they need someone to put bandages on their boo-boos? Mama was especially good at that. She washed it so gentle and then kissed it.

It got really loud in the big room, and she wanted Mama with her. She touched the locket she had under her shirt. Mama and Daddy were in there. So was she, but only as a baby. She didn't know Daddy, but Mama said he was a wonderful man. He had gone to fight in a war to keep bad guys from hurting them. She wished he would come back. Maybe he'd get Mama better, and they could all go to the park. It would be so much fun. Maybe Daddy would push her even higher than Mama on the swings.

She looked around, her eyes searching for Mama. The people sat all around her, and she got frightened they were so close. Some of them cried, and she wanted to cry too. But she didn't. Mama said to stay quiet, and she would.

She looked to the desk, and Mama wasn't there anymore. Where had she gone? She wouldn't forget Tessa. Mama loved her more than anything else in the world. Every night before bed, she told her that. She loved Mama too. Mama always said they didn't have much, but they had each other. She loved having Mama. She was so much fun.

She got scared the more time passed and Mama didn't come back. Too many people here and they were all loud and upset and rushing around. They didn't talk to her. That was good because Mama said never to talk to strangers.

She got tired and rested her head on the back of the chair. She wouldn't fall asleep. She could take a nap at home once Mama was back. But Mama didn't come. She waited and waited, and she was very quiet while she did. Mama had said be quiet, and so she would.

"Mama, where are you? I need you," she whispered so no one would hear her. "Why aren't you coming back? You said you'd never forget me. You love me more than anything in this world. I love you too.

"Mama.

"Mama, come back, please. I'm scared, and I need you. I don't want to sit and be quiet anymore. I want you to come back and be with me." She curled her legs in close and wrapped her arms around them, hugging herself. She needed Mama's hugs, though.

"Mama, please come get me. I need you."

"Tessa? Are you all right? What's the matter?"

She blinked. Erik stood in front of her, his face a mask of concern. Oh no, what had she done?

****

Damn, his hand hurt like the devil. Erik pushed open the waiting room door and attempted to maneuver through it. He'd cut his left hand. The hand he used to hold his cane. The cane he could barely walk without. God, what a dumb fuck he was. His leg had given out just as he was slicing up some carrots, and he'd sliced open his palm instead. Sid was probably furious.

No, actually Sid was too nice for that, though he might be regretting giving him the chef job when he was still so incapacitated. Unfortunately, he had a feeling it wouldn't change. Even after three months, he still had to rely on the cane to keep stable when he walked.

The nurse who'd been helping in the exam room had mentioned Tessa was here waiting for him. Thank God she hadn't brought the kids back to watch the humiliation of getting his hand stitched. Glancing at his watch, he noted it was close to nap time. At least he'd cut his hand toward the end of his shift so he hadn't left Sid too understaffed.

He glanced around the busy waiting room. There they were, in the corner near the children's toys. As he moved closer, his pace quickened. As fast as he could with his bum leg and now his bum hand holding his cane. There was something not right with her. She stared into space, barely aware of the children near her.

When he was only a few feet away, his heart sped up. What the hell was happening to her? Her unfocused eyes were large in her face that showed a mass of emotion, of fear. Tears glistened on her lashes, and she shook. What?

"Tessa? Are you all right? What's the matter?"

She stared at the large room, and he suddenly knew. A while back she'd mentioned being found in a hospital waiting room when she was about four. He knew where she was. Lately, he'd been there a few times himself.

Sitting in the chair beside her, he ran his

unbandaged hand down her arm, trying to snap her out of it.

"Tessa, I'm right here. It's Erik. I'm fine. Just a little cut."

When he pulled her closer, she resisted. Only for a second, though, then she collapsed into him, trembling.

"I'm here, and you're okay. No one's going to hurt you. Look at me, sweetie."

He caressed her cheek. She moved her head a fraction, and her eyes seemed to focus.

"Erik?"

Matty ran over at that moment. "Daddy, you cut your hand?"

Lifting the bandaged appendage, he showed the boy. "They fixed it all up, so no need to worry. I think we need to get your mom home, though. She looks tired."

"Your hand?" She finally seemed aware of where she was and what had happened. She reached for his injured hand and stared at it. What was she really seeing, though?

"Let's get you home. You can take a nap when the kids do."

She looked around, confused. "I'm sorry. I don't know what happened. I kind of zoned out for a minute." When she shivered, he knew they needed to get out of here. The environment wasn't conducive to her well-being.

"Can you manage Kiki?"

Nodding, she scooped up the little girl. When they got to the car, he insisted he drive, though she argued. Not much, though, which told him she was still freaked out by what had happened. Once home with the kids in for a nap, he steered her toward the living room.

"I'm okay, Erik. I should get supper started."

He pulled her toward the recliner. "I can fix supper later. Right now we need to talk about what happened at the hospital."

Her face blushed pink as she looked away. He tugged again. "If you fight me on this, I'll have to go all gorilla on you and pick you up and carry you."

She immediately stilled, her eyes growing wide. "You'll hurt your leg and pull out your stitches."

Yup, all mother hen, like he figured, was actually counting on. But the fact he couldn't pick her up and carry her off rankled. Some hero he was.

"Then come join me for some therapy."

Lowering her eyes, more color crept up her cheeks. They always called their make-out sessions in the recliner therapy. They both knew exactly what it was, though. Therapeutic.

In the chair she turned her face into his chest, as if she couldn't look at him. He reclined all the way back so she couldn't easily escape and wrapped his arms around her.

"I didn't even think when Sid said he'd call you to come to the hospital to get me. I should have arranged for another ride home."

"I'm sorry I had another freak out. I don't exactly know what happened."

"You looked like you were a million miles away when I came out. Reminded me of what happened when I was watching that cartoon where the buildings were collapsing. I immediately got sent back to the shelling of that village. I couldn't do anything about it."

Confused eyes gazed at him. "But that happened to

you recently."

"Doesn't matter when it happened." Kissing her nose, he tucked a strand of hair behind her ear. "You said they found you in a hospital waiting room. Obviously being there today triggered some deep memory you'd forgotten. Or do you remember it?"

She snuggled into his chest, and his heart raced. It felt good to be there for someone. To be the strength she needed. He hadn't felt very strong lately. Not for anyone.

"I hadn't really remembered until we got there. Then it all came crashing back."

He stroked her hair. "What did you remember?"

"My mom. She brought me there because she was sick. She made me sit and wait for her while she talked to a nurse. But she never came back." Her voice cracked at the last few words, and his heart felt like it had cracked too. How that must have affected a small child.

"I kept waiting and waiting, but she never returned. Tons of people came in and sat near me, but I stayed quiet and didn't talk to them. My mom said I shouldn't talk to strangers."

She shifted and touched her locket. It was something she seemed to do when she needed comfort. Someday, could she find that comfort with him and the kids instead?

"Why didn't anyone recognize the woman in the picture as the woman who was at the hospital? At least then they would have known your name and maybe found some other relative to take care of you."

She breathed in a big breath and let it out slowly. "I never showed anyone the locket. I didn't talk to anyone for a long time."

"Because your mom told you to stay quiet?" His heart squeezed even tighter.

She shrugged. "They only knew my name because they gave me crayons and paper and I wrote it down when I colored. When they tried to give me a bath or change my clothes, I'd find a place to hide the locket. Under the cushions in a couch or in my pillowcase or behind an old box. I thought if they knew I had it, they'd take it from me. Later when I was older, lots of the other foster kids took stuff, so I always made sure to keep it safe."

"You showed it to me the night we got married. Or was that only because I saw it and asked?"

"I did show it to Mr. and Mrs. Miller, but they didn't recognize the people in the picture. I also showed it to Gladys."

Shaking her head, she rested it on his chest again. He held her tight and stroked her back and soon felt her relax. Maybe it wasn't super macho or heroic, but he'd been the one to help her today with this flashback.

"I could make an enlargement of the picture and maybe ask around at the VA, if you wanted. Maybe someone would recognize the uniform and patches. We might be able to at least find what unit your dad was in."

She popped up, her face inches from his. "Do you think that would work?"

He kissed her sweet lips, wanting to do everything for her. "I'm not promising anything. Thinking of the timeline, I'd guess your dad was in Desert Storm. Lots of soldiers got deployed then. But I can ask around."

Sighing, she settled back down. It was a long shot,

but if he could get the picture big enough and clear enough, they might be able to read the patches on the man's uniform. That would tell them something. But what if it led to someone who wasn't worthy of her? More likely it was someone who'd been killed over there.

He'd deal with that when and if the time came. Right now, with her in his arms, he knew he'd do anything for her. Anything to make her world better and keep her with him.

Chapter Seventeen

The music from the end of the cartoon floated down the hallway as Tessa peeked in at the kids, then continued to the living room. Erik reclined in their favorite chair singing along to the popular song.

Standing in the doorway, she observed him. Too cute. Watching kid movies was his way to be a solid family unit, he'd said. Yeah, let him think that. The fact he'd rewound this one a bit while she got into her pajamas was a big clue. That and he knew the words to almost every song in most of the movies. Even when the kids weren't around, she'd heard him. The big, tough marine loved children's movies. It pushed him deeper into her heart.

"Is this still playing? I figured it'd be over by now," she teased. "It took us a while to get the kids in bed."

He looked up, his grin sheepish as he fumbled for the remote. "I must have pressed the wrong button when I was channel surfing."

When she looked down to hide her laugh, he narrowed his eyes and glared. Yup, he'd heard. After flicking through a few more stations, he settled on a police drama. This routine was one she loved. Each night, they'd put the kids to bed, she got into her sleep clothes, then they'd snuggle together watching TV. Although how much television they actually saw was anyone's guess.

"Did I tell you how much I like you in my old college sweatshirt?" Settling next to him, she tugged the shoulder of her top back on. The maroon sweatshirt with the gold letters spelling out Norwich University was huge on her to begin with. Erik had hacked the sleeves half off and cut the neck out making it fall off her shoulders if she moved too much. It was super comfortable for sleeping, but she had a feeling he liked it for another reason.

As his lips attached to her exposed neck, she was proved correct. Maybe why she liked wearing it too. And it made her feel closer to her husband. Husband. They'd been married two months now, and it didn't seem real. Never in her life had she imagined being married to Erik Storm. Well, she might have imagined, but she'd never thought it would come true. And that she'd be okay with him nibbling on her neck.

More than okay. With his hands already sneaking under her top, too. No small talk and pretense tonight. Apparently he wanted to get to the action. Maybe it was the action from the cop show on the screen egging him on.

She leaned against him, enjoying his ministrations. When he nipped at a spot on her neck, her head fell to the side with a shiver coursing through her. Quickly, he'd learned what she liked.

Chuckling against her skin, he used his tongue to smooth the spot he'd just bitten. Too soon she'd become a puddle of goo if she didn't try and at least have a conversation to distract herself.

"Your mom called today."

He paused but only for half a second. "Everything

okay? You didn't mention it at supper."

"Sorry, I forgot. The kids keep my mind busy. Nothing major. She wants to make Halloween costumes for Matty and Kiki and was looking for suggestions."

"What'd you tell her?" The kissing hadn't stopped, and she had to remember what they'd been talking about.

"I asked Matty what he wanted to be. The kids have been talking about it at preschool. He said a pirate so he could sail on the ship in his room."

Pushing aside some of her hair that had fallen over her shoulder, he caressed her cheek. Taking his hand in hers, she kissed the palm. It had been a few weeks, and the deep cut had healed, though it was still pink and tender. Thankfully, he'd never let the injury or the bandages get in the way of exploring each night.

"Sounds good. And Kiki? Did she tell you what she wanted to be?"

His hands ran up her torso and cupped her breasts. She sucked in a deep breath and adjusted so he could fully touch her. This was such a sensitive area for her, and it made her head swim when his fingers roamed and kneaded her flesh.

"Well, I'm still trying to interpret the gurgles, but I figured if Matty was going with the theme of his room, then Kiki should too. She'll be a fairy."

He only hummed as his tongue crawled up her neck and his teeth attached to her ear. Her turn to hum. His hands tortured her nipples in such a delicious way it sent coils of desire straight to her core. She still reeled at how much he made her feel. In a very good way.

He shifted, dragging the sweatshirt down, then leaned to press his lips to her breasts. Oh, God, unbelievable.

"Are you in a hurry for some reason tonight?" she teased as his hand slipped inside her loose sleep pants to grip her butt. "Or did the kids' movie inspire you in some way?"

He licked her nipple, then raised his head. "I have PT tomorrow, so chances are good I'll be a bit sore and grumpy when I come back."

"By all means then, take advantage of tonight." Damn, she was getting outspoken, but he didn't seem to mind. Getting in on the act, she let her hands roam over Erik's firm muscles. His back and arms rippled as she ran her fingers over him. Each time he sucked on her, she forgot what she was doing.

As he laved her breasts with his tongue, his hand snuck into her pants but in the front this time. He'd never ventured there before. Not for more than a quick skim through her clothes. Now he dipped deeper and played in the coarse hair between her legs. She kept it neatly trimmed but had never thought he'd be going there. Not if he couldn't have intercourse. What was he doing?

"Oh, shit, Tessa, you don't know what I want to do to you. If this bothers you, tell me now. I want to touch you everywhere. Give you as much pleasure as I can."

Pleasure. Yes, it was. When his fingers stroked into her, she lost the ability to speak. Holy crap, that felt…indescribable. Like nothing she'd ever experienced before.

A tiny moan escaped from her lips, and he paused. She twisted her hips so he'd keep going. He couldn't stop now.

"I take it that's the green light." She could hear the

smile in his tone. Could he possibly be getting something out of this, too? How, she wasn't sure, but no way in hell was she questioning anything. It felt too good.

When his finger slid inside her folds, she gasped at the pleasure. His lips moved back to hers as he did things to her she'd never dreamed of.

"Shit, Tess, I'm dying here. I hope to God this feels good for you."

"Mmm," was all she could manage as he rubbed over the sensitive skin. Dipping in and coming back out, he tortured her feminine region with his talented digits.

"I'm not sure I can stop until I see you go over the edge. God, the look on your face is turning me on and making me want to give you everything."

No words would come, but her hips sure knew what they were doing as they gyrated against his fingers, asking for more. His lips devoured hers, his other hand playing with her nipple. The sensations overwhelmed her, and colors danced across her vision. Except she had her eyes closed. What in the world was happening?

The room started to spin as he continued to plunge his fingers into her in a steady rhythm. There was something she needed. So close, yet not quite there. *Oh, God,* fireworks exploded around her, and she soared through the sky, then plunged toward the ground. Her body shook, and then she was free and floating, drifting softly back to her place in Erik's arms.

Collapsing against him, she tried to get her breathing under control. He pressed a kiss to her forehead as his arms wrapped around her. She hadn't done anything, yet she felt as if she'd run a marathon.

"Holy cow. Is that what the fuss is all about? I had no idea."

"You enjoyed it, then?" His tone indicated his uncertainty.

She ran her hand over his chest and down his arm. "It was intense, but wow, in a good way. If I'd known it was like that, maybe I would have been a little less stringent on the no-touch thing."

He stiffened and frowned. Pushing herself up, she kissed his lips. They softened at her touch, and his hands ran up her back and slipped to her ass again. He sure did like touching her there. She liked it, too.

"I'm glad you didn't know. Being the first one to take you there means a lot to me."

With her head on his chest, his heart raced faster than usual. "Think you might take me there again?" Damn, she was getting downright brazen. He wasn't a good influence on her. Or maybe he was.

He laughed. "We might be able to work that into our touch therapy. I better watch out, though. I may have created a monster."

****

Erik watched as the football soared overhead, and he gritted his teeth. Not that many years ago, he'd been the one running to catch that ball. As receiver for his high school and college teams, he'd scored many touchdowns. Now he'd be lucky to catch the ball if it was lobbed straight at him.

"Heads up!"

Luke ran past as the ball bounced on the ground a few times beyond Erik's feet.

"You didn't even try and catch it," his brother

shouted at him as he bent to pick up the elongated ball.

"You have to grow up and stop playing games at some point in your life," he said tonelessly. He'd never believed that, but he needed some excuse for not diving for the ball the way he used to, and he wouldn't use his cane and crippled leg as an excuse.

Luke glared, then tossed the ball to their cousin Greg who walked toward them in his uniform.

"You sure you guys are okay with Ryan hanging out here for a while? I wasn't on duty today, but someone called in sick. If I want to be considered for that captain's position someday, I need to show I'm willing to pull some extra weight around the station."

"Eat much more of Aunt Luci's cooking, and you'll be pulling all sorts of extra weight." Alex joined them. They all knew Greg's mom, Luci, was the best cook around. She could beat him in a cooking match any day.

"Ryan's no problem at all, Greg. He'll keep my kids company and occupied. They've got so much sugar in them right now, who knows when they'll settle down."

"Thanks, man, I owe you. My mom'll be back in a few hours to get him."

Greg walked off, and Alex shouted after him, "Be safe."

Small town firefighting wasn't quite as dangerous as the bigger cities, but they still occasionally got a call that made Greg's job a risky one. Like his job as a marine. Hopefully, Greg would never have to deal with anything like he had. A crippled leg and scarred face.

"Where is Ryan?" Luke asked, tossing the ball into the air and catching it again.

"In the house," Alex said. "They're sorting through their candy and splitting it up."

They'd come down for a Halloween party at the community their parents now lived in. But the house was small, so they'd come to Alex's, the house they'd all grown up in, to have a family dinner since they were all here. Well, all except Sara who was still on tour. He'd spoken with her a few times, and she seemed to be happy, but he sensed not everything was perfect. Like his own life?

Alex and Luke threw the football back and forth, and he wondered if he should go inside with the women so he didn't have to watch as his brothers ran around the yard. The ball came spiraling toward him, and his instincts had him reaching out for it. But he needed two hands and realized at the last second letting go of the cane would result in his falling flat on his ass. In front of his brothers.

Punching at the ball instead with his right hand, he sent it spiking into the ground and bouncing away. Luke rushed over, frowning.

"Getting rusty in your old age, big brother."

"Fuck off."

Luke glanced at his watch and grinned. "No fucking until much later tonight."

"You really need to grow up."

"Like you? You've been pissy all day. No, thanks."

No denying his mood, though it had mostly been after they'd walked all over the place with the kids. Kiki had gotten tired and wanted to be held, but when he carried her, his hip and leg ached even more. And he felt so damn guilty he couldn't even pick up Matty. The kid was only three. Certainly old enough to be walking everywhere but still young enough he needed a parent holding him occasionally. It wasn't this parent, though.

"Maybe it's hanging around with irresponsible and immature people like you."

Alex came over and picked up the football. "What crawled into your pants and bit you on the ass?"

"I'm fine. Just leave me the hell alone. Maybe I should go hang with the kids. They're more fun than you dickheads."

Alex put out a hand to stop him. He rounded on him, ready to curse him out, but the concerned look on his brother's face made him pause.

"What's going on? Everything okay with Tessa and the kids?"

"They're great. Everything's great with them." It was. For a while now, he and Tessa had been fooling around, but he worried the more she liked his touch, the closer she got to maybe realizing what he couldn't do. And what a disappointment he was.

"I'm glad." Alex let his hand drop from Erik's arm. "You look at her like she's something special. And I know how much those kids mean to you. You're a lucky man, Erik."

Sure, he was. Yet his stupid pride was getting in the way of being truly happy.

"I'm not sure how lucky she is, though."

Alex looked confused.

"She's got herself saddled with a crippled, scarred husband who can barely walk."

"Hey." Luke smirked. "Chicks dig scars."

He glared at his youngest brother. What the hell did he know? He was perfect in every way and could do anything he wanted.

"Not down both sides of your face. We won't even mention what my damned leg looks like."

"I don't hear Tessa complaining," Alex stated, his face serious. "As a matter of fact, she looks at you like you hung the moon. I wouldn't mind a lady staring at me that way."

"You've got plenty of ladies checking you out, Alex. I've seen them."

Alex frowned. "Sure, when they don't know me. None of the women I've dated look at me like I'm everything to them. Like Tessa looks at you."

"That's because you're boring," Luke snorted. "You need to shake things up a bit. Get a little down and dirty. Women love that."

He frowned at what Luke said. "Not all women."

"I like to take it slow and steady in a relationship." Alex crossed his arms. "There's nothing wrong with respect."

"Boring." Luke rolled his eyes.

Thinking of Tessa, he said, "Some women like slow and steady."

A smug smile settled on Alex's face, then he turned to him. "I know you aren't where you want to be, but remember it could be worse. A lot of guys come back with missing limbs."

Or they don't come back at all. He'd lost friends. He knew. And it was more guilt that ate away at him. Why the hell was he dissatisfied with his life? Yet he still felt sorry for himself at times, and that pissed him off too.

"Be patient." Luke tossed the ball in the air again. "You just need time for your leg to heal, and you can lose the cane. It'll all be good."

The ball turned and began to fall. How he felt far too often. Most of the time actually when he thought about what he'd been told.

"It's not going to get better," he blurted. His brothers stared at him, their expressions leery.

"It's only been a few months," Alex pointed out. "You need to give it time."

"I can give it all the time in the world. My leg is fucked up, and it's not getting better."

Luke tilted his head. "Who told you that? Or are you being negative because you can't catch the football right now?"

"The doctor told me, you dumb fuck. The muscles and tendons were too badly damaged. They'll never stretch or bend the same way again."

"What about the physical therapy you're doing?" Alex asked. "Isn't that helping?"

"My therapist, Sue, says she can help make my muscles stronger and possibly not hurt as much when I use them, but even she agrees I won't ever get the range of movement back I had before. There was too much damage."

His brothers remained silent. Damn, he shouldn't have told them. Let someone have hope he'd be back to himself at some point.

"When did you find out?" Luke questioned, his expression solemn.

"The doctors hinted at it when it first happened. They knew what the damage looked like when they did the surgery to put me back together. I didn't want to believe it, though. I figured they were wrong and I'd find a way to walk normal again. I've finally accepted it's not going to happen. I'll need this cane to help me keep my balance. Forever crippled."

Alex narrowed his eyes and lifted his hands. "So now what? You just give up on life?"

"I never said that, but my life isn't going to be what I thought it would be."

"Has Tessa complained? Because she seems happier than I've ever seen her. Hell, she's hugging and kissing the whole damn family. She's never done that before. And don't think I didn't see the two of you groping in the kitchen earlier with a little side of tonsil hockey."

He sighed. That part of his life was wonderful, to a point. But this mobility thing was crap. Especially when he compared himself to his brothers. He used to be able to kick their asses in any sport. Now kicking wasn't even something he could consider.

"You know Tessa's background. She didn't have a whole lot of options for guys."

Alex's eyes widened. "So you're saying she needs to accept the dregs of society for a husband because she's not good enough to get anything better?"

"No!" he roared. "That's not what I'm saying. Tessa is amazing. Any guy would be lucky to get her."

"A guy like you, you mean," Luke said. "Broken down, washed up. Unable to catch a football. Because that's such a useful skill in life."

"She deserves better. A whole man," he muttered, knowing it was true. Yet she still seemed happy with him. Because she didn't know anything else.

Luke turned away. "Yeah, you might as well crawl into a hole and die. You aren't any use to anyone anymore. Because two working legs are the sign of a whole man, right?"

His blood boiled at his brother's words, though he couldn't disagree. At least a whole man would be able to make love to his wife. With more than his hands. She hadn't complained, but that's because of her lack of experience.

"If you're so broken down, I guess you won't be able to play any b-ball with us. I'm feeling like a game." Alex walked away and picked up the basketball sitting on the edge of the driveway.

Luke looked back. "We can get you a chair to sit on so you can watch me wipe the court with Alex."

Alex snorted. "Right, like that's ever going to happen. But I'll go easy on you so you don't look too pathetic. You know, like your crippled brother."

Was steam rising from his ears? His brothers couldn't talk about him that way. He'd show them. Punching the ball out of Alex's hand, he managed to dribble it as he hobbled over to the driveway. When he got his feet as steady as was possible, he tossed the ball into the air. It flew in an arc and came down right through the net without even touching the rim. Yes!

"Not bad for a fucking cripple."

His brothers trotted over, and Luke took the ball. Erik couldn't run but he still got the ball every now and then. And his advantage was he could get it in the net from anywhere. Three pointers had always been his specialty.

They played for a while, and all three of them were sweating and out of breath by the time Matty came out to tell them dinner was ready.

He cleared his throat. "So who was wiping the driveway with whom?"

Alex walked closer and wiped the sweat off his

face with his sleeve. "Not bad for a cripple who's ready to give up."

He laughed. "You did that on purpose."

Luke winked at Alex, and his stomach did a few loops. He had the best damn brothers anywhere.

As he pulled Alex into a one-armed hug, Luke joined in on his other side, and Erik's cane fell to the ground.

"Thanks. For not giving up on me."

"Never."

"Won't happen."

Keeping hold of Alex's shoulder, he glanced at the ground. "You will need to help me into the house or get me my damn cane."

Luke picked up the piece of wood and handed it to his brother, then placed his hand on Erik's shoulder. Alex still held his from the other side. Together they walked into the house to eat as a family.

Chapter Eighteen

"Do you mind if I skip the recliner tonight?"

Tessa paused in pulling the huge sweatshirt over her head, and Erik ogled her generous curves from his position on the king-sized bed they shared. The view was short lived as she let it drop into place around her thighs. He loved she was getting comfortable enough to change in front of him.

Of course, over the last month, he'd been touching and tasting a good deal of those curves. Their routine on the recliner was the thing that got him through every day. But tonight, his leg hurt like a bastard. Today he'd really gone at it during PT, and he wasn't sure why. Maybe playing basketball with his brothers last week had showed him he still had strength and endurance if not mobility, and he didn't want to lose any of it.

But even with her sweet attributes tempting him, he couldn't muster the energy to get off the bed and walk to the living room. Maybe she'd join him here, even though it was barely eight.

She shimmied out of her pants and removed her socks but moved over to the bed before putting her pajama pants on. She sat on the edge of the bed and placed her hands on his knee.

"Is it bothering you again?"

Closing his eyes, he enjoyed the feel of her hands against his bare skin. Even though it was November, he'd kept his gym shorts on after PT. Now he was glad he had.

"I pushed a bit too hard today."

"You've still got some Vicodin if it's really bad."

"Thanks." He wanted to scream he wasn't going to get addicted to that but knew she was only offering to make him feel better. "I should take some of the anti-inflammatory meds. Sue said they help keep swelling down after a hard workout."

"I'll get them. You stay here."

The sight of her long, slim legs beneath his college sweatshirt started his cock aching. Damn, the pesky appendage really liked to play games with him. If only it would hang around long enough to do something useful. Was she ready for that, though? She sure responded to his hands touching her and his mouth kissing her. Did it matter if she was? He had nothing to offer her except kisses and touching.

"Here you go." Like the angel she was, she appeared and handed him a glass of water too. After taking the pills he settled on the bed with her rubbing his knee and thigh again.

"That feels great. Thanks."

Her face reddened as she ducked her head. "You make me feel good all the time too. It's the least I can do."

"I don't expect you to pay me back for pleasuring you." His voice was a touch rough, but he didn't like the idea of her thinking she owed him.

Her fingers continued kneading his skin and muscles. "I like touching you. If that's okay."

There was that doubt again, but the words alone got Mr. Happy dancing. She must have felt it other times as he pressed against her back and played with her, but she'd never said anything.

Slipping his hands under her top, he skimmed his fingers up her rib cage. Shit, she had the softest skin he'd ever felt. He pulled her closer until she was all but lying on top of him. His mouth got busy paying tribute to her full lips while his hands cupped the ass that kept him awake at night dreaming what he wanted to do to it. Maybe someday that might happen.

For now, he would enjoy anything he could get. And that included caressing every inch of her delectable body. Rolling over, he hovered over her, never getting enough of her wide eyes and satisfied smile. When he kissed her again, she clung to him like she'd never let go. God, he hoped she didn't. Could he even live without her? She'd become far more than he ever expected in a fake wife.

Fake wife. No, that couldn't describe her anymore. Not with the way they touched and kissed and the way he made her moan in pleasure as his fingers stroked her to the edge of madness. Watching her break apart was the most erotic thing he'd ever seen. The tiny whimpers escaping her lips were more real than any dramatic screaming he'd experienced. When his name fell from her lips in a pleading whisper, silently begging him to push her over into oblivion, it was the cure for every problem he faced.

Her hands reached for him, and her fingers threaded through the hair he'd let grow from its military style. She used it to hold him close, and he saw no reason to deny her access. He was happy to be held by her, wanted by her. Damn, he wanted her too. "It's getting warm in here. Think we should get rid of this?"

Pulling at the hem of her shirt, he lifted it over her head. Her skin colored from her cheeks down to the toes that had the nails painted a soft peach. Kind of like the color they'd painted Kiki's room.

Damn, he was going soft if he was thinking about paint colors. But that thought didn't last long as he stared down at the beauty before him. Aside from a small scrap of lace around her hips, she was totally bared to his hungry gaze. And boy, could he devour her.

Leaning down, he kissed her again, hands exploring. He skimmed his lips over her neck and shoulders, then moved south to suck on the dusky peaks that always called out to him. Clinging to his head, she arched back as he pulled and laved her nipples. So frickin' responsive and it drove him crazy.

Today he didn't want to stop there. He needed to taste all of her. Every inch of her. His lips lowered farther, traveling down her stomach, and he paused to swirl his tongue around her navel. She sucked in a deep breath but never stopped him. His hands had been on this path, but now his tongue wanted equal access.

Her panties kept him from claiming what he wanted most, and he hesitated, but he'd touched her here before. Using his tongue wasn't all that different. Was it? Or would it be one more thing to dream of during the day?

When his fingers slipped into the waistband and tugged down, she stiffened, so he whispered soft words of encouragement.

"It's okay, sweetie. You'll enjoy this. Promise. I know I will."

The silky fabric dropped to the floor, and his heart

nearly stopped at the sight before him. Tessa, absolutely bare and trusting, prone on the bed, waiting for him. His hip twinged as he slid off the mattress and knelt by the edge. Totally ignoring the pain in his knee, he grabbed her around the hips and pulled until her legs hung over the side. Spreading them apart, he found heaven.

"Erik?" Her anxious voice brought him back, and he caressed her stomach and legs.

"Trust me. Please. God, you don't know how long I've wanted to do this. To bring you absolute pleasure this way."

He kissed along her legs, then the inside of her thighs. Her muscles tensed, but she didn't object. Her hands clenched in the bed covers, and her eyes shut tight. The tiny humming from her mouth let him know it was all good. Safe to proceed.

Draping her legs over his shoulders, he nibbled until he had his target in sight. He parted the folds and stroked his tongue along the soft flesh. Her cry broke the air, and her back arched. Reaching up, he caressed her breast, then moved his hand back down her stomach in a reassuring manner.

He used his tongue to lick along her folds and flick the tiny nub taunting him. As he filled his nostrils with the scent of her ambrosia, she squirmed and moaned and finally grabbed his head. But instead of pushing him away, she held him in place.

Nothing could have aroused him more. He ached with the knowledge he was giving her such sensual pleasure. More licks and nips and a few thrusts into her heated core had her writhing on the bed. His knee hurt, but the pain in his rock-hard cock was far worse. He feasted faster and stronger, then licked her sensitive nerves, and she almost bolted off the bed.

Her whimpers escalated, and she threw her head back, stiffening, holding his head in a death grip. Her body shivered, stilled, then melted, her breathing ragged.

"God, Erik, I don't know how you do that. Get me so I feel like I'm flying and exploding and falling all at the same time."

He pushed himself up, groaning at the ache in his leg. It was so worth it, though. Except his cock was still like concrete. And it hurt like crazy.

After pressing a few kisses to her nose and face, he swung her legs under the covers.

"Be back in a few minutes."

Limping to the bathroom, he pushed at the door. Holy hell. A full-blown erection and no sign of it deflating. Twisting the shower knobs, he let the water warm up. Would this actually work? He dropped his shorts and stepped into the glass enclosure. Holding the wall with one hand, he touched himself with the other.

Still hard as a rock and sensitive as hell. He stroked up and down, and sensations surged through him. It had been way too long since he'd had this happen. Pleasure shot through his body, and he groaned. Faster and harder, but he couldn't quite get there. Shit. To get this far and not finish…that was too cruel.

"Erik?"

Crap. No. She couldn't see what he was doing. "I'll be out in a second." Or he'd be dead from the frustration of jacking off with no happy ending.

"I heard you groan. Are you all right?"

"Fine." His voice didn't sound normal. She'd never

believe him.

"Can I help?"

Her voice was right behind the glass. His head whipped around, and there she stood, the huge shirt hanging off one shoulder, giving him a glimpse of what he'd just devoured. Damn it all. She couldn't know he was this desperate.

She opened the door and looked down. "That seems pretty big. I thought you said it didn't work."

Shit, shit, shit. He had to be honest with her. She deserved that much.

"It doesn't always stay this way. But tonight...you...it got me a little more excited than usual."

Her face turned crimson. "Me, too."

Her tongue poked out and wet her lips. Shit, more blood rushed straight to the member he still held.

"I'd like to help." When she shrugged, the sweatshirt slipped over her tiny shoulders and slithered to the floor. If this ended the way it always did lately, he'd die. But the sight of her beautiful nude body did nothing to diminish his arousal. Just the opposite.

She moved into the enclosure and sidled up behind him. Rubbing her silky body against his back, she slid her hand around his hips and took hold.

Holy hell. Her breasts brushed his back, and his ass settled against her stomach. "Tell me if you need me to go faster or slower."

He leaned against the wall again and guided her hand under his. "You are incredible, Tess. Just like this."

She picked up the rhythm quickly, and he removed his hand from hers. Her other hand ran up and down his torso. The sight of both her hands on him had him coming faster than he thought possible. It had been a long time since he'd last had a woman in the shower with him.

The water trickled over his head as the tension built up. Her warm body snuggled behind him, and her firm hand moved steadily up and down. Finally, shivers ran through him as stars exploded behind his eyes. When he sagged heavily against the wall, she wrapped her arms around him. Was she trying to hold him up? God, she was precious.

"Are you okay?"

Turning, he pulled her against him, using her to keep his balance. "Yes. I can't believe you did that. Thank you."

She lowered her eyes shyly. "You're welcome."

They were standing here naked, and he'd just gone down on her. How could she still be shy? But she was, and he loved that.

"Well, that was the first time I went there since I went off to Afghanistan."

She touched his cheek and smiled. "I'm glad I helped take you there."

"You're getting awfully sassy, aren't you?"

She blushed, and her tongue poked out.

"I definitely want to go there again."

Her eyes gleamed at his words, and she stood on her toes, kissing him. "I better watch out. I may have created a monster."

****

Something warm rubbed against her back, and Tessa snuggled deeper into it. Blissfully. This morning Erik was closer than ever. And if the pressure against her backside was anything to go by, he was happy to be there.

Last night he'd rocked her world in a way she'd never imagined. But then her imagination was seriously lacking.

A muscular arm wrapped around her and slid under her top. Someone was awake. Maybe. A few times in his sleep, he'd done this also. Usually when he had a bad dream. Her heart lightened, knowing she could help ease his suffering. Like she'd done in the shower last night. That had been another first for her. Hopefully, not the last.

She wiggled her butt against Erik and felt skin against skin. She'd only slipped the sweatshirt back on after their shower, but he hadn't put anything on at all. Looking at the light outside, she knew it was still too early for the kids to be up. They did love to sleep. Matty didn't have preschool today, so there was no rush to get up and out of the house. It meant she could stay here snuggled in Erik's arms until they heard from one of the children.

"You smell so damn sexy," he growled in her ear.

She giggled. "How do you *smell* sexy?"

Turning her so she faced him, his hands roamed her backside. "You just do. Or maybe I can smell you on the sheets from last night. Whatever it is, it's working its magic."

The magic he spoke of now pressed against her front, teasing her. As he shifted onto his back, bringing her with him, her legs fell on either side of his hips. It was a strange feeling, skin on skin down there. Strange but good.

"We don't need this, do we?" He skimmed his

hands up her rib cage, relieving her of her top. "I'll keep you warm."

His hair-roughened chest pressed against her as she settled on him. The sensation was incredible. When she moved, the friction sent shafts of delight to her core. It was still early enough. Maybe they could fool around a little before the kids woke up. She leaned down to kiss him, and his lips captured hers as his hands ran over her back and to her ribs.

"Damn, I need to taste you right now." He pulled until her breasts dangled over his lips. Oh, my God, this was decadent. Was he seriously going to do this? She hoped so.

He did. His tongue licked over her taut nipple, causing it to tighten even further. When he sucked on it, she wanted to scream. A good scream. Instead, she bit her lip. This wasn't a picture she needed the kids seeing if the noise woke them up.

As he tortured her with his tongue, the spot between her legs clenched and throbbed. Moving her hips from side to side, she enjoyed the feel of skin against skin. When she twisted again, his arousal nudged her opening. Damn, that felt incredible. If she turned her hips the right way, it rubbed exactly where his fingers always did. Would it feel just as good?

He seemed busy devouring her breasts, so she experimented, seeing how it felt with his erection teasing her folds. It slipped in, and oh, God, the sensation… It was like nothing else. She'd hated when Jeremy had done this. He'd been rough, and it hurt as he kept shoving in and out.

But this, it was sliding and filling her and… It felt like heaven. Maybe just a little more. A little more.

"Tess? What are you doing?" He'd paused his actions. Damn.

"Don't make me stop," she begged. "Please, don't make me stop. Oh, my God, this is... I can't even describe it. Please."

When he chuckled, she finally looked at his face. It looked like he was in agony. "Am I hurting you?"

"Shit, woman, no. It feels freaking amazing. I'm just afraid it won't last."

She wiggled until he was farther inside. "It did last night."

He grinned. Heat suffused her cheeks, but she didn't want this to end. Wanted to see where it would go.

"Have at it, then. It must be the sight of you, naked and aroused, keeping it going." His eyes held a hint of uncertainty.

"I don't care if it works the way it's supposed to. Right now, this is bliss."

He ran his hands all over her. Sitting up, she sank fully onto his erection. She closed her eyes and simply felt. He filled her in ways she never knew existed.

"This is what it's supposed to be like, right?"

"From the look on your face, I'd say yes."

"It wasn't anything like this...the other time, I mean."

His muscles tightened beneath her, and he stroked her arms. "That douche bag didn't give you any souvenirs of that time, did he?"

Souvenirs? What was he talking about?

"I'm totally clean, Tessa."

"Oh, that. No, he used a condom, and I made sure to get checked after. For pregnancy as well. Just in case, you know." Could she and Erik have kids, though? A baby with him would fulfill that elusive family dream.

His jaw clenched, and his hands tightened on her arms. "That won't happen here. I don't remember the exact specifics—they had me on some pretty strong drugs—but apparently the injury affected my semen production. I guess I should consider myself lucky I'm getting this far. I hadn't expected it."

"We've got Matty and Kiki. That's all we need."

His hands spanned her waist. "We do need to get this show on the road, though, if we don't want those two waking up and finding us this way."

She pouted. "I'm kind of enjoying this. What do I do next?"

He smiled. Probably at her complete ignorance. He must be used to women who knew how to please him.

"Just start moving, sweetie. You'll get the hang of it soon enough."

His hands guided her to raise and lower herself, and soon her hips twisted and gyrated, building the pressure inside. She was in control. Slow it down or speed it up, it was up to her. Holy Mother of God, feelings and sensations assaulted her as she raced toward the peak of some unknown goal. More twisting and bucking and she found herself on the edge of a cliff, free falling toward the sensual abyss. Tremors racked her body, and she collapsed against him, satiated beyond her wildest dreams.

Flipping her over, he thrust into her a few more times, rapidly and deeply. "God, I don't want to hurt you, but I need...oh, shit, I need to..."

She wrapped both arms and legs around him and

raked her nails down his back. He shuddered with a deep groan, then fell to his side, pulling her with him.

"Are you okay?" he panted, his nose in her hair. "I didn't hurt you, did I?"

"I don't remember any pain, though my mind is mush right now. Not sure what my name is."

"It's Tessa Storm, my wife." The proprietary tone in his voice had her shivering in delight. "Don't ever forget it."

The sound of her husband's heart racing in time with hers as she nuzzled closer was like music. "Keep doing stuff like that, and I won't."

"Your wish is my command."

Chapter Nineteen

"When's Sara getting here?"

Tessa walked into Alex's living room as Erik asked about their sister. Guiding Matty, who held his cookies and milk like precious jewels, she settled near her husband and glanced around. Alex had only bought the house from Pete and Molly a few months ago, but already made it his own. The furniture was less frilly but still neat and comfortable. If she'd learned anything about Alex, it was he liked things tidy and organized.

"Sofie's getting her at the train station so they can catch up before she comes here," Molly Storm answered, Kiki in her arms. "She told me not to worry." She rolled her eyes. "Like you can actually tell a mother not to worry. Right, Tessa?"

Her heart skipped a beat that Molly would include her in the group of "mother." She shifted closer to Erik. All these people were familiar, yet with so many in one place, her anxiety reappeared. He squeezed her hand and gave her a reassuring smile. Had he sensed she was nervous? And would the butterflies ever stop flitting in her stomach when he touched her? The last few weeks in bed at night...how she hadn't exploded into little pieces was beyond her.

"Alex, did you need any help getting the bedrooms ready?" Molly kissed Kiki's cheek.

"You seriously think he didn't have that done last

weekend, Mom." Luke crossed his arms over his chest. "When has Alex ever left anything to the last minute?"

Alex glared at his younger brother. She loved seeing the banter between these two. All three brothers had their own personality, but their love for each other was apparent. It must have been wonderful growing up in this house.

"The only thing left is the portable crib for Kiki," Alex said, distracted by something out the window. He stood, then scurried into the kitchen. Something must be out of alignment and need straightening.

Luke smirked. "I set up the crib when you first got here. Alex doesn't do everything."

Erik nodded as the sound of the back door opening filtered in.

"Hey, everyone, look who I found wandering around." Alex walked in from the kitchen with a petite woman behind him. Her long, dark hair hung in loose waves down her back, and she was dressed in a flowing, multicolored blouse and denim shorts. She wore black thigh-high boots on her long trim legs. Who was this? Quite exotic and not the type you'd picture for Alex.

"You found?" Luke teased. "You've been peering through the curtains for a few hours now."

Alex scowled but drew the woman farther into the room. "I figured Gina was coming home, and I didn't want her to be alone."

"Honey"—Molly moved in for a hug—"I'm so sorry about your grandmother. We'll all miss her dearly."

Erik pushed himself to standing and tugged on her hand. "This is Gina Mazelli. Her grandmother lived next door. You met her at our wedding. Remember I said the wake and funeral were this weekend?"

The sad-eyed woman was beautiful.

"Gina." He propelled her forward. "This is my wife, Tessa. And our kids, Matty and Kiki."

"A wife and kids, Erik? Wow, you work fast. Gram did mention she'd been to your wedding this summer. Congratulations, to both of you."

She liked Gina immediately. Her smile was warm and genuine, and her eyes held a sincerity that showed how much she appreciated being here with this family. She understood so well. It still boggled her mind she was now a part of the Storm family. A family she'd loved being with and had wanted to be part of since she'd met them.

Would everything stay this way, though? Now that he knew he could perform, would he want another wife? Someone who wasn't a total freak? *But you aren't a freak anymore. You're enjoying sex with him too.*

Deep inside she didn't feel normal, though. Her stomach still clenched and did flips when too many people were around. She worried others could see inside her and know what she was thinking and feeling. Or maybe even see the abnormal background she had. It was silly, but it had been part of her for so long she wasn't sure it would ever completely leave.

Pete stood up and pulled Kiki out of Molly's arms. "We should probably head home and let you kids have some time to yourselves." He kissed the child's head, then handed her to Luke, whose face twisted in a comical expression. He held her stiffly and faked a smile. God help him when he had kids.

Hugs and kisses were given again, and once more she felt swallowed up in a brand-new world. One that was wonderful and so filled with love she knew she never wanted to leave.

"We'll be over early tomorrow morning to start the turkey and all the fixings. Your grandmother already made a few pies today."

"Mom, you don't have to cook Thanksgiving dinner." Alex gave his mom a peck on the cheek. "We're having it here, so I'm happy to do it."

"Don't hang me out to dry just yet, Alexander. I still have a bit of life left in me. Besides, I know how much you like going to the high school football game in the morning."

Alex glanced at his brothers, then at his mom. "If you're sure. I hear the team's pretty good this year."

Once Molly and Pete left, she suggested putting the kids to bed.

"I'll get the crib from the van." Alex stood.

Luke cocked his head. "I got it already. It's in Sara's old room."

Alex narrowed his eyes. "About time you did something to help."

She took Kiki from Luke who looked relieved. The kids went around for kisses, then they strolled toward the stairs. She allowed Kiki to try the stairs herself. The toddler would take a while, and maybe it wouldn't be so apparent Erik struggled with climbing them too.

Once in pajamas, they settled them in their beds. Kiki had half fallen asleep on her shoulder as Erik read a few of the favorite stories.

"We'll be right in the next room if you need us or get scared." Erik fiddled with the baby monitor on the bedside table. "We can hear you through this, so call us if you need us."

"I'm a big boy, Daddy," Matty announced, then snuggled into the stuffed bear he always slept with. He may have been nervous a few months back, but being in this house was familiar, and he felt secure she and Erik would be there for them. She wished she'd felt that way in any of her foster homes.

Erik plugged in a night light, and they moved into the hallway.

"I might stay up here for a while." He glanced nervously back at the door.

She stifled her laugh. "They'll be fine. They were tired. I don't think they'll need us."

He slipped his arms around her waist, and she melted against him.

"What about you?" He leaned down for a kiss.

"What are you asking? Am I tired? Or do I need you?"

A grin split his lips. "Either? If you're tired, we could go to bed. But if you need me, we could go to bed."

Too stinking cute. She bit down on her lip. "What if I said I needed you in bed?"

****

"They clean now, Daddy?"

Erik lowered Matty to the floor and grabbed some paper towels from the dispenser. God, how old was that thing? It looked like the same paper towel holder that had been there when he'd played football for Squamscott Regional.

"I think they're clean, Pal. Let's go find your mom and aunts and uncles."

259

He grabbed his cane tighter in his left hand and reached for Matty with his right. The awkward gait he'd become accustomed to, and the pain was starting to subside, but he still hated he couldn't keep his balance without the damn walking stick.

They made their way through the crowds of the Thanksgiving Day football rivalry with Portsmouth High. Many of the faces were new, though a lot of them looked familiar. Matty held his hand tight and stayed close to his leg. The boy wasn't used to this many people all in the same place. Good thing his mom had offered to keep Kiki at the house with them.

A few more people jostled past, and he leaned down. "Matty grab hold of my neck, okay. I'll carry you until we get back to the family."

Matty slid his arms around Erik's neck, and he lifted the boy to rest on his good hip. Gripping the cane tighter, he walked forward. His right arm tensed, but luckily Matty wasn't too heavy, and his arms were in good shape. Now to find the others. His brothers and sister were here along with many of his cousins. They'd all made plans to sit together in the bleachers and cheer on the old team.

Sara stood by the concession stand with a huge crowd surrounding her. He grinned. Must have something to do with the few articles the local paper had done on her when she'd gotten the opening act gig on tour with Ammunition. "Stormy? That you?"

He turned at his old nickname. His unit had used it while in the marines, but he hadn't heard it around here since high school.

"Tommy. Hey, how've you been?"

He shook hands with the stout, dark-haired man

standing in front of him. Tom had been one of the best defensive linebackers they'd had. A great friend too. Guilt ripped through him he hadn't even attempted to get in touch with the guy since his return home.

"Good, though Sherry's been feeding me a little too well." He patted his stomach, which had grown a bit since their high school days. "I tell her I want to look like her. She's expecting in about a month."

"That's great. Congratulations." He shifted Matty on his hip. "This is my son, Matty. Or he will be as soon as the adoption goes through. He and his sister had a bit of trouble in Kandahar, so I brought them back here."

"That's real great of you, Stormy. And this way you don't have to go through all the cravings and morning sickness complaints I have to listen to from Sherry."

He smiled but knew he'd love to go through that. Images of Tessa all big and round with his child floated through his mind. It would be incredible. But they had Matty and Kiki, and he couldn't love them more. Guilt ate at him for even thinking along those lines.

"So you raising these kids by yourself? Or you got some babe running after you to help?"

Wiggling his cane, he winced. "Not sure too many babes run after guys with scars and bum legs, but luckily one of them didn't seem to mind slumming it with me. She's over there with my sister."

Tom turned, and a grin split his face. "There're two ladies over there with her, and both of them are quite fine. Which one is yours?"

"Come on, I'll introduce you." He shifted Matty higher, then limped to where Tessa stood with Gina, her gaze darting every which way. The game was sure to be crowded, and he'd warned her, but she'd insisted on coming. It was all part of Dr. Sullivan's plans to help her deal with her anxiety.

"Mama," Matty cried as they got closer. Her face relaxed when she saw them, and she reached for Matty.

"Sorry we took so long. There was a line. And I ran into an old friend. Tessa, this is Tom Palmer. Tommy, my wife, Tessa."

"Wife? You went and got hitched and didn't invite me?" Tom laughed, but he figured Tom was hurt. Erik had been his best man a few years ago.

"It was small. Immediate family in the backyard. I'd just got back from overseas and was barely out of a wheelchair at that point."

Tom looked down at the cane, then glanced back up to his face. "You don't look any different except you got this." He pointed to the cane. "It's real nice of you to marry this ugly lug, Tessa. Tell me you didn't fall for the 'pity me, I've got a cane' routine."

She smiled at Tom, then at him. Her smile was genuine, unlike a few he'd seen today, when people had seen his scars and how he could barely walk.

"No, I fell for his humble attitude and shy demeanor."

Tom burst out laughing. Her eyes twinkled, and his stomach flipped a few times. God, she was magical. Tom took off after exchanging numbers. He'd definitely call him. Tom had never been one to care about looks or athletic ability. He was a true friend.

"We should get up to the stands. The game is about to begin. You all set with Matty or do you need me to take him?"

She lowered the child to the ground. "He can walk between both of us."

She always knew what to do and say. How had he gotten so lucky? They made their way through the throngs of people and started up to where the rest of the family was waiting.

"Oh, my God, Erik?"

He looked down to the seat where the high-pitched voice had come from.

"Chrissy, hi." His high school girlfriend hadn't changed much. Blonde hair swept in some messy updo that probably took hours to achieve. Makeup artfully applied to look like she wasn't wearing any. Outfit picked to accentuate her figure. Even in the cold weather of November.

And that look of horror and revulsion when she scanned his face, then lowered her eyes to the cane he had in a death grip.

"Are you all right? I'd heard you got deployed but not that you'd been...injured."

What had she been about to say? Crippled? "I'm fine. It's good to see you." They continued walking up the stands.

He didn't bother introducing her to Tessa or Matty. In high school, he'd idolized Chrissy because she was the prettiest girl around and she'd wanted him. His arrogance had made him believe he deserved her. They'd broken off when they'd gone to different colleges. Looking back, though, he knew she'd been as arrogant as he'd been. Boy, had he been stupid, thinking he'd always be the athletic superstar who could win anyone he wanted.

As he sat next to Alex, Luke, and his cousins, Greg

and Kevin, he glanced down to see Chrissy still watching him. He focused on the game that had begun.

When halftime came around, the guys made their way to wait in line for drinks and snacks while the ladies used the rest room.

"What's up with you dragging Gina all over the place?" Luke nudged Alex.

Alex threw him a look. "Nothing. She lost her grandmother. I'm being nice."

"You've always been 'nice' to her."

"What's wrong with being nice to people?"

Luke frowned. "You're too nice sometimes."

As his brothers bantered back and forth, he scanned the crowd. Chrissy stood on the other side of the large pillar from him. Maybe he should talk to her. He'd cut her off pretty quick earlier. Shoving some money at Alex with an order, he stepped around the pillar just in time to hear his name.

"Have you seen poor Erik Storm? He was hurt in the war. Oh, he used to be so handsome and physically fit, absolutely perfect, but now…he's all scarred and crippled. I can't look at him the same way."

There was no reason to wait to hear more. Turning, he walked right into Tessa with Matty. Damn, she'd heard too.

"I'll take Matty to the bathroom. See you in the stands."

He didn't need any more pity from anyone. There'd been enough today to last a lifetime.

Chapter Twenty

As Erik walked off with Matty, Tessa wanted to go after him. But the men's room was hardly the place for her. He needed some time too. She knew him well enough to know that.

"What a bitch," Gina said from next to her. "Who is that?"

She shrugged, but Sara moved in closer. "That's Chrissy Watkins, Erik's high school girlfriend. I never really liked her, but he thought she was God's gift to men."

Gina cleared her throat. "And here she comes."

"Sara, oh, my God, you look amazing. I've heard so much about your singing tour. It must be fabulous."

Chrissy hugged Sara as if they were best friends. Sara's face showed her confusion.

"Hi, Chrissy."

"It's so great to see you again. I saw the articles in the paper and couldn't believe you've been on tour with Ammunition. Tell me all about Bullet Ryker. Is he fabulous?"

"Fabulous," Sara repeated, though less enthusiastically. "Chrissy, this is Gina, Mrs. Mazelli's granddaughter. You remember her?"

"Oh, sure." Chrissy half glanced Gina's way.

"Have you met Tessa, Erik's wife?"

Sara pulled her closer and linked arms with her.

No, she didn't need to meet his old flame, who was totally gorgeous. The woman had on a short skirt and knee-high boots with a snug leather jacket that showed her figure nicely. The decorative scarf around her neck was the only thing that might have kept her warm.

On the other hand, she wore jeans and a barn coat with one of Erik's old hoodies underneath. It was November in New Hampshire after all. Even Gina, in all her fanciful glory, wore a maxi skirt with thick socks tucked into floral Doc Marten's and a plaid wool poncho. Sara's jeans and thick sweater combo, topped by her dress coat with the fur-trimmed hood, still outshone anything she owned.

"Erik's married?" Chrissy looked at her as if she were examining a piece of furniture she intended to buy. Her dismissive expression and simple "Hi" let her know she didn't pass inspection. Hardly surprising. She never had.

"Oh, Sara, I feel so bad for poor Erik. Is there anything I can do? Start up a collection for medical treatment or something? You know how good I am at charity work."

Gina linked her arm in Tessa's and grinned. "Isn't that sweet of you."

"Well, I've always been known for being a giving person. Why don't you give me your number, Sara, so we can get together to discuss what we can do to help heal these scars and wounds?"

Getting the scoop on Bullet Ryker was probably more in her thoughts than healing Erik.

"That's nice of you. Erik said there are so many guys who need help. We feel blessed he was fine and came home to us, unlike so many others. He's such a great husband and dad." And he was. She hadn't said anything that wasn't true.

Chrissy narrowed her eyes. "You mean that little boy he was with is his?"

"His name is Matty, and we're adopting him and his little sister Kiki. Erik rescued them when they were trapped after a bombing. He kept them alive and made sure they weren't too afraid. They love him so much."

"They love you, too, Tessa." Sara hugged her arm.

Gina placed her hands on her heart. "Erik is so heroic and brave. The thought of it gives me goosebumps. Those Storm men have that effect on women, don't they?"

Heat rushed to her cheeks. Erik sure had some effect on her. No denying that. "It can get a little overwhelming."

"No, no, no," Sara gasped. "I can't listen to that kind of talk about my brothers. They're my *brothers*. I better get in line for the restroom." Quickly, she wandered away.

Gina chuckled and hugged her while she glanced at Chrissy. "I can tell by your blushing just how overwhelming Erik can be. Having a real hero in your bed…"

She bit her lip to stop the groan threatening to escape when she thought about what she and Erik did in bed. Chrissy started to walk away, and she called out, "Thanks for volunteering to raise money for the wounded soldiers."

Gina turned away, and her face scrunched up. Then she took a deep breath and let it out slowly. "I really hate people like that. Think they're so much better than everyone else."

Did Gina feel that way? She wore her confidence out in the open with her wild looks and eccentric dress. But *inside* wasn't always the same as *outside*.

They started walking back to the bleachers, and she leaned in to Gina. "Were you talking generally or do you…did you and Alex…?"

Gina's olive skin flushed as she shrugged. "It was a long time ago. I was his first, and he was mine."

"What happened? Why aren't you guys together?" Although she probably already knew the answer to that. Gina and Alex were worlds apart.

"He freaked out when he realized I didn't have the experience he thought I had. Apologized a million times."

"He apologized?" That totally sucked. The pain in Gina's exotic eyes was apparent. "You still have a thing for him, don't you?"

Gina gazed off into the distance. "Maybe, but let's face it, Felix and I aren't exactly two peas in a pod."

She laughed at Gina's nickname for Alex. The two of them were very much The Odd Couple. Earlier today she'd seen Alex walk around the dining room table, straightening the silverware. Gina had stepped along casually behind him, moving it the tiniest bit. But Alex had noticed and needed to fix them again. It was too bad they couldn't get together because she liked Gina. She'd be a great sister-in-law.

Back in the stands she scooted close to Erik and snuggled into his side for warmth. The game was back in full swing, and most people focused there. Chrissy, though, kept glancing back at them.

She lifted her head to stare at Erik. So handsome. The scars merely accentuated that fact.

"I've never had so many people jealous of me before. I think I like it."

He looked at her curiously. "What are you talking about?"

She reached up and stroked her finger along his forehead and traced the scar that went through his eyebrow. "I'm married to the best-looking guy here. One who's got the attention of every girl around."

He lifted the scarred eyebrow. "I doubt that's why they're looking."

He didn't say any more, but she knew what he was thinking. He was wrong. "I know what I see. And I like it very much."

Pulling at his head, she kissed him soundly. He wrapped his arm around her and held tight. Even after the kiss ended, he still held her close. She leaned into his warmth, not caring if anyone was looking at them or what they thought. Especially Chrissy. Erik was hers now, and that's all that mattered.

****

"I'll let Joe know you're here."

"Thanks." Erik walked into the sparse room at the Veteran's Affairs Division. He pulled out the picture he'd had blown up of Tessa's parents and stared at it. Was this the right guy? And was he actually her father?

Both at the VA in Brunswick and the support group he went to weekly, he'd made it a point to ask around. No one had recognized the man, though a few weeks back, an old timer who'd been visiting had thought the uniform looked familiar. After a bit more digging, he'd finally found what unit the man was in.

Knowing that had brought him to another soldier who thought it looked like Joe Kraznof. And this Joe volunteered a few times a month here at the Portland office. Today was one of those days.

What if it wasn't her dad? So she wouldn't be disappointed, he hadn't mentioned the information he'd gotten. Nor had he said anything since he'd made and enlarged a copy of the locket picture, not sure anything would come of it. He still wasn't.

"Ben said you were looking for me."

When he turned, a slim, middle-aged man with graying hair rolled into the room in a wheelchair. His eyes were the same shade of blue as Tessa's and the smile similar. Glancing at the picture in his hand, he took a step forward.

"Yes, I'm Erik Storm."

The man held out his hand, and Erik gripped it.

"Joe Kraznof. What can I do for you?"

"Is this you in the picture?" He handed him the copy.

As Joe looked at the picture, the smile left his face. He swallowed, his eyes drilling a hole into Erik. "Where did you get this?"

"It's a copy I made from a locket my wife has."

Joe stared at the picture again, his eyes intense. "This is Gail and I right before I shipped out. But Gail died twenty years ago. How did your wife get this locket?"

He pointed to the woman. "Her mother gave it to her. She thinks the man is her father."

Tears filled Joe's eyes, and his lips tightened. "She is alive. I knew it. I've been looking for her for almost twenty years."

"She's twenty-*four* years old." He shouldn't sound accusatory, but dammit, she'd needed a loving family growing up.

"I know. I wasn't in the right shape to contact anyone for a long time when I got back." He looked down at his legs unmoving in the chair.

Gazing at the cane he needed to keep himself balanced, he nodded. "I can understand, though maybe not to the extent you do."

"God, I have so many questions. I don't even know where to start."

He couldn't even imagine what kind of emotions this would bring on. "Her name is Tessa."

Joe looked up, and a few tears rolled down his face. He took a deep breath, then let it out slowly. "That was my mother's name." Closing his eyes, his jaw tensed, and his hands clenched into fists.

Yeah, he should look away, but this was Tessa's dad, and he had to make sure he was someone who wouldn't cause more pain to his wife. In her lifetime, she'd had more than enough.

A few more deep breaths and Joe opened his eyes again, going right down to the picture in his hand. "Actually, she was Theresa, but everyone called her Tessa. Your wife?"

He shrugged. "She doesn't have a birth certificate. She was placed in foster care when she was around four. She's not sure exactly what happened to her parents." He thought about her episode a few months ago. "Something to do with a hospital maybe."

Joe finally looked up. "When I got back, I know I should have gone straight to Gail, but I couldn't bear the thought of her looking at me in disgust."

Like the way Chrissy had looked at him.

"I couldn't walk and could barely lift my arms.

Gail would have given up her life to be with me. She deserved someone better than an invalid she'd have to take care of. I figured it was kinder for me to simply let her go. I didn't know she was pregnant and had my child."

"But you said you've been searching for Tessa for years?"

"It took more than five years and a lot of counseling and rehab, but I finally realized I needed to start living again. The first thing I did was call Gail. Her parents said I was too late. They'd kicked her out once they found out she was pregnant. They hadn't seen her since, though they'd received notification she died a year earlier. When I asked about the baby, they had no answer. Figured she might have gotten an abortion." His mouth tightened into a straight line, and he shook his head. "Gail would never have done that."

Joe glanced around the room, and he could see the man was trying to keep himself in control. *Show no emotion. Show no fear.* He knew the drill.

"I checked with the hospital where she'd died. It was a brain aneurysm probably from an untreated head wound. But it had been crazy in there that day due to a massive car pile up and overturned school bus. There was one nurse who vaguely remembered a small child sitting in the waiting room forever. But when I asked at the local child services, they couldn't find any information on her. I had no idea if the little girl was mine or if Gail had left our child with someone else. Or even if our child was a girl. I wasn't sure who I was looking for."

Joe stared at his hands. "What's she like?"

"She's a beautiful person, inside and out." He

pulled out his phone and scrolled through some pictures until he found one of Tessa reading to the kids. He handed it to Joe.

The man's eyes widened, and he sucked in a deep breath. "She looks just like Gail. So beautiful. Are these your children?" Joe seemed confused. He knew the darker coloring of the kids made many people take a second look.

"These are the children we're adopting. I brought them back from a decimated village in Kandahar."

More tears coursed down Joe's face. "And she's taking them in as her own. That's something Gail would have done. I was so stupid thinking she wouldn't want me and my useless legs. I missed out on so much."

Joe glanced at his hand, and Erik saw the wedding ring. "You're married now?"

"Yeah, for seventeen years. I knew I wouldn't get Gail back, but I never stopped searching for my child. I have two other children now. A boy and a girl. I wasn't sure that would ever happen."

But this guy managed. He would only have Matty and Kiki. It would have to be enough. He certainly loved them as much as he'd love a blood child of his own. No regrets, though. His family was Tessa and the kids.

"Does she want to meet me?" Joe's eyes held hope.

"I didn't tell her I found you. I actually didn't even tell her I was looking. I mentioned showing the picture around, but that was months ago. I don't think she expected anything to come of it. And when Ben told me he thought he recognized you, I didn't want to get her hopes up. For a number of reasons."

"It might not have been the right person," Joe filled in, then frowned. "Or I might not have been the type of person you'd want in your wife's life."

"Exactly. Tessa's had a lot of pain in her life. I won't subject her to any more."

Joe's face crumpled with guilt. "Pain?"

"Lots of foster homes. Not all of them great. She's emotionally...fragile. Since we got married and had the kids, she's been coming out of her shell more. I don't want to do anything to make her go back there. Do you understand?"

Joe nodded. "More than you know. I don't want to do anything to upset her. But if you decide to tell her about me, let her know I already love her more than I ever thought I could. I've missed her every day since I found out about her. And I'm so sorry I never got a chance to see her and be her dad. I'd like to try and make it up to her in some small way. But I understand if she can't forgive me for deserting her and her mom."

Joe was openly sobbing now. Moisture filled his eyes too. Damn. Hadn't he gotten that all out when he'd scared Tessa and the kids? This man had missed so much of Tessa's life and truly wanted to know her.

He cleared his throat. "I'll do my best to get her to arrange a meeting."

Joe dug in his breast pocket and pulled his own phone out. "Would you mind sending me that picture? My wife and kids know all about Tessa, and I know they'd want to see her. And all grandpas want pictures of their grandkids."

Any doubts he'd had before were washed away at Joe's words. The man was already accepting Matty and Kiki. So many others couldn't see beyond where they'd come from.

"What's your number? I'll send them."

After Joe rattled off his number, he sent a few pictures, some of only Tessa, some of the family and one of their wedding.

Joe's phone beeped, and he smiled as he scrolled through his new messages. The wedding one had him looking closer. "Marine, huh? Captain? Sheesh, I need to make sure to salute when you're around."

"I'm still on the disabled list. I'll get an honorable discharge after that."

Sitting up straight, Joe saluted. "You don't know what it means to me my baby girl married a military man. At least I won't have to worry about her."

He wasn't so sure, but he'd try his damnedest not to do anything stupid again. She and the kids meant too much to him. It would kill him if he lost them. It must be how Joe felt.

"I'll call you in a few days after I talk to Tessa. I'll do everything I can to convince her to see you. She needs to know she wasn't abandoned and her parents wanted her." He couldn't go on. The lump in his throat threatened to choke him, and the tears trailing down Joe's face only made it harder for him to gain his control back.

"Can I keep this?" Joe asked, touching Gail's face in the picture.

He nodded.

"Let her know how much I tried to find her, how much I wanted to be with her. That I loved her mom, and I love her. It's been killing me, knowing I failed her. Please, let her know…"

"I will." He patted Joe on the shoulder as the man

wiped at his face. If he didn't get out of here now, he'd have some tears to get rid of too. "I'll be in touch."

Reaching for his hand, Joe gripped it hard. "Thank you for finding me. And for loving my little girl enough to do this."

He took a deep breath and left Joe staring at the picture. After climbing into his car, he leaned his head on the wheel. A few things had come to light today. What happened to Tessa's mom and dad. Where her father was now. But the biggest revelation hadn't been from the past. Joe had said something that got him thinking. Had touched a subject he'd tried to keep hidden. He loved Tessa enough to find her father for her. But more than that...he loved Tessa.

Chapter Twenty-One

"Mama, I have a cookie?"

Tessa looked down at Matty, then up to the grinning face of Gladys as she held up two of her famous chocolate chip confections. She tried to glare at the older woman, but she'd been too wonderful to her since she'd moved here. Even more so since the Millers had passed away.

"How do you ask?"

"Please, Mama, I have a cookie. Kiki too? She can't talk."

Kiki was in fact babbling away in her arms. Lots of unintelligible sounds but "Mama" came up often enough. The word always warmed her heart.

"Yes, you may. Make sure to say thank you."

Gladys handed off the cookies and was dutifully thanked with words and a kiss.

"You haven't been in as much lately. Everything well? You getting your supplies okay?"

She looked around the small store. It was crowded for this time of year. Brianna was working the register, having finished her term at the community college.

"I'm sorry. We usually go to the big chain grocery store in Brunswick after our therapy sessions. It's easier without the kids." She wiped a crumb from Kiki's cheek to hide that her face was heating up. "I need to practice being in more crowded situations."

Gladys reached over the lunch counter and patted her hand. "No need to apologize to me, my dear. I think it's great you're finally finding your wings." She looked over at the register. "I might need to spread mine and help Brianna. Don't know why it's so busy here today."

She let Kiki down and kept hold of her hand as they walked around the store. Matty insisted he carry the plastic basket. Luckily, they were only getting a few things. They needed to meet Erik at The Boat House in a short while for a late lunch, and then they were planning to attempt some Christmas shopping. Nothing for the kids obviously, but she had a whole new family to shop for now. It still felt weird.

She hoped it wouldn't be too much for him. He'd left the house early this morning, saying he needed to meet with someone at the VA in Portland and was heading to work right after. It would irritate him she thought he couldn't handle the full day, but she worried about him. His pain level was getting better, but too often he would wince at times when he was bending or trying to do too much.

"We need more, Mama?" Matty held up the basket, pride evident on his face.

"Mama? That kid is yours?"

Turning, she saw a man possibly forty years older than her, staring at the kids. His face was hard, and his eyes held hatred.

"My husband and I are adopting them." Not that it was any of his business. What was his problem?

"Why the heck would you want to take in some murderous Muslim kids? Leave 'em where they were and let them rot in that hellhole they call a country."

She clenched her teeth and picked up Kiki, then put her hand behind Matty's back to guide him away. Her hand shook as they made their way through the aisle, trying to ignore the rumblings from behind her.

"We should blow up that whole stinking region of the world and kill them all. Then wipe out all the ones who managed to sneak into this country."

She whipped around, no longer able to listen to what this man wanted to do to her precious children.

"The whole region? There are innocent women and children there."

"No one over there is innocent," he spat out. "Not for long anyway. They train 'em young to be killers and keep having more that grow up to be killers. Might as well get them before they get us."

Rage like she'd never before felt pulsed through her. How dare he want to harm these lives that had come to mean so much to her. Or any like them.

"Stop! Just shut up. These are innocent children and have done nothing to hurt you. Just because they come from a place where horrible things are happening doesn't mean they're a part of it. They are victims. Their home was bombed, and their family killed, along with our own people."

Taking a deep breath, she continued, unable to keep her feelings in any longer. "If you think we should hurt them or desert them because of this, you're no better than the people you say you hate."

As she turned to walk away, thunderous applause split the air. Gladys and several other customers grinned as they clapped at her ridiculous outburst. Heat rushed across her cheeks and down into her neck. Damn, she hated being the center of attention, but there was no way she could let this scum talk about her loved ones this way.

The man turned red and scurried from the store. She felt like doing the same. Gladys came over to her and took the basket from Matty.

"Well said, my dear. That blow hard has been spouting nonsense like that since the days of Korea and Vietnam. Time someone took him on."

Gladys put her items in a bag and handed them back to her. "This is on the house today. Go and have fun with your family." She gave her a hug and whispered, "I'm proud of you."

She wasn't proud of her outburst but would do it again in a heartbeat if it meant defending her children. Or Erik. She loved them too much to allow anyone to badmouth them or wish them ill.

As she got the children in the car, she thought back on that. She truly loved this new family. And that included Erik.

****

"The old ball and chain is here," Sid teased as Erik sliced up some mushrooms for the gravy he was making.

"Thanks, Sid. I thought we'd do a late lunch here before we head out Christmas shopping. Can you find her a table that isn't out in the middle of the room? You know Tessa likes it a bit quieter."

"Already done, my friend. She worked for me for quite a few years too. I told her you'd be out soon."

After throwing the mushrooms in a pan with some butter, he finished garnishing a few other dishes. He put them on the warmer, then rang for the waitress.

"The wife and kids are dragging you shopping,

huh?" Darrell, one of the prep cooks, glanced through the window into the dining area. "That sounds fun. Where are they?"

He wasn't thrilled about the shopping trip either, especially since he needed to tell her about finding her dad. Excitement and anxiety warred with each other.

"By the window with the high chair and booster seat."

Tessa slipped off her jacket and bent over to settle Kiki in the high chair. Damn, her ass looked fine in the slim fitting jeans she wore. Straightening, she turned to get Matty a crayon for the children's menu. The snug pink Henley molded her figure, making him forget what he was supposed to be doing.

"Damn, she's hot. And she hooked up with a jarhead like you?"

"Shut up and get back to work. And keep your eyes in your head. She's married, and this jarhead can take you down, even with the cane."

Darrell snickered but went back to work. Erik pushed the mushrooms around the pan, then let them simmer and peeked out at her again. The outfit must be one she'd gotten with Sara at Thanksgiving. All the clothes she'd come back with showed off her assets. Not that he minded. Well, now that she was out in public, actually he did. No one should be getting any ideas about his wife. She was *his* wife.

He poured some stock into the pan with the mushrooms and adjusted the heat.

"Darrell, keep an eye on this for a minute, huh?"

The young man hopped right over and grinned. "You got it, boss." The kid was always looking to have more responsibility in the kitchen. Now was his chance.

He entered the dining room and slipped up behind Tessa. She'd written their phone number down on the children's menu and repeated it with Matty. They'd been trying to teach it to him for a few weeks. The young guys sitting at the next table were paying far too much attention to it for his liking. Maybe he needed to have her wear her old, baggy clothes again.

Or…he wrapped his arms around her and kissed her neck.

"Hey, gorgeous." He glanced at the guys who frowned. *Yeah, she's taken. Hands and eyes off.*

Tessa stiffened and stood. Her smile was forced. His attention was back on her.

"What's the matter? You're awfully tense."

She looked at the children and sighed. "It's nothing you need to worry about. Just some guy was a jerk at Willie's. Made me mad."

Pulling her closer, he rubbed her back. When she looked around, he knew she was aware of people staring at them.

"The place isn't crowded. Don't worry about that. Tell me what happened."

As he sat at their table, she gave a quick explanation of the jerk mouthing off about the kids. He wanted to find him and punch his lights out, but that was hardly an option. Getting Tessa in a better frame of mind was foremost in his thoughts.

"Glad to see you're getting a little spunk in you."

Her jaw clenched and brows drew together. "I won't let anyone hurt the people I love."

Love. She loved the children. Of that he had no doubt. But did she love him too? She'd never said it, but then that hadn't been a stipulation of their marriage.

He stood. "I need to go finish a few dishes, but I'll be out in a minute. Did you order yet?"

She shook her head.

"Then let me take care of it. I know what the kids like, and I'll make something special for you."

She was about to object, so he shook his head and walked away. Knowing her, she was most likely rolling her eyes at him this minute.

As he finished up the orders and threw together the plates for his family, he realized he did know her really well. And he liked what he knew.

Carrying the pasta and veggies out for the kids, he put the platter with the chicken and creamy lemon sauce between them.

Her eyes grew big. "Is this that lemon stuff you made a few weeks ago? God, that was out of this world."

He shrugged and tried to hide his smirk. "Told you I knew what you'd like."

They settled down to eat, and after a while he reached out and patted her hand. "What do you usually do when you need to calm down? You seem so in control when you're with the kids."

She gazed out the window. "I used to paint and draw. That always helped me relax. But when the kids are napping or go to bed, I have to do my billing work, so I haven't had much of a chance lately."

Damn, he hated the thought she'd given up something she loved to take care of the kids. Could he do something for her? First, he had to tell her about her father. Not with the kids in a crowded restaurant, though. It was starting to get busier.

"We'll make sure to find some time. We should go

before more people come in and they drag me back into the kitchen."

They took their last bites and cleaned up the kids. As she slipped their coats on, he excused himself to go get his from the kitchen.

Tonio, tonight's chef, was peering through the window into the dining room.

"That's your woman?"

He grinned, shrugging off his white coat and into his winter one.

"Seriously? You are one lucky man."

He looked back to where she stood with the kids. The guys were gawking at her again, trying to chat her up. After smiling politely at them, she moved toward the door and turned in the direction of the kitchen. Searching for him? He moved to the doorway, and their eyes met. Hers twinkled and gleamed.

"Lucky, lucky man," Tonio repeated.

"You don't have to tell me. I know it."

****

"Tess, you got a minute?"

Tessa looked up from the computer screen. Erik stood in the bedroom doorway, his face serious but handsome as ever. The cargo pants he always wore emphasized his muscular thighs and the T-shirt his solid arms and chest. And here she sat in her pajama pants and his college sweatshirt. The one that never could stay on her shoulders.

Right now his expression wasn't playful, though. What did he want?

"Sure, I do need to finish up this billing, though."

"There's something we need to talk about. It won't take long." He limped over to the window seat, leaning heavily on his cane. They'd done lots of walking in the mall, and Kiki had wanted to be carried instead of sitting in the carriage.

Following him, she tried to assess his mood. After glancing down at his clenched hands, he rubbed them up and down his thighs. Nervous? Anxiety clawed at her insides as she sat next to him. Miss Abernathy had called recently, letting them know the adoption was moving forward. The last checks on whether the children had other living relatives was almost complete. Would Erik want to split up once he had the kids free and clear? Had his being able to perform changed his mind about being married to her?

Yes, she was active in their sex life too, but he didn't love her. Maybe he wanted a marriage like the one his parents had. He always talked about how much they loved each other and would do anything for each other. His envy was apparent. Had he realized he now had everything to offer a woman? One that he loved. Could she live next door to him and a new wife and the kids she'd grown to love as any mother did? God, that would be torture.

She took a deep breath as he picked up her hands and rubbed his thumbs over them. Trying to lessen the blow?

"You know how I made an enlargement of your locket photo."

Her locket? What did that have to do with divorcing her? She nodded.

"I kept showing it to all the guys at the VA and the support group. I finally got a nibble."

"A nibble?" He was talking about the picture in her locket, not splitting up. "You mean the man in the picture?" She held her breath, not daring to say anything else.

"His name is Joe Kraznof. He was with the 1057th Transportation Division sent to Iraq for Desert Storm."

Around the time she was born. "Did he make it back?" She was afraid of the answer.

"I met with him this morning at the VA in Portland where he volunteers."

Her heart stopped, and she couldn't breathe. He sat staring at her, waiting for her reaction, or was there bad news? The man wasn't her father. He didn't want anything to do with her. He hated kids. Something even worse.

"Why didn't you tell me why you were going?"

Squeezing her hands, he leaned closer. "I didn't want to get your hopes up. It might not have been him...or been the type of person I wanted in your life."

"*You* wanted...why is it your decision who I have in my life?" Her voice had risen an octave, almost like when she'd told off the guy at Gladys'.

"I'm sorry, Tess, it's just you've had so much heartache in your life, I didn't want you to have any more."

"So what did you find out?" And what did she want the answer to be? There had been so many scenarios she'd pictured during her life, she wasn't sure which one would be the best.

"Your mother's name was Gail. They were a couple when he shipped out. When she discovered she was pregnant, her parents kicked her out of the house."

She had grandparents. And they hadn't wanted her either. Her stomach rolled and twisted, threatening to send her dinner back up.

"Your father was injured over there, paralyzed."

"So he is my father," she confirmed.

Erik smiled. "Yes, but when he came back, he didn't want your mother being chained to an invalid, so he never contacted her. He didn't know about you until later."

He didn't know. Did that make it any better than not wanting her?

"When did he find out?"

"It took him five years to get his head together enough to stop feeling sorry for himself." He glanced down at his leg and frowned. It still bothered him he couldn't run and play with the kids.

"When he finally called, he found out what had happened. But also that she'd died of a brain aneurysm. It must have been when she left you in the waiting room. There was some large accident, and the place was mobbed."

Her mother was dead. Pain slashed through her heart. It had always been a possibility but to have it confirmed. Why was it affecting her now? She hadn't had a mother in years. Lifting her wrist to her nose, she inhaled the rose scent she liked to wear. Her mother's scent.

"Your mom loved you, Tess. She didn't desert you."

Tears filled her eyes, and Erik became blurry. Her mother had loved her. She had been loved. For far too short a time.

Pulling her to his chest, he rubbed her back. The warmth brought more tears that spilled over and down her cheeks.

"Your dad wanted you to know he started

searching for you as soon as he found out. And that he loved you, even then."

A father. Who loved her. Had loved her for years. How to handle this? Could she even believe it? She'd never had anyone love her. Too many years of being told she was unlovable had closed her heart to that kind of emotion. Except now she loved Matty and Kiki, and they loved her back.

And she loved Erik. Being held in his arms like this had her hoping maybe he could love her too. But he'd known her for too long. Seen her as her total freak self. Some things you couldn't un-know.

"He wants to meet you, Tess. But said he'd understand if you couldn't forgive him for deserting you and your mom. I don't think that's what he did, but he's got some major guilt eating away at him. I'm sure he wouldn't want you to know, but he was crying when he realized he'd finally found where you were and that you were alive and well. You're named after his mother, by the way."

"He cried? Over me?" Someone had cried over her. No one had ever done that.

The sobs shaking her body couldn't be stopped. How many times had she envisioned meeting her parents and having them be hysterically happy to find her? Too many and she'd convinced herself she was delusional even thinking it. But her father wanted to meet her.

"Yeah, he never stopped looking. But he didn't know who he was looking for. Or even if you were still alive. He never lost hope that he'd find you, though. I showed him a picture of you. He said you look just like your mother."

"He wants to meet me." Her chest constricted at the thought. She looked up at his handsome face, so concerned for her. "What if he doesn't like me?" she sobbed. "What if he sees that I'm a freak? I don't know if I can do this, Erik." Too many rejections in the past had colored her thinking.

"You're not a freak, and you know it." He'd put on his fierce marine face. "And he already loves you, Tessa. When he sees how sweet and perfect you are, he'll love you even more. You have that effect on people."

Not on you, though. Swirling thoughts ran through her mind. Her dad, Erik, the kids. Too many and too intense. *Okay, focus on one thing at a time.* Her dad.

"I have a dad. And he loves me." Or said he did. She still wasn't sure she believed it.

She hadn't meant to say that out loud. Erik slipped his fingers through her hair and kissed her cheeks. "You do, sweetie. You do."

As he held her, he whispered soothing words and sounds. Like he did when Kiki or Matty got hurt. After a while he eased back and wiped her face with some tissues. She grabbed them and blew her nose.

"I'm sorry I'm such a mess. Maybe you should have texted me the information and let me do this crying stuff by myself."

Lifting her chin with his finger, he kissed her forehead. "I'd never leave you alone to go through something like this. I'm here if you need me."

He was here for her. That was so far removed from her original thought he wanted a divorce. It seemed like hours ago she'd thought he wanted to discuss that. After wiping her face, she stuffed the tissues behind her.

"It would have been easier for you if you did."

He grinned. "I'm a marine, sweetie. We don't choose easy."

She thought of how screwed up she was, even more since hearing about her father. "You came to the right place, then. Or the right person. I'm definitely not easy."

He gave her a light kiss and ran his hand down her face. "I like the challenge."

When he kissed her again, she clung to his strong shoulders, never wanting to let go.

"Your dad's been waiting all day to hear what your decision is. He's probably going crazy thinking you don't want to meet him."

She stared at the man who had given her so much in so short a time. Who had just given her even more.

"I do want to meet him. I'm just..." The blasted tears started again.

"Scared, I know. But I'll be right there with you if you want. You don't have to do this by yourself."

"You'll come with me? Stay right near me?"

"I'll hold your hand the whole time if you need me to."

She launched herself into his arms and squeezed tight. "Thank you. Yes, I do need you to be with me."

He returned the hug. "I should text him and let him know, and then we can figure out when."

She took a deep breath and eased away from him when she really wanted to stay in his arms, forever. He pulled his phone from his pocket and tapped away.

"When do you want to do this?"

"Tonight. A year from now. I don't know." God, she was so confused. She had a father who supposedly loved her and had been searching for her. It couldn't be soon enough to see him. But the thought scared the crap out of her, and she wanted to put it off. In case it wasn't true. Could she handle that disappointment?

"I'll see when he's free. From his reaction, I'd guess he'd jump in the car and come over tonight too."

Her head whipped up. "I'm in my pajamas."

He laughed. "We won't make it tonight."

"When you're not working." She leaned against him, hugging his arm, needing his warmth.

He finished and pressed send. She froze, her gaze fixated on the phone. Erik nibbling on her earlobe broke the trance. His lips moved to her neck, and somehow her shirt fell off her shoulder. Like it always did when he was around. She leaned back against his solid chest, loving the sensation of his hands moving on her skin.

His phone vibrated, and she jumped up, her heart racing.

His finger swished across the screen. "He's relieved and anxious. He says he'll make it any time we can."

He looked up in thought. "I have Thursday off. How about after dropping Matty at preschool? Then we only need a sitter for Kiki."

Did she need Kiki for protection?

He frowned at her. "I'll be there to keep you safe, sweetie. You don't need to be distracted by our daughter."

She nodded, afraid to say anything. In minutes, the time was set and panic had set in. How did you greet a father you'd never known? Regardless of what her dad and Erik said, she still wondered if he'd like her.

"I don't think I'm going to be able to sleep

tonight."

Erik stood and guided her to their bed. Pulling her next to him, he continued his lips' earlier journey across her shoulder and neck. "That's okay. I can think of some other activities to do instead of sleeping."

As he pulled off her top, she protested weakly. "I have work to do."

"Tomorrow," he mumbled, his tongue tormenting her nipple.

She reached for the edge of his shirt and tugged. When his skin touched hers, the anxiety she'd been feeling eased into the background. Yeah, she'd worry about it tomorrow.

Chapter Twenty-Two

"Are you ready, Tess?"

Tessa walked into the family room where Molly sat on the floor playing with Kiki. She looked down at her skirt with the black leather boots underneath. A purchase Sara had talked her into. As she brushed off some imaginary dust on her blouse, she sighed. Erik stood waiting for her.

"Maybe I should change. This is too fancy. But jeans are too casual." Clamping her lips together, she shook her head in frustration. "Do I look ridiculous?"

He shuffled closer and ran his fingers down her cheek. God, she loved it when he did that.

"You look beautiful, like you always do." Leaning in, he kissed her. It took her mind off her outfit and what they were about to do...for about three seconds.

"Maybe we should postpone this."

Erik touched his forehead to hers, sliding his fingers into her hair. "It doesn't matter what you're wearing, sweetie. Your dad wants to see *you*. He's waited a long time for this."

Molly stood and scooped Kiki off the floor. "I came up here to watch my granddaughter so you could go without worrying. Like Erik said, you look lovely." Molly's eyes brightened as she gazed between Tessa and her son, pride evident at his caring behavior. He'd learned a lot from his parents, and boy, was she grateful.

"Now go and don't worry about anything. I'm in no hurry to get back home. Storm Electric has a big rush job over the next few days, so your father and his brothers won't be around much. Leaves me free to do what I want. Like visiting my grandchildren."

Erik released her and kissed his mother's cheek, then Kiki's. "Thanks, Mom. Matty has a play date after preschool, and that mom will bring him home later. The keys to the minivan are hanging in the kitchen. You've got my cell if you have any problems."

Molly gave him that *mother* look. "I raised four children, three of them boys. I think I can handle one little girl for a few hours. I'll see you later."

She allowed Erik to help her into her winter jacket, the one he'd insisted she buy when he learned she didn't have a good one. Why would she, she'd barely ever left the house before he came along. After hustling her out and into her sedan, they got on the road. He didn't say much but occasionally patted her hand and squeezed it tight. That was one of the great things about her husband. Small talk and chatter weren't needed. He was happy sitting quietly with his thoughts. And allowing her to be alone with hers. Right now, that may not have been a good thing.

As if reading her mind, he turned the radio on, and Christmas tunes floated in the air. The holiday was a week from tomorrow. She listened and looked through the window at the snow on the sides of the road. They'd only gotten a few inches, but Erik had said it made it seem more like Christmas. She wouldn't know. Christmas had never been a huge deal for her. There might have been a small present or two, but she'd never felt the whole spirit of the season like she'd heard so many people talk about. Call her the Grinch.

Until this year, anyway. They'd actually gone out and cut down a tree. Erik had grunted something about proving his worth as a man, then laughed like it was a joke. But she had a feeling underneath it he'd needed to do it to show he wasn't totally useless. And he'd been great. She had to admit she'd enjoyed watching the muscles in his arms and back flex when he hacked away at the base of the evergreen tree. They'd used a little wagon to get it back to the van.

When they'd returned to the house, he'd insisted on hot chocolate while he pulled the box of decorations his grandparents had left down from the attic. She'd watched him like a hawk, worried his leg would give out and he'd plummet to the floor with the box on top of him. But when he'd managed to get the box into the living room, he'd looked triumphant. She'd smiled and mumbled something to the kids about their daddy being such a strong he-man, though she'd made sure to say it loud enough for him to hear. Her reward had been a big kiss.

As they'd decorated the tree, carols floating around them, she'd begun to know what the fuss was about. Christmas spirit wasn't having tons of presents or going to lots of parties. It was having the people you loved around you. This year, for the first time, she'd had that. With Erik and the kids. She'd had a family.

And when the tree was completed, they'd all crawled into the big lounge chair. All four of them draped on top of each other, admiring their hard work, lights twinkling in the dim room. The kids had fallen asleep, and she and Erik hadn't wanted to wake them, so they'd stayed snuggled together for almost two hours, enjoying the feeling of the holiday. It wasn't like anything she'd ever experienced. Like *The Grinch Who Stole Christmas,* her heart had grown three sizes that day.

Now she glanced at her husband's rugged profile as his deep baritone sang along with "I'll Be Home for Christmas." Anytime she was with him and the kids, she felt like she was already home. And she was adding another family member into the mix. She loosened her jacket, not sure if she was sweating from fear or the heat in the car. The fact her palms were also sweaty may have given her a clue.

The last line of the song played out. *If only in my dreams.* So many times in the past, she'd had this family dream, and in so many ways, her mind swirled in confusion.

Reaching out, he squeezed her hand once more. She looked up and was shocked they'd arrived. Dr. Sullivan had suggested they use his office. It gave them some privacy, but he also said he'd be available if she needed to talk afterward.

Her stomach flipped a few times, and she held her hand against it. "I think I might be coming down with something."

"You can do this, sweetie," he encouraged as he opened her car door, guiding her out and into the building. They walked down the hall, and she froze as they approached Dr. Sullivan's door. Erik pulled her into his arms.

She gazed up at him, silently begging him to stay with her. He would, and she knew it, but trust hadn't always come easy. He'd earned it, though. Taking a deep breath, she stepped through the doorway.

Dr. Sullivan sat in one of the chairs, chatting with a man in a wheelchair. He was twice her age, slim with dark hair that was graying in some spots. Her father. Her dad. What was she supposed to call him?

Erik's arm surrounded her, propelling her farther into the room. Dr. Sullivan stood, shook the man's hand, and approached her.

"I'll be down the hallway if you need anything." With that he left and closed the door behind him. This was it.

Moving closer, Erik shook the man's hand also.

"Good to see you, Joe. Thanks for coming to Brunswick."

"No problem. I actually live in Freeport, so it's not far."

The man's gaze never left her face, and heat rushed through her. The room tilted a bit, and she clung to Erik's arm. He looked at her anxiously and held tighter.

"Tessa, this is Joe Kraznof. Joe, my wife."

Eyes, the same color as the ones that greeted her every morning in the mirror, pleaded for her acceptance. His hands wrung together in his lap. He was as nervous as she was. Really?

"Hi, Tessa. You have no idea how much I've wanted to meet you."

Erik tugged the jacket off her shoulders and urged her to the couch. She threw a nervous glare at him, but he only placed both their coats on the chair, then joined her. Leaning toward him, she felt his strength and safety.

"I think I have some idea."

Joe smiled, and again she was reminded of her

mirror. This man really was her father. And he actually wanted to be here with her.

"You look so much like your mother it's uncanny."

Those had been her thoughts about him. But what to say to this man who was her father? All the conversations she'd envisioned had suddenly dried up and blown away.

"Tell us about Gail." Trust Erik to come to her rescue. He may not need small talk, but he knew how to get a conversation started. Oh, to have that ability.

Joe's face lit up, and he reached behind him for a small item. A book or binder or something.

"Gail and I grew up together in Augusta. I think I fell in love with her in the fifth grade. She baked me chocolate chip cookies, and that was it. No one else could compare."

Rolling a bit closer, he held out the book. It looked like a picture album. Did he actually have pictures of her mother? Erik reached out, took it, then settled it in her lap. She didn't dare open it yet.

"I put this together a few years ago. My wife, Nancy, helped me."

She looked up sharply. "You're married?"

Joe nodded, a blush crossing his face. "It was a lot of years after I learned Gail had died. But Nancy helped me move past my bitterness at being paralyzed and at losing Gail. And you."

She stroked her hand over the cover of the album. Erik's arm pulled out of her grip and wrapped around her shoulder. His other hand played with the cover.

"Open it, sweetie."

She did. The pages were filled with pictures of a young girl and boy always smiling into the camera. The same face was smiling at her anxiously now.

"What was she like?" Suddenly she needed to know. Her whole life she'd gone without knowing anything about the woman who'd given birth to her, and she'd been fine. Okay, maybe not fine. A bit of a freak and completely weird about touching. But she hadn't died from the lack of knowledge. Somewhere in the back of her mind, she'd remembered her mom and that she'd been loved. Too bad she couldn't always keep that feeling with her.

"Your mom was the sweetest, kindest person I've ever known. She'd do anything for anyone and never want anything in return. So giving, so loving, such a nurturer. She would have loved you to pieces. You don't remember anything about her, though?"

She flipped through a few more pages, and the face of the girl in the picture aged. Became vaguely familiar.

"Just images, some feelings. I never knew if they were real or something I'd made up to pretend someone loved me."

Her voice cracked. Damn. *Keep it together. Don't fall apart in front of this man, her father.* He'd run away and want nothing to do with her. Like she'd always believed. Only this time she'd know it was true. There would be no lying to herself anymore.

As she kept her gaze on the photos, a hand covered hers. It wasn't Erik's. Joe had rolled closer.

"I always loved you, sweetheart." His voice was as wobbly as hers. Tears filled his eyes as his thumb stroked her skin. "Even when I didn't know who you were or where you were, I loved you."

He took a deep breath. "You were part of Gail and part of me. You were proof our love was real and strong. So I had no choice but to love you. Every day since I found out about you, I loved you."

The room blurred as tears poured down her cheeks. "I think I loved you too. Even though I didn't know if you deserted me or what had happened. I remembered how I felt every time I looked at the picture of you and my mom. I wanted your love so badly I pretended I had it."

"You did, sweetheart, you did. From the moment I knew about you, I loved you. Don't ever doubt that. I'm sorry it took me so long to finally tell you. So sorry."

He was sobbing now too. Like Erik had said he'd done at their previous meeting. She looked at her husband, whose arm still rested along her shoulders. Moisture glimmered in his eyes too. Her big, tough marine had a heart. Lifting her lips to him, she kissed his jaw.

"Thank you for bringing me here. For helping me find love." And not just for her dad but her love for Erik too. He didn't answer, just returned her kiss.

"Would you tell me about these pictures? Please?"

Joe nodded, and Erik handed them a box of tissues. Once cleaned up, Joe moved the chair closer and tilted his chin at the spot next to her on the couch.

"Can I sit there?"

Could he? She shrugged, wondering if she was supposed to help him. Erik started to get up, but Joe waved him away and easily propelled himself from the chair onto the couch. His arms were as muscled as Erik's. She hadn't noticed before.

"I do this all the time. Been doing it for over twenty years."

She put the album between their laps as Joe turned

the pages. Erik had eased back but still rested his hand on her shoulder. When she leaned toward Joe, he looked up sharply, inhaling deeply. "Roses? You smell like roses."

"She's smelled that way ever since I've known her. Ten years." Erik's voice was proprietary. It was cute.

"Gail always smelled like roses too. This exact scent. How——?"

She thought back to when she'd begun using this cream.

"When I was about six maybe, I found this cream at the foster home I was at. The smell of it was so overwhelming and emotional I actually stole the jar. I hid it and never used it. But I would open it every day and smell it. It was about the only thing that ever helped me get through the tough times. I never knew why. When I got old enough and was able to earn some money, I found a place that had some, and I bought more. That's when I started to wear it. I didn't use much. Only enough so the scent was with me if I needed it."

She lifted her hand and inhaled, then brought it up to Joe's face. He held her hand and kissed her knuckles. More tears fell, and neither bothered to even try and hide them.

"I miss your mom so much. I hate I wasn't there for her when she needed me the most."

She looked down at his motionless legs and kissed his cheek. "I know she'd understand. But it seems like you needed her too."

"I should have…I was so stupid." Joe folded, and she wrapped her arms around him and held him. Where the heck were all these tears coming from? So many years of holding back and pretending she didn't care, maybe.

"You were trying to protect her."

"I was in no shape to be with anyone. I was angry at the world and took it out on anybody who was near. I hated the thought of hurting her like that. I hope you can understand."

She glanced at Erik, whose face was like granite. Yes, she knew all about how angry someone could get when their body didn't work the way it always had. How they could take it out on others, even others they loved or cared for.

"I do understand. Completely."

She held Joe with her right hand but inched her left over to find Erik's that had dropped from her shoulder. Squeezing it, she smiled at him. He returned the pressure.

More tissues were passed around, then Joe got down to telling her about the pictures in the book. Erik seemed more relaxed the more they talked. When she turned to the last page, a sheet of paper fell out. When she reached down to get it, Joe sighed.

"I'd almost forgotten that was there."

Opening it, she saw it was a sketch of a young child, maybe three or four years old. The child looked familiar.

"Who is this?"

"That's you, Tessa." Joe's expression grew melancholy. "When I found out about Gail, I went to the hospital where she died, asking if there was a child with her. After a little searching, one nurse remembered a little girl sitting in the waiting room for a long time. With the huge accident that day, no one paid all that much attention to her. To you. Not for a while, I'm guessing."

That feeling of dread, of not being able to breathe, reappeared. Erik stroked his hand down her back and whispered, "It's okay, Tess. You're going to be okay."

Joe's eyes were wide and apprehensive. She hadn't meant to scare him. "Yes, it was a while."

Her father pointed to the sketch again. "I drew this from a description the nurse gave me. It was all I had, and I didn't even know if this child was mine. But I kept it all these years, hoping I'd find you some day."

"You drew this?" It was good. Very good.

"Guess that's where you get your artistic talent from," Erik said. "Tessa's an incredible artist too."

Joe looked curiously at her, but she shrugged it off.

"I used to look at it all the time. My daughter, Madison, found me staring at it one time and thought it was of her. There are definite similarities."

"You have a daughter?" Another daughter, she should have said.

"Yes, and a son. Madison is fourteen, and Brady is sixteen. They really want to meet you."

She had a brother and sister. They wanted to meet her. Her head swam, and her breathing picked up.

"They know about me? About my mom?"

"Yes. I never hid my relationship with Gail from Nancy. She actually helped me look, but I didn't have a name or date of birth, and the social services agency in Portland had no paperwork for you that they could find."

"My foster families were always around here, near the Bay. I have no idea where I lived with my mom."

"The agency in Portland did say they were

swamped and you may have been sent to another agency. Maine isn't that big, but it's big enough when you're trying to find someone with very little information."

What would life have been like if he'd found her? If she'd been raised with his other children. In a loving family. And now that family wanted to meet her.

The fact she had a father who'd tried to find her and loved her was still so new. Her muscles sagged, and she felt like she'd been doing hard labor all day. Totally wiped out, physically and mentally. Could she survive meeting a brother and sister?

Chapter Twenty-Three

"Santa came. Daddy, Mama, Santa came."

Erik opened one eye and turned toward the voice. Matty's curl-covered head rested on the bed next to him. It was too early for this. Glancing at his watch, he noted it was a little after six. But if they were going to open gifts and get down to New Hampshire, they should probably get started.

"How do you know he came already?" Could he buy himself a few more seconds of Tessa's warmth by playing devil's advocate?

"There's stuff under the tree," Matty whispered like it was a secret. Were he and his siblings ever so adorable on Christmas morning? For some reason, he figured they were more obnoxious than anything.

Tessa stirred, her head nestling on his chest, her hand moving to play with his dog tags. He loved when she did this. Though this morning, he couldn't really enjoy it.

"Wake up, my sleeping beauty. We've got some very anxious little elves waiting to get Christmas started."

She pulled herself up and groaned, holding her stomach.

"You okay?" Her skin was paler than usual. Hopefully she wasn't getting sick.

Gently, she shook her head. "I think my stomach is

in knots from everything that's been going on. I'll be fine."

He sat up and kissed her again. "I'll change Kiki's diaper, then get the kids moving toward the living room. That'll give you a few extra minutes."

Her beautiful eyes held gratitude. "Thank you."

He took the cane Matty held out for him, then shuffled his son along. "Let's change your sister's diaper first, then we can check if Santa left anything under the tree."

"He did," Matty whispered again. Damn, he loved this child so much. When he entered Kiki's room, she was playing with her fairy doll. The smile reinforced how glad he was to have taken them in. He'd given them a place to live, but they were the ones who made it a home. The children…and Tessa.

"Daddy, the tree." Matty shifted from foot to foot.

"I need to change Kiki. You don't want to sit next to her in a diaper that's soaking wet, do you?"

Holding his nose, Matty shook his head. He laughed and pointed to the door. "Why don't you use the bathroom too, and I'll have Kiki ready by the time you get back."

Matty skipped from the room, and he got the little girl changed in no time. Lots of practice made him good at this.

"I ready, Daddy." Matty's enthusiastic voice was contagious. No lack of Christmas spirit here.

Tessa met them in the hallway, looking slightly less peaked. She reached for Kiki, and he handed the child over. Often she used the children to make her feel better. No denying their therapeutic value.

"Look, Daddy, I told you. Under the tree."

"They look like presents. I wonder how they got here?"

Matty looked at him strangely. "You said Santa."

"I guess he came, then. Lucky for us."

They settled around the tree, and he handed both children a wrapped box. Tessa helped Kiki open hers, but Matty needed no assistance and tore into his with gusto. They allowed the children to play with the toys for a while, then gave them another present. They'd decided they didn't want to start a tradition of spoiling the children on Christmas. A few nice gifts were all they needed. It wasn't like they were used to getting even this many.

As the third and last gift was opened by the kids, Tessa leaned behind the tree and pulled out a long, thin gift. It looked like a golf club. Did she think he'd be able to golf with his crippled leg?

"I know it's not really what you want, but I thought it might make using it a little more tolerable."

He pulled at the wrapping and smiled when he saw it was a cane. But not any cane. It was red with blue and had the US Marine Corps insignia on one side and the words *Semper Fi* on the other. The black handle was sturdy and comfortable in his grip.

"This is great. Thank you so much." Scooting over, he pulled her into his arms. Her lips met his, and he wished they were back in bed again. Without the kids. But he had a present for her too.

"Matty, hand me that red package, please, pal."

Matty stopped playing with his blocks long enough to get the gift and hand it to him. Tessa smiled shyly, and he hoped she'd continue smiling when she opened it.

"It's not super expensive, but I hope it means something to you."

"It's from you, Erik. That means everything to me."

She carefully pulled off the wrapping paper and opened the box. Cautiously, she lifted the tissue paper and froze, her eyes filling with tears. She touched the content like it was fragile, then stared at him.

"It's my birth certificate. How did you find it?"

He took out the piece of parchment and read the name. "Theresa Gail Kraznof. Once I knew the names of your parents and added in the approximate date of your birth, I was able to find it. Your real birthday is first of March, though, not March tenth like it says in your locket. You must have been ten days old when your mom took the picture."

She touched the names of her parents. "Gail Marie White. Joseph Anthony Kraznof. My parents. Here in black and white, all official and everything." Watery eyes stared at him. "I have a mother and a father and a real name that wasn't given to me by some social worker. I'm somebody. I'm real."

He leaned his forehead against hers. "You've always been somebody real for me, whether you're Tessa Porter, Tessa Storm, or Theresa Gail Kraznof. I'm kind of partial to the Mrs. Erik Storm moniker, though. Lets me know you're mine."

She licked her lips, and a huge smile broke out on her face. "You make me so happy, you know that, Erik Storm?"

"Kind of been my mission from the start. For me and you."

"I thought it was to have someone help you with

the kids." Her lips quirked in amusement.

"Anyone can take care of kids. The happiness part comes from you."

She leaned forward and kissed him. The kids chattered on in the background, happily playing with their new toys. This was what family was. What Christmas should be about. He'd been pissing around so much about how he'd never be able to be like his dad, have what his dad had, and yet he had it. It had snuck up on him at some point and had only hit him in the head at this moment.

He loved his wife. His kids. There wasn't anything more he could have asked for. Maybe a leg that worked, but Joe Kraznof seemed to do the family thing quite well, and he didn't have the use of either leg. What did he have to complain about?

"Tessa." The words *I love you* were on the tip of his tongue, but they wouldn't come out for some reason. He did love her, but did she love him back? No doubt she cared for him, but would he be adding more stress to her life if he said it and she didn't love him? This past week alone had brought so much turmoil, he couldn't bear the thought of giving her more.

She looked at him expectantly, so he kissed her again. Softly, sweetly, gently, trying to show her his love even if he didn't say the words.

"You make me incredibly happy too. I'm so lucky you're in my life. I'm not sure what I'd do without you."

"I'm hungry," Matty piped in. "We eating today?"

"You'd be feeding these kids on your own, that's what you'd be doing."

They both chuckled and dragged themselves to

their feet. His new cane was the perfect height for him, and he felt his steps lighter because of it. And because of the perfect woman who had given it to him.

Chapter Twenty-Four

"Tessa, it's going to be fine."

Tessa looked over at Erik as he drove through the streets toward her father's house. Her nerves were in shambles, and she'd been trying to hide just how much. He still knew. Although not that she'd actually thrown up this morning. Her stomach had been in knots ever since he'd told her about finding her dad. It had been ten days since she'd met him, and they'd spoken on the phone every day. It was getting easier to talk to him, but now he wanted her to meet his wife and kids. Her brother and sister. Well, half-brother and half-sister. He hadn't called them that, though.

Holding her hand against her stomach, she wished she could order it to behave. She'd tried. It didn't listen. She'd barely touched the great meal at Alex's on Christmas.

"He said they were eager to meet you. You have nothing to worry about."

He patted her hand, but all her old insecurities came flooding back.

"I shouldn't have worn this outfit. I look stupid. His wife will think…I don't know what she'll think. But it won't be good."

"You look absolutely gorgeous."

She glanced down at the black wool skirt that fluttered around her thighs and the cropped, burgundy sweater topping it. Dark sweater tights and knee-high boots were added for warmth. The short gray peacoat he'd gotten her complemented the outfit. But she felt like a fraud. This was something Sara would wear...or Alex's friend, Gina. Well, maybe too tame for Gina unless it was in brighter colors. It wasn't her, though.

"The guys at the gas station didn't think you looked stupid," he growled, his eyes leaving the road only long enough to glare at her. "Their tongues were almost hitting the ground."

While Erik had filled the tank, she'd run into the gas station convenience store to get some gum to settle her stomach. Two young guys had made some comments to her.

Her face heated. "They were making fun of me." Like everyone always had.

He shot her a look. "Take my word for it, they weren't. If they'd ogled you any more, I would have had to smack them around a bit."

Peeking into the back seat, she made sure Matty and Kiki were okay. Well, that was an excuse, but it gave her something to do. Besides think about what her siblings or her dad's wife would think of her. Would the wife feel threatened his old flame's child was back in the picture? Would the kids resent her for taking his attention away from them?

What would she do if a child of Erik's from some old girlfriend showed up? Oh, yeah, she'd feel threatened. Especially if the old girlfriend showed up too.

"Number fifteen, blue house, gray shutters."

She looked out the window and trembled. They were here? Already? How was it her father had lived less than thirty minutes from her, and she hadn't known? Life was so unfair.

As Erik got Matty out of his car seat, she didn't move. She should get going. Get Kiki out too. But her hands shook. How the heck could they unbuckle a car seat?

Her car door opened, and Kiki was thrust into her lap as Erik undid her seat belt, then leaned forward to kiss her cheek.

"We're all right here with you."

Taking a deep breath, she climbed out of the van, holding Kiki close. The house was a low rambling ranch with a ramp up to the side door. A conversion van sat in the driveway close to the house. Her dad had said he was able to drive using the specially adapted vehicle. His job as a pharmaceutical sales rep must be a good one.

"Why couldn't you have found me before?" Her voice was low, but Erik heard and slipped his arm around her shoulders and squeezed.

He guided Matty up the walk and to the door. They hadn't even rung the bell when the door was pulled open. A teenage girl with long, light-brown hair bounced on her toes.

"Hi, you're Tessa?" She turned and yelled, "Dad, they're here!" Then stood back from the door.

"Come on in. Oh, my God, I have been waiting for you all day. I was afraid it would snow and then you wouldn't be able to get here."

Joe Krasnov rolled into view, and she held her breath. This was her father. Her dad. She still couldn't quite grasp the fact. His face lit up when he saw her, and suddenly he was blurry. Damn, she was crying

313

again. Her emotions were totally out of whack.

"Tessa, it's so good to see you again. I can't tell you how much I missed you."

Heat crept up her face, but the words made her feel lighter than air. "We've talked every day."

He took her free hand and tugged. Slipping Kiki to the floor, she hugged him. It felt like home. His arms held tight for a while, then finally let her go.

"But I haven't *seen* you." He looked past her to Erik and held out his hand. "Good to see you again, too."

"Thanks for having us over. The kids have been excited to meet you."

She scooped a wandering little girl from the floor and held her near the man in the wheelchair. "This is Kiki. And the one hiding behind his father's legs is Matty."

The teen who'd answered the door bounced up and down. "My name is Madison, but my dad sometimes calls me Maddy. Oh, my God, sorry. Our dad. He's ours."

Madison had her head spinning. But she didn't seem upset to have a new sister show up.

Joe laughed. "As you probably figured out, this is your sister, Madison. Brady is helping Nancy set the table. Follow me."

They walked past the living room and into a large open kitchen. A petite blonde stood at the stove, stirring a pot. A teen boy finished placing utensils on the table.

"Nancy, this is my daughter, Tessa, her husband, Erik, and their children, Matty and Kiki."

The woman walked toward her, and she froze but only for a second. The warm expression on Nancy's face melted the fear she'd felt all day.

"It's so wonderful to finally meet you, Tessa. Joe's been desolate not knowing what happened to you." Nancy leaned in slowly like she was about to hug her. She stiffened. She hugged and kissed the Storm family all the time now, but she wasn't sure if her newfound spatial awareness was ready for someone else. Nancy seemed to realize this and patted her arms, then stood back.

"This is Brady."

She nodded at the teen with sandy-colored hair, but Erik stepped forward and shook his hand firmly.

"Dinner's about ready. Why don't we all sit down?" Nancy pointed to the dining area. The whole house was very open with lots of space between furniture. But as her father maneuvered to the table, she realized why.

Erik glanced around the room, and his face relaxed a bit. Was he finally realizing how lucky he was he could still walk? Maybe not as perfectly as he wanted, but he wasn't confined to a chair like Joe. Her dad. Would she get tired of thinking that?

The conversation flowed easily, mostly due to Erik and Nancy. She watched everyone carefully, looking for any signs they didn't want her here. They weren't apparent, but her stomach still revolted as they ate.

"Don't you like chicken, Tessa?" Nancy asked, looking at her half-eaten meal. "I would have made something else."

"No, it's great. I'm just...uh..."

"A little nervous," Erik filled in for her.

"Nervous? About what?" Madison asked. "That you wouldn't like us?" Her pretty mouth pouted.

"Oh, no, that you wouldn't like me."

Erik patted her hand under the table.

Joe frowned. "I told you they were eager to meet you. They've known about you for years."

"Yeah," Madison piped in. "Do you know how long I've wanted a sister? Forever. And to have one as cool and pretty as you, it's like a dream come true. The best Christmas present ever."

"Speaking of Christmas presents," Joe said, "I got you all a little something."

"That wasn't necessary, Joe," Erik said. "We're thrilled to be invited into your home."

Nancy chuckled. "Be thankful it's only a little something. He wanted to get Tessa a present for every Christmas and birthday he's missed. I told him maybe he should spread them out a bit. I can't guarantee what he'll do in the future."

Her head spun at Nancy's words. Her dad stared at her with such love and warmth in his eyes, she felt hers fill with more tears. This emotional crap needed to get under control. They were talking about the future. It was finally dawning on her this wasn't some one-time thing and then they'd go their separate ways. She had family. Blood family.

"I think it's cool I'm an uncle now." Brady pushed a small car next to Matty's plate.

Madison had insisted on sitting near Kiki and helping her eat. "I wish we had met sooner. Maybe I could have been a bridesmaid at your wedding. That would have been amazing. My friend, Amanda, was a bridesmaid, and she always brags about it. But she's not an aunt yet, and I am."

"We'll have to take lots of pictures of you, Tessa,

and the kids," Erik suggested. "You can show them to your friends."

Madison's head bobbed up and down. Tessa picked at her food some more. Okay, maybe these people did want her here. Her new sister was certainly enthusiastic.

They finished the meal and moved into the living room where Joe handed out presents. They were little things, but she could have cried again—not hard these days—when she opened a framed picture of her mom with her dad.

"That was a few months before I shipped out. I had it in storage, but I thought you might want it."

"Thank you. I love it." Blinking a few times, she bit down on her lip to keep from bawling all over this new family she'd found. Luckily Madison started chattering away again.

"Do you think you could help me pick out an outfit for a New Year's party I'm going to? And I have some stuffed animals I'm trying to wean out. I thought maybe Matty and Kiki would like some."

"They may already have a million of them, like you do," Joe said.

"They've only been here since July," she told him. "Erik's family has spoiled them, but not too many animals yet. I'm sure they'd love some."

Madison led her and the kids down the hall to her room and pointed to a pile of stuffed animals in the corner. The children's eyes opened wide.

"You can each pick one. Only one. Then make sure to say thank you to your Auntie Madison."

Her sister looked like she was going to explode at the title. She pulled her to the closet and started going through outfits, asking for opinions.

"I might not be the best one to ask. I'm hardly a fashion statement."

"Are you kidding me? Look at you. You're totally gorgeous. And oh, my God, Erik is so hot. And he's my brother-in-law now. This is the coolest thing ever."

Madison whipped her head around to stare wide-eyed at Tessa. "Oh, I probably shouldn't say that. That Erik is hot, huh? I mean, he's your husband."

Heat rushed into her face, and she chuckled. "Well, he is hot. I can't deny it. But we can keep that between us. He thinks his scars make him less attractive."

Madison made a face. One that clearly said Erik was still hot, even with the scars. She couldn't disagree.

"I'd expect you to have a totally hot guy for a husband, though. You probably had every guy falling all over you in school, huh? You're beautiful and trendy, and do you think maybe we could go out shopping together someday? My mom takes me, but let's face it, shopping with an older sister is way cooler, right?"

She sat on the bed and smiled. She'd never had an older sister or a mother to take her shopping, so she couldn't answer Madison's question. The teen was so excited, though, so she didn't say anything. No way was she bursting her bubble. And her little sister thought she was cool and beautiful.

They spent a few more minutes with Tessa looking through Madison's clothes and commenting on them. Once Matty and Kiki each picked a stuffed animal, they wandered back to the living room. Erik sat chatting with Joe, Nancy, and Brady, but the look he gave her warmed her blood. Yes, Madison was absolutely right. Her husband was hot.

When she settled on the couch next to him, his arm automatically lifted to her shoulder.

"You look like you're dreaming."

"I sometimes wonder if I am."

"No dream, sweetheart. We're all real. We're not going anywhere."

Needing his warmth and strength, she leaned against him. Being here with family, she hoped, if it was a dream, she'd never wake up. She wasn't sure she could handle the heartache if it ended.

****

"What is it with people going to the front door?" Erik grumbled as the buzzer rang again.

He pulled on the handle and froze. Miss Gulch stood there with her face as somber as ever. Oh, shit, what did she want?

"Miss Abernathy."

"Is your wife at home? I'm sorry to come unannounced, but I have a few things I need to discuss with you both." She actually looked uncomfortable instead of her usual confident demeanor.

He opened the door wide and stepped back. She entered and stood waiting for him to close it.

"Tessa and the kids are in the family room. Can I take your coat?"

She forced a smile but shook her head. "I'll only take a few minutes of your time."

Tessa looked up and frowned as they entered, then scrambled to her feet from her place on the floor reading to the kids.

"Miss Abernathy, we didn't know you were coming. Please, have a seat. Let me move some of these."

She pulled the toys off the chair and piled a few more onto the shelves, clearing a spot on the floor. He clenched his fists, knowing by the time he shuffled over and attempted to get down to pick anything up, she would have it all done. No, he wasn't in a wheelchair, but his damn leg sure was inconvenient at times.

"Please don't worry about cleaning up for me. It's obvious you're enjoying some quality family time. I don't want to disrupt that."

Abernathy sat stiffly on the edge of the chair, and Tessa joined him on the couch. Matty sat at their feet, pushing one of the cars Brady had given him around the carpet. He scooped Kiki up and deposited her in his lap. They might need her calming effect. Maybe Gulch was only here to let them know the adoption was going through, but her expression told him otherwise.

"What can we do for you?" he asked, running his hand up Tessa's back. She'd stiffened too, and he could almost see her trembling.

Folding her hands primly in her lap, Miss Abernathy cleared her throat. "Well, you know we've been running checks on the children to ascertain you have total claim on adopting them. We recently became aware of some possible relatives. They contacted our office and are flying here in two days, on Friday."

"From Afghanistan?" He'd die before he let the children go back there.

"No, from England. You had mentioned their grandfather was a British soldier. These are apparently some cousins of his. They seemed quite keen on taking in the children."

"They want to take the children," Tessa squeaked, her body tightening up further. "But they don't even know them. Why in the world would they suddenly want them?"

"I don't ask for motivation, Mrs. Storm. I deal with legalities. If everything is in order and they have a legal claim on the children, they would, in their right, be able to become the children's legal guardians."

His heart pounded faster at the thought of losing the children. "They've been living here, happily, for six months. They can't possibly love these children more than we do."

Miss Abernathy's face actually softened. "I have a feeling you're right, however my job is not to judge who is a better guardian."

"You were awfully judgy when you first came here." He should have softened his words, but he was pissed. They almost hadn't gotten the kids because of this woman.

"True. It's my job to make sure the homes the children are in are safe. But the legal aspects of this case supersede that. If these people check out, then they will bring the children back to England, and they're out of my jurisdiction."

"Erik?" Tessa looked at him, fear in her eyes. "What are we going to do?"

"I'll be here Friday afternoon with the relatives. I believe it's two male cousins, and one is married, so his wife will be with him as well. The children will spend the weekend with them, and if their papers are in order, they'll spend a few weeks here getting things in order to take the children back to England."

Tessa's whimper caused his stomach to tighten and flip. What the hell were they going to do about this? They'd gone through so much only to have the kids ripped from their grasp.

"But Matty started preschool this year. He has friends and is learning so much. What about that?" Tessa whined. Her agony tore at his already painful heart.

Miss Abernathy stood up, her face somber. "I'm very sorry to have to give you this information. Unfortunately, my hands are tied with legalities. I will make sure to do a thorough background check on these people, the Richards family. Unless they have a solid, legal claim, they won't be able to leave the country with the children. You have my word. I'll see myself out."

They sat there until the door clicked shut. Tessa glanced at the children, then ran from the room. He herded them to the bedrooms for a nap. He needed some time to think.

Tessa was still in the bathroom, her sobs interspersed with vomiting. She'd done this a few times lately when she'd been meeting with her new family. It was something he should mention to Dr. Sullivan when they saw him again. God, he hoped she wasn't picking up some weird nervous side effect due to stress.

He waited until she appeared in the bathroom doorway and pulled her into a hug.

"I'm going to call Nathaniel and see if he can give me any information on what our legal recourse should be."

She looked at him with such sadness in her eyes, he felt as if he were bleeding inside. How could he make it better for her? For him too. Kissing her forehead, he left to get a notebook in case Nathaniel gave him any information he needed.

His cousin was sympathetic, but since he wasn't a family lawyer, he didn't have any immediate action that could be taken. He did promise to contact a few friends from law school and get back to him soon. He couldn't ask for much more than that. Then he called his parents to let them know what had happened. They were devastated but said they'd pray for the right thing to happen and were available if they were needed.

When he shuffled down the hallway, he heard Tessa's voice in their bedroom. Pausing in the doorway, he watched her as she sat in the window seat sobbing. Talking to her father. Something she'd done often in the past few weeks. She'd also taken her sister shopping a few times as well. Madison and Tessa seemed to have clicked, and he loved watching his wife grow in confidence with the love of her new family.

As he stood there, a horrible thought came to his mind, and he felt like puking himself. She had her own family now. If the kids were taken from them, would she still need him? She cared for him deeply, he had no doubt. But they'd originally gotten married for the children. If they weren't here, was the reason for their marriage valid anymore?

They'd been perfect for each other, though. Him physically disfigured and crippled and her emotionally and physically untouchable. But she wasn't untouchable anymore. Not by a long shot. He thought of what had happened after they'd gotten back from a New Year's Eve party at his work last week.

He'd been sitting at the kitchen table going over some menus for work when she'd come in to tidy a few things before bed. His large sweatshirt with the cutout neck and sleeves was the only thing she wore. The one that fell off her so easily. As she bent over the table to wipe off some crumbs, he'd grabbed her hips and pushed his chair back enough to stand her in front of him.

"I need to clean off the table, Erik," she'd laughed and leaned over, exposing her incredibly long legs to his gaze. It had been more than he could handle. He'd run his hands under her top and caressed her breasts as they swayed freely. She hadn't moved out of his grip as his hands explored further.

It wasn't long before he'd had the panties down around her knees and was tasting her. Pure ambrosia. He'd unzipped with one hand and managed to stay on his feet long enough to push inside her and give them both the ride of their lives. His shy little rose had certainly blossomed. But they had that chemistry now too, didn't they? Or had he helped her bloom into the passionate flower she truly was, and now it was time to explore other gardens?

She'd always been pretty, but since she'd become more confident, with his help, she was stunningly attractive. It was more than apparent at his work party New Year's Eve. She hadn't clung to his side all night, and he'd been thrilled she was showing more effort in socializing. But when more than a few guys hit on her, he'd been wishing for some of her timidity to return.

To her credit she hadn't flirted back, but she had blushed furiously and gotten flustered. The innate innocence was such a turn on, though, it had only egged the guys on more. Moving in, he'd made it clear she belonged to him. Maybe it was why he'd taken her as he had later that night. To show her he could give her what she needed. That he wasn't just some scarred, crippled soldier.

But he was. And now she had a new family, her own blood family, and new sexy clothes and more confidence, maybe she'd want to explore other possibilities. Ones that weren't scarred or incapable of walking.

As she spoke softly to her father, she glanced up at him, then wiped the tears from her face. He wanted to kiss them away. Let her know how much she meant to him. He'd never told her he loved her. Should he do it now? Would it matter? If the children were taken away, would he lose her as well?

Chapter Twenty-Five

"You're going into work today?"

Erik buttoned his white work shirt. "I traded shifts with Tonio the last two days so I'd be here with the kids. I'll work as much as I can this weekend so I'll have time with them next week."

"Do you really think they'll take them away permanently?" Tessa couldn't bear the thought of losing the children. But she wondered if she'd lose him too. The last few days he'd spent tons of time and been close to Matty and Kiki but had been somewhat distant from her. They were both stressed about possibly having the kids taken away, but was it more than that?

He looked up, his jaw tight. "I don't know. I told you what Nathaniel's lawyer friend said. International adoptions are tricky. Any blood relative has priority over a nonrelative. There's not much we can do."

"I miss them already, and they've only been gone one night. Matty was being brave, but I know he didn't want to go."

He turned away, but not before she saw the fear cross his face. "There's nothing I can do. I guess I'm a failure in that department too."

"A failure? What are you talking about?"

"Nothing." Shaking his head, he scowled. "Are you going out today?"

She gazed out the window. "The snow's coming

down pretty hard. I really don't want to drive in it. Why, did you need me to do something?"

"No, you just look all dolled up. I was wondering if you were meeting someone."

She glanced at her leggings with the loose flowing top. Hardly fancy especially with the short boots she also wore. Yes, she'd put on a bit of makeup this morning, but mostly because she'd thrown up again and her face had been super pale. This stress was getting to her.

"You know I don't like driving and definitely not in this weather."

"Someone else could be picking you up."

"Who? My dad is working, and Madison can't drive yet. Who else do I know around here?"

"You got pretty friendly with some people at The Boat House party last week. You could have made plans to go out with them."

"You mean those guys who were flirting with me? Is that what you're accusing me of? I barely even talked to them. I certainly didn't flirt back."

"No, you didn't. But you seemed to like their attention. You were blushing like a virgin."

"It's embarrassing when I hear things like that. I haven't often gotten compliments from men."

"Sorry I lacked in that department as well." After shoving his wallet in his pocket, he straightened his coat.

"Erik." God, why was he being so exasperating today? "I'm not planning to go anywhere. I'm usually with the kids during the day. It's not like they're the easiest things to drag around with me."

"They aren't here now, though. Are they? Makes

your social life a bit freer."

"I don't want a social life. I want the kids back. What the hell is your problem?" How could he even suggest she go out and have fun when they might have the children taken away and never see them again? If the kids moved to England, it wouldn't be easy to visit, and they were so young they'd probably forget who they were.

"But you can have a social life if the kids aren't here. Especially now you don't have your no-touch rule. You've come a long way from the timid girl who married me."

"Married you because of the kids," she muttered under her breath. He seemed to catch it, though, and frowned. Was he trying to push her away with his belligerence? Now he could perform, did he want a wife who wasn't a freak? A woman a bit more experienced sexually than she was. Yeah, she was certainly no expert in the sex department, but she thought what they'd been doing was amazing. Maybe it was still tame to someone like him. Without the kids he could have more excitement.

"I suppose if we don't have the kids, the reason we got married disappears. Is that what you're saying?"

"Don't put words in my mouth," he growled. "We don't need to make any decisions right now. We don't know for sure the kids are being taken away. I just wanted you to know I'd understand any choice you made regarding staying here."

"Do you want me to go?" Was that what he was getting at? Hinting she should leave?

He let out a huge sigh and closed his eyes. "I don't want you to go, Tess. But *I* need to, or I'll be late for work. Try not to think too much about the kids. We'll have them back tomorrow night. I think."

"I'll try not to run off with any guys in the meantime." That had come from left field, but he was being a jerk.

Grabbing his keys from the dresser, he rushed off, his limp more pronounced. When she heard the van drive away, she finally moved. What the hell had happened? Her gaze roamed the room, trying to figure out what Erik had been getting at.

It wasn't the time to think about it, though, not with her heart in pieces, knowing they might lose Matty and Kiki. The people who had come to the house had seemed pleasant enough, but they were a little older and very proper. What would they do with two young children? She didn't see them getting on the floor and playing blocks or cars. Or reading them nightly stories. But if the children had stayed with their mother, they most likely would have been running from the dangers of war.

The first thing she needed to do was laundry. With Christmas and the new year, she'd gotten behind. The thought of handing all of the kids' stuff over to these people grated on her, but she wanted Matty and Kiki to have everything that was familiar to them. After gathering the clothes from the children's rooms, she took her stuff along with Erik's.

Once the clothes were in the laundry room, she sorted through the stuff in her closet. With her new wardrobe, she might not wear some of it again. Much of it was baggy and old and definitely not in style any longer. All the clothes she knew she wouldn't use, she put in bags and brought it over to her old house. Later, she'd decide what to do with it.

If Erik was indeed trying to encourage her to leave him, she couldn't live near him. Not if he was planning to parade new women around. She'd have to sell the house and move. Maybe closer to her father.

Snow swirled around her as she sank down on the steps, and tears came to her eyes. Damn things were out of her control these days. But what else could she do if he wanted her gone? Anger reared up inside he'd made her fall in love with him, taught her what it was like to feel passion, and now he wanted to toss her aside.

Damn it, no. No way in hell she'd let that happen. They were good together. If he wanted something more exciting, then he could teach her. She'd be more than willing to learn. And if the kitchen table antics a few weeks ago were anything to go by, she'd like it.

Getting to her feet, she marched back into the house. After changing the laundry around, she pulled the last few things out of her closet. She'd been wanting to put some new shelves in there to give her more space, but she'd never had the time without the kids. Now she did. Painting the inside first might be a good idea, though. They had some of the leftover peach from Kiki's room.

The phone rang as she was sandpapering the rough spots in the closet. The connection was spotty, probably due to the storm, but she stopped breathing. It was Matty.

"Mama, I don't want to be here."

"I know, baby, I want you home, too, but we have to do what we're told." Damn, this was so hard. And Kiki was crying in the background. She sounded distraught.

"You get us, Mama?"

"Matty, do they know you're calling me?"

"No." His voice softened. "They watching TV in the other room. But I remember our number, so I call home."

"What a great job, Matty. Why is Kiki crying? Why aren't they making her feel better?"

"They yell at us, Mama. I don't like it here. You come get us."

She could hear conversation in the background but couldn't quite make out what they were saying with Kiki screaming. "Try to get Kiki calm, honey. I need to hear what the people are saying."

Matty started talking to the little girl, and she managed to hear the background.

"Thank God, she finally shut up. Once we get our inheritance, that brat is being shipped to some unpleasant and very cheap boarding school."

"Oh, how about that place you went to for a few months when you were young? Where they still used corporal punishment. Can't have them learning bad manners, can we?"

Her blood began to boil. It didn't matter what the friggin' law said. There was no way these people were getting her kids. She had to do something.

"Matty, listen to me. I'm going to come get you both, but you need to do something for me, okay?"

"Yes, Mama, come get us."

"I need you to hang up the phone, put it back where it was, and don't say anything to them. I'll be there as soon as I can, but don't let them know. And try and keep Kiki happy if you can. I hate to hear her cry."

"Okay, Mama, I'll sit in her crib with her."

"I love you, sweetie. Be there soon."

After hanging up the phone, she dug in the drawer for Gertrude Abernathy's number. Within minutes, she relayed the conversation she'd heard and had the name of the motel the people were staying at. Picking up the phone again, she dialed The Boat House. Nothing. The line didn't connect. She tried once more, but the same thing happened. The lines must be down at the restaurant due to the snow.

She dialed Erik's cell number, hoping he'd pick up. If he was in the middle of cooking, it wasn't always possible. His ringtone echoed from across the room where his phone sat on his dresser. When he'd rushed out earlier, he must have left it. Damn. She couldn't wait for him, though. Their children needed her.

Grabbing her coat and keys, she hurried out into the storm.

****

Tessa's car was missing.

Erik pulled into the driveway and frowned. She'd said she didn't like driving in the snow, yet she'd gone out anyway. Where? The new snow, where her car had been, indicated she hadn't been gone all that long.

As he sludged into the house, his heart ached. God, he'd been such a bastard earlier. Started that fight, no doubt about it. He still wasn't sure why. Maybe he was feeling her out, trying to see where she stood on their marriage. When had he become so unsure and needy? About the time he realized he loved his wife but that wasn't the reason they got married. And their purpose for getting married might be stolen from them.

"Tess?" Stupid, she wasn't here. Her car was gone, and so was she. Now what did he do? The power had gone out at the restaurant, and Sid had sent them all home. There was nothing to do here, though, not with the kids gone and Tessa missing. What had been so important she'd needed to risk driving?

In the bedroom, he pulled off his shirt, unbuttoned his pants, then sat on the bed, kicking off his boots. Leaning back, he relaxed, hoping she would be back soon. He needed to apologize. And tell her he loved her and didn't want her to leave. His mind filled with all the delicious ways he could show her how he felt. It all started with peeling her clothes from her warm body. That was one benefit of not having the kids here. Though it certainly hadn't stopped them once the kids were in bed at night.

"Damn." Pushing himself off the bed, he changed his pants, leaving his shirt off for now. Maybe Tessa would come home and he'd be halfway to convincing her they belonged together. His cane dropped as he threw his dirty pants in the hamper, and when he bent to retrieve it, he saw the closet door partway open. Tessa's closet. He moved closer and opened the door. It was empty.

All the air dried up in his lungs, and his heart stopped. No, she couldn't have left. Not moved out already. Would she have done that without saying anything?

She asked if you wanted her gone.

"I said I *didn't* want her gone." His voice echoed in the empty room.

Why hadn't he said something earlier? Told her he loved her before the damn thing with the kids happened. It would kill him if he lost them and her, too.

Throwing on a shirt and shoes, he hobbled through

the house. Her footprints led to where her car sat, but there was another set that seemed to go...to her old house. There were no lights on there, and her car was gone, so going over there seemed stupid. But right now he wasn't feeling particularly smart. He grabbed a coat and the keys and slid his way through the snow and icy build up. Calico hopped up the stairs and rubbed against his legs as he pushed the key in the door.

"Where'd she go, Calico?" Not that he expected an answer, but he took comfort in the fact she hadn't gone far. Not without her cat.

The house was cold but not empty. A bag sat on the kitchen floor. As he tugged on the top, some of her clothes spilled out. Had she actually been moving out? Started packing and leaving? He had to stop her. Get her back. Someone with her background needed reassurances they were loved. Too often she'd been told she wasn't lovable. Even now, she still hadn't fully believed her father and his family would be permanent fixtures in her life.

The snow sloshed under his feet as he trudged back to their house. The one they'd made into a home with their love and togetherness. The children had been a large part of it, but Tessa had been integral, too. He couldn't lose her. He wouldn't. Whatever he had to do to convince her they belonged together, he'd do it.

****

The car slid to a stop in the motel parking lot. Miss Abernathy had said it was room 127 and she'd meet her there. Tessa wasn't waiting for anyone. She was getting her kids. Period.

The snow had gotten heavier as she drove, but she'd been determined to get to the children. Kiki had sounded terrified, and Matty's sad voice had cut straight to her heart. Her feet pushed through the snow just as Miss Abernathy pulled in. The woman moved fast for someone her age. They met at the door.

"I'm terribly sorry this occurred, Mrs. Storm. My supervisor pushed to have this visit happen. I have a feeling some palms got greased. But I got the information back on the Richards family. Apparently, there's a nice-sized inheritance up for grabs. These cousins are actually related to the sergeant's second wife and aren't blood. They're only eligible for the inheritance if they have custody of the children, or the children have passed on."

A chill ripped through her that had nothing to do with the icy wind and snow. "Do you think they would have…?" She couldn't finish the thought.

Miss Abernathy knocked firmly on the door, and she held her breath. A child cried in the background, and she started breathing again. When the door opened, she didn't wait for an invitation. Pushing past the woman who answered, she zeroed in on the crying.

"Mama! You came."

She rushed to hug Matty who sat in a portable crib with Kiki. The poor girl had tears streaking down her face. When she pulled them both up, she realized why Kiki was so upset. She was soaked.

"When was the last time you changed this diaper?" Not that she was expecting an answer since the Richards were arguing with Miss Abernathy in the other part of the room.

"Matty, where's the diaper bag I sent?"

The boy grabbed the bag from the floor and hauled it over. She went to work, stripping Kiki from her sodden outfit. She really needed a warm bath, but baby wipes would have to do for now. After bundling her in a new warm outfit, she snuggled her close. Matty climbed on the bed next to her, and she pulled him in, too.

"I missed you both so much." Her heart beat rapidly as she thought of the near miss they'd had. She kissed the children as they clung to her.

"I miss you, and Daddy, too. I don't want to visit here no more. We go home?"

"Yes, we're going home." Although she wasn't certain what she'd find with the way Erik had been this morning, but he'd be happy to see the children. His feelings for them had never been in question. And with them back home, she'd have time to fight for his love.

She had Matty use the bathroom while she gathered the stuffed animals they'd brought, the ones Madison had given them. She swung the bag over her shoulder, then picked up both children. Miss Abernathy was still giving the three adults the stink-eye. When they caught sight of her with the children, the woman moved forward.

"You can't take those children. We have every right to that inheritance, and you're not going to take it away from us."

"I don't give a shit about the money," she growled, hoping Matty and Kiki wouldn't pick up on the swear. "But I do care about these children, and I'm taking them home. Try and stop me."

"I'll be in touch, Mrs. Storm. Again, I'm sorry for the inconvenience. I don't imagine we'll run into any further snags with your adoption. I'll make sure of that." Miss Abernathy actually smiled at her, then turned a sour face back to the Richards.

Once she'd gotten the children buckled into their car seats, she carefully pulled onto the icy road, glancing at her GPS to get her someplace familiar. When she made a few of the more difficult turns, she put the phone back down.

"Mama, I play a game on your phone. Kiki want to see it."

"Let me get through this snow first, sweetie. I really should call your father, too."

"I call him, Mama."

"He's at work right now, and the phones were down. He left his cell phone at home, too. We can try again when we get there."

Kiki started to fuss, and she knew she'd be distracted if the child was cranky. Getting distracted wasn't a smart idea with these road conditions. Picking up the phone, she thrust it back until Matty took it.

"Play a game for her, okay, sweetie. We'll be home in a little while."

Beeps and bells sounded from the back, and she gave a tiny sigh. Now if only she could get through this storm and safely home. As she drove along the stretch of road, the car started to skid. Damn, she wasn't used to driving in this kind of weather. She'd always stayed home. Even in good weather.

Her phone signaled she'd gotten a text, and she tensed, turning slightly. But as the car skidded some more, she straightened back again. Damn, a small tree lay across the road. She tapped the brakes. The car didn't stop. She yanked on the wheel to avoid the branches, and the tires slid. The steering wheel was useless. She couldn't get the car under control again.

No, she had to get the kids back to Erik. Back home. As they went over the bank and rolled down a hill, she yelled in fear and frustration. This wasn't fair. She'd gotten so close. They couldn't take her family from her now. As the car flipped and crunched to a stop near a tree, the world turned black.

Chapter Twenty-Six

Erik paced the floor as he waited for the water to boil. Might as well get dinner ready for when Tessa came home. If she came home. He'd texted her a few minutes ago to see if he'd get an answer. Nothing yet.

As he pulled down a box of angel hair pasta and started to open it, the house phone rang. He grabbed his cane and limped to where it sat on the wall.

"Hello."

"Daddy!"

"Matty, where are you? What's the matter?" Kiki screamed in the background. His heart stopped.

"The car went down, and it turned and turned and scared me."

"Whose car? Who's driving?"

"Mama, but she's sleeping, and Kiki is crying. Mama won't wake up."

Holy shit. Tessa had gone to get the kids. Something must have happened. No time to explore now, though. Sounded like she was unconscious. Or worse.

Stop. Think. Do something.

"Okay, Matty, I'm going to hang up the phone for a minute but hold onto it. I have to call the rescue people, but I'll call you back. Press the red button like we taught you, but then the green one when it rings again. Can you do that?"

"Yes, Daddy."

"Are you hurt, pal? What about Kiki? Is she bleeding at all?"

"We in our car seats and all crooked, but I don't see no blood. I want to get out."

"Don't try and move now. I'll be there as soon as I can." Fuck, where the hell were they, and how long would it take to get there? After hanging up, he used his cell to check the app he'd installed on Tessa's phone. He'd wanted her GPS location in case she ever broke down and needed help. Thank God he'd done that.

He dialed 911 and provided the location as he scurried into the van. He refused to stay on the line any longer than it took for a few questions, then called Tessa's phone again.

"Daddy, you coming?"

"I'm in the car now. It'll take me a bit to get there. You have time to sing that song to Kiki like we did before. Remember it? Can you sing it now?"

Matty began to sing, and he attempted to join in, but his throat closed, and he could barely breathe. Matty had said the car had turned and turned and it was twisted. Had it rolled? The kids were in padded car seats but Tessa? She always wore her seatbelt, but would it even matter if the car had rolled? What if she—no, he had to stay positive. She was okay. She had to be.

He lost track of time as he raced through the icy streets. The snow was slowing down, but the plows hadn't gotten everywhere yet, so the roads were still slick. He slowed down as the GPS indicated he was close but didn't see her car. Where the hell was it?

The skid marks by the low hanging branch sent

shivers down his spine. They'd gone over the side of the road into the ravine. Holy fuck, this wasn't good. Jamming the car into park, he didn't even bother shutting it off. He grabbed his cane, though it wouldn't do much good on the downward slope. Who knew what he'd find at the bottom of the hill?

As he pushed through the snowbank, he saw it. The car rested on its side near the bottom. Propped against a tree. Shit, fuck, damn. When he'd left the house for work earlier, he'd been so freakin' mad he'd forgotten his phone. If he'd been with her getting the kids, this wouldn't have happened.

The frigid snow slid into his boots as he slipped down the incline. Grabbing at small trees and shrubs, he managed to get most of the way without landing on his ass. A few more yards and he'd be— *Bam!* His weak leg shot out from under him and twisted sideways. Scorching heat sliced through his knee and thigh as he took a header into the ice-covered ground.

Tortured muscles screamed in agony, and he tried to pull himself to sitting. Stars swam before his eyes, and the scenery tilted. God almighty, the pain was so bad he was afraid he might pass out. But he needed to get Tessa and the kids. The shock of sticking his face in the snow brought him back to life. He looked around for his cane but must have dropped it as he fell.

Reaching for the closest tree, he pulled himself up. When he bit his lip to keep from crying out, he tasted blood. A few more steps. One more and he'd be there.

"Matty, I'm here."

Kiki's cries escalated, and he used his arm muscles to get up the side of the overturned car. The door took some strength to get open, and he wasn't sure where it came from. No way he'd leave them inside, though. *Get them out. Find out how Tessa was.*

"Tessa? Can you hear me?" Maybe she'd come to since he'd talked to Matty. "Tessa, dammit, answer me."

"She still sleeping." Matty's voice shook, and he saw the fear on his son's face. Tessa was slumped over the steering wheel. As he started to climb in, the vehicle shuddered and swayed. He jumped clear as the car fell back and settled on its wheels. The breath was sucked out of him as he landed on his back with a thud. The children's screams tore through his soul. Damn, had it done more damage to Tessa when the vehicle moved?

"It's okay, the car's down now so I can get you out easier."

He had to crawl back to the vehicle using only one leg. The other throbbed like a bastard and refused to move. When he finally got the car seats undone, he set the children between them on the seat, Kiki in Matty's lap.

After a cursory check on the kids, he held them tight and kissed their heads.

"Sit right here and hold your sister while I check on Mommy."

It was difficult to ease out of the back seat, but he had a mission to complete. Through sheer determination he got the front passenger door open and slid in. Tessa now rested against the side window, her face slack and eyes closed. Blood covered part of her face.

"Please be okay," he muttered to himself. *Don't let her be dead.* Reaching out, he pressed his fingers against her throat, searching for a sign she was still with them. Blood pulsed under her skin, and tears flooded his eyes. She was alive.

Sirens screeched from up the hill, and he finally released the breath he'd been holding since he'd gotten Matty's call.

"You're going to be fine, sweetheart." He didn't dare move her, but he had to touch her, to convince his frozen heart she'd be okay. Stroking his fingers over her cheek, he pressed kisses to her nose. Blood dripped from under it, but he didn't care. It was all part of Tessa, the woman he loved more than anything. The woman he needed and who had helped him regain his masculinity and pride. She'd never allowed him to feel sorry for himself. Her life had been a worse hell, and she wouldn't put up with his ridiculous feelings of inadequacy.

"I love you, Tessa. Please wake up and let me show you how much. I'll tell you every day for the rest of our lives if you just wake up and show me you're all right."

"Sir, are you hurt?"

A rescue worker poked his head into the back seat of the car. Kiki and Matty had calmed somewhat, but tiny whimpers still escaped their mouths every now and then.

"I wasn't in the accident. My wife and the kids were. I didn't want to move her. I don't know what her injuries are."

"Is there a pulse?" The man's eyes flashed between the kids and Tessa.

He nodded. Another paramedic showed up and started talking to the kids as the first one carefully opened Tessa's door and began examining her.

"Sir, why don't you come out with the children, and we'll get them up into the ambulance. It will give us more room to work on your wife."

He didn't want to leave her, but they were right. He was in the way here. A third rescue worker held the door behind him, and he grimaced as he pulled himself out of the car. His leg screamed in agony, and his good one almost buckled at the pain. The rescue worker grabbed him by the elbows and kept him up.

"Are you injured? You said you weren't in the car when it went off the road."

He clenched his teeth so hard he was afraid he might crack a tooth. "I have a previous leg injury and twisted it again on the way down the ravine. I'll be fine."

The man slid into the seat he'd just vacated. Half a dozen men appeared, some carrying stretchers, others holding ropes that worked their way down from the top of the hill. The children were strapped into the stretchers and pulled up. When they offered to get him up that way, he shook them off. He stood to the side until they had Tessa on a backboard and loaded onto another stretcher. The ropes were pulled from above, and he grabbed hold of one. Two of the firefighters flanked him, and he could have kissed them. They didn't say anything, just got him up the hill.

"We can have someone drive your vehicle to the hospital for you, sir. The children might be more comfortable in the ambulance with you."

He was helped into the back of the large vehicle, but he didn't care if they thought of him as a cripple. His family needed him. Matty and Kiki sat on one of the benches, and he slid in beside them. They both crawled into his lap as Tessa was raised onto a gurney and loaded into the middle. One of the paramedics crawled up behind her and closed the door.

As the vehicle maneuvered through the streets, the paramedic focused on Tessa.

"We checked the children for obvious injuries. They'll do more thorough tests at the hospital."

She lay still and colorless, and he reached out to touch her hand. "What about my wife?" He choked on the last word. She'd become so much more than that.

"She's alive. We'll know more when we get to the hospital."

The paramedic started an IV, and Matty began asking him questions. As they rode, he took the opportunity to lean down and whisper into Tessa's ear.

"The kids are here, and they're fine. But they need their mom. I need you too, Tessa."

The emptiness in his chest seemed to grow bigger the longer she remained quiet. Even the soft babblings of Kiki couldn't alleviate his fear.

It seemed like hours before they reached the hospital. A wheelchair was produced for him, and the children climbed in his lap and clung to his neck. Tessa was wheeled away with a promise of news soon. As they waited for a doctor to come into his exam room, he called his parents and Tessa's dad.

"Hi, I need to get some information from you." A young woman in cartoon-covered scrubs appeared in the doorway of the cubicle. "You're with the woman the paramedics brought in from the car accident, right?"

"Yes, she's my wife," he answered, tightening his hold on the children. "I'd like information too, as soon as they know anything."

The woman smiled, pulling in a laptop on a rolling cart. She peppered him with questions. Name, address, birth date, health insurance, medical history.

"Does your wife have any allergies you know of?"

Damn, he knew so little about her in that aspect. She was his wife. He should know if she was allergic to something. When they got out of here, he'd make sure he learned every little detail.

"I'm not sure."

The woman looked at him strangely but continued on with more questions. Luckily, he'd read enough of the children's medical history to know about them. She left, and soon a nurse entered and handed him a hospital gown. She took his blood pressure, temperature, and checked his pulse, then repeated it with the children.

"The doctor will be in soon. Get them out of their coats, and you can slip this on. You don't have an injury besides your leg, correct?"

"I'm more worried about my wife and the children. I just twisted my knee."

"We'll make sure to get everyone checked."

When she turned to go, he slipped the kids off his lap. "Take your coat off, Matty. Can you get Kiki's off too, please?" He then removed his own coat, boots, and pants, which were covered in snow and mud. He pushed them into a corner, then lifted the children onto the gurney. He grimaced as he slipped the johnny on, then maneuvered onto the soft surface next to them.

"Where's Mama?" Tears dripped from his son's eyes, and he felt like he'd been sucker punched.

"They're taking care of her in another room. We need to stay here so the doctor can make sure you and Kiki are fine."

The little girl snuggled into his side and closed her eyes. It was nap time, and these two had been through quite an ordeal today. Thank God they seemed okay. Now he needed to see Tessa and reassure himself she was fine too.

The curtain swung aside, and a man a few years older than him pushed in another laptop. "Erik Storm, Matteen, and Kinah. I'm Dr. Lavoie. Let's check and see what we have here. Car accident, correct?"

"The children were in the accident. The car rolled down a ravine. I wrenched my knee trying to get to them. But it was already messed up. I'm sure it's no worse."

"We'll still take a look. Why don't I start with you, so the children see how brave you are?"

Dr. Lavoie manipulated and prodded at his leg as he asked questions about the previous damage. It took all of his control not to growl at the pain, but he didn't want the kids getting scared.

"I had a fractured pelvis and shattered knee cap along with damage to the muscles and ligaments. They inserted a metal plate to piece my kneecap together again."

"Metal plate. That leaves out an MRI, then. I would like to get a CT scan, though, to see what we're dealing with. Let me check the children first."

The doctor examined both of the children while they were sitting in Erik's lap. He had a gentle bedside manner and had them laughing within minutes.

"Aside from a few cuts and bruises, I don't see anything to be concerned about. They were obviously strapped tightly into their car seats."

"My wife would have made sure of it. Do you have

any information on how she is? We're more than a little worried."

"I can imagine. Let me take a peek." He clicked away at some keys on the computer, then looked up. "Dr. Abbasi is in with her now. They've ordered a full blood work up and have her on fluids. There's nothing else in here yet, but I'm sure they're doing everything they can for her. I'll let them know you're concerned."

The nurse poked her head back in. "The paramedics dropped off your keys and wondered if this was yours." She held up his marine cane. When he nodded, she handed them over, then added, "Your in-laws are out in the waiting room. Do you want them to come back here?"

Dr. Lavoie nodded. "You'll need someone to watch the children while you get your CT scan."

A few minutes later, after the nurse had cleaned up the children's slight injuries, Madison, Nancy, and a very worried looking Joe came in, causing the small space to get even smaller. Madison reached for Kiki and snuggled her to her shoulder. Like Tessa always did. Joe stared intensely at him.

"They won't give me any information on my daughter. How is she?"

His jaw tightened. "I wish I knew. All I got is they're running blood work. She was unconscious when we came in. I don't know any more."

"You and the kids are fine, though?" Nancy asked.

It was embarrassing he was even in the mix. Damn, freakin' leg. "They're a little bumped and bruised but no worse for wear. I reinjured my leg trying to get down the ravine. It's nothing."

"Did you want the kids here with you, or would it

be easier if I took them home?" Nancy offered.

He hated to let them go, not after what had happened, but a hospital really wasn't the place for them.

"Do you mind taking them back to our house? They need something familiar, and I think they could use food and naps."

"I'd be happy to."

Once the nurse provided release papers for the children, he fished out the keys and gave them to Nancy. "Take my van, it has car seats for the kids. The house keys are on the ring too. Although I left in such a hurry, I'm not sure I actually locked the door."

After giving Matty and Kiki kisses and hugs, they left. "I don't know when I'll be back. I'm not leaving until I know Tessa is okay. My parents are on their way up. They'll be able to take over later. Thank you."

Nancy gave Joe a kiss and asked Erik to keep her informed. When she left with Madison, Joe looked around the enclosed space, lost.

"I just found her. God wouldn't be cruel enough to let me lose her now, would He?"

Even though he wanted to assure the man Tessa would be fine, he'd seen too much cruelty and had lost too many guys oversees to be able to say it.

The wait took forever, even with the interruption of being taken for a CT scan. Once done, they wrapped a brace around his knee for support, gave him some scrub pants to wear, and brought him to a private waiting room where Joe sat staring into space.

"Don't we look a pair with our matching wheelchairs?" Joe joked, though his heart wasn't in it. Erik knew how he felt. His gut clenched tight every minute that passed with no word.

"Erik Storm?"

A dark-haired woman in her forties stood in the doorway. When he tried to stand, she waved him back down.

"No, don't get up. I'm Dr. Mellina Abbasi. I've been taking care of Tessa."

"How is she? I'd like to see her. Is she awake?"

The woman's neutral face scared the pants off him. Maybe all doctors took a class in expressions so they didn't give anything away.

"I'm Tessa's father, Joe Kraznof."

Dr. Abbasi shook his hand, then looked down at her clipboard. "Before I get into details, I need to know if Tessa had an advanced directive?"

Advanced directive? The military made you complete one before you shipped out, but he was going to a war zone. He couldn't breathe. Was it that bad?

"She's only twenty-four. Is she—?" The words wouldn't come.

"It's a standard question in these types of situations. She's holding her own right now."

"But she's not in good shape," Joe stated, his eyes on the floor.

The doctor rattled on about blood tests, hemoglobin, red blood cells, and hematocrit. He didn't care about that. He wanted to see his wife and have her be fine.

"...no broken bones, but we're keeping an eye on her levels since there's a possibility she has some internal bleeding. My biggest concern is the head trauma she sustained. We're seeing increased intracranial pressure, and we need to relieve that. I've got her on a drug that should help, but we've also sedated her. She regained consciousness for a short while but became very agitated."

"My wife doesn't like hospitals."

"That explains the agitation, though I think she was also concerned for the children. I assured her they were fine."

"They're at home with family."

"They wouldn't be allowed in to see her now anyway. Any exposure to light, sound, or even movement could be detrimental and cause severe pain. We need to keep the stimuli to a minimum."

"Can I see her?" Yes, he sounded pathetic, but he didn't care.

"She's on her way to have an MRI at the moment, then she's being sent to ICU. She's allowed one visitor at a time, and it's immediate family only."

"I understand." He and Joe might have to duke it out as to who went first.

"The other thing I should mention is she's had some light spotting. At this point we have no idea if the accident caused any damage to the baby, but we'll do everything we can to keep the fetus from terminating."

Chapter Twenty-Seven

"The baby? What?" What was this woman talking about?

Dr. Abbasi frowned, then looked at her notes again. "We did a full blood panel when she first came in. According to HCG levels, your wife is about seven weeks pregnant. You weren't aware?"

"No."

"Not a planned pregnancy, then?"

"I didn't think I…I shattered my leg and pelvis in Afghanistan about seven months ago. They said I couldn't…" *Stupid,* she didn't need to know everything. "No, it wasn't planned."

"Sometimes swelling and inflammation can cause temporary impotency and sterility. Did the doctors tell you it was permanent?"

"I was so drugged up I don't remember. I just assumed, so we never used any birth control."

"It looks like it's all working again."

"But she still might lose the baby." He choked on the words. Like Joe had said, God couldn't be cruel enough to give him and Tessa a child, then take it away.

"She's far enough along we could do an internal ultrasound. But I'd like to get her stabilized first. The increased intracranial pressure, if not controlled and relieved, can be fatal."

Fatal. Closing his eyes, he took a deep breath.

Good thing he was already sitting because he didn't think his legs would hold him.

Joe patted him on the arm. "She'll be all right. We have to believe that."

"I'll send someone down when she's settled in ICU. There's a waiting room right outside the ward for any overflow visitors."

The quiet of the room surrounded him, pushing in on him, suffocating him. Sweat trickled down his neck and back, and his aching limbs shook. Only now was he feeling the effects of the tumble down the ravine. What the hell would he do without Tessa? She'd become as essential to him as air.

Joe's head was bowed, and his hands clasped together. Was he praying? It couldn't hurt. Letting his eyes close, he asked for Tessa to recover. The children needed her. Hell, who was he kidding? He needed her just as much.

How much time passed, he wasn't sure. Eventually an orderly came in to tell them she'd been admitted to ICU. When he tried to put any pressure on his leg, the pain was excruciating. Crutches were procured, and both he and Joe took the elevator up to the third floor where ICU was located. Glancing at his watch, he couldn't believe the accident had happened hours ago. Best text his mom to let her know where he'd be. No details yet, though, as this wasn't the type of information you could give over the phone. When they got here, he'd tell them personally. If he could manage to get it out.

When they got to the intensive care unit, Joe rolled toward the waiting room.

"I'm not even going to try and fight you for first

right to see her. Tell her I love her, and I'll be right here if she needs me."

"Thanks. Can you call Nancy and find out how the kids are? They've been through a lot today. I should be there, but…"

"I get it. Go."

He stepped through the door into the unit. A nurse's station sat to his left with rooms surrounding it in a large semicircle.

"My wife, Tessa Storm, was brought up here."

The petite brunette pointed to a room on the far left. "Room six. She's sedated, though, so don't expect much. The instructions are to keep the lighting low and noise to an absolute minimum. Phone on vibrate if you need it."

"I just want to sit with her." He must have looked pathetic because she gave him a sympathetic smile. Maybe it was the crutches or the fact he was still wearing the hospital scrub pants with his gray marines T-shirt.

"If you need anything, let us know."

Hobbling over to her room, he made sure to enter quietly. Another nurse, this one older with short white hair, fussed with the IV bag near Tessa's head. His wife lay there, still and pale, but as beautiful as ever. He swallowed hard, wanting to pull her into his arms and kiss every inch of her. Tell her he loved her and needed her.

"She's sleeping peacefully." The nurse patted his arm. After positioning the chair close to the bed so his left side was on the outside, she left.

Easing into the seat, he put his crutches on the floor. Taking Tessa's hand and stroking the soft skin, he brought it to his mouth to kiss her fingertips.

"Hey, sweetheart," he whispered, his voice choking on the endearment. Why hadn't he used it more often? Something else to fix when they got home. He stared at her, frowning at the huge bump on her forehead, though they'd cleaned up the blood from her face.

"The kids are fine." He kept his voice low. If he caused her any undue pain, it would kill him. "You don't need to worry. Your sister and Nancy are with them at home." *Our home. The one you helped create. The one that will feel so lonely if you don't wake up and come back to us.*

Memories of her flittered through his mind. Tessa when she first moved in next door. So young and painfully shy she couldn't even look at him. Then later when she'd snuck glances at him when she thought he wasn't looking. Flattering yes, though at the time his ego hadn't needed any more boosting. It had still felt good to see her timid smile when he helped her at work or stood up for her against some stupid teens. That same grin had shown up years later when he'd landed on his ass and she'd been there to witness his fall from grace.

He'd loved seeing her as she opened up and discovered new possibilities as a wife and mother. Yeah, the wife part had been great. Slowly realizing touch wasn't always bad and often it could be quite satisfying. How she'd blossomed into a sexual creature who rejoiced in pleasing him as much as she was pleased.

Then there was her laugh. It had been infrequent at first but became a bigger part of her personality. Especially when she was with the children. God, she was such a great mom. So naturally loving. And now she'd be a mom again. To their child.

Reaching out, he gently caressed her flat stomach. If the baby survived. If she survived.

Dropping his head, he closed his eyes, drowning with the thoughts of losing this woman he loved so much. She'd slipped under his defenses and infiltrated his heart. This wound was one he wouldn't recover from.

"I love you, Tessa. I should have told you before. I wish I had. I hope you can hear me and understand how much you mean to me. You're my world, and without you, life has no meaning. Please, don't leave me. I need you."

He rested his head on the bed and held her hand to his mouth. Maybe if she felt his presence, she'd fight harder to get better.

The vibration in his pocket a while later woke him from the stupor he'd fallen into, and he pulled out his phone to check the text message. His parents were in the ICU waiting room.

Hauling himself up, he leaned over and kissed her perfect lips. "I'll be back in a few minutes. I'll have your dad come in to see you. I love you, sweetheart."

Adjusting his crutches, he made his way to the waiting room. His parents sat talking to Joe. When they saw him, they hustled over, anxiously eyeing the crutches.

"I thought you weren't in the accident," his dad commented.

"This happened when I climbed down the ravine to get to the car. I'm sure it isn't any worse than before. It just hurts like...the dickens." *No marine language near*

Mom.

"How's Tessa?" His mom leaned in for a hug.

His throat clogged when he tried to say the words. He coughed, then waved at Joe.

"You've met Tessa's dad."

"I introduced myself when they came in," Joe said. "Now answer the question. How is she?"

He attempted a smile. "Why don't you go spend some time with her? I'll fill my parents in on the details."

"Fair enough. I wish we could have met under better circumstances."

As Joe rolled out of the room, his parents turned their attention to him. They didn't say anything, just stood waiting. Could he even get any words out? Tears filled his eyes, and he was afraid he'd lose it right there. *Look around the room. Focus on something. Keep the fear in check.* Shit. It wasn't working. The fear was too great, and it was winning.

"She's got...got a serious head injury. They've got her sedated so it doesn't get worse. It's like she's simply sleeping, all peaceful and innocent. And so damn beautiful it makes my heart ache."

His mom leaned in and hugged him. Holding tight, he accepted her strength. How long had it been since he'd needed his mom's support? He needed it now.

"Would it be more comfortable sitting, Erik?" his dad asked, his face no less concerned.

He felt lost. Nothing made sense. Maybe sitting would give him a few minutes to get himself under control. Maneuvering to a bench, he eased into the seat. His dad sat across from him and his mom next to him. Again, they waited, never pushing.

"They've got her on some medicine that should help get the brain swelling down. If it doesn't, she could—"

His mom squeezed his arm and sniffed. "We've got everyone in the family praying for her. You know your grandmother thinks she has a direct line with how often she goes to church."

He chuckled, though it sounded hollow. Like his heart without Tessa in it.

"She, um…she…" He couldn't say it. Didn't even want to think about it. Taking a deep breath, he managed, "Tessa's pregnant."

His parents exchanged a look, then his mom rubbed his arm. "I suspected she might be."

What? "How?"

His mom raised one eyebrow. "At Christmas, she seemed tired and pale. And it was mostly the chicken she was avoiding. I couldn't eat chicken for the first few months with all of you. And you mentioned she'd been sick to her stomach."

"I don't think she even knew. I can't believe you did. You didn't say anything."

"It wasn't my news to tell. Did they say how far along she is?"

"About seven weeks." He did the math quickly. "It probably happened around Thanksgiving."

His dad snorted. "I do remember your brothers teasing you about how thin the walls were in the house. Sounds like they got an earful."

Heat rushed to his face, and he grinned. It was just like his dad to try and alleviate the tension in the air. Even if only for a few moments.

"What did the doctor say about the baby?" his

mother asked in her gentle voice.

Pain slashed through him as he thought of this. "She's spotting. What that exactly means, I don't know. But it sounded like she could lose the baby."

"Oh, Erik. I'm so sorry, honey."

He let the tears fall. The fear had won, and he couldn't fight it any longer. His mom leaned against him and wrapped him in her arms.

"But right now, they're…they're more concerned with losing Tessa. I don't know what I'll do if I lose her. God, I love her so much."

****

The world came into focus a bit clearer this time. Tessa had been floating in and out of a dream she hadn't been able to wake from. Erik and the kids had been there. And her dad. He'd been sitting near her, talking to her about her mother. It was the weirdest dream. She never spoke back to them, only stayed in one spot listening.

Beeps seeped through her foggy brain and integrated with the medicinal odor in the room. When she moved her eyes, they didn't hurt as much as they had. Was she still dreaming, or had she woken up? As she looked around, she took in all the details of where she was. Definitely not at home. Either at her place or Erik's.

Erik. They'd had a fight, and he'd gone off to work. The kids were gone, someone had taken them. Images of driving through the snow flashed through her mind. She'd gotten the children. Where…?

The snow. The car. Oh, God.

She struggled to sit up, but her body wouldn't cooperate for some reason. Why did she feel like she was stuck in molasses?

"Whoa, sweetheart, settle down. I'm right here. It's okay." Erik's handsome face appeared in the doorway.

Slumping back, her eyes filled with tears. "Where's Matty and Kiki? I went to get them. The snow was bad, though. Hit a branch in the road."

He sat on the edge of the bed and lowered his crutches. What happened to his cane? She'd bought him a new one for Christmas.

"The children are fine. They're at home with my mom. She took Matty to preschool this morning so I could be here with you. I went to grab a cup of coffee. I'm sorry I wasn't here when you woke up. You've been in and out of it for a few days now."

"A few days?" What the hell had happened? "I dreamed of you and the kids. And my dad. Talking to me."

"I brought the kids in yesterday. You opened your eyes a bit, but I wasn't sure if you realized we were here. They've had you sedated for a while. They only started easing off this morning."

"Sedated. Why?"

As he picked up her hand, he leaned over and kissed her forehead. "You have a severe head injury from the accident. They needed to keep you still and relaxed so it didn't get worse." His voice cracked at the last words. Shaking his head, he cleared his throat. "We've all been really worried about you, sweetheart. I've been worried about you."

"What day is it?" She'd gotten the kids on Saturday.

"It's Tuesday. We've had someone here most of the time with you. Your dad's come a lot. Even Gladys sat with you for a while. We had to lie and say she was your grandmother, though. ICU only lets family in."

"ICU? Intensive care. I'm in that bad a shape?"

"You're getting better. You've got what they call increased intracranial pressure. It means your brain started to swell."

Leaning closer, he pressed his forehead to hers. "God, Tess, we could have lost you. *I* could have lost you. And I never told you the most important thing."

The room started weaving again, but she needed to hear what he was saying. "Important."

He kissed her lips gently, then stroked her face. "I love you, sweetheart."

"You do?" He loved her. Erik Storm loved *her,* No-Touch Tessa, the freak.

"I do. I love you so much, and it nearly killed me thinking I might lose you."

The words sounded familiar. Maybe that dream she'd kept having. Lifting her hand, she touched his face. He closed his eyes and sighed.

"I'm not going anywhere, Erik. Not that I know of. You said I was getting better, right?"

He nodded, then kissed her again, though he didn't linger. Not that she had the strength to kiss him back, but she loved the feel of his lips on hers.

"You won't leave me. Please tell me you'll stay."

"You're scaring me, Erik. Did they say I might still die?"

His eyes narrowed, then widened. "No, I meant because you'd packed up your clothes. I know I was a bastard and said some stupid things. I don't want you to move out. I want you with me."

She'd packed her... Oh, the bags of clothes. "You

mean the closet I cleaned out. I wanted to paint it and put in some shelves for more space. I took some of my older clothes and stuck them at my house. I figured I could donate them somewhere."

"You weren't planning on leaving me?"

"No." It was her turn. Was she brave enough? She'd never said this before, not to anyone. "I love you, too, Erik."

He pressed close again, and his lips skimmed her cheek. She still couldn't believe he loved her. First her dad and now her husband. Kind of silly since those were the people who were supposed to love you, but then she'd never had anything normal in her life. Finally, she was getting there.

"You're sure the kids are all right? They weren't hurt in the accident."

"They're fine. A few bumps and bruises. They miss their mom, though."

"When can I get out of here and go home?"

He frowned. "You're on medication to help the swelling go down. You have to be off that for two to three days and stay in the normal pressure range before they'll let you go anywhere. They might let you out of ICU, though. They wanted you awake without too much head pain before that. The regular ward isn't as quiet as here."

"I kind of remember you here as I was floating in and out. I wasn't sure if it was a dream or not."

"I didn't want to leave you until I knew you'd be okay."

"It's Tuesday. Shouldn't you be at work? You usually do the dinner crowd on Tuesdays."

He glanced at his crutches and grimaced. "Sid gave

me a few weeks to get my knee in better shape."

"What happened to it?"

"The car went into a ravine. I twisted it when I was trying to get to you and the kids. It's no worse than before."

She could barely keep her eyes open, though she wanted to watch Erik. Her husband. The one who loved her.

"You look tired, sweetheart. I shouldn't have talked to you so long. Why don't you get some sleep? I should go home and take a shower. I'm beginning to smell."

She reached up with both hands and pulled his shoulders closer. "I like how you smell."

Laughing, he settled himself in her arms yet didn't put any weight on her. As she held him tight, his lips nuzzled her neck. She loved him so much, and now she was free to say it any time she liked.

"I love you, Erik."

"I love you, too. I've missed you so much these past few days. Especially in my bed, holding me close. I didn't have anyone to chase the nightmares away."

She stiffened, and he eased back slightly. "Are you having nightmares again?"

His lips nibbled her ear. "Mostly about the car accident and losing you. I can't wait until you're home again. And to do that you need to get some rest."

She kept her arms around him for a few minutes. It felt so good she started to drift off.

His moving away roused her. Leaning over, he kissed her again. "I'll be back later. I promise."

Her eyes drifted closed. Before she succumbed to sleep, Erik's words floated over. "I love you."

****

The tug on her IV line woke Tessa from her drowsy state.

"Good morning. I'm Annette. How are you feeling?"

She took stock and realized she didn't hurt as much as before. Her head seemed clearer, and the aches had lessened.

"Better."

Annette fussed with her IV. "They're transferring you to a general med/surg floor. I need to check a few things first. And I think you're awake enough now maybe we can take that catheter out."

"Can I get up and go to the bathroom, then?" She hated to even think of what she looked like. Erik kept telling her how beautiful she was, but she'd felt her limp, straggly hair and the bump on her forehead, which was probably in vivid Technicolor by now.

Annette fiddled under the sheets, removing the catheter. "I can get you a bed pan if you need one. You haven't had any spotting in a few days, but they don't want to push it with you walking around. The baby seems to be holding tight, but too much movement could still cause a miscarriage."

"A miscarriage?" What was she talking about?

"It's been four days since the accident, so the chances are slimmer now, but the doctors don't want to take the risk. Your husband's been quite worried."

She was pregnant. And Erik knew. Well, that explained all the puking she'd done the last few weeks. And obviously her period wasn't just being its irregular self. It wasn't coming. She was having a baby.

A baby? Holy shit. Never had she imagined this

happening, especially after he'd implied he couldn't—Well, he'd been mistaken on the having sex part, so why not the sterile part, too? She and Erik were having a baby of their own.

He knew but hadn't said anything the last two days she'd been conscious. Well, he'd said he loved her. Damn, was that only because of the baby? Then he'd begged her not to leave. Said he needed her. Was that so she didn't go anywhere with his child?

At Christmas, Erik had a conversation with his cousin about appreciating having a child of his own blood. At the time, she hadn't thought anything of it. He wanted a child of his own. Yes, he loved Matty and Kiki, no doubt. But having a child of one's own was also something special. Special enough to pretend to love your pregnant wife?

Tears threatened to fall with the confusion in her heart. Could she accept his pretense, if that's what it was? She loved him, and he did care for her. If it wasn't love, could it grow to love? And if it didn't, could she still be happy?

Of course, she could. During the past five months of their marriage, she'd been happy, and she'd never fooled herself that he loved her. But she'd also gotten used to the last few days of him telling her. Maybe she was spoiled now.

As they moved her to a new room and got her settled in, she kept her mind on other things. The transfer had tired her out. This injury thing sure was sapping her strength. When she closed her eyes, sleep wouldn't come. Her mind was too occupied with thoughts of the baby…and Erik.

A soft tap on the door had her looking up and

Kari Lemor

pasting a smile on her face. Alex stood there, an uncertain expression on his face.

"Are you up for a visitor? If you're too tired, I can come back later."

She waved him in. "Seems I'm always tired these days. I'd love some company, though." She really liked Alex. He was always more in tune with people's emotions and moods.

Walking in, he sat in the chair near the end of the bed. "Erik needed to spend some time with the kids. They've been clingy lately with you gone."

"I miss them, too. I wish I could go home. All I do here is sleep."

Alex patted her foot under the sheet. "Soon, I'm sure. The fact they moved you out of ICU is a step in the right direction."

"What are you doing up here in Maine? Please tell me you didn't come up just to visit me, because Erik is a mother hen."

Alex laughed. "He's gotten more that way since he got married and had the kids. And no, I've been helping Erik with a little project, so I was already here."

She wanted to ask, but Alex didn't offer, so maybe it was a surprise. Erik knew she had thought about repainting the closet and adding shelves, so maybe he was doing that for her. That would be sweet.

She and Alex chatted a bit about the family and what was going on in everyone's lives. They all sent their regards and warm wishes for her to get better. Molly and Pete had been staying in her old house so they could keep an eye on the kids while Erik had been here. And her dad, Nancy, Madison, and even Brady had taken turns helping out, grocery shopping, and cleaning. It amazed her how everyone pitched in. This feeling of family almost overwhelmed her, but she never wanted to go back to the way things were before.

"I honestly never expected to see my tough marine brother so totally whipped. The emotion coming out since your injury… It's really weird but nice to see."

Emotional about her…or the child she carried.

"I know he's worried about my losing the baby."

Shaking his head, Alex gave a sad smile. "He's worried about losing *you*. When the accident happened, and he called home, he was a mess. He knew the kids were safe, and it was before he found out you were pregnant. You've been so good for him, Tessa. Erik always had everything come easy to him. Everyone wanted to hang out and be seen with him, the popular jock. Especially the girls. Now with his scars and the leg…he questions things more. I don't see the confidence he used to have."

Alex gazed around the room, then smiled at her. "You accepted him even with all that happened. I know he hasn't been easy to live with, yet you put up with his moods and bad attitude. That shows me just how right you are for him. And how much you love him. He feels the same way."

She couldn't keep the tears from welling in her eyes. Damn hormones. Between the stress of the accident and the pregnancy, she was doomed. "Thank you, Alex. I do love him."

"You better be talking about me, or I might have to get nasty here," Erik growled as he walked in the room. His grin told her he was only kidding. Pulling out a folded piece of paper, he handed it to her.

"Matty made you a picture and wanted me to give

it to you right away."

The paper in her hands showed a picture of stick figures. Two large and two small. There was a huge heart in the middle of them. The words *I Love You* in childish print covered the top. She couldn't even pretend to hold the tears in check.

"Now you made her cry," Alex teased, then got up from his chair. "Hey, bro, make sure this lady knows how you feel, huh? She isn't one I'd be letting get away."

"I'll try my hardest. Thanks for stopping by."

"Babysitting." She rolled her eyes.

Alex laughed. "It's time for me to head back to work. I'll see you both later."

Erik perched on the side of the bed and leaned his cane against the chair. He bent down and kissed her.

"How are the kids?"

"Missing you. Like me."

"Tell the doctors I should come home."

He frowned. "I wish I could, but that brain pressure thing still isn't where they want it to be. I don't want anything happening to you."

"Me or the baby?" Damn, she'd gotten brave. But she had to know.

"The baby? You know?"

"Why didn't you tell me?"

He pushed her hair out of her face and kissed her forehead. "You haven't been awake that much, and the doc said to keep you calm. I know you, sweetheart. Losing a child would be devastating. I didn't want you upset and having a setback."

"You didn't want to lose your baby."

"I didn't want to lose *you*. Yes, I want this child. I

won't lie. But not at your expense. And I want the baby not because it's mine but because it's *ours*. It's part of both you and me."

The love shining from his eyes couldn't be denied. She didn't want to deny it either.

Shifting her on the mattress, he slid on the bed next to her. He pulled her to rest on his chest like they'd done at home. The IV was a little different accessory, but the position still felt wonderful.

When his lips touched her hair, she closed her eyes. "I'm sorry for doubting you, Erik. I still have a hard time believing anyone could love me. It's too new."

"Believe it," he whispered near her ear. "I love you, and that's never going to change."

Shivering at his closeness, she hoped she always had this reaction to him. Hoped he'd always be there for her. It looked more and more like he would. Her attitudes and fears of the past had to go, and she needed to embrace this new love and new family she'd been thrust into. Snuggled next to his warmth, knowing he loved her and they'd have Matty and Kiki back with them, she started to believe it.

As she touched her stomach, she wished and prayed this child would be okay. Erik was right. The baby had been created with their love. Nothing could be more perfect.

"So if I lost the baby, were you ever going to tell me?"

"I don't know." Shrugging, he pulled her closer. He kissed from her cheek down to her neck. "Maybe I'd just try harder to get you there again."

As her husband held her, kissing her gently, she knew she couldn't argue with that.

Chapter Twenty-Eight

"We're home."

Tessa unbuckled her seat belt and reached for the door. Reaching across, Erik stopped her.

"No, wait for me. You aren't supposed to be on your feet yet."

After grabbing his cane, he came around the side of the van. She worried he'd slip on the ice, but the driveway had been scraped clean and sanded. And there was a strange truck in her driveway. Before she could question further, he opened her door and leaned in.

"Now this is going to be a little tricky, but I think we can do it. Put your arms around my neck. I'm going to pick you up with my right arm, but you need to hold on. I need my other hand for the cane."

"Erik, this is silly. I can walk into the house. It's been nine days since the accident, and there's nothing wrong with my legs."

"I'm not taking any chances."

He didn't move back. Man, he was stubborn. And worried about her. She couldn't fault him for that.

"You were there for the ultrasound. The baby is fine. His heartbeat is strong."

He grinned. "Her heartbeat."

She laughed. They'd been having this faux argument for the last day. It was too early to find out the sex of the baby, but it had been so amazing to actually see their child. Hear the baby's heart beating so rapidly. Who would have imagined something so tiny would already look like a little human? And be moving around. The child she and Erik had made.

"I love you, Erik."

"I love you too, sweetheart, but you're still not walking into the house. Besides I have a surprise for you."

She hid her own grin. Had he redone the closet, giving her more space? When she looped her arms around his neck, he slipped his hand under her legs and lifted. Only a slight stumble then he started walking, his hand clenched around his cane. Heading in the wrong direction.

"Where are you going?"

"I told you I had a surprise for you."

They were headed to her old house. "Is this a subtle hint you *do* want me to move out? You could have just told me." She kept her voice light.

As he climbed the stairs, he grunted, and she felt guilty. He shouldn't be carrying her. If it made him feel better, though, she'd let him. It was only a few steps.

The door opened, and Alex stood there, smiling. A handsome, dark-haired man stood behind him, wearing a tool belt and carrying a tool box.

"We just finished up and cleaned our mess. Tessa, this is John Michaels, a friend of mine."

She held her hand out and shook the one John offered. "Happy to be able to help. If you need anything else, Alex or Erik, let me know."

Erik nodded at the man, and he left.

"I think you can put me down now." What had they done here? The kitchen and dining room looked the same.

"Not yet. Can we put chairs in there, Alex?"

Alex grabbed some chairs from the dining room and lugged them down the hallway. It looked lighter than it usually did. As he moved slowly toward what had been her den, her eyes almost popped out of her head. The small room that had been down here was now open into the living room and sported floor to ceiling windows on two sides.

"What in the world? Why...?"

Settling her on one of the chairs, he sank into the other one with a groan. "I wanted you to have a place where you could work on your art. But with the kids, that isn't always possible. So Alex and I got our heads together, and he drew up plans for this alteration."

Alex came around from the other direction and leaned over the half wall that separated the living room from this room. "This big room now has the lighting you'd need for any drawing or painting you want to do. And this part"—he bent down and came back up with Matty and Kiki clinging to him—"is for the kids. We replaced the carpet and made everything child safe. The TV is mounted up high, and the remote can be kept on your side. We brought some of the kids' toys here and created low shelves for them so they'd be able to reach. There's a portable crib and couch for naps too."

Erik reached over and took her hand. "I wanted a place you could do your art and still be able to see the kids. Not that you can't come here and work if I'm home with them. But I know you haven't allowed yourself time for what you love."

"I love you and the kids, Erik. I'm very happy being your wife and their mother."

"Good, I'm glad. But I also remember how excited you were when you got to paint the murals in Matty and Kiki's rooms. You should have that too. This way you can."

"It's beautiful, Erik. Thank you." As she looked around the room, she saw all sorts of possibilities. "You know I could start with painting the walls in here. And maybe do a few fun things on the walls in the living room."

"All in good time, sweetheart. You still have some healing to do."

"We didn't do anything to the upstairs yet," Alex said. "Erik thought it might be a nice idea to keep them bedrooms. For when your favorite brother-in-law comes to visit. You know, so I don't have to sleep on the couch at your place."

"Who says you're her favorite brother-in-law?"

"That's a perfect idea for this house. Could you set up my computer in here too, so I can do some of my billing?"

Erik cocked his head. "I was thinking maybe you should start cutting back on your hours. My job is more than enough for what we need. And Gladys says she'd love to have you start creating things for her to sell at the store. I'd bet lots of the touristy gift shops would take your artwork if you offered it."

"Really? Are you sure?"

"I want you to do what you love, Tess. Taking care of the kids and art."

She bit her bottom lip. Could she seriously have everything she wanted?

"I really don't love doing billing. It was easy, and I could do it at home."

Erik walked closer and scooped her up again, depositing her on the couch in the living room section. Matty and Kiki crawled into her lap as he settled next to her. Alex gave a wave and disappeared.

"I don't mind doing the billing if it'll make things easier."

"Stop worrying about money. Between my job and my military disability, we're doing okay. Plus, Miss Abernathy paid me a visit while you were in the hospital."

She stopped breathing. He didn't look upset, though. "What did she say?"

"Mostly she let me know the adoption was moving full speed ahead. She's one determined lady, and she's determined we have these children."

"It's nice to have her on our side now."

He slid his arm around her shoulders and pulled until she rested her head there. "She's been in contact with the lawyers for Sergeant Richard's estate. They're aware we have custody of the children. They've made arrangements for the inheritance to come here. I tried to refuse, I didn't want any more trouble, but they insisted. So I had Nathaniel set up a trust fund for both kids. They can use it when they get older and go to college."

"Wow, really? And you don't want to run out and buy something big?"

He kissed her cheek. "I don't need fancy things or a lot of money. I've got everything I need right here with you and the kids. I can't think of anything I want more."

The children snuggled in their laps as she rested in her husband's arms.

It was a feeling like no other. But like one she'd so

often longed for.

Her dream of a family had finally come true.

A word about the author...

Kari Lemor has always been a voracious reader, one of those kids who had the book under the covers or under the desk at school. Even now she has been known to stay up until the wee hours finishing a good book. Romance has always been her favorite, stories of people fighting through conflict to reach their happily ever after.

Writing wasn't something she enjoyed when young and only in the last few years began putting down on paper the stories that ran rampant in her head.

Now that her kids are all grown and have moved out, she uses her spare time to create character-driven stories of love and hope.

https://www.karilemor.com/

Thank you for purchasing
this publication of The Wild Rose Press, Inc.

For questions or more information
contact us at
info@thewildrosepress.com.

The Wild Rose Press, Inc.
www.thewildrosepress.com

To visit with authors of
The Wild Rose Press, Inc.
join our yahoo loop at
http://groups.yahoo.com/group/thewildrosepress/